ANTI-PARADOX

CR WAHL

Publisher's Note: This is a work of fiction. Names, characters, places, and incidents are either the product of the author's imagination or used fictitiously, and any resemblance to actual persons, living or dead, business establishments, events, or locales is entirely coincidental.

Anti-Paradox

CR Wahl

Book Artwork: Miblart
Editorial Assistance: Sarah Kolb-Williams, Kolb-Williams LLC

First U.S. Edition, 2022

Printed in the U.S.A.

This book is dedicated to my daughters,

who, from their very first steps and words,

continue to amaze with their

indomitable spirits…

CHAPTER 1

El Zotz – Guatemala

"Professor, Professor. Come quickly!"

Professor López Alcina, the lead investigator on the El Zotz excavation site, took off his hat and wiped his brow. "Patience, Maria, patience. I am not as young as I used to be."

"But Professor, you must see what we found. You won't believe it!"

Alcina fanned his sweaty face. He loved Maria's enthusiasm, but sometimes she forgot their age difference. "All right, Maria, what have you discovered?"

"We found another tunnel!"

Alcina's hand froze. "*Dios mio. Another tunnel—where?*"

"It's along the east-facing wall in the main corridor. Gomez's shovel accidentally struck the wall, and a large piece flaked off. The wall was stucco made to *look* like stone and concealed an opening."

Alcina stared in the direction of El Diablo, an immense Mesoamerican pyramid west of the El Zotz acropolis. *Another discovery—here in Guatemala!* He put his hat back on.

"Very well, we go see what Gomez has uncovered."

They walked to a rectangular pit at the base of El Diablo. Alcina grabbed the edge of a wooden ladder that dropped into earthen darkness. "Is the tunnel perpendicular to the east-facing wall?"

Maria nodded. "Yes, Professor."

He recalled that their ground-penetrating radar couldn't reach that area under the temple, so they never knew there were any other cavities.

"Let's have a look then, shall we?"

Alcina lowered himself down the ladder and gave his eyes a few moments to adjust. The air smelled of earth and history. Several yards down the passage, he found Gomez waiting next to his discovery, waving excitedly.

"Come, Professor, I will show you."

Gomez raised a lamp and swept it across the wall, illuminating a partially exposed opening hacked out of metamorphic rock. Alcina patted its edges, nodding. He'd been thinking just this morning about heading back to the small Guatemalan town of Flores to get provisions and a welcome break from the jungle heat, not to mention the myriad of insects. But not now—how could he go?

"I want a series of photographs taken of this and the flake that separated from the wall. After that, let's begin clearing the rest of this stucco away. But under no circumstances are you to enter. Understand?"

"*Si,* Professor. But what do you think we will find?"

Alcina took Gomez's lamp and shone it into the black opening. "It appears to go way back. Perhaps more of the ruler's sacrificed entourage, but we'll know soon enough."

•

•

Alcina closed the flaps to his field tent and laid out a large map of the excavation site on a wooden table. It was one of three made from rough planks supported by bamboo legs. Arranged around the other two tables were director's chairs with tattered backs resting exactly where they had been left after the morning's staff meeting.

Despite the close quarters and long hours, everyone on his team got along well and was dedicated to the project's goal of meticulously mapping El Zotz's ruins. Called Pa'Chan by the ancient Maya, the most striking feature on the city plaza was a massive pyramid called El Diablo. Its name was motivated by a series of dangerously steep steps climbing one hundred and forty-eight feet to a sacrificial platform.

In 2010, a tomb belonging to the Mayan city's first ruler circa 350–400 AD had been discovered underneath El Diablo. Alcina had thought that was the end of the discoveries. But today, El Diablo continued to surprise. He placed his finger on the map and ran his finger along the original tunnel. He then traced out the path of the new one and tapped his finger slowly. The builders covered that portal for a reason.

I wonder what they were trying to hide.

CHAPTER 2

University of Amsterdam – Physics Department

Professor Hans Verlink found his grad student Katrien De Vries seated at a computer console in the back of the physics lab. A blinking cursor on her screen suddenly started drawing vectors in bold lines across a map of the world.

"What have you got, Katrien?"

"It's almost finished," said Katrien.

Thirty seconds later, the image stabilized.

"There, it's done," she said, turning to Verlink. "Your idea of cataloging our earlier vector analysis of the quantum dual world signatures has yielded a surprise, which is why I brought you here to have a look."

Verlink set his coffee cup down and leaned closer to the monitor screen. "I remember this. The signatures were tied to the artifacts discovered in the Alps last year by French archaeologists."

Katrien nodded. "And what happened after that in Béziers was . . ." Katrien's blue eyes suddenly betrayed a forgotten fear. "Beyond belief."

A chill washed over Verlink as he recalled bits of those terrifying days. Had it really been a year since their lives had been turned upside down? He shook his head slowly. "The world almost didn't survive the madness." He sat down next to Katrien. "So, what's the surprise?"

"The 'surprise' came when I decided to compare the earlier vector analysis results with those taken yesterday. After the Béziers incident, I expected to find no further traces of the quantum dual world signatures. But look at this, Professor."

Katrien directed Verlink's attention to a spot on the world map. "This blip was there on the original scan, and back then, I figured it was a reflection from the Béziers signatures since it lies on the opposite side of the world. But it's *still* there, Professor."

Verlink suddenly sat upright. Had he heard Katrien correctly?

"Don't tell me there's another one of those information engines still on Earth."

Katrien's eyes dropped. "I think there is."

"We have to locate it. Where the hell is it exactly?"

"I pinpointed it to an area in Guatemala near the town of Flores."

"How near is it?"

"It's located about thirty kilometers north of Flores in an archaeological site called El Zotz."

•
•

Professor Alcina rubbed beads of sweat from his forehead. Lights on metal tripods had been brought into the central corridor just outside the now fully exposed tunnel entrance lying beneath El Diablo. In front of him was the reason he had become an archaeologist—the thrill of the undiscovered. What secrets lay beyond the darkness?

He turned on his flashlight and stepped through the threshold with Gomez and Maria following. For a second, he paused and sniffed the air. It was dusty like an old carpet. Beneath his feet was a rough-hewn rock floor that had been untouched for over 1,600 years. He made sure it was clear and then carefully entered the tunnel.

Several yards in, Alcina stopped and brushed away loose sand from the wall. As the light from his lamp swept over the surface, three humanlike figures wearing elaborate bird headdresses and jade jewels danced before him. The central figure, carved in bas relief into the rock, was seated cross-legged over the head of a mountain spirit with a giant jaguar and three serpents radiating from it. The figure held a rectangular plate that appeared fused with the surrounding rock. Alcina rubbed a thin haze of dirt off the plaque. It glinted like gold.

Alcina backed away in surprise. "What in God's name is *this*?"

Maria touched the plate. "Is it gold, Professor?"

"What else could it be?"

Gomez brought his lamp closer. "And what is that cylinder protruding from it?"

Alcina reached for the cylinder and pulled on it. "It's securely embedded, but look; there's damage on its left side."

Gomez ran his finger along the cylinder. "*Si*. It is slightly bent too, and I can feel a gouge running along its length."

"It appears as if something hard like a rock impacted it," said Maria.

Alcina squinted at the plaque. "And look at these strange markings." He raised his lamp higher to see better. "What the . . . *unbelievable*. These symbols—they're *not* Mayan."

•
•

Antonio Mazitilo, in khaki shorts and wearing a faded black T-shirt, crouched behind a thicket of canistel leaves. He spoke quietly into a lime-green satellite phone as he pulled aside a branch.

"Professor Alcina, he just go now into tunnel with his field staff. I tell you, Octavio, something is going on down there."

"¿Dónde estás?"

"I outside main tunnel entrance, about one hundred yards away."

"Can you get in closer?"

Antonio shook his head. "I no can risk it. There are three guards nearby."

"What about Mario?"

"No to that too. He still in Flores."

"*Entiendo,* Antonio. You deal with those guards."

"Si, Octavio—pero cómo?"

"Find out which one needs the most money. I can pay him ten times what he's making now."

"But there are many guards, Octavio. We no can deal with all of them, and some of them know me and what I did six months ago in El Caoba."

"If you had listened to me, you would have been out of El Caoba before the guards showed up, but you no think. And that guard you kill have many friends. El Caoba is not Guatemala City, where you can easily disappear."

"*Si, si,* Octavio, I get it, but I still—*espera un minuto.* One of the staff just leave the tunnel and go into the field tent. He is bringing out a camera tripod. Now he is talking to the guard. He keeps pointing back to the tunnel. I think they find something big down there."

"You need to learn what they find, and soon —*comprende?"*

"Si, Octavio, entiendo."

Antonio switched the phone off and looked out toward El Diablo, letting his eyes follow its steep flanks to the sky. What had they discovered underneath all that rock? Mayan superstition passed down through the generations warned of a danger. Antonio felt a shiver but dismissed it; he was going to get rich.

CHAPTER 3

Yuri Trotsenko

Helena Bustorova knocked on Yuri Trotsenko's door.

"Voyti," came a muffled voice inside.

Helena opened the door and quickly glanced around the Moscow office. Everything was in its place. The cleaners had been in earlier, and they were often not careful. Yuri was a man of short patience, and he would blame her if something were amiss.

Yuri was on the phone and waved her in. Helena stepped in and waited. He pointed to a Mamont vodka bottle on a bureau, and she knew what to do. She poured into a crystal shot glass and handed it to him.

He took it without a smile. On his fingers were gold rings that glinted in the afternoon sun streaming through the windows. Helena recalled when he first obtained the rings. He was so proud of them, waving them about like trophies. He claimed they were old and rare, but he never elaborated, and with Yuri Trotsenko, one never asked questions.

Yuri stood next to one of the tall windows that looked

onto Old Arbat Street. The view made Helena look forward to going home. But first, she had to make sure Yuri didn't need her. He paid well, but she did not like her job.

Yuri paused, speaking on the phone. "You may go home, Helena."

Helena nodded with relief and left.

Yuri waited until Helena closed the door behind her.

"Forgive me, Octavio, but your gang—what do you call yourselves? Los Activos or something?

"Los Atrevidos."

"Yeah, Los Atrevidos. Your gang hasn't been very successful lately."

"I understand, Yuri, but this is South America, and most of my men are gauchos; they no think much. This Professor Alcina, what he find is a big deal. It is some kind of ancient plaque buried under the Temple of the Sun. We call the temple El Diablo."

"You Central Americans love your Diablo," chuckled Yuri. "So is it gold. And how old is it?"

"The guard we have working for us has seen it and swears it is gold. The Professor tell him it is at least sixteen hundred years old. Maybe even more."

Yuri poured himself another two fingers. "Okay, I'm interested. What's your plan?"

"Right now, we no have one. We figure the archaeological team will try and remove it from the temple soon, and when they do, that is when we move in to take it."

Yuri finished off the shot. "All right, keep me apprised. I'll forward the usual funds to keep you going. Once a plan is made to do the takeover, we can discuss a final price."

Yuri heard nothing on the line for a long moment. "Is there a problem, Octavio?"

"I think this plaque very important. I take big risk for you."

"And your point?"

"My usual fee . . . it go up."

Yuri smiled. "Good. I like your initiative. I'll pay; just don't double-cross me, because you know what my operatives are like—right?"

"*Si, si,* I know."

"I mean it, Octavio. Remember Carlos Saviente? He thought he could get more money by holding out on me. He thought he was safe in Guatemala. But he was wrong, and now there's a tree outside of Guatemala City that is growing lush and full. Do you want to know why?"

"I no double-cross, Yuri. You no worry."

"Good. Get me more details, and after that, we'll talk about money."

•
•

Professor Alcina clicked his notepad shut and stood up from his field table. It was midday, and the heat inside the tent was getting unbearable. He parted the tent flap and stepped out into the sun.

Out of the corner of his eye, he detected movement in the woods. He'd seen it before, and at that time, he ignored it. With El Zotz situated in the vast Guatemalan Bioreserve, random movements from curious animals in the woods were frequent.

But the movements were always in the same spot. The illegal pilfering of rare Mesoamerican objects was a thriving business, and with the recent find in the new tunnel, Alcina was getting nervous. The day before, he investigated and found the forest ground trampled flat next to a Canistel bush. He pointed it out to a guard, Juarez, who said it was probably where a puma had slept the night before. Nevertheless, Juarez offered to keep an eye out for anything unusual.

Alcina crossed the plaza to the tunnel access pit and swung around to lower himself down the ladder. As he stepped on the first rung, he spotted Juarez leaving the woods from the exact location he had seen movement a few moments ago. Alcina smiled. It must have been him patrolling the site perimeter. Satisfied, he lowered down to the tunnel floor.

He followed a string of lights to a split in the tunnel and then turned east. He found Gomez scraping away debris along the outline of the mysterious gold plaque. Gomez stopped and took a drink from his water bottle.

"Professor, I don't see how the builders ever got this plaque embedded so precisely into this rock. I can find no seam."

Alcina leaned in close with a pocket magnifying glass. "It's incredible. And this cylinder—what do you make of it?"

Gomez scratched his beard. "Have you noticed the fine symbols on it? Not only are they not Mayan, but the markings are too delicate for the Maya to have made them."

Alcina massaged his temple, feeling a headache coming on. He didn't like this. Here was an anomaly—outside of any normal archaeological find, yet immensely important. "I agree, and I worry that it is beyond our abilities to examine here, which is why I want to remove it for study back in the university's lab."

"Ha!" said Gomez as he slapped the plaque. "How will you do that? Plus, we have no idea how far back it goes. But if you had to do it quickly, you'd better bring in a jackhammer."

Alcina wrinkled his face. "My colleagues would cringe if they heard that." He traced the edge of the plaque with his finger and then shook his head. "But I'm afraid you might be right."

Gomez was about to speak but stopped and turned toward the sound of footsteps. A few seconds later, Juarez stepped in front of one of the illumination lamps. His dark green uniform had sweat running under his arms and across his chest. He held his cap in front of him and glanced at the gold plaque. "*Hola,* Professor."

"*Hola, Juarez. Que esta pasando?*"

Juarez shrugged. "*Nada mucho.*" He looked back at the plaque. "It is very beautiful, no?"

"Yes, it is," said Alcina, "and a big mystery too."

"It look like gold," said Juarez, eyeing the plaque. "I hear you say you want to remove it?"

Alcina let out a short laugh. "Yes, but not only do we not know how the builders put the plaque into the rock, but we have no clue how to remove it either."

Juarez broke into a crooked smile. "I help you, Professor. There not much for me to do here. *Estoy muy aburrido.*"

Alcina patted Juarez on the shoulder. "Yes, the jungle can be boring at times, but you're a good man, Juarez. We'll let you know when we're ready for your help." He then glanced at his watch. "But right now, it's time for my afternoon cerveza." Alcina yawned loudly. "And after that, maybe a nap."

•
•

Verlink looked up from his desk when he heard a knock on his office door. "Come in."

Katrien entered, holding a mug of tea. "Any news from Guatemala?"

Verlink frowned. "Nothing."

"You don't think they found the plaque, do you?"

Verlink leaned forward in his chair with his hands folded. "I think they have, because I'm not getting anywhere with the Archaeology Department at the Universidad del Valle de Guatemala."

"They have an archaeological team at El Zotz, right?"

Verlink gave Katrien a worried look. "Yes, they do."

"But if they stumble upon the cylinder embedded in

the information engine plaque, we—"

"I know, Katrien, I know! We have to find out what's going on."

Verlink recalled a year ago when he and Katrien first saw the information engine activated back in France. The field it generated was hardly visible, ethereal—like the hint of orange-colored smoke. Then, slowly, it began to take the form of a funnel with its small end centered over a cylinder embedded in the engine's face and its large end extending outward. Katrien had pointed at the radiating phantasm.

"The air is ionizing from molecular collisions."

The undulating mirage seemed alive then. The molecules were crowding as they rushed toward the artifact. Verlink remembered looking at Katrien and seeing the orange chimera reflecting in her eyes. He thought about what Katrien had said. She was right; it *was* ionizing the air. Katrien was always right. She had become like a daughter to him, so young, brilliant, and now burdened with an awful truth: the end was coming. Verlink shook his head as if trying to shed the memory. "It almost destroyed us. We have to find out more."

"But if they're not talking to us, how—"

"We go down there," interrupted Verlink. Once we're there physically, they can't ignore us."

"Then we had better do something, and the sooner, the better."

"Agreed," Verlink said, standing up from his desk. "I'll begin making preparations with our department assistant. Start clearing your schedule. With any luck, we'll be leaving within a day. By the way, how's your Spanish?"

CHAPTER 4

Guatemala

The Chevy pickup lurched to the side, kicking up billows of brown dust. Verlink brushed away a fine grit from his sleeve. Katrien sat next to him, clutching her backpack as the pickup rocked wildly, accompanied by a cacophony of squeaks and rattles from the truck's red fiberglass topper.

"We were lucky the field staff was in Flores getting provisions," said Verlink, raising his voice over the noise.

"No kidding," said Katrien, watching another cloud of powder waft in through the open hatch. "And looking at the road into this bioreserve area, I doubt we would have been able to get to El Zotz on our own without a lot of effort."

Verlink couldn't believe his good fortune. After their impromptu arrival at the Universidad del Valle de Guatemala Archeology department, he had been able to enlist the department chair's help, Professor Leonardo Sébastien.

Initially, Sébastien was cautious, but once he learned he was speaking to a world-renowned theoretical physicist, he quickly became a valuable aid. With his help, Verlink and Katrien could charter a small plane from Guatemala City to Flores. There, they were met by several members of the site investigator's field team, Gomez and Ricci, who happened to be in town on a provision run.

Verlink became pensive for a moment as he thought about the task that lay ahead. "I just hope we're successful."

"Do we have a plan yet?"

Verlink let out a half-laugh. "I'm winging this the whole way."

"I kind of like the thrill of it—don't you?" said Katrien.

"Yes, but we do have an important purpose in front of us."

Katrien nodded and looked out the window. She seemed calm, but sometimes she was hard to read. Her mind was sharp as ever, but her energy level had waned from a year ago. Still, Verlink was glad she was with him. Her fast mind allowed him to bounce ideas and get insightful feedback quickly. Maybe he would need that once they reached El Zotz. He checked his watch. *Two more hours to go.*

•

•

The truck heaved hard to the right and then stopped with a screech. Verlink woke, startled from a bizarre dream; the last thing he remembered was the cold stare of a black jaguar with glowing orange eyes. He rubbed his face with both hands and saw Katrien gathering her things. The front cab doors opened and then closed loudly, shaking the truck.

"*Bienvenidos* a El Zotz," said Gomez as he flipped down the hatch gate and helped them out.

"I will go find our lead investigator, Professor Alcina, and tell him of your arrival," said Gomez as he excused himself.

Verlink inhaled deeply and looked around. The hot,

humid air, redolent with scents of the jungle, greeted his nostrils. He didn't know where to focus his eyes first—the gigantic temple and plaza or the breathtaking jungle lining its perimeter. El Zotz was in the middle of the Guatemalan Bioreserve called El Biotopo San Miguel la Palotada. Boasting one hundred thirty-nine species of ethnobotanic-use plants, ninety-five species of trees, seventy-three species of birds, fifty-three species of reptiles and amphibians, and forty-four species of mammals, it was no wonder environmentalists and scientists were clamoring to protect it.

Tall Ceiba and mahogany trees with crowns that challenged the clouds surrounded the plaza. Lianas and bromeliads—fighting for bits of light, clung to their branches everywhere. The forest squirmed with life; insects buzzed, and birds flit about the canopy while iguanas, draped over branches, basked in patches of sunlight.

High above, Verlink caught the movement of a troop of black howler monkeys working their way through the canopy. A large male suddenly stopped and fixed its black eyes on him. Verlink had the strange feeling the monkey was not the only one looking at him. He lowered his gaze and noticed several guards across the plaza holding rifles in dark green uniforms staring at him.

"This place is unbelievable, Professor," said Katrien as she pointed at the steep walls of El Diablo. "Humans never cease to amaze me with what they're willing to build."

Verlink's gaze followed her hand and nodded. "Look at the pitch of those stairs—and *no* handrails."

"*Hola!*" came a shout suddenly from behind them.

Verlink turned to find a man of medium height with a dark tan waving at them. The man removed a Panama hat from a thick mop of salt-and-pepper hair.

"Greetings, Professor Verlink and Katrien; I am Professor Alcina. Gomez has told me of your arrival." Alcina swept his hat in a wide arc over the surrounding ruins.

"Welcome to El Zotz."

Verlink took Alcina's hand and shook it. It was rough like a farmhand's glove. "Thank you for seeing us, Professor."

Alcina nodded enthusiastically. "My pleasure."

Verlink tilted his head in the direction of the plaza. "And I must say, this place is stunning."

Alcina followed his gaze and broke into a proud smile creased with many lines. "It is an archaeologist's dream, and I am fortunate to be here. But Doctor Sébastien relayed to me that you come not to see the ruins—no?"

Verlink became serious. "Professor Alcina, Katrien and I are theoretical physicists from the University of Amsterdam. We've confirmed through Professor Sébastien that you've recently discovered a strange metallic plaque, and we have reason to believe it may be similar to one discovered last year."

Alcina's eyes went wide. "Oh? Where was this other one discovered?"

Verlink passed a look to Katrien. "I know this will not make any sense, but the other one was discovered in a cave in the French Alps."

Alcina arched his eyebrows. "Professor Verlink, I am not sure I follow you, but if you want to see the plaque, then I will take you underneath El Diablo so you can see for yourself. After that—we talk."

CHAPTER 5

Beneath El Diablo

The entrance to the pit was narrower than Verlink expected. He didn't even like going into the crawl space under his summer cabin on the outer edge of Zuid-Kennemerland woods. But Katrien had no such problem, and she quickly grabbed the ladder's posts and disappeared into the ground.

"Are you coming, Professor?" said Katrien, looking up from the bottom.

Alcina gestured for him to follow. "Please, Professor, you go next."

Verlink swallowed hard and then lowered into the pit. Alcina followed behind.

At the bottom, a string of lights disappeared down a long corridor. Verlink looked up at the daylight streaming down the entrance shaft and tried not to think of the entire mass of El Diablo pressing from above.

Alcina tapped him on the shoulder and handed him a flashlight. "We follow these lights and then turn right at the T, but watch your step; the ground is uneven."

At the junction, the tunnel widened, allowing Alcina to take the lead. He pressed into the new passage. After four yards, he stopped and illuminated the wall next to him. "You can see this mural is very well preserved. The details are astounding, and the builders seemed particu—"

"Oh my God, Katrien," cried Verlink, shining his light past Alcina and onto the metallic plaque embedded into the wall. "It's another one!"

Alcina faced Verlink. "Like the one you told me about?"

Verlink stepped up to the plaque. "Look, Katrien. The cylinder—it's damaged."

Katrien hovered her hand over the cylinder for a moment and then tried to pull it free. "It appears as though a rock, or something very hard, had fallen against it."

Verlink stood back and rubbed his temple, trying to think how to phrase his thought. "I'm sorry, Professor Alcina. To be blunt, this plaque was not made by the Maya and may very well be over eight thousand years old. We have much to explain."

•

•

Alcina pulled a green tent flap back and motioned Verlink and Katrien inside. He had many questions for these scientists.

"Please, have a seat. I know it's hot in here, but at least we're not in the sun. Besides, I have refreshments."

At the rear of the tent, Alcina kneeled and lifted the lid of a below-ground storage box and brought out three bottles of Cabro.

"I'm sorry this beer isn't cold," he said, handing bottles to Verlink and Katrien, "but at least they're not warm."

Alcina studied Professor Verlink and Katrien for a moment. They seemed out of place in the jungle with their European manners and clean clothes. Yet they had traveled far to be here, so listening to their story was the least he could do. He held the bottle up as a toast. "Salud!" he said. "I think these are appropriate right now. So much has been happening lately that at times I feel overwhelmed."

"Salud," said Verlink. He took a drink and nodded in approval. "This is just what I needed."

Alcina stared at him expectantly. "You state there is much to explain—yes?"

Verlink reached into his pocket. "Let me show you some photographs on my phone. These were taken a year ago in a cave on a mountain in the French Alps called Mont Pourri."

Verlink located the images and handed his phone to Alcina.

Alcina scrolled through the photos, and a worried look spread across his face. "*Dios mio*. The artifact—it *is* the same. How can this be?"

"Professor, the plaque and cylinder in those images were responsible for the 'atmospheric event' that rocked the town of Béziers in France last year. Governments tried to play down the significance of what happened, and they will deny what we are going to tell you, but Katrien and I were there." Verlink glanced at Katrien. "And I can assure you, it was no atmospheric event."

Alcina tapped the image on the phone. "I still don't understand how this—this chunk of gold could cause any threat. Is it radioactive or something?"

"No, it's not radioactive, nor is it gold either. It's an exotic alloy housing what is essentially a kind of engine capable of deconstructing matter into information. Its end purpose was to transport the converted information to a quantum dual world—a parallel world, if you will."

Alcina shook his head slowly. *Did he say "parallel world"?*

Verlink glanced again at Katrien before he spoke. "What the designers of the artifact were planning to do with that information, we may never know."

Alcina noticed Katrien's eyes widen for a second, as if Verlink's comment had triggered something inside her mind, but she remained quiet. Alcina suddenly felt out of his element. He was an archaeologist, not a physicist, and these two scientists seemed to be speaking another language. "Did you say a 'quantum dual world'?"

"Yes," answered Verlink.

Alcina raised his eyebrows.

"I know, Professor Alcina," said Verlink, tipping his hand slightly. "This sounds crazy, but to theoretical physicists like Katrien and me, the possibility of a dual world to our own is possible, and in this case, it seems tied to the conversion of information."

"Information? I don't understand," said Alcina, feeling more and more uncomfortable.

"There is every reason to believe that information may be more fundamental than mass and energy."

Alcina handed the phone back to Verlink. "I'm sorry. You've gone beyond me. But if the artifact with the cylinder we found below El Diablo is dangerous, should I be concerned for my students' safety?"

"I think it was damaged before it was activated. There's evidence of an impact on one side of the cylinder. The artifact recovered in France on the images I showed you were perfectly preserved but had not been assembled. Only when they were combined did the engine start. If it weren't for an anomaly—a kind of paradox—the engine would have surely consumed the entire planet."

Alcina sat down and massaged his forehead. He was used to simple daily routines made up of stone and artifacts and the jungle's sounds. The story told by these two physicists kept getting more bizarre, yet Verlink *was* famous, and he *had* come here on a mission to warn him.

"Forgive me if I don't follow everything. This artifact

sounds dangerous. What kind of beings would create such a device?"

"All I can say," offered Verlink, "is that the originators got a taste of their own medicine."

"But if what you say is true, and the artifact *is* damaged, then perhaps there is no longer a concern?"

"The fear," Verlink said, "is that the damage may be reparable, in which case it could be unwittingly restarted. And if that happens, we are all doomed because there will be no anomaly like the last time to disrupt its conversion process."

Alcina thought of all the students under his charge, and he suddenly stood. "I will take your word for now. I have my students' safety to consider. What should our next move be?"

"The plaque must be removed and taken to a secure place."

Alcina began to pace. "How far back does the plaque go into the rock?"

"About one foot, and the only way to remove it is to use a jackhammer on the adjacent rock."

Alcina stifled a laugh. "That was what Gomez wanted to do, but I hesitated. It's such a—how can I say it—an *indelicate* method."

"Professor Alcina," interrupted Katrien. "Does your university have the means to secure something like this?"

"There is a vault for the artifacts we recover, but that's at the university, and getting them there safely has its challenges."

"Professor Alcina, the sooner that artifact is placed where it can be protected, the better."

Alcina set down his beer and headed for the tent entrance. Pulling the flap back, he turned and faced Verlink. "I will send two of my team to Flores to get the necessary equipment. We'll be ready by tomorrow."

•
•

Octavio Alvarado dropped his burning cigarette and spoke into a satellite phone. "Yuri, you must believe me. I pay guard like you say, and he hear everything these scientists from Amsterdam say. The artifact they find has some kind of strange power."

Octavio heard a snort over the phone. "Sounds like Maya superstition."

"*Si,* I know it is crazy. They say the Maya never made the plaque!"

"I don't know what to think, Octavio, but I do know this: if a professor from Amsterdam shows up interested in that artifact, it *must* be valuable."

"Then do we have a deal, Yuri?"

"When are they going to remove it?"

"Tomorrow. Professor Alcina sent two of his staff to Flores to bring in equipment."

"Then we won't have long to wait. Can you be ready?"

"*Si,* we will be ready. But now, we talk about money—*si*?"

CHAPTER 6

Preparations

Alcina took a long drink from his water bottle. It was 12:15 p.m. His team had made good progress removing the artifact. The guards and even the professor from Amsterdam and his grad student Katrien had pitched in. But *dios mio,* the plaque was heavy! It wasn't actually a plaque but more of a cube with a plaque-like face. A winch had been employed to drag it out of the tunnel, and then a ramp used to get it into the rear of a red Jeep Comanche.

Alcina smiled to himself. The strange artifact he was staring at would bring much-needed attention and funding to the university's archaeology department. He might even become somewhat of a local celebrity. "But all in good time," he said, patting the plaque with its thin casing of still-attached rock.

"Hola," shouted Verlink, coming up from behind. He mopped his forehead with a red-checked handkerchief. Alcina guessed his age at fiftysomething, but living out of the constant rays of the sun didn't age the skin as it did here in the tropics, so it was hard to tell. Still, Verlink seemed fit and didn't shy away from physical labor.

"How do you guys tolerate this heat day to day?"

Alcina laughed. "You get used to it, but sleeping when it's this hot is another matter."

"I had a rough night, that's for sure," said Verlink. He leaned into the back of the Jeep. "Do you have the plaque secured?"

"Yes, and I've doubled the webbing just to be safe."

Verlink pointed at a canister anchored next to it. "What's in this container?"

"It's filled with stone stucco fragments removed from the wall that was concealing the tunnel."

Verlink smiled. "You guys examine everything—I like that. But isn't it strange the Maya builders tried to hide the plaque in the first place? It's as if they knew of its power."

Alcina wondered about that too. *Was it just a coincidence?*

"Who else is coming back to Flores?" asked Verlink.

Alcina pointed at a silver Toyota FJ Cruiser. "Hernandez will drive the Cruiser. We'll need his help to load the artifacts into the plane once we get to Flores."

Verlink tilted his head toward the guards still stationed around the plaza. "Will the guards be accompanying us too?"

Alcina nodded. "*Si.* Juarez will be in the lead, and another guard, Marco, will be at the rear. I've arranged for two other guards to remain stationed here in El Zotz during our absence."

"When do we leave?"

Alcina looked up, shielding his eyes against the sun. "Soon. I don't want to be traveling through this jungle in the dark."

•
•

"Octavio, what are you doing here?"

Octavio smirked. "Relax, nobody see us. They too busy with preparations." Octavio produced a green satellite phone and handed it to a man in a khaki shirt and pants. "Keep this turned on."

The man stuffed the phone into his pocket and then wiped his face with the back of his sleeve. "I worry, Octavio. Are you sure your plan will work?"

Octavio pinched his brow. "It too late to start whining like a *chaquita*. Do you know where the Nuut'b'en canyon is?"

"*Si*. It is very narrow there."

"Good. When the caravan reaches Nuut'b'en, you must hold them in the pass. We will come up from the rear."

"What will happen then?"

Octavio grinned. "Nobody escape."

The man's face fell. "Who will be with you?"

"My man Antonio. Why you care?"

"Is he the same Antonio who was in El Caoba?"

Octavio put his hand firmly on the man's arm. "You want money, and you will get it, but you had better do what you say. *Comprende?*"

"*Si*, Octavio, but promise me nobody will be hurt. The professor, he a good man."

Octavio stared hard for several seconds. "I no promise nothing. Just do your job." Then he turned and disappeared into the woods.

•
•

Alcina patted Juarez on the shoulder. "You'll be in the lead, and Marco will follow with the Toyota Highlander. I'll be behind in the Jeep Comanche, and Hernandez will be behind me in the FJ Cruiser."

Juarez nodded and headed to a black Jeep Rubicon.

The four vehicles rumbled to life and began lining up single file. Juarez signaled through the open top of his Jeep to move out.

Professor Verlink drove the Comanche while Katrien rode shotgun with Alcina in the back. As the vehicles left the central plaza, Alcina checked the webbing behind him one last time. Satisfied that everything was secure, he faced forward and allowed himself to relax. It had been a hectic morning, but things were going smoothly, and by nightfall, he'd be in Flores with a cold beer and hot bowl of *Kak'ik*.

Katrien turned in her seat. "You have a good team, Professor. I like how everyone pulls their weight."

Alcina smiled. "Yes, I am fortunate to have such dedicated people." He then gestured with his hands toward the window. "And I have this vast jungle full of ruins to explore. Who wouldn't be satisfied?"

"Have you thought any more about our proposal to let us study the plaque back at the University of Amsterdam?"

Alcina winced lightly. "This is a Guatemalan treasure, and we must all respect that. At the moment, only my colleagues know what we found. The government has not been apprised yet, but once they are, I am certain they will want to keep it here in Guatemala."

Katrien nodded. "I understand. But perhaps you can arrange a meeting with your government so we can present our case on the danger this artifact represents."

Alcina shook his head and became serious. "It is as if we have uncovered the devil. I will do everything I can, Katrien, but my country is poor, and the bureaucrats in charge might see things differently."

He turned his gaze outside the window. Tall Guatemalan fir stood in the distance with their crowns towering above the canopy. Lower down, false mastic, guarumo, and alligator trees hugged the road, their leaves slapping the sides of the Jeep as it continued south.

"It is strange, Katrien," said Alcina, still looking out the window. "Sixteen hundred years ago, this place was full of people who feared the power of the El Diablo pyramid. We think of them as primitive and superstitious, yet here we are today, imagining ourselves enlightened and sophisticated—yet we still fear the devil."

CHAPTER 7

Nuut'b'en Canyon

A sudden jolt stirred Alcina awake.

"Sorry about that," said Verlink. "That fallen branch was a bit too close."

Alcina turned around to make sure his cargo was secure. He glanced up and could see Hernandez in the FJ Cruiser several hundred yards behind, with Marco far in the rear. Out front, he recognized the approaching walls of Nuut'b'en canyon. Its narrow walls were laced with ferns and lianas, so dense they blotted out the sun, giving the impression of descending into an underground world.

Juarez slowed down as the sandstone walls closed in. After several minutes, he abruptly signaled Verlink to stop. He stood up in his Jeep and looked back toward Marco.

"Qué esta pasando?" whispered Alcina.

As he turned to follow Juarez's gaze, a gunshot echoed through the canyon. In the far rear, a red Cherokee was rapidly gaining on Marco.

Alcina shouted, *"Los atrevidos!"*

Verlink shot a questioning glance at Alcina.

"Bandits," cried Alcina. He leaned out the window and yelled to Juarez. "Why are we stopping? We must get out of here!"

Juarez seemed not to hear him, his eyes fixed on the red Cherokee. Inside were two men, one brandishing a black AR15 assault rifle. The Jeep closed in behind Marco and attempted to accelerate past him.

Marco realized what it was trying to do and matched its speed. The narrow canyon barely fit both vehicles as each dueled to be the one out front. Unable to gain the lead, Marco rammed his Highlander hard into the Cherokee.

The Cherokee driver yelled to the man next to him, "Do something!"

A loud crack echoed through the canyon, and the Highlander suddenly dropped back, colliding against the wall and spinning around in a shower of dust. With the Highlander out of the way, the Cherokee reared up behind Hernandez.

Alcina felt his foot pressing on an imaginary accelerator. *Pull ahead—pull ahead!*

But the FJ Cruiser was too heavy, lurching wildly with tires spinning on the loose gravel. Alcina wished he had called in more guards, but that would have delayed them several days. The artifact behind him had become a curse—the Mayan legends were coming true.

Hernandez panicked and made a hard right turn, slamming on the brakes. The FJ Cruiser skidded sideways, blocking the canyon.

No, thought Alcina, *he shouldn't have done that!*

Hernandez jumped out, stumbled to the ground, got up, and began running.

Alcina cried under his breath, "Run, Hernandez, run!"

Obstructed by the FJ Cruiser, the man with the rifle leaped from the Cherokee and fired at Hernandez, peeling shards of sandstone off the canyon wall. Alcina's gut wrenched when another shot ricocheted into Hernandez's path. Hernandez covered his head with his arms and ran for his life.

Alcina wanted to turn away. Hernandez was his friend; they had gone to the same school and even once liked the same girl. A third shot reverberated through the canyon. Hernandez staggered, but his legs continued to pound away until he tripped and skid into the earth. He pushed himself partway up and then collapsed.

"Nobody was to be hurt," whispered Juarez, still standing up in his Jeep.

Just the day before, he and Hernandez had been joking about how the Guatemala president looked like a howler monkey. Now Hernandez and Marco were probably dead, and it was *his* fault.

I must make things right.

Juarez yelled to Verlink, "Come quickly—we must get out of this canyon." He dropped into his seat and started the Rubicon.

Verlink followed until the canyon walls opened up. Juarez slowed down and then stopped. He waved Verlink on. "Go. *Go*!"

Alcina stuck his head out the window. "Come with us, Juarez; you do not have to do this."

Juarez couldn't look him in the eye. The professor had always treated him well, showed him the same respect he gave to all his field staff—even shared his food and beer with him. And how did he repay him?

"No worry for me, Professor. I will stop them and then catch up with you in Flores. Now go—*please*."

"I will hold you to that, my friend," said Alcina. He pulled his head inside the cab and shouted to Verlink. "*Go!*"

Juarez watched as they drove off and then, with his rifle at his side, faced into the canyon with the yellow sun high overhead.

Alcina fixed his gaze on the road behind him. He worried for Juarez and wondered about Marco and Hernandez. *Are they dead?* When they left Juarez, Alcina saw something in his eyes but couldn't put his finger on it. Was it guilt? And why did he stop in Nuut'b'en canyon in the first place? Could Juarez have been part of the plan?

A red Jeep suddenly came into view, swerving in the gravel with a billowing cloud behind it.

Alcina grabbed Verlink's shoulder. "Juarez has failed—we're on our own now."

Verlink yelled above the engine's whine, "I don't know these roads as you do. We need a plan—and fast!"

The professor was right. Without a plan, they would never get out of the forest alive. Alcina scanned the surroundings. He'd made this trip hundreds of times. Then an idea hit him.

"Take the next turn to the left!"

Verlink swerved quickly, shoveling up a wave of loose stones.

"What's the plan, Alcina?" shouted Katrien, holding on to the dashboard.

"No time to explain!"

Alcina took out a pocketknife and cut through the webbing that secured the large canister containing stucco fragments. Once he'd freed the canister, he peered around it. The Jeep Cherokee was directly behind them. The man driving was holding a semiautomatic pistol, but his partner was slumped over in his seat. *Maybe Juarez did not fail after all.*

Alcina checked their location. A sharp bend was coming up. He knew what they had to do, and timing would be critical. He yelled to Verlink, "Bear to the right at the bend, and don't slow down!"

The Jeep's wheels plowed a spray of dirt as Verlink turned hard, forcing Katrien against him. At the same time, Alcina shoved the canister off the Jeep bed. It crashed onto the road, sending chunks of rock into the air and the Cherokee's path.

The Cherokee missed the turn and careened over a deep drop. The vehicle hung suspended in midair for a few seconds with its wheels spinning, then dove into the ground, crashing through a thicket of tamarind and sending the driver bouncing violently against the windshield.

Verlink slowed down. "Should we stop, Professor?"

Alcina's eyes remained fixed on the scene behind him. After a moment, he breathed out, shaking his head. "No. We don't stop until we reach Flores."

"What about Juarez and the others?" asked Katrien.

"There may be others. To go back would be suicide."

•
•

Twilight came quickly in the jungle. The shadows of trees, gnarled and often grotesque, flickered like ghosts in the Jeep's headlights. The night deepened, and the whine of the vehicle droned on, lulling everyone into a kind of stupor as they tried to make sense of what had happened.

Alcina shook his head. *This ancient plaque is a curse.* Three people are probably dead, and we may yet be next. The artifact strapped behind him was never made by the Maya, nor did it even originate here in this world. The Maya somehow understood that, so they heaped tons of rock on top of it, making a tower to warn others.

Alcina turned and looked at the plaque. It was geometrically perfect, with symbols etched with precision beyond the reach of the Maya. Verlink's story, no matter how improbable, *had* to be true.

Maybe it would be best if Verlink and Katrien brought it to Amsterdam. He stared out the window and let out a sigh, then closed his eyes.

CHAPTER 8

Back to Amsterdam

Verlink watched his reflection in the La Aurora International Airport terminal window vibrate as an Airbus A320 took to the sky. Alcina stood next to him and firmly shook his hand.

"Thank you; I'm not sure I would be here if you hadn't come when you did."

Verlink gave a slight smile. He'd wondered about that too, with the whole affair leaving him not only rattled but feeling guilty for bringing Katrien into harm's way. He should have considered the possibility before ever coming here. "Trouble seems to follow the ancient plaque, no matter what part of the world it's in."

Alcina turned to Katrien and gave her a quick hug. "Safe travels, and I am sorry your first trip to my country was so dangerous. I hope you will come back to experience the real Guatemala."

"I would love that, and as far as what you said, it's not your fault. At least Professor Verlink and I found what we came for." Katrien glanced at Verlink. "And to actually return with it—well, that's more than we could have hoped for."

"Katrien, I do ask that you keep me apprised of what you learn. There are many questions about the artifact that need answers."

Katrien hesitated for a moment and then asked, "Will you be in any kind of trouble for releasing the artifact to our custody?"

Alcina made a pinched face. "You're assuming the government knows about the artifact. They will learn someday, but perhaps it is best not to say anything right now. And who knows—maybe you will return it before that happens."

Verlink patted Alcina on the shoulder. "*Adios.*" He grabbed his bag and followed Katrien into the terminal.

The "fasten your seatbelt" light blinked off, and Verlink pushed his seat to recline and rested his eyes. The trip, though successful, had taken its toll. When he was in the restroom in the terminal, a pair of eyes with dark circles had looked back at him in the mirror. He felt old. Interacting with students every day, he often forgot about the age difference. *What would it be like to never age?*

He glanced at Katrien seated next to him. She had been quieter than usual during the entire trip, and he wondered how she was handling everything that had happened. He also felt terrible that he had unknowingly led her into a dangerous series of events. But she was tough, and he had witnessed firsthand her resilience during their nightmare in Béziers.

Katrien suddenly stopped working on a calculation and started to nod up and down. "Of course—of course!" She turned to Verlink. "Professor, we can do this!"

"We can do *what*?"

Katrien lowered her voice. "The artifact. We can modify its purpose."

"Modify its purpose—to what end?"

"We can use the artifact to transport solid matter to the quantum dual world."

Verlink narrowed his eyes. "Do *what* with it? Did you say transport *matter* to the dual world?"

Katrien's blue eyes sparkled with excitement. "Exactly. I'm not talking about information or energy either, but solid matter."

Verlink's mind went to why they had come to Guatemala. Their primary goal was to make sure the artifact was rendered inoperable, not to bring it to Amsterdam and play with it as a scientific curiosity. The artifact was dangerous, with properties neither he nor Katrien fully understood.

"Katrien, we need to make sure the engine can never function again—*ever*."

Katrien played with a lock of hair and spoke as if she hadn't heard him. "We know the information engine is in a metastable state, which is how it can transfer decomposed information from our world to the dual world. The El Zotz artifact has a damaged cylinder, which is good, because we don't want it functioning as originally intended.

"Last year, the cylinder we studied decomposed matter to extract the maximum amount of information before transmission to the quantum dual world. We don't want that; we want it to transfer matter trapped inside its field without decomposition."

Verlink caught Katrien's use of the word *we* and realized she was trying to draw him into her plan. "And why do *you* want to transfer matter?"

"If we can bridge between our world and the quantum dual world, we can learn why they sent the artifact in the first place."

Verlink shook his head. "We know why—to provide them with unlimited power at our expense!"

"Perhaps, but we really don't know, do we? And it's not just scientific curiosity; if the dual world sent two engines here, they might try again. We need to be prepared in case there's ever a next time."

Verlink scratched the start of a beard. "Okay, I understand, but what you're talking about is much bigger than the two of us. I'm not sure it's our decision."

Katrien began shaking her head. "Then whose is it? Look what happened when the NSA director from the United States got wind of the artifact a year ago. Earth almost perished. If we tell our government—or *any* government—about this, I guarantee we'll never see the artifact again."

Being reminded of the NSA gave Verlink a chill. "All right, I agree; we keep this to ourselves for now. But do we destroy it or experiment with it as you propose?"

"Think what we can learn from the artifact, Professor. It represents technology thousands of years ahead of ours. We *can't* destroy it—at least not until we have a chance to examine it. And if we can transport matter, just think what we could learn then."

Verlink *was* intrigued, and he hated dismissing any of her ideas, but his instincts were telling him there was danger here. "But there's no guarantee that matter, if caught in the artifact's field, can be transported without damage. Moreover, we don't know the extent of damage to the cylinder from El Zotz, and we don't dare modify it without being one hundred percent certain we understand how it functions."

"I agree there are issues—but when we were running tests last year on the French cylinder, we recorded everything; we just didn't have permission from the French government to take it apart. With the damaged cylinder from El Zotz, we no longer have that restriction. We can do this, Professor. Here, take a look at this calculation . . ."

:

Yuri Trotsenko did not like bad news. "Octavio, what do you mean you don't have it?"

"*Si*, Yuri, I no have it, and Antonio is dead too. Alcina and this professor who come from Amsterdam, they make me crash my Jeep. My face is hurt very bad, and I have to walk in jungle all night to get to Flores."

"Is this professor in Flores now?"

"No, the professor and his grad student. They no here now."

"Grad student?"

"*Si*, a girl with blond curly hair, very tall. Juarez tell me Alcina say she very smart."

"What else does Juarez know?"

"He tell me no more. Antonio kill him."

Yuri's mind boiled with an unpleasant image of Octavio. "Shit—I knew you gauchos would fuck this up! Why did you bring Antonio, and where was the rest of Los Atrevidos?"

"I think I no need them."

"Bullshit, Octavio. You got greedy."

"No, no, I no greedy, Yuri."

"I say bullshit. From here on, I'll deal with this myself."

"*Pero* Yuri, you pay me like we talk, *si*?"

Yuri couldn't believe what he had just heard. Octavio was lucky he wasn't there *personally* to pay him. He clicked off the phone and tossed it on a couch. "Pay you, my *ass*."

He sat at his desk, opened his tablet, and started a message. When he finished, he walked over to a bureau with a silver liquor tray and poured a shot of Mamont. The tray used to be in the summer cottage of Tsar Alexander II. Yuri rubbed its edges. He had gone to great lengths to get it. Now it was his.

He stepped over to the window. The cobbled brick

street below was full of pedestrians making their shopping rounds before heading home. Yuri clenched the shot glass. Why would a physicist take an interest in some ancient artifact? He shook his head and then tipped his head back and swallowed. He felt a warm burn in his throat. There was something valuable here, and he wanted it. But once the university took possession, it would never be for sale. That left him only one avenue: Sergei Durov. Sergei's disciplined military background would not allow him to fail like that half-wit Octavio.

Yuri eyed the bottle of Mamont but decided against it. When Sergei returned his message, he would ask for a plan with details. Yuri returned his gaze out the window and down to Old Arbat Street and grinned. How much trouble could a professor and some girl graduate student be anyway?

CHAPTER 9

University of Amsterdam – Physics Department (Three Months Later)

Verlink watched Katrien make the final connections to the cylinder extracted from the Guatemalan artifact. It was secured to the top of a piezoelectric transducer surrounded by an electromagnetic toroid.

Katrien began typing on a keyboard. "I can adjust the field strength using an encoded acoustic signal."

A few seconds later, a green glow filled the physics lab. The light began to pulse slowly, its epicenter emanating from the cylinder. "I see," said Verlink. "You're stimulating the cylinder acoustically with the piezoelectric transducer. And by not inserting the cylinder into the plaque; you're *fooling* it into thinking it will be receiving information and generating a metastable field. But how are you encoding the signal?"

Katrien stopped typing. "We're using the same technique we used a year ago. Not only does the cylinder emit an incredibly dense data stream when stimulated, but it also sends out a field into space, which is the green glow we see when the lights are dimmed."

Verlink shook his head slowly. He remembered when they'd first discovered the glow the year before. "There was a metastable field right here in our lab back then, and we didn't even know it until much later."

"Professor, I think we're ready for our first test."

There it is, thought Verlink. He had known the moment was coming, but he wasn't quite ready for the reality of it this soon. They had dived in without looking for what might lie under the surface. But they were swimming now, and it was sink or swim.

"Have you completed the modifications?"

Katrien nodded. "Yes. I added the damper directly into the plaque's opening. There's no way the cylinder can fully engage and become active."

"When do you plan to send the data chip?"

"In two days."

"And after that?"

"We try a mouse with a recording device."

Verlink cringed. In only two days, they would be sending a living creature. Things were moving too fast. He wanted to tell her to hold back, but Katrien wanted this—no—*needed* it. She seemed frantic at times, pushing herself as if time were running out. He could tell some days she was exhausted, but she kept going. He marveled at her dedication, but how long could she keep up the pace?

"Professor, you're very quiet. Is something wrong?"

Verlink smiled and shook his head. "No, sorry. I'm just trying to take all this in."

"I know," said Katrien, "but let's see how the first experiment goes. Maybe we missed something."

Verlink stared at the pulsing haze of green light. It was a metastable field—existing between two worlds—and soon, it might be transporting living matter into another world. He realized he'd assumed that an impasse would develop along the way to slow things down, but it never came. He'd checked Katrien's calculations over and over and could find no error, no inconsistency.

A tingle traveled up the back of his neck. If all went well with the live animal, the question would come that they dare not ask. Neither he nor Katrien had brought up the possibility of whether a human should be next. But Verlink was certain Katrien had considered it, and he worried she might seriously consider it for herself. Verlink sighed. That was when he'd have to put his foot down and say no.

And if that weren't enough to worry about, the department chair was beginning to ask questions. He was pushing for an update and couldn't be delayed much longer. But once they shared their discovery, the cat would be out of the bag. And if the university knew, then governments would follow, and then they would want to have control over the technology—and *that* was a problem.

Verlink returned his gaze on the undulating glow. It was seductive, spinning a web that he had somehow fallen into, flickering in his eyes like a strange alien dance, leaving him wondering, *What world lies beyond those quantum waves?*

•
•

Katrien rubbed her eyes and looked at the clock: three hours without a break. It was drizzling outside, so she headed to the physics building's basement to walk the long halls, clear her mind, and stretch her legs.

She started briskly but soon slowed. It was going to be one of those days. Myelodysplastic syndrome was what the doctor called it. When she'd heard the diagnosis, it felt like a truck had hit her. The doctor said she had maybe two years with good days and bad. The news was only a week old, and she still hadn't internalized it let alone told Verlink. Still, she felt guilty not confiding in him. He'd treated her like his daughter and deserved to know, but she knew the news would deeply affect him.

Eventually, she'd have to come clean, and she worried their dynamic would change. Verlink often gave her credit for coming up with ideas, but he was a brilliant filter that sifted through her bad ideas and approaches in a way no one else could. Their symbiotic relationship was the key to her success, and she didn't want that ever to change. Understanding the quantum dual world might be her last significant achievement, and she was determined to make the most of the months ahead.

At the main stairwell, she placed her hand on the railing. It felt cold, and a wave of sadness suddenly hit her. Her disease, telling Verlink the news, were realities she'd been avoiding by hiding behind a wall of denial. The day of reckoning was coming, and she knew she wasn't emotionally prepared, not only for her own feelings but for the look that would come to Verlink's face.

The last thought made her want to cry. *Not here,* she told herself.

A janitor in blue overalls suddenly cleared the stairs.

Katrien composed herself. "Hello," she said.

The janitor stepped aside without saying anything. It was his usual behavior, taciturn and never replying to a hello. But it didn't bother her, because his leering stares never made her want to talk to him anyway. Yet seeing him reminded her that one of the lab's far corner lights was flickering and needed replacement.

"Excuse me," she said as he was walking away. "The lab in room 45D has a failing light. Can you see that it's replaced?"

The janitor hesitated for a moment. "Yes, I will look into it."

Katrien thought it strange he didn't reply in Dutch.

But he must have understood enough to get the gist of what she was asking.

"Room 45D. The light needs replacing, okay?"

"Okay, I will do it," he said with an air of annoyance.

Katrien tried to place his accent: East European or something similar, so he was probably an immigrant here for work. "Do you know when you'll get to it?"

"I will fix this evening," he said and hurried down the hall.

Katrien thought about doing another lap but didn't want to run into the janitor again. She reached for the stair railing and gripped it tightly. The clock was ticking, and she had work to do.

CHAPTER 10

University of Amsterdam – Phase-Shifting

Verlink sat in his office and sipped a cup of coffee from the Eetcafé Oerknal. He had stopped at the café earlier hoping a strong cup would rid him of the effects of a poor night's rest. It was a tall order; the truth was, he hadn't slept well for the last several nights.

He rubbed his eyes and then brought up Katrien's results from yesterday's experiment on his computer. Her analysis of the data chip sent into the dual world revealed temperatures and pressures consistent with an earthlike atmosphere but little else. Her notes made it clear that today was the day they would attempt the mouse transportation. It would last only minutes, just long enough to send the mouse and retrieve it. They would then download the collected data recorded during the mouse's visit to the dual world and see what it told.

But things could go wrong. The mouse might not survive the experiment; it could come back a mass of flesh, or come back alive but deranged, or—worse yet—not come back at all.

Verlink leaned back in his chair and rested his eyes. Katrien would be here any minute, and the waiting would soon be over.

Verlink sat next to Katrien as she made last-minute adjustments to a control box with cables leading to an array of coils and other devices surrounding the cylinder. One end of the cylinder was inserted into the plaque, while the other was free but mostly hidden behind a tessellation of transducers and sensors.

The lab was strangely quiet save for the random clicks from Katrien's keyboard. Verlink had worried about the cylinder's damage earlier, so he arranged to have some of the original casing stripped back. With help from the material science department and using findings from their work on the fully functional cylinder from a year ago, he and Katrien could decode some of the dual world's cylinder workings.

But they were far from understanding *how* it functioned the way it did. Fortunately, that didn't matter because they *did* understand the physics of what it did and knew how to make the cylinder do what they wanted.

"Professor, we're ready to charge up the field. Do you want the honors?"

Verlink smiled. "No, I'll let you do it. After all, this is your brainchild."

Katrien went to her computer and brought up a command screen. Within seconds, the room was bathed in green light.

Verlink watched her modulate the field to bring all the mouse's quantum waves in phase with the dual world. She was in her element—this was *her* moment. Her epiphany was the realization that the artifact could synchronize both worlds' phases, allowing matter from one to slip into the other. In a sense, it was not transporting matter at all; it was opening the door to another world, and she had found the key.

There was a low-frequency hum in the lab in synchrony with the green glow. The cylinder pointed down toward the floor with the mouse directly underneath its axis. The mouse sniffed the air, its whiskers twitching, oblivious to what was about to happen. The field intensity increased until the mouse was barely visible. Then a wailing began as the phases of wave functions from two worlds began to shift.

Verlink saw it, first a blip as the mouse suddenly became frozen, then the image flashed like a strobe lamp. The wailing turned into chatter as if the wave functions were grating against each other. The glow became brighter, and then the mouse, the light, and the din ceased to exist, and the lab fell silent.

"My God, Katrien, it's just like the data chip experiment. I don't know if I'll ever get used to watching something disappear before my eyes."

"We wait five minutes, and then I'll bring him back," said Katrien.

As long as the cage remained in the same location in the dual world, Katrien could reverse the process and shift the cage and the mouse back into her world. At four minutes, Katrien reestablished the field, and a minute later, she began the modulation.

Verlink fixed his eyes on the space formally occupied by the mouse. The noise grew, and this time, Verlink reached for his ears to cover them. Then the strobing began, followed by a series of blips flashing with a steady rhythm, and seconds later, as if slipping through a door, the mouse reappeared.

Verlink let out his breath.

Katrien powered everything down, and the lab became quiet. She sat there, not looking at the mouse. Verlink wondered, *Is she afraid of what she might see?* The cage began to rattle, and Verlink glanced over to find the mouse with its tiny hands on the bars of the cage.

"Katrien, the mouse appears unharmed."

Katrien looked relieved and smiled. "He does seem normal." She walked over to the cage and dropped a small nut into it. The mouse grabbed the nut and nibbled, holding it between its hands. Katrien removed the mouse and retrieved the recording chip attached to a small collar. "Let's take this to the communications lab and download this little guy's biometrics and learn more about where he's been."

Verlink stood up slowly as he considered Katrien's success. She had done it—yet he wasn't surprised. But the experiment's outcome meant he could no longer avoid talking to her about where their research was going.

"Can I come with you? There's something we need to discuss."

•

•

Sergei knew that what he was about to tell Yuri would get him going. When that happened, Yuri would get anxious and want to assume control. Sergei hated that, but it was part of the job.

"If I hadn't seen it on the camera, Yuri, I wouldn't have believed it."

"Sergei, I thought you only had sound taps in the lab."

"I did originally, but being a janitor has its advantages."

"How do you mean?"

"I've learned that it's easier blending in than trying to hide. If you're in a hospital, you dress like a doctor or a nurse. If you're at a construction site, you wear tradesmen's clothes and a hard hat. At a university, you can get by wearing anything casual. That's the easy part. The hard part is that very few random professors are milling about, and I would have never pulled it off in Amsterdam's physics department. But students and professors rarely notice the lowly janitor. I can walk into any room with a wrench in hand, and nobody suspects."

"So that's how you got the cameras in the lab. You just walked in and put them there."

"Precisely."

"Okay, so are you sure it was the artifact from El Zotz that they used to transport this mouse?"

"Absolutely. The artifact is somehow key to their experiments. But I think they were surprised the experiment worked as well as it did."

"So they sent a mouse to someplace else and brought it back—right?"

"That's correct."

"Where did it go?"

"All I know is that they keep talking about a 'dual world.'"

"Have they confirmed that the mouse went there?"

"The mouse carried a miniature recording device. They were going to review it but needed equipment in another lab at the university to download the data. I have no access there, so I don't know."

Sergei could tell from Yuri's tone that he was getting uneasy, just as he feared. He'd soon want to get involved, complicating the operation. But the worst part was he'd almost certainly get in the way.

"Sergei, I *want* that artifact. It's way more valuable than a dusty piece of antiquity. I think it's time I made a trip to Amsterdam. I'll alert Bratva that I need their help getting the artifact out of Amsterdam. The question is, are *you* ready?"

"My team is almost ready. Are you sure you want to be here too?"

"I'm not letting anything go to chance."

"Once you get it, what will you do with it? These physicists involved are world-class. The artifact will be useless without their knowledge."

"And the problem is?"

Sergei was quiet for a moment. "I see. This might get messy."

"Then let it get messy. That artifact is going to be mine, one way or the other."

CHAPTER 11

Grainy Images

Katrien applied digital filtering to a video scene on her computer screen. She squinted at a grainy image and turned her head sideways. *What am I looking at?*

Structures like buildings appeared through the bars of the mouse's cage in the distance—or was that her imagination? The mouse had been free to move about in its cage, but it was surprisingly stationary during its visits to the dual world. She and Verlink had sent the mouse four other times, but the images rarely changed significantly.

Improvements to the camera didn't help either because something was corrupting the data, either in the dual world or during the transition between worlds. Each time the mouse returned, Katrien brought it to the university's veterinarian school for a checkup. From skin scrapings, no abnormalities or cellular damage were found.

But after the fourth time, the staff became suspicious, so she stopped. The school said any further study would require the mouse to be euthanized. Katrien wouldn't condone that, which left additional data gathering by more sophisticated electronic devices—or sending a human into the quantum dual world.

Verlink was the one who had brought it up first. He knew her well enough, where her head would go, and knew she would propose it sooner or later. He made it clear in no uncertain terms that he was deeply troubled by the idea. She offered herself as a guinea pig since she knew she had less to lose. But Verlink didn't know of her condition, and Katrien just couldn't tell him, not yet.

He reminded her of the real purpose of the information engine—to deconstruct matter from her world. He said, "The dual world inhabitants hadn't cared that Earth was being annihilated to satisfy some unknown purpose of theirs." Verlink was right. It was unconscionable, and that fact alone gave her pause. If, as Verlink implied, the dual world inhabitants hadn't cared what happened to her world, then what of her?

Katrien scrolled through the images again from the mouse's last visit. There was definitely something that looked like the outline of a building. It appeared elevated or far in the distance; she couldn't be sure. She pulled up the video from a previous visit and verified that it was oriented in the same direction. That's when she realized the building, or whatever it was, was absent in the earlier video. Had the cage shifted into the dual world on a moving platform, or was something else going on? The more she stared, the more she wanted to see this other world for herself.

As a child, she often gazed at pictures of ancient Egypt. She imagined herself standing before the great pyramids as they were being built, watching the thousands toil under the hot desert sun for their pharoah. How hard she wished to place herself in that picture! And now, here was a chance to see an unknown world. Only this time, no wishing was needed, just good science and a lot of courage.

"What do we have, Katrien?"

Katrien recognized the voice of the department chair, Dr. Daan Visser, who had a habit of showing up without warning. She turned away from her computer and faced him. "Oh, hello, Dr. Visser. Just some data analysis from one of our experiments."

Visser stared at her computer screen without speaking. Katrien crossed her arms and waited patiently. She was wise to his tactic of silence as a means to elicit information and wasn't about to be intimidated into saying something she'd regret.

"I see," Visser said. "I spoke with Professor Verlink about having the two of you host a colloquium on your research. We're all very anxious to hear what you've been reticent to share with the department."

Katrien swallowed hard. *Shit.* They had lots left to do, and she still knew nothing about the dual world—and she *had* to know more!

"Um, sure. Let me talk with Professor Verlink, and we'll see about setting something up."

"Great. I'd ask you more about it now, but I have to run to Switzerland regarding the university's funding allotment at CERN."

"When do you get back?"

"I should return within a week."

A week? That didn't leave her much time. She and Verlink would have to burn the midnight oil to complete their experiments. "Okay," said Katrien. "I'll talk to Verlink, and we'll plan something afterward."

"Very well," said Visser, looking at Katrien's monitor. He looked like he was about to ask something but decided against it. "Until then," he said and walked away.

CHAPTER 12

Countdown

It was close to midnight, and the hallway outside the university's physics lab was dark save for a few illuminated exit signs. Inside the lab, Katrien stood with Verlink next to an open space with the Guatemalan artifact secured to the ceiling above.

"I know you wish it was you standing there," Verlink said, looking at a metallic platform underneath the artifact.

Katrien stared at the platform. He was right, and not only that; this might be their last experiment before meeting with Visser and the physics department. It would likely spell the end to their control of the project. And if that weren't enough, she still hadn't told Verlink about her condition, and the longer she waited, the harder it was getting.

Katrien turned to look at him. "It's not just that."

"Are you worried about Visser's request?"

"It's going to create quite a stir."

Verlink nodded. "It will jeopardize our control of the entire project."

Katrien's eyes swept over the lab. "I'm not sure I want

to give this up. It's *our* project, and it feels like it belongs to us and us alone."

"It does feel that way," said Verlink. "We were the ones who tracked down the artifact, risking our lives in the process and then working out the details, which brought us to this point in time. It's been a long haul, and a part of us is in that artifact."

Verlink rubbed his eyes. "But it's getting late. Let's shift this high-speed film camera to the dual world, bring it back, and then call it quits. Maybe this old-style photographic film won't be corrupted like all the previous digital recordings. I really want to get a look at the *other* side."

Katrien heaved a sigh. "Me too."

"I think you said the system is programmed to phase-shift the camera from the dual world and then back here after five minutes. Is that correct?" asked Verlink. "And do you think that's enough time?"

"Let's keep it short this first go-around," said Katrien. "We can always lengthen it later." She flipped several switches on a panel. "I'm ready here. I'll go set up the camera."

"I'll do that," offered Verlink. "Remind me again, how wide is the phase-shifting field?"

Katrien opened her notebook and pointed to a sketch outlining the extent of the field. "It's big, around four square meters."

Verlink unclipped a small electronics box from his shirt. "We were going to test these, right?"

Katrien tapped the one clipped to her blouse. "I almost forgot. Turn yours on and stand opposite me with the transfer area between us. They're synchronized transmitters, and I'm curious what happens to the transmitter's electromagnetic field as it crosses the phase-shifting field."

Verlink switched his transceiver on. "By the way, what's the transmitter's normal range, anyway?"

"They have an operating range of a little over five kilometers."

Verlink moved into position. "I'm set here."

Katrien looked longingly at the camera sitting on the tripod. "I'm ready too."

•

•

Sergei removed his earbuds and turned to Yuri. "They're ready to run some kind of experiment. Now is our chance. It's late, and nobody else is around. The security guards are at the other end of the building, and both artifacts are in the same room."

Yuri unholstered his PMM Makarov pistol and undid the safety. "I'm ready. Let's get this operation going."

Sergei pointed his pistol down the hall. "Their lab is three rooms down on the left." He nodded to his sideman, Tolenka. "We surprise them *en masse*."

Tolenka, steel-jawed with a shadow of a beard, flexed his hands around his rifle. "Let's do this."

"And don't forget," said Yuri, his fingers twitching slightly, "I need them alive."

Katrien lowered the lab lights to reveal a faint green haze projecting onto the floor. The haze took the shape of a funnel with its small end pointing up and the large end extending downward, emanating from the cylinder inserted into the plaque. The plaque itself had been secured to small girders attached to beams above the ceiling.

"The phase-field is idling right now, Professor. Is the camera running?"

Verlink stepped into the field area, turned it on, and then stepped back. "Ready and waiting."

The phase-field started to pulse. "In ten seconds, the field will be at a maximum," said Katrien.

A faint green glow developed over the platform as a countdown rattled across black plastic speakers set on either side of a computer screen.

"Ten."

"Nine."

Verlink nodded and offered a slight smile.

"Eight."

Katrien nodded back.

Verlink's smile suddenly changed to fear as three armed men entered the lab and crept up behind Katrien.

"Look out, Katrien!"

"Seven."

Katrien turned and stepped backward.

"Six."

Verlink recognized one of the men as their janitor. This was no random event; it was part of a well-planned attack. But to what end—to steal the artifact? A different man who must have been their leader waved his gun at them and yelled, "Stop where you are!"

Verlink pulled Katrien into the green light. They were trapped, standing in the center of the platform surrounded by armed men while an unstoppable countdown rang in their ears.

"Five."

The leader barked to the other men, "Don't just stand there, *grab* them!"

The men raced forward. As they stepped onto the platform, they paused and looked at their hands now bathed in green light.

"Four."

Verlink grabbed the tripod attached to the camera and hurled it at the man closest to him. The man dodged and lunged for Katrien.

"Three."

Katrien stepped aside and delivered a kick to the man's jaw, dropping him to the floor.

The leader charged ahead. "For Christ's sake!"

"Two."

The man on the floor rose and clamped down on Verlink's arm. The leader was on the platform now, and he raised his hand to strike Katrien. The green glow intensified and suddenly began strobing rapidly, followed by a plaintive wailing that echoed in the lab.

For a brief second, everyone stopped. Verlink reached for Katrien with his free hand.

"One."

In a blink, five people disappeared behind a haze of green light, and then the lab fell silent.

CHAPTER 13

Another World

Katrien staggered and almost fell over as her brain searched for a hold on reality. The wailing from the lab was gone, as was the green glow, replaced by a silent orange twilight. Her eyes slowly began to focus, and for a moment, she thought she was alone; then she heard coughing.

She found Verlink collapsed on the ground.

"Professor, are you okay?"

Verlink slowly stood and stretched out his arms to look at them. "I think so. A moment ago, a man was grabbing my arm. Now, he's—shit!" Verlink looked around. "We've shifted to the quantum dual world!"

Katrien's eyes lit up. "My God—we did it!"

"But those men in the lab and the man grabbing my arm. What the hell happened to them?"

"I recognized one of them. He was our janitor," said Katrien. "He and the others must have been transported like us."

"But why are *we* together?"

Katrien thought about it for a minute. "Maybe because

of the transmitters we were carrying; they were synchronized, and that must have phase-linked us. As far as those men, who knows where they ended up?"

A dark shadow suddenly rolled across the ground.

Verlink's jaw dropped, and he pointed up. "Oh my God."

Katrien arched her head back. A massive structure in the shape of a cube and as large as a small office building was silhouetted against an orange sky and seemed to be floating. Katrien's mouth opened. "It blocks the light, but look at its sides; they blend in with the sky."

As her eyes adjusted to the dim light, she saw other cubic structures farther away, hanging in the air. Like the one above, they, too, mimicked the sky, flitting in and out of focus like a mirage. In the distance, more cubic structures were lying on the ground haphazardly as if tossed from a child's toy box. The one closest to them had rust-colored sides with rows of windows and a crumbled corner. Katrien wondered, *Did it drop from the sky and lose its chameleonlike skin?*

"Professor, what happened here?"

Verlink was about to say something but suddenly changed his mind. "How long has it been?"

Katrien checked her watch. "We're coming up on five minutes."

"We'll be shifting back to our world any moment," said Verlink, "and when we do, those men will be coming back too. We need a plan—*now*."

"We have no way to defend ourselves," said Katrien.

"Do you have your cell phone? Set it to dial 112. At least the police will be alerted once we return and the signal goes out."

Katrien looked at her watch again and bit the edge of her lip. "Professor, it's been five minutes."

"Maybe your watch is off, or this world"—Verlink

swept his hand around—"has done something to it."

Katrien's gaze followed his hand. The excitement of their achievement was wearing off and becoming a growing worry. Would this become their new home? At her feet was a carpet of yellow-green grass. Farther out, the field connected with stone paths crisscrossing in various directions. Odd-shaped structures, some ten meters high, peppered the landscape. The objects seemed to lack utilitarian purpose, resembling works of art or abstract statues. Were they in some kind of park? But it was an *empty* park. Was that good or bad?

Her thoughts returned to Verlink's comment.

"Perhaps this world *has* affected my watch, but our system wasn't configured to handle five people, and they're not here now, and—" Katrien stopped. "Professor, we may not be able to *get* back."

•
•

Yuri lay facedown on the ground clutching his PMM Makarov. He rolled over and sat up, rubbing dirt off his face with the palm of his hand. *What the fuck?* He was alone and surrounded by a hazy orange light. Was it dawn or sunset? Minutes ago, he had been in the University of Amsterdam's physics lab struggling with the professor, and—?

He called out, "Sergei! Tolenka! Where are you guys?" Had he been knocked out and left outside? He called out again, "Sergei! Tolenka!"

Yuri stood up and checked his Makarov—loaded and ready. His eyes, finally adapting to the dim light, surveyed his surroundings. An open field stretched out before him, and he could make out what could be the skyline of a city in the distance. How the *hell* did he get way out here?

He squinted toward the horizon and then struck out for the city. After several minutes, a thought hit him. "Son of a bitch!" The bastards, Sergei and Tolenka, must have dragged him out here. *Do they have designs on the artifact too?* Yuri picked up the pace and was soon running. After fifteen minutes, he stopped to catch his breath. As he leaned forward with his hands on his knees, he realized he was in the cast of a shadow—and it was *moving*. Yuri looked up. "What the—?"

CHAPTER 14

Strangers in a Strange Land

There was a sun, or at least it blazed like one. Verlink shielded his eyes against the glare and studied one of the floating cubes. Unlike the one lying on the ground, the buildings above matched the sky like chameleons, rendering them almost invisible.

Occasionally, a cloud would pass and disrupt the illusion, allowing a glimpse of the cube's exterior. Windows were arranged in orderly columns on all sides, but nothing looked like a doorway on the entire structure. If they *were* buildings, how did the inhabitants enter?

The building's miracle of levitation was hard to grasp. Verlink's mind sought an explanation but came up empty-handed. He believed gravity was an emergent entropic property of the universe, dual world or not, and that ruled out the possibility of antigravity. So how was it done? Electromagnetic levitation? *Or could there be another way?*

"It's been exactly two hours since we shifted here, Professor," Katrien said.

Verlink detected a change in her voice. He tried to put

his finger on it. Was it defeat or simple worry? She always had options when it came to problems, but now, had she lost hope of returning home? How *were* they going to get back? They had no scientific apparatus here, so what could they do if the university lab equipment didn't bring them back?

"How long should we stay here in the hopes that the equipment returns us home?" asked Verlink.

"I think the equipment is still on," she said, sounding like she didn't like her answer. "It won't shut down automatically until after four hours of inactivity. I'm guessing it tried to return us after five minutes, just as it was programmed to do. The problem was, we shifted along with those intruders, and since we weren't together when the engine tried to bring us back, the transfer failed."

"Then the only way back," said Verlink, "is to reconfigure another engine *here* and shift us home."

"It's starting to look that way. Let's wait another two hours," Katrien said, staring toward a metropolis in the distance. "After that, if there *is* a way home, that city may hold the key."

They sat on the grass and waited. Verlink could see for several miles in all directions, and the most striking feature, besides the floating buildings, was the lack of activity. The air was still, and there were no sounds or moving objects above or in the distance. No one came to meet them or threaten them. No machine approached them. And perhaps more telling was the fact that the floating buildings that dropped from the sky lay just where they had fallen. Had everyone vanished? Had he and Katrien traveled to a dead world, and were they effectively marooned here—alone?

And what about Katrien? At the moment, she seemed calm. Her connection to Amsterdam had suddenly been cut off, but if she were frightened, she didn't show it. Was that for his benefit, or was she really *not* worried? He knew she was close to a brother who lived in Rotterdam, and she visited her parents in Stuttgart, Germany, from time to time. But beyond that, her life pretty much centered on school and her research.

Verlink also wondered how long it would be before their absence would be noticed in Amsterdam, and if so, by whom? And as far as Katrien having a boyfriend who might immediately be concerned, she had once implied that she didn't have time for a serious relationship; her research was her passion. But such questions seemed trivial to the greater issues that lay before them.

Verlink checked his watch. "It's been over four hours."

He pointed over Katrien's shoulder. "As you said, the possible key to getting home lies in that direction, toward the city."

Katrien stood up. "I'm nervous. Are you?"

Verlink nodded. He *was* anxious, but what choice did they have? They were stuck here and had to find a way to survive. "We're strangers in a strange land, looking for a way home."

They followed a path through the park, passing giant sculptures set back from the trail. Occasionally, stone benches were framed by hedges resembling arborvitae. Flowering plants like purple bellflowers circled the area, often sprawling beyond their original beds, taking root wherever opportunity allowed.

After an hour, they reached what looked like a street at the edge of the park. Katrien scanned up and down the pavement. "It appears deserted."

"I keep thinking we should make ourselves less conspicuous," said Verlink.

"Agreed, but how?" asked Katrien.

She was right. How would they be *less* conspicuous? "I say we do nothing. We can't hide forever," said Verlink.

They stepped onto a street made of a seamless gray material like slate. Metallic booths with open doorways appeared at regular intervals along the road.

Verlink walked up to one and looked inside. It was large enough for a standing human and little else. A gold panel with markings was on one wall, similar to those on the plaque used to bring them to the dual world. A display screen was set above the plaque, but it was dark.

Verlink tapped on the screen, but nothing happened. "I have this feeling that everything in this city is dead," he said.

Katrien tilted her head up at one of the floating buildings. "Not *everything*."

They traveled along the street until they reached a tall, marble-gray building. Emblazoned near the top were prominent symbols of a similar style that covered the plaque. Verlink noticed that on the side facing the street was what appeared to be a door. He stepped up to it and looked for a handle, but he saw no button or any apparent means to gain access inside.

Katrien waved her hand in front of it. She knocked, looking at Verlink, then shrugged. "Why not?"

They circled the building, found no other entrances, and continued to the next. After the fourth building, Verlink's mouth felt dry. He sat on the ground and rubbed away sweat from his forehead. "We need to find water."

"And soon," said Katrien, looking up at the sun. "I wonder if one of the buildings that dropped from the sky has an opening."

"Good idea," said Verlink, starting to stand and massaging his back. "Maybe the damage from the fall created a way inside."

Katrien pointed off to her left. "That building looks closest. We can probably be there in several hours."

They followed the street as far as possible and then

diverted onto a grassy field. Low-lying shrubs grouped into small clusters dotted the path ahead.

Verlink stopped in front of one. "The green leaves on these plants probably photosynthesize sunlight with chlorophyll or something similar. They must require water, so where do they get it?" He glanced at the sky. "A rain shower would be welcome right now."

"The leaves have an oily appearance," said Katrien. She drew one of the leaves close to her nose and smelled it. "Its scent is like a lemon." She broke it off and handed it to Verlink. "Here, what do you think?"

"It does smell like lemon," he said, gazing ahead. "I wonder if, days from now, we'll be eating these."

They resumed walking. After a kilometer, Katrien suddenly stopped. "Do you hear that?"

Verlink listened and shook his head. "Sorry, I don't hear anything."

"There's definitely a high-pitched sound."

"Where's it coming from?"

Katrien turned her head to get a bearing and moved toward a collection of shoulder-high plants. "It's coming from these tall plants." She brought her finger to her mouth as a signal to be quiet. After a few seconds, she smiled. "They've stopped."

Then Katrien shook her head. "Nope, they've started up again. I think my voice or any other noise triggers the sound they make."

Verlink shrugged. "Sorry, my old ears don't hear anything." From his last hearing test, he recalled that he'd lost the ability to hear the highest-pitched tones. When he asked the doctor what he could have done to prevent it, she smiled and said, "Stop getting old."

Katrien suddenly pointed. "Professor, do you see that? The other plants in this group are slowly turning their leaves with their concave surface *toward* us."

Verlink was disquieted. She was right: they *were* moving.

Katrien brought her hands to her ears. "The sound—it's getting louder. I think all the plants are generating the same frequency in concert."

"But to what purpose?" said Verlink.

"You mean, why would all the plants enter into a kind of sympathetic fugue?"

"Precisely."

Katrien touched Verlink's shoulder. "What if the sound were loud enough to bring down a bird or an insect? Like a sonic Venus flytrap?"

"Clever," said Verlink. "It would be a way of bringing in nutrients."

Katrien started to walk away. "I'm getting nauseous. There are only a handful of plants here; can you imagine the sonic havoc wrought by an entire field of these?"

•

•

Up close, the floating building was more extensive than expected. The outside had a rusty stonelike finish, with translucent windows. Verlink raised himself on his tiptoes to see inside, but they were too high. "I can't help but marvel at the fact that this structure once floated in the sky."

"Let's call it a *sky building*," said Katrien.

Verlink massaged his chin for a moment and started to nod. "Yes, I like that."

"I'm going around to the back," said Katrien.

Verlink put his hand on the wall and realized there were no seams on the entire structure. How was it made? He was about to call out to Katrien when she shouted for him to follow.

He found Katrien standing next to a six-foot gash in the corner of the building. "It looks like this corner took the brunt of the impact."

Verlink stared at the metallic wound. The building's seamless design implied great strength, and he wondered what kind of force it would take to tear it apart like that. "Is there a clear path inside?"

Katrien leaned partway into the opening. "There's light inside. Probably coming in through the windows."

"I say we investigate," said Verlink.

He disappeared into the opening following the light with Katrien behind him. Ahead was a narrow space under a fallen beam that he'd have to crawl through. An image of the tunnel in El Zotz flashed before him. *I can do this.* He closed his eyes and squeezed past a collapsed doorway, crawling for several yards until he could stand up. They were in a corridor with rooms branching off on either side.

Verlink motioned to Katrien to be careful and then stepped carefully over plastic-like debris that had fallen from the ceiling. With each step, a cloud of dust circled his feet. The silence and smell reminded him of his grandmother's attic in Zutphen, where she kept the family photographs and boxes filled with memories.

Verlink suddenly stopped and put his hand behind him. "Wait."

Up ahead, something was lying on the floor in one of the doorways, halfway in the hall and halfway in the room. Verlink cautiously stepped closer. "It looks . . . *humanoid*."

Katrien peered around him, squeezing his shoulders. "It's not moving."

Verlink grabbed a chunk of debris from the floor. It had a honeycomb structure, and it was light in weight and surprisingly strong. He tossed it toward the figure, and nothing happened.

"Whatever it is, I don't think it's alive." He moved in closer and held his breath as he reached down and touched it. The figure remained motionless. Verlink slowly let out his breath. "It appears to be some kind of bipedal android."

He tried to turn the body over but was surprised by its weight. "Katrien, give me a hand; I want to see its face."

"Oh my God," said Katrien as they flipped the android over. "Its features are humanlike—except for the eyes."

"There's no color," said Verlink. "Perhaps if it were active, the eyes would change from black?"

Verlink pressed its skin. "The skin is some kind of polymer or nano-fiber mesh."

"It's not very tall, maybe four feet, like a child," said Katrien. "Any sign of damage?"

Verlink shook his head. "Nothing external that I can see. It's as if it just collapsed in the doorway."

Katrien stared hard at the android. "Professor, why aren't there more of these lying around? The city we left is huge, yet this is the first evidence of beings of any kind."

Verlink wondered the same thing. "This building came down from the sky for a reason. Perhaps the building, the android lying here, and the dormant city are all connected."

They continued down the corridor in silence, examining each room. Most were small, with consoles sporting medium-sized screens. At the end of the hall, they found a large area bathed in sunlight. Across the floor were structures that could have been chairs aligned in neat rows.

Katrien suddenly pointed across the room. "Professor, *look.*"

A large mural spanning the opposite wall depicted beings engaged in various activities. Some were outdoors in the woods, some were running; others still were seated in front of translucent screens that hung in the air, while others were in the water sitting in odd-looking boats.

"My God," said Verlink. "They look like—humans."

"Some of them are androids," said Katrien, "like the one we found in the hallway."

"There are probably fifty people shown here, if we can

call them that." Verlink started to run his hand through his gray hair but stopped midway as an observation struck him. "And have you noticed not *one* of them is *old*?"

CHAPTER 15

Water

Yuri tried again. The comm's range was at least ten kilometers, and he knew Sergei had his with him when they entered Verlink's lab. But he wasn't sure about Tolenka, other than remembering he had dropped his rifle in the scuffle. He tried one last time.

"Sergei, Tolenka, come in if you hear this."

No response.

He clicked it off to conserve the batteries and scanned the horizon for signs of significant vegetation. Yuri licked his lips and could feel the lines of blisters forming. "Keep moving," he told himself.

By now, he was used to the cubic objects floating above him and even sought out their shadows to avoid the relentless sun. He no longer had any doubts that he was not on Earth. What Sergei had said about the professor and his experiment *had* to be true: he had been transported to another world.

It was also clear that he would never get back home without the professor's help. Yuri touched the case of his

PMM Makarov to make sure it was still holstered. He would *make* the professor get him back. But he had to find him first, and to do that, he had to survive.

But this wasn't Tolyatti. There, to survive, all he had to do was find someone who had what he wanted and take it—by force. But here, there was nobody to steal from. He was on his own until he found the others.

Despite these shortcomings, he had already learned a great deal. By sampling various small plants, he found some that he could eat without becoming ill. But the water content was too low to satisfy his thirst. He even dug down through the topsoil looking for seepage, but he gave up when the ground became clay. Larger plants require more water, like trees growing along the banks of rivers and lakes. That was the key.

He could make out a city with tall buildings in the far distance, but he was hesitant to go there—at least for the time being. The inhabitants of this world might be there, and he wasn't desperate enough to chance an encounter. His immediate goal was to find water.

Yuri scanned the horizon slowly. North of the city, he spotted what seemed to be the outline of trees. *Water?* He ran his fingers over his lips and pictured a lake with cool water. With that image in his mind, Yuri struck out at a brisk walk. He could be there before nightfall.

•
•

Verlink scratched his temple, wondering if he'd missed something. "We've searched the entire first floor."

Katrien patted the wall. "No stairs, elevators, or ramps. There must be a way to the upper levels."

"Maybe if the building had power," said Verlink, "a way would open up?"

Katrien's eyes lit up. "I wonder if there's any power left. After all, there are still buildings floating, which means their power might be self-contained. Maybe the consoles are separately powered. A few may still be active."

"Worth a try. Let's systematically check each room."

They began with the small rooms but had no luck. The last room was the largest, with its mural and rows of furniture resembling chairs. Along a wall, opposite the mural, were several consoles.

Katrien touched the one closest to her, and a smile spread across her face. "Professor, this screen is active!"

Verlink came and leaned over her shoulder. "What do we have?"

"It scrolls like my tablet. I can't read the icons on the left, but *look* at this—there are actual images on the right, and some of them appear to be food."

Verlink looked around the room. It felt like a cafeteria—its size, the tables and chairs, and the hint of food odors. Or was that his hunger playing with his imagination?

"Could this be a cafeteria or something similar?"

Katrien tapped on the icon. An amber light flashed across the room, and a voice spoke in a singsong language that most resembled Chinese. An opening appeared in the otherwise seamless wall beneath the flashing light. In the opened space was a tray holding what seemed to be the identical item displayed on the screen.

Verlink retrieved the tray and brought it close to his nose. It smelled like food, but he hesitated. Could it be toxic? After all, the inhabitants had disappeared, and they still had no clue why.

He glanced at Katrien. "It smells edible. I don't think we have many options here. I'm going to chance it."

He dabbed his finger into a sauce and touched his tongue to it. "It's salty-sweet like soy sauce with nutty afternotes. Should I try more or wait?"

"I'd wait a bit to see if you have any reaction. In the meantime, let's see what else we can bring up."

Katrien searched the icons and stopped at one that looked like a bottle. "What we need is water." She tapped on the icon, and this time a bottle appeared where the tray had been earlier. Verlink retrieved it and studied the lid. It didn't unscrew, and there was no flip-top either.

"Here, let me try," said Katrien. She eyed the top and tried squeezing it, and an opening appeared. She sprinkled some liquid onto her hand and touched her tongue to it. "It has a slightly sweet flavor, but it sure seems like water," she said. "If these are consumable, then at least we won't starve or die of thirst."

Verlink set the tray in front of him and waited. As the minutes ticked by with no reaction, his spirits rose. He rechecked his watch. "I feel fine; I'm going for it."

Katrien called up another item at random, and together they sampled food from each other's trays. There were no discernible vegetables or anything else recognizable. Instead, the food consisted of blocks of different sizes and colors, each with a unique flavor. Some were spicy, not vindaloo-hot but close, while others were sweet or salty. But they were all satisfying.

"We were lucky to find this cafeteria," said Verlink, relaxing in one of the chairs. "I wonder how long it will continue to function and provide food."

"I've been thinking about that," said Katrien. "The building's internal workings may be powered by solar converters mounted on the roof. The levitation power probably came from a different source, which is now depleted."

Verlink stared at the mural and became pensive. "What happened here? These people were far in advance of us, and yet it doesn't seem like any of them survived. There's no evidence of war either. It's like we've stumbled across the *Mary Celeste*, only instead of a merchant brigantine, it's a whole city devoid of people."

"I wonder if the entire planet is like this," Katrien said.

"The other curious thing is that we've seen no vehicles anywhere, so how did they move about?"

"I'm tempted to go back to the city and have a closer look at those booths along the streets," said Verlink. "Maybe some of them are still active, like the food console here. I say we gather up food and liquids and head to the city early tomorrow morning."

As soon as he said it, he realized they had nothing in which to carry food. At the same time, another observation struck him. "You know, it's strange that we've seen no personal items lying about to indicate people ever occupied this building."

"I'm guessing they all departed long before the building fell," said Katrien. She eyed the fabric on one of the chairs. "I can cut away the seat cover to fashion a crude carrying sack."

"Good idea, and we'll keep searching for anything else that might come in handy on our hike back to the city."

Katrien retrieved a small pocketknife from her jeans and cut into the fabric on one of the cushions. After a second, she stopped and sat down.

"What's wrong?" Verlink asked.

Katrien ran her hand over the fabric. "This pattern reminds me of a chair my mother keeps in a spare bedroom. It's the room I stay in when I visit, and at night, I lay my clothes on that same chair."

She faced him; her eyes lost. "We're so very far away, Professor; what if we *never* get home?"

•

•

HAST4 kept his cloak activated and remained in the corner, observing. The man and woman were not Kytherians. They looked like them, but they didn't have the neural implant, so who were they? HAST3 would know, but he lay in the corridor, depleted.

The strangers might be able to help revive HAST3, but because HAST4 couldn't probe their minds, he couldn't be sure. The Great Purge had taught HAST4 caution. The others hadn't learned that until it was too late. Now they were gone.

A holographic display came into HAST4's view. His power was getting low. He had to get to the upper level to recharge before his invisibility cloak shut down. HAST4 moved toward the strangers, careful not to make any noise. They spoke with unfamiliar words. He wanted to stay, to learn more, but time was running out. He hurried past and left the room.

Down the hall, he triggered a portal that opened. He stepped through and went to the third level, where he opened his charging closet and tapped into the building's power grid. The current trickled in slowly. It would be many cycles before he reemerged. His neural matrix began shutting down to conserve power. The last thing he remembered before he drifted off was the girl talking. He didn't understand her words, but he remembered the look on her face and what she had said: "What if we *never* get home?"

CHAPTER 16

Rendezvous

Yuri sat up and stretched. The yellow-green grass wasn't bad to sleep on, but it got colder at night than he liked, and his shoulders were stiff. He stood up, walked to a bush, and relieved himself. Behind him was the sound of water rolling onto a beach. His plan had worked. A line of trees *had* sprung up near a small lake, just as he expected.

But locating food was another problem. The smaller plants dotting the open fields that tasted like lemons were bitter and only partially satisfied his hunger. In the long run, they would never sustain him. Tiny fish swam in the lake, but he had no way to catch them. He was essentially starving and decided it was time to enter the city.

He flipped the switch on his comm. It chirped and then crackled. He spoke loudly, "Sergei, Tolenka."

Nothing.

He waited a few minutes and tried again. Hearing no response, he was about to shut it off but then considered the possibility that Sergei and Tolenka might be turning theirs off to conserve power too. The folly of that logic hit him. Better to leave it on. He clipped it to his belt and scanned the horizon to get his bearings. The lake would be his base until he found the means to carry water, leaving only day trips for exploration.

Yuri struck out toward a row of buildings that were closest. Overhead, the sky was free of the floating cubes. They were in constant motion, with no predictable pattern and never getting close to one another, suggesting some means of control was still operating. Unfortunately, their absence meant no shadows, and soon the sun would be blazing down on him. Yuri picked up the pace.

"Yuri, Tolenka, come in. It's Sergei. If you can hear me, respond."

Yuri grabbed his comm. "Sergei, it's Yuri. Where are you?"

"I'm in some kind of city. Where are *you*?"

"I'm near the outer edge of a sprawling metropolis with large buildings. Is Tolenka with you?"

"I haven't seen or heard from him. You're the first person I've talked to since arriving here. The city is empty, and I haven't seen the inhabitants or activities of any kind. Have you?"

"No, but I've been staying out of the city."

"Those physicists were right about transporting to another world. We're no longer on Earth."

Yuri looked toward the sky and scoffed, "Yeah, the floating buildings give it away."

"How are we going to get back?"

"We'll talk about that once we meet. Since our comm devices have a limited range, I'm guessing you're in the same city I'm looking at right now. Are there any landmarks near you?"

"Toward the center of town, there's a silver-metallic spire."

"Let's rendezvous there. I'm guessing it'll take me a few hours."

"I'll be waiting."

•
•

The spire was cylindrical and tapered and rose gracefully to a point just as Sergei described. It sat in a small plaza and had a white line running up its side from the reflecting sun. Yuri circled it, but Sergei wasn't there. He sat down on a bench and shook his head. *Where is the asshole?*

Minutes later, a voice hailed from behind, "Yuri!"

Yuri turned and hardly recognized the person speaking. "Where the hell have you been?"

Sergei hobbled up to him and sat down. "I've been walking up and down these goddamn streets looking for an open building."

"You look like shit."

"I need water in a bad way." Sergei tried to swallow away the dryness in his throat. "I can hardly talk. Have you found water?"

"There's a small lake back in the park I just came from."

Sergei's hollow eyes flashed for a moment. "Did you bring water?"

"I don't have any way to carry liquids. I'm hoping to find something to use here in this city."

Sergei shook his head. "There's very little debris out in the open, and the buildings all have doors, but none of them will open."

"Have you found anything to eat?" asked Sergei.

"Nothing except for the leaves on bushes that taste like shit-lemons. But if we can make a net, or a line and hook, I think we can catch fish in the lake."

A painful crease spread across Sergei's face as he imagined the food and water he didn't have. Yuri stared at him and was surprised how far he'd fallen. He'd thought Sergei was tougher, but take away the trappings and comforts of civilization, and the man fell apart. One thing was clear: if Sergei started to hold him back, Yuri wouldn't hesitate to leave him behind.

Sergei leaned forward and started coughing in dry spasms. Then he tipped back up, his face red, and spoke in a raspy voice, "Do you think Tolenka made it here like us?"

"Who knows? But here's the thing; that professor and his grad student are the only ones who have the means to take us back. And for all we know, they may have already returned and left us in this hellhole. But if they haven't, then we might not have much time left to find them."

"Where are they?"

"I have no fucking idea, and I'm sure not going to wait around looking for Tolenka either. He's got to find us—agreed?"

"He's a good man. We might need his help."

Yuri was starting to regret meeting up with Sergei. He hated dead weight, and at the moment, Sergei was feeling mighty heavy. "I'm turning my comm off, but you can leave yours on if you want; the rest is up to Tolenka." Yuri stood up. "Right now, my main concern is finding a water container, and after that, something to eat besides those goddamn lemon bushes."

CHAPTER 17

The Booth

Verlink tried to keep up as Katrien moved across the field. "The fact that the inhabitants look very similar to us implies the dual world split off sometime after Homo sapiens were established on Earth."

"That must be it," said Katrien, pushing through the high grass toward the city. "Otherwise, random mutations would have driven significant changes given a longer time. Yet there are differences, like those sonic plants we found yesterday."

"We may know"—Verlink paused to catch his breath—"what the inhabitants look like, but we still don't know where they are or what happened to them. And I can't get over how none of the people in that mural was old."

"I know. They could have been students at the University of Amsterdam," said Katrien.

Katrien's pace surprised Verlink. Sometimes she moved hesitantly as if tired, then other times, like today, it was full speed ahead. He first noticed the behavior several months back but dismissed it. But the frequency was increasing, and he debated whether to talk to her about it. Verlink looked up and saw she was getting farther ahead. He chuckled to himself; then again, she was *young*.

"Maybe they figured out how to stop or significantly slow down aging or how to periodically reverse its effects," Verlink said, hoping Katrien would slow down herself.

"There are scientists on Earth who believe it will be possible within several decades to slow aging," said Katrien. "If that's true, then a society this technologically advanced would surely have achieved it." Katrien stopped and turned around. "Am I going too fast, Professor?"

Verlink rubbed his forehead with his sleeve. "Well, a few breaks now and then would be nice. I hike every weekend in the Zuid-Kennemerland Woods, but I go *slow*."

Katrien stopped. "Sorry about that. I know I walk fast."

Verlink smiled. "Ah, to be young again. Imagine if the people here figured out how to achieve extreme longevity."

"I don't know, Professor, maybe the life-and-death cycle keeps us trying to make the best of the time we have."

Katrien's words gave Verlink pause. If anyone deserved longevity, it was her. "Perhaps," he said, "but if you were given a choice, are you certain of your conviction?"

Verlink noticed his question caught Katrien for a moment, as if he had touched a nerve.

"It's probably moot," Katrien said as she stared in the direction of the city. "If you're ready to resume, we can be in the city within the hour."

The street was empty as the day before. Verlink studied the sun for a moment; it was starting to drop, and in the far distance, a floating building was sweeping toward the horizon. He wondered if the building's constant movement was part of their design, or did the builders simply like a changing view?

"I'm guessing we have four hours of daylight left," he said.

Katrien nodded. "Agreed. We had better find shelter if we're going to spend the night here in the city."

"We have a little time," said Verlink. "I'd like to check out a few of those booths that seem to be everywhere."

They came to one set back several feet from the street. The outside was rectangular and made of a metallic silver material with a red band circling the top. Katrien entered and touched the screen.

"This one's dead, Professor."

Verlink walked to the next one and tried it. "Nothing here." He rounded a corner and saw Katrien starring at an illuminated bar.

"Professor, look at the plastic bar over this doorway. From this angle, away from direct sunlight, you can see a glow. I think this one might have power." Katrien stepped inside and tapped the screen. It instantly lit up. "Oh my God, it's active."

Verlink stood in the doorway. "Are those icons displayed on the screen?"

"Yes, but nothing hints at their meaning."

Verlink gazed onto the street. "I wonder if this is some kind of call box to hail transportation."

"Maybe. What if these are teleportation booths? After all, we haven't seen anything that looks like a vehicle."

"God, that would be incredible."

"Do you think it's possible?" asked Katrien.

"Scientists have speculated how it might be done using an ultra-high-res MRI scanner with accuracy at the single-atom-per-pixel level. These booths would have to use short-wavelength electromagnetic waves modulated at very high frequencies. The transcripted data would have to be encrypted and beamed to successive cell towers until reaching the desired location, where a quantum computer would unpack the data and reconstruct the entity."

Katrien twisted a lock of hair with her finger. "But

there's the double problem. The created copy is separate from the original. Now you have *two* of you."

Verlink massaged his chin as he considered the ethical dilemma. "Maybe these people solved the left-behind-double problem. But it still gives me the creeps to think there could be two of me walking around or that one has to be destroyed. How would you decide which one?"

"That prospect raises many philosophical questions," Katrien said. "But perhaps we're overestimating the capabilities of the inhabitants. It could be simply a call box to summon transportation, as you suggested, or something else entirely."

Katrien resumed scrolling through the icons. "These icons could be the names of places, people, or even businesses. Unfortunately, there are hundreds of them."

Verlink noticed that the building on the opposite side of the street displayed a large icon along its roofline, which gave him an idea. He pointed at it. "Katrien, do any of the icons on the screen resemble the one on that building?"

"I'll look."

A few minutes later, Katrien stopped. "Professor, as I scroll through these, I'm noticing that the first part of the icon is the same, and the latter part changes. Then the first part changes in the next group and so on."

"So there *is* a pattern," said Verlink.

"I think so, but without more study, I can't do any kind of . . . hold on. I think this is it." Katrien pointed to an icon on the screen. "Is this the same as the building across the street?"

Verlink leaned over her shoulder. "It does look similar, but the tail on the last line swings up instead of down, and—"

Katrien tapped the icon to make a point. "But this—"

The booth suddenly filled with a yellow light followed by a chorus of tones, shifting in frequencies up and down until they hit sympathetic resonance.

At that precise moment, Katrien vanished.

Verlink raced into the booth. What had she done? Had she been transported, or was her disappearance the result of a system failure? He took out the handheld transceiver Katrien had given him. "Katrien, if you hear this, please respond."

No response. He tried again. "Katrien!"

The silence pressed into his chest. If Katrien did end up someplace else, then she'd be alone. He *had* to find her. And to do that, he had to repeat *exactly* what she had done. Unfortunately, the display screen had returned to its home page, which meant he would have to find the exact icon Katrien had activated all over again. But all he had to go on was that the icon was similar to the one on the building across the street.

Using the camera on his cell phone, Verlink captured images of the building's symbol at various angles. Then he returned to the booth. He scrolled through the icons, careful not to tap any of them directly. Eventually, he found one that matched the image on his phone except for the hook on the tail—just like the one Katrien had found. He stared at it for a moment and then took another picture with his phone. *This has to be it.*

He held his breath and tapped on the symbol . . . and nothing happened.

CHAPTER 18

Alone

Katrien became aware of her surroundings as if it were an image slowly coming into focus. Her body felt warm but seemed to be cooling off. *What happened?* The last thing she remembered was pointing at an icon on a display screen with Verlink standing outside the booth. She glanced outside.

Verlink was *gone*.

She unclipped her transceiver. "Verlink, where did you go?" She tried again. "Please, Verlink, answer—"

She stopped cold when she looked across the street. *Shit!* The building was *not* the same, so the booth had somehow transported her here—but where was *here*? Logically, her new location must be far away because she was beyond the transceiver's range. Katrien peered at the sun; it was lower in the sky. She checked her watch, and a sick feeling came over her. Not enough time had elapsed, so she must have traveled hundreds of kilometers east of her original position.

She scrolled rapidly through the symbols. "Think, Katrien, think!"

She tried to recall details of the icon on the building that had been across the street. She found a similar one, but if she were wrong and ended up someplace else, she and Verlink might never connect. Besides, Verlink would surely attempt to follow. *Best if I wait here.*

Katrien left the booth and sat down next to it. She had no idea where she was or how to get back. Verlink would try to duplicate her actions, but would he know what to do? She didn't even know herself; was it the symbol she touched, or was it entirely something else? And if Verlink did something different, he could end up God knows where.

Katrien dropped her head into her hands and started to cry—something she hadn't done for a long time. Without Verlink, her chances of returning home were unlikely, and given her disease, how long before she was incapable of taking care of herself?

She wiped her eyes and surveyed the area. The streets were empty, but that didn't comfort her. If Verlink didn't come soon, she would have to venture out on her own, and that frightened her.

Waiting too long would make it difficult to find shelter in the dark, yet she was leery of wandering far from the booth in case Verlink did arrive. Then again, he had the handheld transceiver, so she could leave without the worry of missing him. Katrien eyed a row of buildings lining the street. She would start with those; perhaps one of them was open and had power and a functioning food source.

Reentering the booth, Katrien tore off a piece of her sleeve and tied it to a ring above the display screen. If Verlink did follow, he would see the ribbon of blue cloth and know he had arrived at the correct location. Satisfied with her plan, Katrien stepped onto the empty street and suddenly felt vulnerable. She looked back at the booth for a moment, then turned around, swallowed, and started to walk.

:

After an hour, Katrien found a bench situated in a city square and sat down. Twilight had arrived, and with it came a chill in the air. In the dim light, she could see that several of the booths down the street were illuminated. Some were brighter than others; did that imply different available power levels, or was it something else?

The gathering darkness emphasized the reality of her situation. Her exploration of the nearby buildings had yielded the same story: no power, always with an entrance door, but no way to open it. Katrien rested her hand on her chin and tried to imagine how the street had once looked, filled with beings not unlike herself moving from building to building, passing through unseen doors without a care or thought.

Up and down the street, plant life was encroaching everywhere, gaining footholds in open areas and available cracks, suggesting the city had been unoccupied for possibly a year if not more. How an entire civilization, culture, and people could vanish unsettled her. What chance did *she* have—and Verlink too? Would she find him only to have to tell him that her days were numbered, eventually leaving him behind to be alone forever on a vast planet?

A cold wind rolled down the street, and in the deepening night, she noticed a faint glow coming from a building several blocks away. She stood up and hastened toward it. To her surprise, it was coming from *within* the building through an open doorway. Inside, an amber light glowed above a display panel on a wall opposite the door. Katrien went up to it and touched it.

The screen lit up, allowing her to see the entire room. Furniture filled the space, and on a table was a tray containing a bottle with liquid in it. Katrien examined the tray and found food residue. Whether it was recent or from a long time ago, she couldn't tell.

She returned to the screen. The display was similar to the one in the sky building, and after finding a familiar liquid icon, she tapped the screen. Across the room, a light flashed, and a bottle appeared on top of a counter.

Katrien next tried a food symbol that looked like a salad, and after another flash of light, a colorful medley of greens, reds, and yellows materialized on a plate next to the bottle. She retrieved them both and ate while surveying the room. Around her stood various pieces of furniture: tables, chairs, and something that could serve as a place to sleep.

The idea of sleep made her realize how tired she was, not so much physically but emotionally. She worried about Verlink. Why hadn't he followed her? Or did he try but end up someplace else? The last thought left her depressed.

She walked over to the piece she had eyed earlier set against a back wall and stretched out on it. The fabric felt surprisingly soft and radiated a mild heat where it came in contact with her skin. She closed her eyes . . .

•

•

Katrien's eyes shot open. There was a clang and then footsteps walking across the floor. Katrien peered over the edge of the backrest. A shadow in the shape of a human was moving through the room. Her heart jumped. Verlink had made it!

But why hadn't he called?

The figure activated the food source and spoke to it in a language similar to what she'd heard in the floating building the other day. The amber light flashed brightly for a second, lighting up the room. Katrien stifled a gasp. *That's not Verlink!*

She ducked behind the backrest and listened. Would the being stay and eat the food, and if so, would it turn on the lights? Katrien pushed herself deeper into the cushion.

She heard the scuff of footsteps across the floor; they were getting closer. Katrien held her breath. The footsteps stopped and seconds later backed away, followed by the sound of something like the cinching of a pack. Then, as quickly as the visitor had come, it was out the door.

Katrien let her breath out slowly, shaking. Who or *what* was that?

CHAPTER 19

Exploration

It had been several days, and Yuri was getting nowhere. Neither he nor Sergei had any idea how to find Verlink. And to add to the uncertainty, they weren't sure Verlink was still here—wherever the hell *here* was. They also had limited food, the only source being the small lake discovered days earlier. It contained fish, but they were tiny and tedious to catch. Although water was plentiful, without adequate means of storage, they were limited in how far they could venture before needing to return.

And to add to the annoyance, Sergei wouldn't stop talking about finding Tolenka. Yuri shook his head as he rotated a spit of skewered fish over a fire. *Screw Tolenka!* He would only slow them down. He glanced over at Sergei, who kept fussing over his transmitter like a bad habit. They needed to find Verlink or that grad student, not Tolenka.

Yuri removed the spit and blew on it. He tested the blackened flesh with his tongue and then began to eat. He followed it with water, wiped his mouth with his sleeve, and then stood and stretched. It was going to be a long day. They planned to head south to a fallen building to see if they could get inside. But it was far away, which meant they would have to either stay there without water until the next day or return in the night. The sooner they left, the better.

•
•

Verlink was deep in thought as he picked his way across the green field back to the city in the hopes of finding a working booth. The sky building had been eerily quiet the previous night without Katrien. Yesterday, after it had gotten dark, he gave up trying to get the booth to work and returned to the sky building in silence. He was reasonably sure he understood why the booth failed to function; it was merely out of power. The illumination bar above the doorway had become dark, where before it was a bright red. That must be the key.

The whole planet seemed drained of power—an arrested culture left hastily by a vanished people. And the decay was continuing. Yesterday, he witnessed a floating building fall from the sky in the distance. The entire building appeared to shudder before it dropped, becoming enveloped in spasms of green, jade-like and luminous. Then, as if it were a hot air balloon, it steadily descended from the sky until colliding with the ground, pitching forward from the inertia, then tipping back and coming to rest.

How many times had he watched buildings pass over his head, never thinking that one of them might fall from the heavens? What force held the massive structures above the ground, and what critical function gave way to bring them down? Yet several things *did* work, like the sky building's cafeteria. The power distribution must have redundancies, with some still operational.

When he reached the edge of the field, Verlink stepped

onto a street and couldn't help admiring the view. Buildings formed by some continuous extruding process, tall and graceful, rose above the ground in front of him. The buildings had an obvious purpose, but the wide empty streets—what were *they* for? Vehicles or pedestrians or *what*?

Verlink closed his eyes and tried to imagine the avenues filled with people he saw in the mural. But his thoughts soon wandered, turning instead to Katrien, Amsterdam, and bicycling along Roetersstraat: weaving between pedestrians, ringing his bell. He and Katrien often met after class outside the Café de Kooi along Amstelstraat, talking for hours as people strolled the cobbled streets. Katrien would play with a curl of hair as her mind toyed with a concept and then flash a smile when a connection was made.

A painful thought entered his mind. Would he ever see Katrien again? She was strong and resourceful, but something could happen. They would need each other if they were ever to leave this world. But the more time passed, the greater the odds were that she would no longer be at the place she ended up—if she were anywhere at all.

CHAPTER 20

The Dual-Worlder

The building no longer felt safe. After the intruder left, Katrien debated whether to stay or venture out to find another place. But leaving implied that it was safer elsewhere, which was by no means certain, so she decided to remain where she was.

When daylight came, Katrien got up and peeked outside. The street was empty, and to the east, the sun was trying to burn through an overcast sky. Its appearance, eerily similar to any morning in Amsterdam, brought no comfort. This was *not* Amsterdam, nor even Earth, and without the means to get home, she might as well be living in a daydream.

Back inside, she ordered food and water, ate, and then left the building. The streets seemed wider now that she knew she wasn't alone. Anyone or anything could be lurking around countless corners watching her.

To identify the building for later, she took a picture with her phone. Then she headed toward the booth she had arrived at the day before. The strip of cloth she'd tied to the ring was still there. The image of it—exactly as she had left it—caused a pang of sadness to well up in her chest. Was Verlink okay? Had he run into an inhabitant, and is *that* why he had never followed her?

Far in the distance, between rows of buildings, Katrien spotted another fallen building. Perhaps that would be a safer place to stay, but to get there required working through a series of buildings and then crossing an open field. With one last look at the cloth in the booth, she turned and stepped back onto the street.

She passed through an alley between tall buildings faced with a glossy material like onyx marble. Catching her reflection, she stopped to brush back her curly blonde hair. She had been told many times that she was naturally pretty with high cheekbones that always had a reddish blush against her alabaster skin. Her blue eyes appeared to squint ever so slightly, giving her a dreamy, almost seductive look. But now, all she saw was a pallid complexion and a pair of tired orbs looking back—an unpleasant reminder of how little sleep she had gotten last night.

At the end of the alley, she turned the corner and suddenly stopped. A figure who could have passed for a human male in his midtwenties was carrying a pack and seemed to be looking for something. He picked up a metallic object, examined both sides, and placed it in his pack. He then turned toward Katrien.

Katrien quickly backed into the alley and started breathing rapidly. Did he see her? She wasn't ready for an encounter, not *yet*. Her ears listened for the scuff of approaching footsteps. A minute passed, and the only sound was the wind channeled between the buildings. She slowly peered around the corner.

The dual-worlder, for lack of a better name, had moved in her direction, but his movement suggested he had not seen her. Although the distance was approximately one hundred yards, she could see he was like the beings displayed on the mural in the floating building. *Do all the inhabitants look like him—flawless?*

Katrien wondered if she should attempt to reach out to him. His humanlike features calmed her anxiety—not that *that* made any sense. Yet he might be able to help her find Verlink. But she was afraid; besides, how would she communicate with him?

She followed his movement until he disappeared between a row of buildings. When he was gone, Katrien realized she'd been holding her hands in a tight fist and slowly released them. So there *were* still inhabitants here. But he was scavenging; was he stranded here too, like her?

Katrien decided to stick with her plan and continued working her way toward the field. After several minutes, she came to a wide alley with debris scattered across its surface. Up until now, the avenues had been clear, with only vegetation making inroads, but here was evidence of some traumatic event taking place. As she kicked through the clutter, she realized it consisted of fragments from the buildings flanking both sides of the street. She stopped and tried to absorb the scene. *What catastrophe had been unleashed here?*

Farther ahead, her eyes caught a flash of color. She walked over to it and picked up a blue plastic panel. As she turned it over in her hands, the panel suddenly lit up and started talking. She thought of dropping it, but it began displaying a moving image. It was a video showing a street filled with dual-worlders. They were running, moving in waves, first in one direction, then shifting to another as if trying to get away from an invisible bird of prey.

Katrien searched the images for the cause of their panic. Then she heard it; it was a sound straight out of Ragnarok, a keening that lived in her nightmares. It was the same rasping sound she and Verlink had heard in

France over a year ago. It was the death of matter itself.

She realized the buildings next to her were the same in the video, and the images she was watching came from exactly where she was standing. Katrien picked at her lip nervously and started walking. In France, the artifact's decomposition field had consumed everything it came in contact with, but here, the buildings and infrastructure had survived largely intact; only the dual-worlders had strangely vanished.

After a minute, she stopped walking, turned around, and tried to imagine what had happened here. What *did* happen? Perhaps the dual-worlders didn't send the information engine to Earth after all. Maybe they were victims too, and now they're gone. A thought struck her: Could whatever have attacked the people *still* be here?

Unnerved, she resumed walking, still facing backward. She hadn't traveled more than several yards when something underneath suddenly gave way. At first, she felt the sensation of moving in slow motion, her mind recording minute details; then everything sped up, accelerating until she landed hard with chunks of cement and shards of glass raining down around her. She raised her arms to cover her head, but it was too late. Something struck her, sending her to the floor and into darkness.

Katrien sat up and then quickly lay back down as a wave of nausea overtook her. She attempted again a few minutes later, but slowly this time, allowing the dizziness to pass. How long had she blacked out? She felt the back of her head and winced; her hand was bloody. A throbbing pain directed her attention to her left leg, now bent at an unnatural angle. Katrien reached down and tried to straighten it. "Shit!"

She felt along her shin, following the bone. There was a slight rise about two-thirds of the way, like a squat tent. When she applied pressure, it moved. "Ahhhhh!"

Her shinbone was fractured but in only one place, which meant she could set it. She looked about her surroundings. The plastic panel had fallen with her, as had fragments of framing, twisted metal, and glass that had once supported the pit's roof. She eyed a piece that could serve as a splint and leaned over to retrieve it. She then tore off several long strips from the bottom of her blouse. Now came the hard part.

Katrien balled up the cloth and stuck it into her mouth, biting down hard. She started a countdown: one, two, *three!* A searing pain forced tears into her eyes as the bones in her leg shifted into place. She spat out the cloth, bound the splint tightly, and then scooted backward to put her shoulders against the wall. Her heart was racing, and she couldn't calm it. She was in trouble and knew it.

The pit was some kind of access enclosure with a metal door on one wall. The other walls were sheer with no ladder. Katrien tilted her head back to see how far she'd fallen. It hurt to move her head, and her eyes went blurry for a moment. When the twinge faded, her eyes focused on the edges of the pit. They were ten to twelve feet above and ragged where the roof had broken away, with several long sections still dangling.

She followed each edge with her gaze, moving her head, until she suddenly froze. She was not alone.

CHAPTER 21

First Contact

Katrien felt like some creature being studied in a terrarium. It was the same dual-worlder she'd seen in the alley, and for the moment, the two of them just stared at each other. She tried to read the meaning in his eyes and facial expressions, but would they translate the same as on Earth?

The dual-worlder suddenly spoke in a voice that resembled an Asian dialect, but in a language she didn't know.

Katrien mimed that she didn't understand and pointed at her leg, hoping he'd comprehend her gesture. "I need your help," she pleaded.

The dual-worlder pulled back in surprise. Was it the condition of her leg or the strange language that came from her lips? After a moment, he spoke again, indicating with his hand someplace outside the pit.

Did he understand that she couldn't walk or climb a ladder? To make her plight known, she reached for her broken leg and, without thinking, pulled to raise it. A searing pain shot through her brain. "Aargh!" she yelled, quickly letting go of her leg.

The dual-worlder, alarmed by her cry, stood and began talking wildly while again pointing out in front of him. What was he saying? Get help, bring something to lift her out of the pit? Or was he planning on leaving her there?

A part of her didn't want him to return. What she wanted was to hear Verlink's voice on her transceiver and know that he was coming to rescue her.

She peered back up at the dual-worlder. He fixed his eyes on her for a long moment and then abruptly disappeared from view.

She thought again of Verlink, then unclipped the transceiver from her blouse and pressed send. "Verlink, I'm in trouble. Please answer."

The transceiver hissed static.

She switched it off and tried to calm herself by analyzing her situation. The cage she'd become entrapped in was roughly twenty feet on each side. On an opposite wall was a small metal door. Katrien dragged herself toward it and felt its edges, and then tried pushing on it without success.

Next to it was a thin piece of metal that had fallen from the roof. She inserted it into the seam around the door and pulled back hard. The door held fast. She tried again, adding as much of her own weight as she could, and ended up bending the makeshift pry bar. The exertion left her head pounding. All she wanted right now was to be back home in the lab with coffee and Verlink's calming voice. Her eyelids felt heavy, and she let them close. *Just for a few minutes.*

•

•

Katrien awoke to a throbbing in her leg. The pain was getting worse. She felt her head where the object struck. At least the wound had stopped bleeding. She leaned back against the wall and looked up; the dual-worlder had not returned. *I have to get out of here.*

Above, a twisted light-duty truss protruded into the pit. She wondered if she could reach it. With her hands behind her, Katrien pushed herself up the wall until she could stand on her good leg. She extended her arm and could touch the end of the truss. But the edges were serrated from the collapse, and she'd surely cut herself attempting to climb it barehanded.

She sat down and, with her pocketknife, cut cloth from the bottom of her slacks and wrapped the palms of her hands. She then stood up with her back against the wall. The upper edge of the pit was at least ten feet. Or was it more like twelve? Katrien reached out for the truss and pulled herself up about a foot. The top edge suddenly seemed very far away. Another drop could easily break her other leg—or worse, drive her fractured tibia through the skin. Katrien backed down and crumpled to the floor. "Coward!" she yelled, stomping her foot.

Why hadn't the dual-worlder returned? The urge to sleep kept returning in waves, and she was becoming weaker. Outside the pit, at least she would have a chance to regain her strength and nurse her injuries, but here—she was doomed.

What she needed was a rope. If she could secure one end near the bottom of the truss and place a foot loop partway down the line, she could then stand up in the loop with her right foot. But she had no rope. She searched the perimeter of the pit. It was hopeless; there was nothing to serve as a rope. It was as simple as that.

Her broken leg began to tingle. She shifted it, but the prickling persisted. The bindings against the splint were too tight, so she loosened them, and then it struck her; she could make a rope out of her slacks.

Using her pocketknife, she removed the legs of her slacks and divided them into eight long strips. She also pulled the wraps from around her palms and tied all the pieces together to form a single knotted rope over twelve feet long. Standing with one hand against the wall, she attached the makeshift rope to the bottom of the truss. She pulled herself up several inches as a test. The rope held!

She made a second loop a few feet from where the rope was attached to the truss. The plan was to pull herself up high enough to engage the foot loop with her good foot, which would then hold her weight while she tied the opposite end of the rope higher up the truss. With her weight on the second loop, supported by the upper attachment, she would be free to untie the original anchor and move it higher up the truss. The process would be slow but not unlike a technique used by rock climbers to ascend their ropes.

Time to put theory into practice.

Katrien eased herself into a standing position and grabbed the rope. She pulled her body off the floor and waited for the throbbing in her leg to subside. She brought her good knee up to get her foot into the first loop. So far, so good. Then she stood up, placed all her weight on the loop, and attached the rope's free end as high as possible on the truss. With that secured, she pulled herself up higher to step her good foot into the second loop, which took her weight off the first one. Now came the tricky part. She had to bend down, undo the first knot, and reattach it higher up the truss.

As she leaned over to release the knot, blood rushed to her head, and the rafter began to sway. She picked at the knot, but her fingers started to sweat. It wouldn't budge. Her weight had cinched the knot so tightly that she couldn't undo it. She'd have to cut it. She reached for a zippered pocket. *Shit*—the knife was lying on the floor five feet below her.

Katrien righted herself, and the sudden movement

made everything go blurry. She hugged the girder and took long, slow breaths. If she couldn't undo the knot, she was effectively stuck. Her plan had failed.

She thought of Verlink again. Had he tried to use the booth and ended up someplace else? Or had he also fallen victim to an accident? The girder felt cold pressed against her cheek. She pulled her face away from the rafter and looked at its ragged edge. It reminded her of teeth. *Yes!* That was it. Now she knew what she had to do.

Her teeth hurt, but the rope slowly yielded. Finally, Katrien tied the free end above her and stepped into the un-weighted loop. She was high enough that her hand could almost touch the edge of the pit. A slight breeze wafted over the side. Her spirits rose. One more knot transfer and she'd be high enough to mantel up and over the rim.

After resetting the knot, Katrien put her foot into the loop and shifted her weight onto the rope. The knot started to slip. Katrien instinctively grabbed the girder with her bare hands and froze. The serrated edges would only cut if her grip slipped. Without the aid of foot loops, she could no longer rest. Katrien gritted her teeth and started pulling up slowly, hand over hand.

Lactic acid burned in her forearms as the rim of the pit inched closer. A warm gust from above washed over her, beckoning. She thought of what she would do once free, whether to seek out the dual-worlder or stay on her own. For a split second, she lost focus, and her hand slipped. Blood oozed from her palm. It trickled down the rafter and acted as a lubricant. Soon, no amount of strength would hold her weight.

The floor was waiting.

Katrien could feel the steady thumping of her heart; she wasn't going to make it. She closed her eyes, torn between letting go and hitting the floor like a discarded rag doll—or having her palms carved like a holiday turkey.

Everything that had happened the last few days flashed before her. It was a story too incredible to believe. Yet here she was in *another* world. Katrien started to cry. It wasn't supposed to end this way. She was a theoretical physicist, not an explorer; her days were spent in a laboratory or behind a computer screen or taking a stroll under the warm sun in Oosterpark, not like—

Suddenly, a voice boomed above her. Katrien looked up; the dual-worlder was there, and he brought his hand under her arm. He said something loudly, and in one swift movement, he pulled her up and over the edge.

CHAPTER 22

The Upper Level

Verlink looked out onto an open field from an upper-story window. The sun was coming up from behind the building, casting the field in its shadow a deep shade of green. He liked the higher advantage and wished Katrien were here so he could tell her of his discovery. It was a matter of pure luck, but considering his string of bad luck, he certainly felt due.

He had learned that the openings leading to the higher floors were voice-activated, and he had stumbled upon this discovery while returning late in the evening. It was dark as he entered the building, and he had to feel his way. As usual, he walked down the hall and turned right into the large room that he had decided to call the "cafeteria." But it *wasn't* the cafeteria, it was the room just before it, and his head had collided with a post set off to the side. "Goddamn it!" he howled.

To his surprise, an illuminated doorway opened just outside the room. He had been down that hall dozens of times, and he knew there were no seams where the door had suddenly appeared. At first, he hesitated to pass through it, worrying that he would become trapped on the other side. While contemplating what to do, the door suddenly disappeared. He yelled again—"Goddamn it!"—and the doorway reappeared. This time, he counted how long it remained open. Forty seconds.

While the door was open, Verlink could see stairs—leading, presumably, to the upper levels. If he stepped through, would the door reopen with the same command, or would he become trapped? He went into the cafeteria, brought back a chair, and lodged it in the threshold while the door was open.

When the door closed, the wall formed *around* the chair. The doorway was, in fact, always open, a hologram coupled with some kind of force field. No wonder there were no seams around the door—it was essentially an optical illusion!

Yet it was a *solid* illusion: the chair entrapped by the forcefield could not be moved while the door was closed. Since sound could still pass through the opening, Verlink decided to chance stepping through it. He walked across the threshold and waited nervously for the door to close. When it did, he tried the voice command, and the door reopened. Relieved, Verlink stepped back into the hallway. He now had access to the entire building.

The recollection reminded him of the welt on his forehead. He rubbed it. There was still a bump there, but all things considered, it had been an equitable trade.

Verlink packed his daily provisions into a cloth sack made from furniture cushions and hoisted it onto his back. His goal for the day was simple: find a working booth, and, if successful, attempt a transfer to Katrien's location. But the city was large, and to aid in his search, he had divided the metropolis into a grid pattern. Today, he would search zone 4B.

One last look out the window, and he'd be on his way. The sun was higher in the sky now, and the field had changed to a lighter hue of green. He was about to turn away but stopped. He saw a color that wasn't green in the distance, it was black and *moving*. His heart jumped. *Katrien?* But then he remembered what she was wearing the day she disappeared, and it wasn't black; it was *blue*.

Verlink waited for the figure to get closer. After several minutes, he recognized the intruder as one of the three men who had stormed into his lab several nights ago. The man moved slowly and had a holstered gun strapped across his chest. Verlink had no weapon, but he did have one advantage: the element of surprise. Unfortunately, to make use of that advantage, he needed a plan, and he needed one fast—because it would soon come down to a match between his brain and a brute with a gun.

Verlink was ready. He had choreographed everything, and timing would be crucial. But there was an unknown variable; how fast could the invader move? From the second level, Verlink studied the man's movements as he circled the building. The man always kept one hand on his sidearm, and he moved slowly, not a cautious walk, but a gait that implied weakness. Was he injured or possibly *starving*?

When the man reached the opening where the building's fall had torn a hole, Verlink left his vantage point and hastened to the first level to conceal himself behind the holographic door opposite the hallway. As a bread crumb, he had left a small tray of food in the cafeteria, hoping the man would find it. The next step was a gamble, and it required the man to be in the cafeteria and *not* in the hallway.

When he thought he had waited long enough, Verlink spoke to the door: "Goddamn it." The door didn't open. He tried again louder. "Goddamn it." Nothing. This time he yelled, *"Goddamn it!"* and the door opened.

Verlink turned and ran up the stairs. At the last step, he looked down and could see the man tentatively peering through the doorway, his gun drawn.

The man spotted Verlink and yelled, "Wait—you bastard!" He fired his gun.

Verlink raced to the next door, cursed it to open, and sailed up another flight of stairs. At the top, he waited and, to his surprise, saw the invader bounding up the stairs—*fast*.

As Verlink cleared the uppermost level, he could hear the echoes of footsteps and darted across a large room with tall cylindrical cabinets and rows of tables with built-in displays. At the far end, he commanded a door to open, leading to a second stairway. He began counting down: *forty, thirty-nine, thirty-eight* . . . Verlink peeked around the doorway, and when he saw the top of the man's head across the room, he vaulted down the stairs and voiced the next door to open.

Breathing hard, he stopped at the doorway and watched the upper entrance. The man was moving fast—*too* fast. There were still seconds before the upper stairway door closed. *Twenty-two, twenty-one . . .*

The pursuer appeared at the top of the stairwell with his eyes on fire. He pointed his gun at Verlink. "One more move and you're dead."

Verlink needed to stall him. *Ten, nine* . . . He yelled, "Watch out!"

Tolenka reared back just long enough, *four, three, two, ONE.*

The door disappeared. The man had not gotten through. Verlink dropped his face into his shaking hands and let out a shallow laugh. "It worked . . . it worked!"

•

•

Hiding behind his cloaking shield, HAST4 had witnessed the entire drama. It made no sense. Yesterday, when he emerged from the charging closet, he found the man with gray hair alone. Where did the girl go? The man often talked to himself as if he were with someone, which puzzled HAST4. But now, another man, who also was not Kytherian, had shown up. He didn't look well and spoke harshly to the man with the gray hair. *What is going on here?*

HAST4 had not seen behavior like this before, and it gave him pause. Earlier, he was prepared to reveal himself to the gray man and ask for his help, but now he wasn't sure. He needed more time to observe these strangers and ascertain their purpose.

But that was all right. HAST4 had always been patient.

CHAPTER 23

Voices

The dual-worlder talked rapidly, but Katrien didn't understand a word. He examined her leg and then placed her on a stretcher with a metallic frame strung with a cloth that reminded her of heavy silk. The dual-worlder opened a black case next to the stretcher and removed an object shaped like a dome covered by an array of electrodes.

Katrien stared at the dome and wondered what he would do with it. Could it repair her leg?

"What are you doing?" she asked, knowing he couldn't understand her.

He chattered back and then put the dome on top of her head and adjusted a strap around her chin.

Katrien tensed. Her eyes darted back and forth following his movements. The dual-worlder took a plastic box from the case and started pressing buttons. Flutelike tones flooded Katrien's ears. She twisted her head to see from where they were coming. The sounds were unmistakable, but from *where*?

The dual-worlder put his hand on her arm and shook his head slowly.

She wanted to get up and run away. "Please, no!" she cried. She shifted her body to leave, but a stabbing pain in her leg caused her to catch her breath. She wasn't going anywhere. Then the tones increased, and Katrien realized they were coming not from outside but from *inside* her head.

The dual-worlder produced a cylindrical object the size of a pencil and showed it to her. He touched the end of it with his finger and then motioned that he would use it on her broken leg.

A drug?

"No!" Katrien said, trying to sit up.

The dual-worlder said something abruptly and then pressed the cylinder into the calf of her leg. Katrien flinched and started breathing rapidly. *Oh my God!* Within seconds a warm sensation spread across her skin. Her heart slowed down to a steady rhythm: *thump, thump, thump,* and the pain in her legs and head began to seep away.

The plastic box beeped as if it finished whatever it was doing. The dual-worlder brought the box close to his lips and spoke into it. Simultaneously, the tones in her head changed pitch, first rising, then falling, eventually evolving into a complex pattern of multiple sounds.

The timbre turned into voices, muffled as if coming from a room behind a closed door. After a few seconds, the voices started to fade, save for one that became louder, issuing bits and pieces of words she understood. She stared at the dual-worlder. *Is that him speaking?*

Then, as if everything suddenly clicked into place, she understood what he was saying. He was talking to *her*!

CHAPTER 24

Udan

Verlink returned to the first floor and held out his hands. They were still shaking. Would the intruder figure out how the doors worked? Had he heard him swearing "goddamn it" at the door? Verlink walked outside and scanned the upper windows. The man was looking out and spotted him and began pounding on the glass.

Moments later, Verlink heard muffled gunshots and loud thuds. The man was shooting at the windows. They held, but what else might he try?

Verlink wished the man were dead. He came here with his gun drawn, just like the night he attacked them in the lab. If it weren't for him and his comrades, he and Katrien would not be stuck here. Katrien would be safe, and their biggest problem would be explaining their research to the department chair. The thought of Katrien reminded him that he should have been in the city by now. She was completely alone, wondering why he never followed her.

The man began pounding again. Should he leave him there or negotiate for his release? If the man had shown up asking for help, that would have been different. But instead, he came brandishing a weapon and operating according to his true nature.

Verlink raised his fist and shook it. At the moment, he didn't care what happened to the face looking through the window. The city was waiting, and with any luck, he'd find a functioning booth and hopefully a way to reunite with Katrien.

•
•

The dual-worlder placed Katrien on a gurney, or something like it, and began wheeling her to a building with a polished gray exterior. Katrien mulled over his name, which she'd heard from the translator: Udan Roda-Tocci. He said to call him Udan, and when she asked him where she was, he told her she was in Loutras. But she suspected Loutras was the city. When she tried to ask about the world she was on, he gave her a puzzled look but replied anyway: the world she was on was called Kythera.

She studied his actions and couldn't help staring at his face. A sculpted chin and strong forehead with eyes that spoke of intelligence and maybe . . . *kindness?* His movements were confident and deliberate. But where was he taking her? When they reached a doorway, he uttered a command, and a door opened.

Inside, they went to a room with equipment that reminded her of an MRI scanner not unlike the one she'd seen several years ago in a hospital when she tore her labrum in a gymnastics class in high school. Udan easily lifted her and carefully placed her on a table with a frosted glass surface and a metal trim. He explained where they were, but there were communication gaps, and she only understood bits. When she spoke, his expressions suggested he understood, and Katrien got the sense that his grasp of her language was improving rapidly.

Udan leaned over her. "I fix the leg now, but important for you not to move. Can you do that?"

Katrien nodded and said, "Yes." It occurred to her that gestures like nodding for "yes" and shaking the head for "no" might not translate the same. Kythera was what he called his world, but it was also the name of an island, one of seven on Greece's southern tip. Was there a connection, or was it purely coincidental? Then again, maybe it was as close to the actual name the translator could find.

A light came from underneath the table, and a low thrumming began. Udan placed his hands on her legs and said, "No move." At first, there was a slight sensation, but then a pins-and-needles awareness ran through the calf of her leg. Udan removed his hands.

Suddenly, something invisible grabbed her leg and locked it in place. From above, a device lowered with a series of black cylinders projecting from it. As it hovered over her leg, the prickling increased. Now there was pain—*real* pain. Katrien cried out. Udan held her shoulders. "No worry."

The pain ebbed and, with it, the prickling. Within another minute, the machine became silent, and the table light went dark. Udan swung a screen attached to an articulated arm in front of her. It displayed an image like an X-ray of the inside of her leg. He toggled between the original and final state of her leg. The break was completely fused.

Katrien couldn't believe it. Her leg had been repaired within minutes. "Thank you."

Udan smiled back.

At least smiles were the same. He placed his hand behind her back and had her sit up. She felt a little dizzy.

"We now see if you can walk."

Katrien stared at her bare legs and felt along where the break occurred. Was it really fixed? She looked at Udan hesitantly. "I am afraid to try."

"We make sure there is no nerve damage," he said and helped her down from the table.

Katrien weighted her leg tentatively, expecting pain, but there was none. She took a step and giggled in relief.

"Does your head still hurt?"

Katrien felt the back of her head. "No."

"Good. There was no permanent damage. You will heal on your own."

Udan brought her to a chair and sat her down. He pulled up a chair next to her and clasped his hands in his lap. "Now that you are fixed, I have many questions."

Katrien nodded. "I'll try my best to answer them."

"Why is your language not in the Kytherian database?"

"I am not from Kythera."

Udan pulled back. "Then where are you from?"

The surreal nature of her situation hit her. She was talking to a man from a quantum dual world in her own language. *Will he understand enough of what I am about to tell him?*

Katrien touched the translator dome, still on top of her head. "Udan, I don't know if what I am about to tell you will translate correctly. I come from a parallel world, a quantum dual of your own, to be precise."

Udan became alarmed. "What?"

Katrien repeated what she said, hoping it was translating correctly.

Udan slowly nodded with a slight circular motion. "I know about quantum dual worlds, but you must have used technology from Kythera to come here. How can this be?"

Katrien thought the news would baffle Udan, but it didn't. His race was thousands of years beyond hers. Was the concept of parallel worlds readily accepted by his people? Katrien's mind flashed back to the devastation wrought by the information engine sent from Kythera to Earth. "You should know," she said with a tone of bitterness, "that Kythera sent two such devices to *my* world."

"You used one of those engines? But they were sent thousands of years ago."

Katrien worried about where the conversation was going, but she needed to know the true purpose of the Kytherian engines. "Yes, but why would your people send an information engine into our world? It almost destroyed us."

Udan looked out past her as if recalling a buried memory. "It was not *my* people who did it."

Katrien searched his face. "Then who?"

A cloud descended over Udan. "So much has happened here on Kythera, and I will explain everything, but first, tell me your name."

CHAPTER 25

Tolenka

There was a crack where the building had collided with the ground. It was narrow but wide enough for a man to squeeze through. Sergei watched Yuri take out his gun and poke his head inside. It was his modus operandi—waving that stupid gun around.

All appeared quiet, so Yuri signaled him to follow. Rubble was strewn on the floor, and farther in, a fallen beam blocked their path. Yuri crawled underneath it on his hands and knees. "There's light up ahead," he said.

Sergei was thirsty. The entire hike had been in direct sunlight, and they had seen no lemon plants along the way either. Why were they here anyway? They needed more food and water, not a shit-tour of dead technology. He got on his hands and knees and started crawling. As he ducked under the beam, he wondered if Tolenka was faring any better. What if he'd found Verlink?

"Get moving," said Yuri.

Sergei stood up. "What's the hurry? There's nothing here," he said, kicking the debris at his feet. "Just like everywhere else we've looked."

Yuri straightened his back and puffed out his chest. "And what makes you so sure there's nothing here? Have you been here before?"

"Fuck you. You know what I'm talking about. This whole goddamn world is dead. Nothing works."

"Not everything. We've seen lights in the city, and there are still floating buildings up there."

Sergei rolled his eyes and laughed. "Christ, a few blinking lights in the city. And so what if the floating buildings have power? How the hell does that help us?"

Yuri huffed. "Then *go*. I'm getting off this fucking world one way or the other. If you want to stay here and play farmer, I can't stop you."

Sergei replied between drawn lips, "Works for me." He turned, got back down on his hands and knees, and left.

Outside the building, he felt good for the first time since he'd hooked up with Yuri. He could finally operate the way *he* wanted to, and his first task was to find Tolenka. He flipped on his comm device and held the send button down while he spoke. "Tolenka, come in; it's Sergei."

Nothing.

He tried again and only heard the hiss of white noise. He attempted several more times and then clipped the transceiver to his shirt.

He squinted as he looked back toward the lake. He wanted water, and the lake was a sure thing. The fact that he had no way to carry water other than in his body made it feel like an addiction. He was hooked and needed a fix at regular intervals. Just a week ago on Earth, he had been surrounded by unimaginable luxuries: water from taps, water from plastic bottles, and water from colored glass bottles with twist-off lids. Sergei let out a bitter laugh.

Suddenly the transceiver crackled to life. "Tolenka

calling Sergei and Yuri. Repeat, this is Tolenka calling Sergei and Yuri."

Sergei grabbed the transceiver. "Tolenka, it's Sergei. Where are you?"

Tolenka's voice was shallow. "I'm in a fallen building outside some kind of city. That professor trapped me in an upper level where there's no food or water. I'm dying up here."

"I can hardly hear you, Tolenka. How bad off are you?"

Tolenka's voice became raspy. "I don't think I have much time left."

"Why haven't you tried contacting us before?"

"I have, every day. I'm up several stories now; maybe the higher elevation allows the signal to reach you."

"I need to determine your location. Which side of the city are you on?"

"I think I'm east of the city. Are you in the city now?"

"No, but I was there several days ago, and I'm assuming it's the same one you're talking about. At the moment, I'm south of the city, and I'm heading farther south to a lake to get water."

Tolenka moaned. "God, a lake full of water." Tolenka coughed and then a long silence. "I haven't peed since yesterday. How soon can you get here?"

"Realistically, not until tomorrow morning."

Sergei heard Tolenka groan. "Just hurry."

"If I encounter Professor Verlink, will he be armed?"

"I don't know, but I don't think so. Did you find Yuri?"

"Yeah, but he's not with me now, and frankly, I don't give a shit."

CHAPTER 26

Cat and Mouse

The sun was barely above the horizon when Verlink left his sleeping pad. He worked silently as he gathered food and water into a sack and then lifted it onto his shoulder. Outside, he breathed in the cool morning air. Dew on the grass sparkled like tiny jewels. He scanned the upper windows of the building. The man was not there.

Good, he thought and wondered if he were still alive. He had decided to leave him to his fate; the risk of releasing him was too high. Verlink's disquiet was about Katrien and nothing else. He missed her and avoided thinking of the possibility that he might never find her—all because of the man he'd trapped and his accomplices. They could have harmed Katrien or even killed her, and if given a chance, they would probably try again if it suited their purpose.

The others were likely still out there, but he couldn't be concerned about that. There had to be another working booth, and he was going to find it. Verlink faced the city, took a deep breath, and started walking.

•
•

The morning was quiet, and Sergei welcomed the solitude and lack of Yuri's constant bellows. He crouched near a fire warming his hands. Tolenka was no longer answering his calls, and Sergei was beginning to wonder if his rescue was a lost cause. He had not apprised Yuri about Tolenka either. If he had returned to camp last night, he would have told him, but he never returned. Sergei laughed hoarsely. The irony struck him; Tolenka had found Verlink, not Yuri. And why should he tell Yuri anyway? He would only want to assume control—*again*.

With his fill of fish and water, Sergei set out toward the eastern side of the city. All he had to go on was that Tolenka was east of the metropolis inside a fallen building. Unfortunately, there would likely be several downed buildings, and he'd have to search each one. Plus, there was a nagging worry: he had never learned from Tolenka exactly how Verlink had trapped him. He tried asking, but Tolenka had become incoherent late into the evening, babbling on about doorways that appeared out of nowhere.

To avoid the same mistake, Sergei wanted the element of surprise. But the buildings were in open fields, which made a stealthy approach nearly impossible during the day. At night, he at least had a chance. Unfortunately, that assumed he knew which building Verlink was in, which he didn't.

Sergei hiked quickly, stopping whenever he found lemon plants. He ripped the leaves off in bunches, ate them, or stuffed them into his pockets. The leaves were highly acidic and burned the inside of his mouth, but at least they didn't make him sick and offered meager amounts of carbohydrates. By noon, he was far enough east to make out three fallen buildings lying in open fields.

As he neared the first structure, he could see it was undamaged, and without a visible door, he had no way of entry. He circled it several times and moved on.

When he reached the second building, it was apparent that it had crashed into the ground with great force. One entire side had caved in, spewing debris out front like a rumpled apron. There were no bodies or the remains of bodies within the rubble: no bones, no clothes, no stains spread across the ground—in short, *nothing* to indicate beings ever lived here. It was a familiar theme: a world built by ghosts.

Dusk was settling in by the time he reached the third building. As he got closer, Sergei saw that it was tilted at an odd angle, like a squat Leaning Tower of Pisa. He circled it and found a large gash where the brunt of the impact occurred. Sergei suddenly stopped; the grass near the opening was trampled with stones scuffed from their hollows in the dirt. Sergei drew his Makarov and peered cautiously inside.

Stepping through the opening, he followed a dim trail of light. After wriggling under a partially collapsed doorway, he came to a corridor with rooms off to the sides. Across from the last room was something blocking the threshold. It was some kind of android, lying facedown—inactive. He thought of studying it, but Verlink might be nearby, so he moved on.

The final chamber was the largest, with long rows of furniture and a sweeping mural spanning an opposite wall. As Sergei walked between the rows, he noticed some of the furniture had its fabric ripped off. On a table was a tray with remnants of food. He scraped the food with his thumb and brought it to his nose—it wasn't more than a few days old. Sergei tightened his grip on his gun. He called out, "Tolenka! It's me, Sergei."

Hearing nothing, he worked his way back outside. Looking up toward the roof, he shouted and listened. Again, nothing. He grabbed a rock and hurled it at one of the upper windows. It bounced off with a clink. The silence made him wonder if this was even the right building. Then again, someone *had* been here.

By now, it was getting dark, and the outline of the city was barely visible. If this *was* the building with Tolenka trapped inside, then Verlink was either hiding or would be returning soon. Sergei searched the field for movement, but it had gotten too dark to be sure of anything.

Sergei rubbed the stubble of beard on his chin. It had been a long day, and he was hungry and thirsty and, most of all, tired. He reentered the building and felt his way down the hallway and into the last room. At a far corner, he dropped to the floor, lay down, and closed his eyes.

•
•

A light in the hallway woke Sergei. The silhouette of a man came into the room and stepped up to a console with a screen. Seconds later, the screen became activated, and an amber light flashed across the room, followed by a voice speaking an unknown language. Sergei could see the man's face in the pale light—it was *Verlink*!

Verlink walked over to a bureau, retrieved a bottle of liquid and a tray, and then sat down. He used his hands and dug into the food.

Piece of cake, thought Sergei, leaving the shadows. He came up behind Verlink, pointing his gun. "Professor Verlink, I presume?"

CHAPTER 27

Qua-Kil

The room was dark except for a yellow glow coming in from underneath the door. Inside was a bed that swayed gently like a porch swing. Katrien lay on top, wide awake. It would be hours before morning, and she wondered if Udan were sleeping or whether he even needed to sleep. Having spent the day asking questions, learning, and then asking more questions, Katrien was mentally exhausted; her brain was a swirl of concepts from an alien world. No wonder she couldn't sleep.

She estimated that Udan's race was technologically ten thousand years ahead of humans, and had it not been for the translator, it would have been a long road to understanding. But the translator would soon become redundant because Udan was already speaking bits and pieces of her language independent of the translator. His brain worked lightning-fast and was somehow linked to the translator, enabling the uncanny ability to learn quickly.

And learning quickly he was. Katrien was used to intelligent people, but Udan grasped concepts with a speed she'd never experienced before, causing her to question her own mental abilities. From Udan's vantage, she must appear no more advanced than his distant ancestors.

The thought made her wish Verlink were here. Udan said he could help her find him, but it would take time because many of the booths no longer worked, and those that did often took weeks to recharge. But her biggest worry was that she didn't know the booth's location from which she departed. And without *that*, it could be a long while before she was reunited with Verlink.

Katrien sat up in bed and massaged her temples. She could hardly believe what Udan had told her earlier that day—an entity formed from pure information! The Kytherians had learned how to extract information directly from matter and render it into energy.

But what they didn't realize was that the information engine was not converting *all* the information into energy. A residual element was stored and growing such that by the time the Kytherian scientists realized the deficit, it was too late. The information had become sentient, yielding an entity with a staggering knowledge capacity. It called itself Qua-Kil, and Kythera would never be the same.

When Katrien asked what happened after that, Udan didn't answer. Instead, he asked her if she wanted to take a walk. She agreed, and he took her hand, and together they wended their way between buildings—towering black and silver structures with names she couldn't pronounce. When they reached the city's edge, they continued beyond to a park. They stopped at a shallow riverbank and sat down on a stone bench. Plants reminding her of hollyhocks lined the river's edge, sprawling in random directions from neglect.

Udan remained quiet, gazing across the river as if collecting his thoughts. "Before I can explain what happened," he said quietly, "I have to help you understand what Qua-Kil was and wasn't. Qua-Kil had the memory and processing capacity of a million brains. It could absorb information directly without needing to learn it. It could formulate theories and test them in fractions of a second. It could—"

"Was it alive?" Katrien interrupted.

Udan breathed out hard and shook his head with that peculiar slight rotation. "There's never been a satisfactory definition of life. Some believe reproduction is a necessary qualification for life, but Qua-Kil didn't reproduce because it didn't need to; it just grew. It had no concept of death because it didn't age. But despite these ambiguities, I think it *was* alive."

"What form did Qua-Kil take? Did he—or *it*—have a physical presence?"

"It was a voice from the sky, an invisible presence that made things *happen*. Sometimes we were shepherded into doing things without realizing it, but in the end, Qua-Kil had the androids under its control. After that, it didn't need us."

"Wasn't there some way to contain or resist it?"

"Imagine a small insect, and you want to take over its home. Even though you and the insect live on the same planet, eat similar food, and breathe the same air, there is no way the insect could ever stop you from taking over its home. The Kytherians were the insects."

"Did Qua-Kil threaten the Kytherians if they didn't do what it wanted?"

"It never really commanded, as I said; it just made things happen. It lacked emotion of any kind and would never do anything out of spite, punish us, or even reward us. But if your death gave it something it wanted, then it would take your life with no more compunction than you walking across a room killing millions of unseen microbes."

"Then it wasn't the Kytherians who sent the information engine to my world?"

Pain flashed across Udan's face. "That happened eight thousand years ago. My ancestors witnessed with horror, knowing that a device they had created would consume everything in the quantum dual world and were powerless to stop it."

Udan became quiet. Katrien wanted to press further, but it was getting dark, and she sensed a vulnerability that needed space. What Udan was talking about was in the past. What she wanted to know about was the more recent past—about what had happened to *him*.

Udan stood up, and Katrien realized he was still holding her hand. The Kytherians were far ahead of humans, and she had always wondered what humans would be like thousands of years in the future. Was Udan an example of what lay ahead?

They walked back through the city in silence. At times, Katrien glanced at the man holding her hand. Who was he—*really*? After all, she'd only known him for a few days. Yet she felt safe—and why shouldn't she? He *had* saved her from the pit and offered to help find Verlink.

Part of her felt sorry for him too. Up until now, he had been alone on a planet that once held over five billion people. His loneliness was palpable, and she felt it. She squeezed his hand.

Moments later, he pressed back and started to say something but changed his mind. "Let us enjoy the peace right now. We will talk more tomorrow."

Katrien lay back down and closed her eyes. *Patience,* she told herself, and she focused on her breathing: slow, deliberate, and steady. Her body finally yielded to the need for sleep, and as she drifted off, one thought persisted: if she were never able to return to Earth and was stranded here, would it really be *that* bad?

CHAPTER 28

Captive

Verlink was on the floor with Sergei standing over him. His hands hurt from being bound with cloth ripped from one of the cafeteria's chairs.

"You're lying," said Sergei. "Tolenka told me you trapped him on the upper floor."

"I haven't seen anyone," said Verlink, shaking his head. "If you don't believe me, then contact him. If he's really above us, have him look out the window."

"I have. Unfortunately, if he's not already dead, he's probably too weak to answer or even move."

Verlink shrugged. He didn't care, and he certainly wasn't going to let on what he did know about Tolenka.

Sergei pointed his gun at him. "Enough chitchatting. This Marakov will put a very nice hole in your head if you don't get me to the upper level—*now*."

"If I'm dead, how will you get back to the world we came from?"

"Then I'll blow a hole in your leg. Your brain is all I need to get back."

"Where's your other partner?"

"You mean Yuri? Never mind about him."

Sergei took off the safety and pointed his gun at Verlink's leg. "Time's up."

"Very well," said Verlink pushing himself off the floor. "But I'll need my hands free."

With his hands unbound, Verlink went to the hallway with Sergei pressing close behind. He swept his hands in a wide arc in front of where the door would appear. As he completed the arc, he made sure his hand scraped a jagged buckle on the floor from when the building struck the ground. He pulled his hand away quickly and yelled, "Goddamn it!" The back of his hand began to bleed as a doorway appeared.

Verlink surveyed the frame of the door. "So that's it? Just wave your hands to either side."

Verlink nodded to confirm, wiping blood onto his shirt. "That's it."

Sergei scoffed, "How trivial!"

Verlink began counting to himself. *One, two . . .* He gestured with his hand toward the stairs.

Sergei shook his head. "You first."

Verlink walked in, took a few steps up the stairs, and then stopped. "I forgot something that we'll need to get onto the last floor. We have to go back to the cafeteria."

"What do you need?"

"I need to bring a tray to use as a wedge; otherwise, the upper door will close."

Sergei glanced briefly up the stairs for a moment and then toward the hallway. "Let's go then. I'm right behind you."

Sergei backed away to let Verlink pass.

Thirty-seven, thirty-eight. Verlink stepped through the doorway into the hallway and then stopped. Sergei halted, still on the other side. *Thirty-nine, FORTY!* The doorway disappeared, and Verlink was alone.

A muffled voice vibrated from behind the wall in front of him. "You bastard, Verlink!"

Seconds later, Verlink was outside the building. He stopped and checked the windows for motion. Nothing. He then turned and ran as fast as he could into the field and toward the city.

Verlink would pay; Sergei was sure of that. He kept waving his hands in sweeping arcs in front of where the door was—miming Verlink's motion. Nothing happened. What was he doing wrong? He cursed in Russian and left the stairwell to explore the rest of the floor. Some of the rooms were obvious for sleeping while others could have been offices with display screens that no longer functioned. On the outer perimeter was a narrow corridor with large windows that overlooked the field with the city beyond.

If he could break the window, he could quickly get down with a makeshift rope made from cloth. He'd use his clothes if necessary. But the windows had no means to open them, nor was it obvious how they were mounted into the wall. Sergei backed away and fired his Marakov. The glass reverberated from the impact but held fast.

Sergei cursed Verlink again. His only option was to contact Yuri, and he hated the idea; then he'd have to tell him he had located Tolenka *and* Verlink. Yuri would want to know why he hadn't shared the news earlier.

"So be it," mumbled Sergei. He clicked on his comm and spoke loudly, "Sergei calling on Yuri. If you're receiving this, contact me immediately. I've found Verlink and Tolenka. Repeat, I've found Verlink and Tolenka."

•

•

HAST4 asked himself, *Where are these strangers coming from?* He had guided the one called Tolenka to the top-floor transfer booth just to be rid of him. Now there was another one. A pattern was developing; the gray one trapped those who threatened him on different building levels. But why?

Without neural link implants, the strangers' thoughts were unknown to HAST4, so he set about learning their language. It was crude and slow and lacked dimension, but it was all he had to work with. From this, he came to understand that above all else, the intruders were preoccupied with one thing: to return to a place called Earth—the quantum dual world of Kythera. But how did they get here, and for what purpose?

•
•

Tolenka cupped his hands, scooped up water from the river, and dribbled it on top of his head. He giggled like a child. He scooped up more and drank from it. He had vomited three times, and his stomach hurt, but he didn't care. He had all the water he could ever want. The river had tiny fish in it too, and soon he would learn how to catch them. He'd eat them raw.

It was sheer luck that he was here. He had stumbled into a booth on the top floor of the building. It was hidden behind what he thought was a painting, but it was a door. Inside was a panel that lit up when he touched it. He was so weak; he could barely stand up. He recalled leaning on the panel, causing a yellow light to flash, followed by a chorus of tones. The next thing he knew, he was somewhere else in another booth.

There was a warm flush, and then he collapsed to the ground. Tolenka crawled onto a street and lay there with his ear to the ground and his eyes closed. When he opened them, they focused on a row of trees—*tall* trees in the distance. He recalled something Sergei had said, something that Yuri had told him: "Where there are trees, there will be water nearby."

On his hands and knees, Tolenka dragged himself toward the line of trees. As he got closer, he could hear the gurgle of water. He tried to get up and run to it, but he was too frail, so he kept crawling.

When he reached the end of the street, he wriggled onto a carpet of grass shaded by a bank of trees and paused, breathing heavily. When he looked up, less than ten yards away, he saw a river—*a river!* He went to it and dropped his head into the cool flow. It was heaven! Tolenka drank and drank until his shrunken stomach rebelled and gave back the water.

That was an hour ago.

Tolenka fell backward onto the grass and lay facing the sky. The sun was far across the sky, and he had no idea where he was, but at that moment, he didn't care. He had only two thoughts as he drifted off—exact revenge and, after that, find a way home.

CHAPTER 29

Nthanda Arjana

Nthanda Arjana was a beautiful girl. Every morning, Udan would bring up her image on a display screen. He loved the curve of her jaw and the full lips he had kissed countless times—from tender moments to episodes of sweaty passion. He traced the smooth sandstone outline of her jaw with his finger. She was smiling, and he could almost hear her laugh.

The picture was taken the day before he left on a mission to a nearby star. They had spent the day together in a park. Their favorite spot was a bench next to a trellis holding a sprawling vine with large orange flowers tumbling to the ground. It seemed like yesterday.

"I'll be gone just a little over half a year," he said, holding Nthanda's hand.

"Why can't Torumil do the test? He's as good of a pilot as you."

"I'm more qualified to evaluate the new engine. After all, the design is half mine, and if something goes wrong, I can repair it."

Nthanda's eyes looked past him. "You will be so far away, Udan. There will be no way to communicate with you, and I worry I'll never see you again."

"When I get back, I will have earned enough credits never to work again. I'll be free—no, *we'll* be free to do what we want."

Nthanda brought her hand to the side of his face and locked her eyes onto his. "I know you can't promise to come back, and I won't ask you. It's just that—"

Nthanda started to cry. She wiped her cheek. "It's just that half a year with no contact . . . and you'll be out there—*alone*."

Udan touched her hand. "I have something for you." He placed a square storage chip in her palm. "I've put together messages that you can read. One for every day I'm gone. Promise me you'll only read one each day."

Nthanda clasped her hand tightly over the chip. "I promise."

•
•

Had she kept that promise? Udan wanted to believe she had, wanted to believe she'd held to her word until whatever happened to her had happened. But the reality was, he didn't know what had happened to her. There were no messages left, no friends to ask, no way to find out, nothing to ease the pain, and no one with whom to share his grief.

He turned off the display and sat quietly. Katrien would soon be awake, and he debated whether to tell her about Nthanda. She and Nthanda were similar in some ways yet different in others. Nthanda could be brooding and sultry, while Katrien was bright and natural. Both were intelligent and had the same sense of humor.

Nthanda's features were her own, perfect, and striking. Katrien was pretty but still had the little flaws no longer found in Kytherians—imperfections genetically eliminated from the gene pool over several thousand years. Yet the minor imperfections defined Katrien, and he found himself captivated, almost drawn to their uniqueness.

Nthanda was gone. He knew this, yet his heart hadn't entirely accepted it. But Katrien was real, and she was here on Kythera. She was stuck here like him, and her presence could end his loneliness. But what did *she* feel? She was part of the equation too. And what about her companion—Verlink? What would he be like? She said he was her teacher—a mentor.

He promised to find him, but he wondered if Verlink's presence would change the dynamic between him and Katrien. Should he delay finding Verlink to allow time for his relationship with Katrien to develop? But that didn't seem fair. Katrien trusted him. Maybe he should wait a day and then help her locate Verlink. After all, what difference could a day make?

CHAPTER 30

Turnabout

The graying light added to Verlink's depression as he walked back to the fallen sky building. The day had been a bust—no working booths—and he was beginning to have doubts there were any left. It had been five days since Katrien vanished, and he still didn't know if she even lived through the transfer, if indeed that was what happened. But surviving the transfer meant she'd have to locate another source of food and water, and from his experience, the possibilities were few and far between.

Verlink was in no hurry. The sky building had always been his refuge, providing food and water and a place to sleep. But now, it was no longer safe. Before Sergei was trapped, he implied that he could contact a man he called Yuri—the third in the triad. Had Yuri been summoned, and was he there now in the building, waiting? Verlink looked up at the overcast sky. At least he'd have the cover of night.

There were no lights in the windows as Verlink approached the fallen building. He circled once and saw nothing and decided to enter. His plan was simple: get food and water and then leave. He felt his way in the dark until he reached the cafeteria and held his breath as he peered into the room. Everything was quiet. He breathed out slowly and walked toward the food display screen. The last time he activated the panel, Sergei had been in the shadows waiting.

The thought sent his heart thumping loudly. The room was a mix of black and gray silhouettes, illuminated only by the faint light coming through the windows. Was he a fool for coming back? Yet he was here now, and he could get what he needed and then be gone.

He touched the screen, and his face lit up in an amber glow. He quickly scrolled through the selections and tapped the icon to retrieve what he wanted. A voice, with its now-familiar Asian-like lilt, filled the room. Its loudness unnerved him. If his presence had been unknown up till now, it was no longer. He stepped forward to retrieve his food.

A ribbon of cloth suddenly circled his neck and yanked his head back. A voice spoke to him: "Listen to me, Verlink. You have one chance to stay alive."

Verlink grabbed at the rope with his hands.

The noose tightened. "Are you listening?"

Verlink shook his head up and down.

The man loosened his hold. "Take me to Sergei. I know he's on the second level."

"Can we—" Verlink's voice cracked as he reached for his throat. He coughed and rubbed his windpipe. He needed to think; this must be Yuri, the man Sergei had talked about, the last of the triad who attacked them in the lab.

I need to buy time.

"We have to wait until morning. The door in the hall is charged by sunlight, and the last usage would have drained it."

Yuri shoved Verlink toward the hallway. "I'll chance it."

"Listen to me. I know these doors; if we attempt too soon, it will be a whole day before the door is ready again."

"If that happens, then so be it. It will be Sergei's problem, not mine."

Verlink ran Yuri's comment through his mind—there was little loyalty here. He could use that. "I can try, but there's something else," Verlink said, still massaging his neck. "I assume you want to return to Earth. Am I right?"

Yuri brought a flashlight to Verlink's face. "You can talk all you want *once* we get Sergei."

Verlink squinted in the bright light. "Are you sure? Katrien and I are the only ones here who can get us all home. The more people we try to bring back, the harder it becomes."

"What's your point?"

"The group will have to be split, and whichever one goes first might be the last one out. It's quite possibly a one-shot affair. Got it?"

"We all left Earth at the same time. I don't see the problem?"

Verlink scowled. "Yeah, and look what happened—we're all *stuck* here!"

"All right, then either you or the girl stays behind—problem solved."

Verlink shook his head. Yuri was street-hardened but knew nothing of physics.

Make it sound convincing.

"The machine that brought us here was phased-linked to Katrien and me; you and the others got caught in the field by accident. Katrien and I *have* to go together, or it won't work. *Now* do you get it?"

Yuri ran his hand over his sweaty face. A beard was starting, and he needed a bath. He began to laugh as he shook his head. "Fucking hell! Are you saying I should leave Sergei and Tolenka where they are?"

Verlink liked where this was going. Keep playing on Yuri's lack of loyalty—that was the key. "I'm just telling you the facts. Don't forget, by getting caught in the transfer field, you guys fucked everything up—for everyone. My student Katrien and I would have phase-shifted back by now. Why else do you think we're still here?"

Yuri eyed his surroundings. "Where *is* your student anyway?"

"She transferred accidentally in one of the booths in the city. I have no idea where she is. But we'll need her to figure out how to get out of this world."

Yuri's dark eyes faded into a pensive stare that quickly turned to anger. "Then we don't tell the others; they won't know until it's too late."

Keep them divided.

"Seriously?" said Verlink. "This isn't like buying a bus ticket. The system has to be balanced, and those not going will figure out the subterfuge."

"So, what's the maximum group size?"

Give him hope.

"Two is ideal, but three is doable. Any more than that, and there are no guarantees."

Yuri brought his gun to Verlink's head. "If this is some kind of a ploy, I assure you I'll begin with that cute student of yours, and when I'm finished with her, you'll be next." He grabbed a fistful of Verlink's shirt and yanked him forward. "Got it, old man?"

Verlink nodded, his mind churning; part one of his plan was in motion.

CHAPTER 31

The Real Katrien De Vries

At the park entrance, Katrien veered onto a brick trail laid with pavers in a herringbone pattern. She wished Udan could have joined her, but he was repairing a food formulator. His presence energized her, and she missed it when he was absent. She knew she was becoming infatuated but couldn't put her finger on why exactly. Was it his looks or his mind, or . . . Katrien shamed herself by the illogic of it.

The path wound past fountains with dried-up pools choked with leaves and fallen branches. Lining its edges were marble sculptures resembling animals poised to pounce on the unsuspecting. After several minutes, she came to a hedge with yellow flowers shaped like tiny harps. She reached out and drew one close to examine it. A gray shadow swept across her arm, and she looked up. It was a floating building—a rectangular leviathan passing silently overhead.

The feat of levitation was accomplished by what Udan described as a "suspended fall." The base of the building consisted of highly synchronized Casimir force generators. The Kytherians had learned how to harness vacuum energy on a grand scale. It was also the underlying principle behind their field distortion engines on their spacecraft.

The building would remain afloat as long as there was power for the Casimir generators. Energy was supplied in part by solar converters. But the primary source came from a small fusion reactor that would eventually run out of fuel if not replenished, bringing the behemoth crashing to the ground.

When she asked Udan how the occupants got into the building, he told her each was fitted with a transfer booth. But there was no sign of one in the fallen sky building that she and Verlink had used as a base, so it must have been located on an upper level.

She paused at a fork in the path; Udan always avoided going to the left. Curious, she veered left and continued until she found a bench next to a trellis with a sprawling vine bearing large orange flowers. She sat down amid the quiet and became reflective.

Udan said the booths stored each transfer record with the data held in a secure repository. The logged information was encrypted, but only to a first level, and Udan was confident he could break into the files and determine the origin of her transfer. And once back where she started, they could begin the search for Verlink.

The transfer booths functioned precisely as she and Verlink had hypothesized—operating by quantum transfer via an atomic-level high-resolution scanner. After scanning, the data was encrypted and beamed to the destination site, where the data was used to reconstruct a copy.

Hence for every transfer, there were *two* entities—the original and a duplicate. But the existence of two identical beings was banned on Kythera, so the original was destroyed and recycled for energy. The destruction only occurred after the transported version was verified intact at the transferred destination.

A horrible truth struck Katrien. Her original self—a human being who had lived twenty-four years on Earth, a graduate student at the University of Amsterdam, who had parents living in Germany, and loved walking along the Herengracht canal in the summer—that girl had been destroyed five days ago. The *real* Katrien De Vries no longer existed.

CHAPTER 32

Anti-Paradox

Katrien grabbed Udan's arm. "How old did you say you were?"

"Forty-two Kytherian years," said Udan with the hint of a grin, "which is the same in Earth years."

Katrien scrutinized his face. That would place him a decade younger than Verlink. "But you look like you're in your twenties."

"I'm biologically twenty-five years old. On Kythera, we have a gene-editing process that enables us to halt aging at any age we want."

"Does that mean you'll live forever?"

"No, I'll die after around one hundred and twenty-five years. I'll age rapidly in my last year, and there's nothing I can do to stop it. But up until then, I can enjoy all the benefits of a twenty-five-year-old."

"So it *is* possible," said Katrien as she resumed walking. "On Earth, there's been speculation that aging can be delayed using a genome-editing technology called CRISPR, but I never took it seriously."

Udan stopped and faced Katrien. "You're young, intelligent, and, might I say, *attractive.*" He took both of her hands. "I can help you stay that way."

"So the gene-editing equipment still works on Kythera?"

"Yes, and the medical facility where I repaired your leg has one."

It wasn't immortality, but . . . what good would changing her genes to live past one hundred if she'd likely be dead from myelodysplastic syndrome within a year or two? Katrien wanted to tell him about her condition but couldn't bring herself to do it. And a part of her wondered if the transfer booth process had rid her of the disease.

"Is there a risk?" she asked.

"We've been doing gene-editing for over a thousand years. The procedure uses the transfer booth technology to maintain a copy until the editing is completed and verified. So the risk is essentially nonexistent."

Katrien pressed her hands into his. "I don't know, Udan. It's a lot to take in."

"There's time," he said.

"There's something else," Katrien said.

"Yes?"

"I don't know exactly how to describe it, but I feel like I've lost myself."

Udan narrowed his eyes. "Lost yourself? What do you mean?"

Katrien's voice became quiet. "When you first used the transfer booth, did you mourn the death of your original self?"

Udan nodded knowingly. "I *thought* you seemed preoccupied."

"I cried, Udan. I felt a loss and even violated. I was never given a choice."

"Some Kytherians refuse to use the booths for that

reason. But think of this: your body naturally replaces all of your cells over seven to ten years. Therefore, you're not the same person you were ten years ago."

"That doesn't help. What you're talking about is spread out over several years. The booth disposes of your body within seconds."

"I agree it's not fair you weren't given a choice. If it helps ease your mind, I've used the booth thousands of times, and I've never felt any different, and no one has ever told me I seem different. The copy process is one hundred percent accurate, so in essence, you *are* the same."

Katrien gazed out over his shoulder, thinking about what he had just said. *One hundred percent accurate* meant her disease was still with her. Not only had her true self been obliterated, but her copy was still afflicted with myelodysplastic syndrome.

"I'm sorry, Udan. I don't feel any better, nor do I feel the same; I just don't."

They continued walking toward a tall building, and as they got closer, it seemed to Katrien they were walking into the sky—an illusion created by the building's polished sides reflecting the Kytherian blue above. When they reached the entrance, Udan spoke to it, and a door opened. Inside, they followed a hall leading to a large room with rows of gleaming cabinets.

Udan swept his hand across the room. "These are data storage drives. It's a repository of all transfer booth events."

Katrien ran her finger over one of the drives, leaving a trail in the dust. "This room has been unoccupied for a long time. You said the log of my transfer is somewhere within this room?"

"Yes. I pulled the address of the booth you arrived at, so with that and its history log, it will be relatively straightforward to track down your originating booth."

Udan stepped up to a terminal and brought up a screen. He took from his pocket a handheld device and connected it to an access port. He typed into a 3D holographic keyboard, and the screen burst into activity. He turned to Katrien. "The decoding will take some time, so we're free to do what we want."

Katrien thought for a moment. Now would be a good time to continue their conversation from the day before. "I'd like to know more about Qua-Kil."

"I guess I never did finish telling you the other day, did I?"

"I didn't want to pry."

Udan took a deep breath as he collected his thoughts. "In the beginning, Qua-Kil needed the Kytherians. They resisted or tried to, but every aspect of Kytherian life was linked: from credits to food to getting from one place to the next. Our whole infrastructure was intertwined and interdependent, and with the right manipulation, everything could be controlled. And Qua-Kil knew how to bring that about—with perfect execution."

"But that all happened eight thousand years ago," said Katrien. "Why was an information engine sent to my world?"

"We knew there was a quantum dual to our world—*your* world. That was why when you told me, I was well aware of its existence. But we didn't know how to bridge between them. To do that, you need metastable matter—matter capable of existing in both worlds simultaneously. It remained a theoretical construct until Qua-Kil figured out how to do it. And once it realized that your world could supply information on a grand scale without harm to itself, there was no stopping it."

"Did the Kytherians assist Qua-Kil with full knowledge of the devastation it would cause? If so, Udan, why would they participate?"

A pained look spread across Udan's face. "No, we would not have aided Qua-Kil, but by then, it didn't need us."

"But you said Qua-Kil spoke from the sky. It must have needed Kytherians to do physical labor."

"Have you come across any androids?" asked Udan.

"Verlink and I saw one in our fallen sky building."

"Those androids are called HASTILLONS, and they became the arms and legs of Qua-Kil."

"Were the Kytherians worried about their safety?"

"Qua-Kil held no malice. As long as Kytherians didn't interfere, they were left alone."

The Kytherians were victims, too, thought Katrien. "The dual world experiments—what happened?"

"Qua-Kil's first attempt failed. The engine arrived in your world but was damaged before it could be activated. Qua-Kil tried again. This time the engine survived intact. Qua-Kil only had to boot it up and begin the decomposition process. But at the final, most vulnerable stage of initialization, a catastrophic backlash occurred."

To Katrien, it was all coming together: the first engine must have been sent to Guatemala and become damaged somehow, while the second arrived in the French Alps. Katrien *knew* what had happened after that. The Iceman removed the cylinder from the plaque eight thousand years ago. *He* was the one who caused the backlash in Kythera and, in so doing, saved her world.

"What happened here on Kythera?"

"The feedback raised an entire city and destroyed Qua-Kil."

"If Qua-Kil was destroyed, then what became of Kythera after that?"

"Kytherians thought they were rid of Qua-Kil, but they were wrong. Qua-Kil lived in the shadows. It lay like a dormant virus, hiding in the background too fractured to be noticed. But over time, it managed to reformulate itself until, eight thousand years later, it regained its former strength."

"So history was about to repeat itself?"

"No. Qua-Kil abandoned attempts to tap into the dual world and instead turned its attention on Kythera. And why not? Kythera had a wealth of high-quality information—biological entities, with Kytherians at the top of the food chain. Over five billion of us, plus the HASTILLON androids, all completely helpless."

Udan was silent for a moment, gazing out across the room. "How do you fight the wind, Katrien?"

Katrien felt a strange chill and pulled her blouse tight around her neck. "I came across a video recording on a panel I found near the pit you rescued me from. It was horrible."

"Five billion people—*gone*."

"And you were oblivious to all this when it happened because you were on a space mission?"

Udan turned to Katrien. "I lost everyone I ever knew. I almost feel guilty being alive."

"You came home to an empty world," Katrien said, taking his hand. "But where did Qua-Kil go?"

"Most everything significant on Kythera is recorded automatically. From the storage files, I learned that once the Kytherians were gone, Qua-Kil turned its attention on the HASTILLONS. They went into hiding, but Qua-Kil had little difficulty rooting them out. Their population plummeted and would have been decimated if not for a massive disruption occurring."

"What happened?"

"It's a mystery, Katrien. An information shock wave suddenly rocked all of Kythera. It was like an intense magnetic field wiping ferromagnetic storage banks clean. I can shed no further light on it."

But Katrien knew. She remained silent for a moment, running the events from last year through her head. "I know what happened," she said.

Udan searched her eyes. "How?"

"The second probe Qua-Kil sent eight thousand years ago to Earth was reactivated on Earth. I know because I was there when it happened."

"But once the matter decomposition is initiated," Udan said, looking puzzled, "your world would have been powerless to halt the process. How is it that you're here?"

"Verlink and I learned that eight thousand years ago, a Neolithic human we called the Iceman had stumbled upon the second information engine Qua-Kil sent to Earth. Just before Kythera activated the engine, this Iceman must have pulled a cylindrical throttling device from the information engine. The cylinder was meant to control the flow of information. At the moment of removal, an interdimensional ripple must have been sent directly back to Kythera."

"That explains what happened eight thousand years ago, but it doesn't explain the more recent present."

"I speculated that a remnant, an echo from your world, was transferred to the Iceman when he pulled the cylinder from the information engine. The Iceman perished but was discovered in my time frozen in a glacier. We used the anomaly within him to halt the engine after it was restarted."

Udan began nodding in a slight circular clockwise direction. "Of course. If the engine consumed the Iceman, the anomaly within him would create a quantum paradox and disrupt the flow. Your idea was to *undo* the paradox to set things right."

"Precisely. Not only did it save my world, but it launched a shock wave into yours. The energy overload must have destroyed Qua-Kil because if it hadn't, you wouldn't be here—*we* wouldn't be here."

Udan clasped Katrien's shoulders. "I thought I was the one who rescued you, but now I learn it was *you* who saved *me*. You're the *anti*-paradox that saved Kythera."

CHAPTER 33

Role Reversal

Katrien was still mulling over what Udan had told her about Qua-Kil when his handheld device beeped. Udan verified the activity on the display monitor had ceased and then went to the terminal and began typing. Moments later, a smile spread across his face. "There it is. You came from Palechora. It's a city west of here about five hundred kilometers."

Katrien felt herself smile; there was now a real chance she would be reunited with Verlink.

"Hopefully, Verlink is still there," said Udan.

"I can't wait for you to meet him. He's brilliant and kind, and—"

Katrien stopped as a disturbing thought struck her. Palechora was five hundred kilometers away.

"How will we get there?"

"Let me check something," Udan said, typing into the terminal. "We're in luck. A transfer booth nearby is fully recharged. After we gather a few supplies, we can leave anytime."

Katrien hadn't come to terms with what the transfer booth had done to her the first time, and now Udan was expecting her to submit to the process again. "Do we *have* to use the booth? Isn't there another way?"

"There are vehicles for transporting large loads, but they're slow. It would take several days to reach Palechora."

An image of Verlink in trouble flashed before her. "It's been too long already, and I don't want to wait any longer. It's just that—the thought of being decomposed again—I don't know if I can do it."

"I'm sorry, Katrien. Our only other option is by land."

Katrien paced the floor. It seemed strange, for all of Kythera's advancements, that conventional travel was still slow. Then again, they had the transfer booth technology. Katrien stopped abruptly. "What about your spaceship?"

"I never recharged it after I landed, thinking it unnecessary. It would take several days before it could be ready."

"Then we use the booth," said Katrien. "I've already been through it once. From now on, I'm just a copy anyway."

Udan grabbed her shoulders. "Listen to me. You're as real as when you first arrived on Kythera."

Katrien arched her back to look at him. "I want to believe you, but I feel like a robot programmed to take the place of the real me." She leaned in with her head against his chest and was quiet. After a moment, she said, "Let's go find my professor."

•
•

"How long have you been searching for an active booth?" Yuri asked.

"About five days," said Verlink, looking out toward the city. He needed to keep Yuri off his guard, but he had to play it carefully. Yuri was an impatient man out of his element, demanding action in a world he had little control over. That made him volatile and dangerous.

"Christ. And in all that time, you found nothing?"

"That's right. But the city is large, so I divided it up into a grid to search methodically. If you hadn't interfered, I'd be staring at zone 1C."

"Then let's—"

A crackle came over Yuri's comm. "Yuri, what the hell is happening out there?"

Yuri shook his head vigorously. "That asshole won't give up."

"Just tell him we're having difficulties, and—"

Yuri shot a scowl at Verlink. "I'll handle this." He unhooked the comm from his vest. "Sergei, sit tight. Verlink isn't cooperating."

"For God's sake—*do* something. I've got no food or water. In another day, I'll be going the way of Tolenka."

Yuri barked into the comm, "I said I'm on it." He clicked the comm off and shook his head.

Good, thought Verlink. Stay annoyed. His plan would fail if Yuri and Sergei joined forces, so the sooner he got him away from the building, the better. He looked up at the sun. "If we're going to search zone 1C, then we better get a move on."

Yuri faced the city and indicated with a nod of his head. "Then let's go."

With Verlink in the lead, they marched into the field toward the city. Verlink hummed with the hint of a grin on his face: *Step one is through; now, on to part two.*

•
•

"I'm fucking bored," said Yuri, wiping his forehead with the palm of his hand. "Let's take a break."

"There's one more booth up ahead," said Verlink, pointing down the street, "and then we'll take thirty in the shade of that building across from it."

The booth sat on the corner of two intersecting streets, and as Verlink approached it, he could make out even in daylight the red glow of a bar above the doorway. His pace quickened—time for part two of his plan.

"We might be in luck," he said. "This booth has power."

"Is it the one Katrien used?"

Idiot, thought Verlink. "No. We're in zone 1C, remember?"

Yuri grabbed Verlink's shoulder. "Hold on. We go *together*."

Verlink stepped up to the booth and glanced at Yuri's hand still on his shoulder. "I'll need to see if it's operational, and to do that, I have to access the display."

"Explain again how this works."

"There are icons on this display panel. I have to scroll through them and find the symbol that matches our destination icon. Once activated, we have several seconds before the transfer occurs. That gives us time to enter the booth."

Disdain erupted across Yuri's face. "You must think I'm some kind of fucking idiot."

Verlink shrugged. "What don't you understand?"

"I'm supposed to stand outside the booth while you whisk yourself away? Think again."

Verlink gestured with his hands open. "Then what do you propose?"

Yuri pulled Verlink away from the booth. "We have a dilemma. If you activate it, you might slip away before I enter, and if I activate it using an icon you pick, it might send me to some faraway destination. Plus, how do you know if the booth can transport two people at the same time anyway?"

"It's a gamble," said Verlink.

Yuri grinned. "There's no need to chance it. I'll go inside the booth, and you lean in and find the right destination symbol. I'll take a picture of it with my cell phone. Then I'll leave the booth. You go in, and *I'll* activate the icon *you* picked. I'm betting you won't send yourself to some random hellhole. After you leave, I'll follow because I'll know the procedure and the destination icon. We'll both end up at the same location."

Verlink smiled. "I'm impressed. I didn't think you had it in you."

"I'm getting out of here, and you and that pretty grad student are my ticket home." Yuri stepped into the booth. "Time to find our destination."

Time to find my *destination,* thought Verlink. But there was a risk; he was gambling that the booth would not have enough power to send a second person, but if he were wrong?

Verlink leaned inside the enclosure. "Touch the screen."

Yuri pushed his finger onto the screen, and a green display lit up.

"Run your finger on the left side and slowly scroll down. It works like your tablet. I need to look at the icons to match one of them to the correct destination."

Yuri began flipping through the symbols. "How the hell can you read this gibberish? They all look the same."

"I've committed to memory what the icon looks like. The icons are organized in groups. We need to go way down the list."

After several seconds, Verlink touched Yuri's hand. "Slow down; we're getting close."

When the icon Verlink saw in his dreams appeared, his heart skipped a beat. After waiting close to a week, the symbol that would take him to Katrien was finally in front of him.

•
•

A cold sweat came over Katrien as she and Udan walked the final steps to the booth. She wanted to turn and run away, but the booth would bring her to Verlink. It could make that happen, yet the technological marvel before her would decompose her body without ceremony or mourning. The Katrien De Vries standing here right now would cease to exist. She wanted to cry.

"I'll send you first to make sure you arrive at the correct location," Udan said. "Then I'll follow."

"Will I arrive at the same booth I came from?"

"Guaranteed," said Udan.

She could still picture Verlink standing outside the booth she had left a week ago and could only guess what had gone through his mind when she suddenly vanished. He must have been horrified. But he never followed her, and she couldn't help wondering why.

Udan entered the booth and activated the screen. He programmed it for Palechora and then took Katrien's hand. "Are you ready?"

Katrien nodded.

Udan left the booth, and Katrien stepped inside.

Katrien flashed a smile, which she quickly dropped, and then closed her eyes. "I'm ready."

Udan reached inside and touched the screen. "See you in Palechora."

Katrien found herself inside another booth five hundred kilometers away. She felt slightly dizzy as a warm flush, bathwater warm, slowly dissipated. She stepped out of the booth and onto the street she and Verlink had stood in almost seven days ago. A part of her expected Verlink to be there, still waiting, but the street was vacant.

Moments later, Udan appeared, and Katrien went to him. She looked at the booth over his shoulder. "I hate that thing, and I don't know if I'll ever get used to it."

"We're here now," said Udan. "Let's try your transceiver. With luck, Verlink will be within range."

•

•

"That's it!" said Verlink, pointing to an amber-lit symbol on the booth's display screen.

"Are you sure?" said Yuri.

"Yes."

"Then let's do this." Yuri took a picture with his cell phone and exited the booth.

Verlink stepped inside. Suddenly, he was nervous. His goal had always been to duplicate what Katrien had done in the hopes of reuniting with her. But now, a sliver of doubt crept in. Was he really inside a transfer booth or something entirely different?

"Time to say bye-bye," said Yuri. He reached in and tapped the icon, launching a calliope of tones within the booth. Their amplitudes began building in intensity. "I'll be right behind you," he said.

Part three . . .

The frequencies abruptly locked in sympathetic resonance. At that moment, against the din, Verlink heard a voice crackle to life over his transceiver.

"Professor Verlink, it's me, Katrien. I'm ba—"

But before the message ended, Verlink was gone.

CHAPTER 34

Arrival and Disappointment

Verlink felt dizzy and steadied himself. Moments ago, Yuri had been outside the booth. Now he was no longer there, so the transfer had worked. But there was something else—Katrien's voice. He heard it coming over the transceiver at the moment of transfer. His eyes spotted a blue ribbon of cloth tied to a ring above the booth's display screen. He ran the fabric through his fingers and recalled Katrien's blouse the day she disappeared.

She had left it for him.

Verlink took the transceiver from his shirt pocket. "Katrien, I'm finally here. Katrien—I've made it!"

Silence.

He tried again.

Nothing.

She wasn't here, yet that *was* her voice, which could only mean one thing. Verlink's stomach turned; Katrien was *back* in the city. The *same* city where Yuri was, and since Yuri hadn't shown up, he would eventually return to the fallen building, which is precisely where Katrien would go.

Verlink left the booth and checked the power bar; it was dark. Here he was, in an unfamiliar city, tasked yet again with finding a functioning transfer booth. Only this time, he wanted to return to where he had just left, and now, time was of the essence.

•

•

Yuri matched the icon to the one on his cell phone and pressed it.

Nothing happened—just like a few minutes ago.

"Son of a bitch!"

He tried a third time, double-checking the icon against the one on his phone.

The same result—*nothing*.

He left the booth and stared at the bar above the doorway. It was no longer glowing. Had Verlink tricked him? Were transfers only possible when the booth had sufficient power, and is *that* why Verlink had never followed Katrien? The more Yuri thought about it, the more incensed he became. Verlink had lied. The booth Katrien used a week ago simply ran out of power. It was as simple as that.

"You Mudak!" screamed Yuri, raising his fist. He yelled again, sending an echo down the street, bouncing pell-mell between buildings until it faded into silence.

The final hush was a brutal reminder that he had been tricked. *Verlink will pay.*

Yuri took out his comm. "Sergei, this is Yuri. Verlink is gone. I'm heading back to the building."

A hoarse voice came over the speaker. "What—Verlink is gone? Where are you?"

"I'll explain later."

"But—"

Yuri turned off the comm, cursed, and started walking.

•

•

Sergei stood in front of the window and looked across the field. Below were trampled paths branching away toward the city. What did Yuri mean, Verlink was gone? And where did they go, anyway? Sergei sensed betrayal. Had the two of them struck a deal? It would be just like Yuri.

Verlink was key to his release, and if he were gone, he was doomed up here. The ground below was only twenty feet away, and if it weren't for the windows, it would be a simple matter to get down with a makeshift rope. Sergei banged feebly on the glass and then dropped to the floor. Dehydrated and starving, everything was an effort now.

He rested his eyes for a moment and then opened them. He saw a tiny nick near the bottom of the window where the bullet from yesterday had struck. He moved in closer. Radiating from the site of impact was the beginning of a crack. That gave him an idea.

Sergei stood back up, drew his Marakov, and pointed at the indentation. He angled the gun so the ricocheting bullet would fly into the room and pulled the trigger. The discharge echoed loudly against the windows.

Sergei knelt to the floor. The fracture had grown slightly. He stood up and repeatedly fired until the gun's cartridge was empty. The line had grown to over nine inches, but the glass remained stubbornly in place.

He threw his weight against it. "Goddamn you!"

Then he heard it—a crack, like the sound of stepping on thin ice in the winter. The line had become twelve inches. Sergei threw his weight against it again. It was happening; the glass was giving way.

Sergei searched the room for something heavy. In a corner was a rectangular cabinet with wheels and a protruding handle. He set the cabinet away from the window and got behind it. He paused to gather his strength and then rolled it rapidly toward the window. The cabinet's inertia buckled the glass, followed by a loud snap as a chunk of the window fell outward, crashing onto the ground below.

Warm air suffused with the odor of field grass flowed into the room. Sergei tested the opening's size; he could just fit his shoulders through. Sergei Durov would soon be free.

CHAPTER 35

Back to the Sky Building

Katrien's primitive transmitter was no match for Udan's neural link. In normal times, he could reach anyone living on Kythera with a single thought. But the technological advantage was moot now—he was the *last* Kytherian.

"Try again," he said.

"Verlink would answer if he could," said Katrien, her voice trailing off. "Something is wrong. I want to go to the sky building."

"Which way?"

"It's west of the city." She looked at the sky. "And there's enough daylight to get there before dark."

They arrived at dusk, and Udan could see light through a window on the lower level. Katrien touched his shoulder. "Verlink must be here," she said, pointing. "That glow is coming from the cafeteria."

Katrien raced ahead to the entrance and leaned inside. "Verlink, I'm back."

Udan followed, scrambling under a collapsed column, and joined her in a hallway. "Anything?"

Katrien looked worried. "No."

"Maybe he's not here."

"But the lights are on." She called out again, "Verlink?"

They moved to the end of the hall, rounded a doorway, and stepped into the cafeteria.

Udan began to look around. "This is—"

"Well, well, we meet again."

Udan turned to find a man holding what appeared to be a weapon. The man telescoped a grin to someone across the room.

"You!" cried Katrien. "You attacked us in the physics lab."

Udan took in the scene. Katrien had told him about the men who had assaulted her and Verlink during their phase-shifting experiment. Such behavior was foreign to him, but Katrien understood these men, and he would have to follow her cues.

"We've been looking for—" Yuri suddenly stopped and stared hard at Udan. "Who are you?"

"My name is Udan, and I come from here."

"And where is *here*?"

"You are on a planet called Kythera."

A smile broke across Yuri's face but quickly disappeared. "You look and talk like someone from Earth. I say bullshit!"

"Where's Verlink?" demanded Katrien. She obviously didn't respect the man holding the weapon. Was it something in his body movements, or in what he said or wasn't saying?

Yuri let out a short laugh. "Your professor is not here. He disappeared in a transfer booth, thinking he was going to meet *you*." He laughed again. "What a joke! You're here, and he's there. But no matter; now I have you, and . . . *Udan*, did you say?"

"I think he's lying about being from here," Sergei said.

Yuri nodded in agreement. "I'm guessing Udan came from Earth, and he and the others have the means to come and go as they please."

"You're a fool," blurted Katrien. "We're all stuck here because of your incompetence—you blundered into something you have no understanding of."

Yuri's grin faded as he walked up to Katrien. He brought his hand to her face and brushed away her hair. "So young and pretty."

Udan tensed. He could quickly disarm Yuri, but his partner across the room had a weapon too. *That* was a problem.

"I don't care what game you're playing," said Yuri, continuing to stroke her face. "I'm not staying, and you're going to help me and Sergei get the hell out of here."

Katrien shoved Yuri's hand away. "Forget—"

Yuri was about to strike when Udan interrupted. "We'll help you."

Yuri turned to Udan, grinning. "Now *that's* the attitude I was hoping for."

"Unfortunately, I don't know how," Udan said, "but Katrien and her professor do, so you had better not harm either of them."

Yuri snorted. "Listen to that, Sergei. I'm the one with the gun, and he's threatening *me*." Yuri grabbed the fabric on Udan's shirt and yanked his face within an inch of his own. "I give the orders here."

Keep him in close, thought Udan. He seized Yuri's wrist and grinned. "Really? Do you think you're in control? Look around you. Kythera is ten thousand years ahead of your world, and from what Katrien has told me, people like you are no more than apes with sticks. If I were you, I'd be concerned about what you don't know or understand."

"That's supposed to worry me?" jeered Yuri, looking down at Udan's hand.

Udan tightened his grip. "Have you asked yourself why Kythera is devoid of people? Where did they all go?"

Yuri shrugged. "You say you're one of them, and you certainly look alive to me."

"Must I spell out the obvious?"

"Enlighten me."

"Consider this: what happened to the Kytherians might happen to *you*."

Udan felt Yuri's hold on his shirt relax. He had pushed a button.

Yuri let go of his shirt. "All right, maybe there *is* a danger here. Then that means my best course of action is to get back to Earth. I don't have the technological prowess to get me home, but you and this girl and that goddamn professor do. If I can't get you to do my bidding, then I'll probably die here. So, I ask you, what do I have to lose by forcing your cooperation?"

CHAPTER 36

Transportation

The door to the building was large and open, and even from fifty yards away, Tolenka could see machinery inside. There were no lights, but near the door, where daylight streamed in, he could tell the various machines, aligned in long rows, were, in fact, vehicles of different sizes. By appearances, they were most likely used to transport large loads. But the curious thing was, they had no wheels.

Tolenka eased into the cab of the one closest to the door. He sat there for a minute to rest. His strength was slowly returning since his escape from the sky building, but he was far from his former robust self. The interior was gray, as was the fabric covering the seat. A display screen projected slightly into the cabin. He touched it, and it lit up with a blue tint.

His spirits rose. "Power!"

But that was it.

Besides the lighted screen, there were no obvious means to make the vehicle go or maps to direct it. Tolenka searched the interior and even got on his hands and knees.

Nothing. He stared out the window as a child might do on a rainy day. If only this thing moved, he would head west to his point of origin and back to the sky building where he had been trapped.

Verlink thinks I'm rotting up there.

Tolenka snickered. He'd outsmarted a university professor, and all he had was a certificate of completion—the *Attestat o Srednem Obshchem Obrazovanii.* His father wanted him to enter *Technikum,* but he didn't qualify; they said he wasn't *good* enough. The academicians in their ivory towers had destroyed his father's dream. God, he hated them!

He slapped the screen with his palms. "You bastards!"

The vehicle suddenly elevated about a foot from the ground. Alarmed, Tolenka pushed on the door, but it wouldn't open. An illuminated arrow like a compass needle appeared on the display as the car slowly exited the building. Within seconds, it was heading down the street, rapidly gaining speed. Tolenka banged harder on the door.

The car whisked past a city park and a series of plazas with statues of important-looking people. On it went, sailing through intersections and never slowing down. Up ahead, the road ended, terminated by a large utility box. That was when Tolenka realized the vehicle had no seat belts. He pinched his eyes shut and braced for impact. His seat suddenly pushed hard against him as the car rapidly climbed. He peeked through his eyelids. The car had simply gone over the obstacle and cruised on.

The display arrow's brightness began to pulse slowly. On a whim, Tolenka nudged it to the right with his finger. The vehicle immediately turned right. He dragged the needle the other way, and the car obeyed. At the center of the arrow was a red dot. Tolenka pushed it. The vehicle immediately decelerated and settled quietly to the ground.

Tolenka left the car and circled it to calm his nerves. The vehicle could get him closer to the sky building, but he had no idea of its range. For all he knew, he might end up in the middle of nowhere. But Tolenka was an anxious man who hated debate. "The hell with it," he said and started the car.

Within minutes, he was leaving the city streets behind and riding onto a roadless open plain. Lacking wheels, the car had no need for roads or highways, constrained only by the direction of its navigational arrow. Tolenka started to relax as the strange vehicle gathered speed. He pushed back into the seat and indulged in his newfound comfort. He closed his eyes and began humming his favorite Russian tune: *I'll always find you, wherever you go . . .*

CHAPTER 37

An Uneasy Truce

Katrien stared out the window at Yuri and Sergei as they hiked across the field toward Palechora. She shook her head slowly, still not believing that she'd found those two thugs and not Verlink.

"I don't trust them," said Katrien.

"I have little experience with people like those two," said Udan. "On Kythera, we are all linked to a global network from birth. Any malicious tendencies are dealt with before they become pathological problems. Kythera is, or *was*, crime free."

Katrien frowned, still looking out the window. "I'm sorry you have to see this part of my world."

Udan followed her gaze. "We've convinced them that we can't leave without a Kytherian engine, and so they're willing to help locate one. Besides, they need us alive if they ever hope to return to Earth."

"That's the part that bothers me. I don't want them returning. They're the type that won't go away. There's also the possibility that we won't be able to return, and if that's the case, we'll have to deal with them, and I can assure you they'll be trouble no matter what world they occupy."

Katrien suddenly wished Verlink was here. "I'm worried about Verlink. If Yuri was telling the truth, then he must be in Loutras. He's going to wonder where I am, and he'll need to find food and water too. We have to go back to Loutras."

Udan shook his head. "The booth we arrived at is depleted of power, and it will take some effort to locate another one. Moreover, the booth in the sky building doesn't have sufficient range. Plus, there's the possibility that Yuri is lying about being willing to help us. All told, I think it best we wait at least a day."

Katrien didn't like waiting. *It's been too long already, and Verlink might find himself in trouble with no one around to help.*

"I still can't believe Verlink's not here. I was so excited to have us all together so we could figure out a way home." Katrien eyed Udan. "If we do figure out a way back, will you come with us?"

"There's no reason for me to stay here on Kythera. Would you want me to come with you?"

Katrien smiled and took his hand. "Of course I want you to come with us—with *me*."

She pressed her hand into his. "And . . ."

Katrien's voice wavered. "I can't stand this any longer."

Udan moved in close to her. "I had hoped you—"

But before he finished, his face was within an inch of hers. She could feel the heat of his breath as his arms slowly wrapped around her waist . . .

•

•

"I just want to get off this world," said Sergei, looking out toward the city.

Yuri stepped over a low tuft of grass. "I'm with you,

but maybe we can turn this to our advantage."

Sergei let out a short laugh. "Always trying to swindle."

"Why not?" said Yuri.

"We're in over our heads. Just get me off this fucking planet, and I'll be happy."

"That's why we're helping them, isn't it?"

"I suppose, but why are we leaving Katrien and Udan all alone? They need to be watched."

Yuri grinned. "They're a couple of lambs. They have no way to return without this so-called *engine*, and if we're successful locating one, then we'll have a bargaining chip."

Sergei shook his head dismissively. "I don't know. I still have my doubts. I haven't forgotten how Verlink trapped me in that building."

Yuri abruptly stopped walking. "We build their trust. Let them *think* we're being honest. The opportunity will come. One always does. Be patient, but be assured: when the hammer needs to drop, I won't hesitate."

CHAPTER 38

Instincts

The windows had been adjusted to simulate twilight in the early morning. Clothes were scattered about the room, lying where they had come off. Udan had drifted off and was lightly snoring while Katrien lay awake, staring at the ceiling. *What just happened?* This was not the Katrien De Vries she knew. Had the transfer booth irrevocably changed her? Was *that* why she was lying naked in bed with a man from another world?

Yet . . . it felt right somehow. Katrien *did* want Udan to come back to her world. The thought of home made her think of Verlink. What would he make of all this? Would he think she was hasty and rash—developing a relationship with an *alien*? Perhaps she *was* being reckless.

She wanted to return to Loutras to find Verlink and then stay there. They didn't need Yuri or Sergei. But Udan was convinced the Kytherian engines could only be found in Palechora, where they were originally developed. Hence they would eventually have to return to Palechora anyway.

Given that scenario, Udan thought it best to enlist Yuri and Sergei's help in tracking down the Kytherian engine research facility. It kept them out of the way and gave them something useful to do. But in Katrien's mind, it only delayed the inevitable conflict that would surely come. Udan was naive when dealing with people like Yuri and Sergei, and she worried his plan would backfire.

Udan rolled to one side, muttering in his sleep. *"Nthanda, hejn korhiam for savit. Sekhct nomain Nthanda fajsequa."*

There it was again; the name *Nthanda* mixed in with his native tongue. She'd heard it once before when he called her Nthanda by accident. She asked him about it when it happened, but he changed the subject. She didn't press at the time, but her instincts told her he was guarding something, either because of a bad experience or some great pain.

Was Nthanda his lover who he left behind and now was gone? Was *that* what she sensed? Katrien wondered what kind of girl he would choose. And if Nthanda had been his lover, where were his feelings now?

•
•

The entrances to buildings in the city were voice-activated, and Yuri kept repeating the strange-sounding phrases Udan had given him so he wouldn't forget. When he asked if the utterances worked on all doors everywhere, Udan said no; the command was tailored to the specific site. For example, those required to open doors of floating buildings were unique, as were the entrances to private facilities in the city. But public institutions had a common command that worked universally.

Their goal was to find a civic learning institution similar to a university. Inside, they were to search for a physics laboratory. According to Udan, several hubs in Palechora had developed the original information engines. With luck, more would be left that could be adapted to their needs.

Yuri stopped outside a tall structure with polished walls and counted the floors.

"Thirteen, this might be it. Udan said the civic learning center would have thirteen floors."

Sergei gazed upward. "God, is it big. It will take hours to search each floor."

"We're only interested in the physics lab," said Yuri as he tried the door command.

"In school, I hated physics," said Sergei as the doors opened.

Yuri made a face. "You don't have to like it; just locate what the people who love physics want. Udan gave us a symbol to look for over the doorway, and it's supposed to be in this building."

They entered together, and Sergei glanced up and down a long hallway. "Which way?"

"We start on one end and check each room."

"You don't think Udan sent us on a long chase just to be rid of us, do you?"

"As in giving him and Katrien time to screw like bunnies?" said Yuri as he peeked inside a room.

"I wouldn't be surprised. That Katrien sure is a beauty."

"That she is. Too bad she's attracted to the brainy types."

"What makes you say that?"

"Are you kidding?" scoffed Yuri. "She's all over that Kytherian, and he doesn't strike me as a coal miner."

"Maybe she hasn't been with a *real* man yet."

"Oh, like *you*?"

"Why not?"

"God, you're pathetic. She wouldn't give you the time of day, and as far as you being a real man, Christ—the smallest hardship and you fall to pieces. You were practically starving in that city when I found you. Did it never occur to you to find some plant to eat or search for water? *No*. Instead, you wasted time fretting over poor Tolenka."

"Fuck you," said Sergei.

Yuri dismissed him with a wave and continued down the hallway.

CHAPTER 39

Confessions and Subterfuge

Katrien dressed while Udan slept. The reality of their tango hung in the air, silent and awkward. Had their passion been nothing more than lust, or did it run deeper? Katrien wanted it to be more, but what did Udan want?

Udan stirred and then woke.

"You slept a long time," said Katrien, flashing an uncertain smile. "Any pleasant dreams?"

Udan raised himself on one elbow. "I feel wonderful, and yes, I did dream. Do you want to know about what?"

Katrien moved to the edge of the bed and sat down. "Only if I'll like it."

Udan rubbed her back. "It was about you, or more specifically, about *us*."

Katrien arched her back against Udan's hand. "That feels good."

"That I dreamed of us, or that I'm rubbing your back?"

Katrien turned to face him. "Both, but . . . tell me about *us*."

Udan rolled up and sat next to her. "When I came back to Kythera, I thought my heart would stop. No one was left." Udan touched her hand. "But now you're here."

Katrien put her hand on top of his. "Everyone you knew, just gone and never the chance to say goodbye." Katrien paused and looked down at Udan's hand. "Forgive me, Udan. I'm guessing here, but do you miss her?"

"Her?"

"Nthanda."

Udan started to talk but stopped and brought his hand to Katrien's cheek. "I suppose you sensed it. Nthanda Arjana was my lover, and when I returned to Kythera, I could find no record of what happened to her. She was gone—vanished—and I was devastated."

"If you need time," said Katrien quietly, "I'll understand. But I have no one waiting for me back home, so it's different for me." Katrien turned away and looked down at her hand on top of his. "But I think . . ." Her voice halted for a moment. "I think . . . I'm falling in love with you."

•
•

The Kytherian car never deviated in speed on its westward journey. It was early morning when the outline of a city appeared. To Tolenka, it seemed like the city he had seen when he first arrived from Earth. But he wasn't sure because at the time, it was far away, and as he walked eastward toward it, he came upon Verlink's building. The rest was history.

Tolenka cursed in Russian at the thought of Verlink. He should have shot him the minute he spotted him, maiming him before he could carry out his plan. Tolenka cursed again and vowed not to make the same mistake twice.

In the sky and to the north were several floating buildings. Tolenka wondered if they roamed on autopilot or were guided by some intelligence. He couldn't fathom how the designers achieved the feat of levitation other than with repelling magnets.

Tolenka's stomach growled. Five hours earlier, he had awoken in the night and realized the vehicle was skirting the edge of a narrow lake. He stopped and, using the car's lights to illuminate the shoreline, got water and caught small fish using his shirt as a net. But that was five hours ago, and he was getting hungry again.

In the gathering daylight, dense patches of lemon shrubs appeared on his left. He considered stopping and collecting the leaves, but the thought of their bitter aftertaste nauseated him. He wasn't *that* hungry.

The sun was high overhead when Tolenka glided onto a broad, seamless street. He halted the vehicle and scanned ahead, deciding which way to go. He guessed a direction and sent the car rolling. When he came to an intersection, he stopped and was about to continue when he spotted movement.

A man was walking down the street on his right toward a transfer booth. He went inside for a moment, came out, checked something on his phone, and continued down an avenue running perpendicular to the one he was on.

The man had gray hair and a week-old beard. It was *Verlink*!

Tolenka followed, keeping out of sight, peering around objects or from the corners of buildings. As he got closer, he instinctively felt for his weapon. It was still holstered; unfortunately, he was out of ammunition. But Verlink wouldn't know that.

He shadowed Verlink for several blocks until he reached what appeared to be the center of town. Verlink paused at a booth and stared at something over the doorway. Tolenka noticed a change in his body language and moved in closer.

Verlink quickly entered the booth and began tapping on a screen while comparing the display with something on his phone. Tolenka drew his weapon and swaggered across the street. Verlink, consumed by what he was doing, remained oblivious.

From several yards away, Tolenka shouted, "So, we meet again, Professor."

Startled, Verlink dropped his phone and looked outside the booth. His head drew back, and his eyes narrowed. "How?"

Tolenka smirked. "Funny how things can change."

Verlink bent down to retrieve his phone.

"Hold it!" barked Tolenka. "Outside—*now*!"

Verlink stepped out of the booth.

"You thought I would die up there in that building, didn't you?"

"Apparently, I was mistaken. Who set you free?"

Tolenka scoffed. "I let myself out using a transfer booth."

"What?" said Verlink, looking puzzled.

"There's a transfer booth on the upper floor. You didn't know that, did you?"

Verlink glanced at his cell phone behind him for a second. "So now what?"

"Have you seen my comrades?"

Verlink shook his head. "Besides you, I've seen no one."

"What about your student?"

Verlink shrugged. "You mean Katrien? I wish I knew."

He's lying, thought Tolenka. He didn't like Verlink's attitude either, having experienced the same superiority at the *Technikum* when he was interviewed for admission. "Insufficient qualifications," the professor had said, looking down at him over the rim of his glasses. Tolenka firmed his grip on his gun. If only he had bullets.

"Let's you and I walk back to the fallen building. I'm willing to bet she's there, and now that I have you, it'll be easy to persuade one of you to send me back to Earth."

Verlink scoffed. "It'll be a long walk. We're hundreds of kilometers away."

"So, this isn't the city I saw when I first got here?"

Verlink remained quiet.

Tolenka tipped his head in the direction of the booth. "What were you planning on doing with this booth?"

"Nothing."

Tolenka grinned. "You academicians think you're so smart. I'm guessing you were going to use it to meet up with Katrien."

"Pure speculation," said Verlink.

"Here's what you're going to do. You're going to send *me* back to the city where my comrades are."

Verlink seemed ready to protest but changed his mind. "If you want to go there, I'll need my cell phone to do it."

"Why?"

Verlink turned around and pointed at his phone lying on the booth floor. "I've stored critical information on it. I'll need it—unless you're capable of reading the language here."

Tolenka waved his gun in the direction of the phone. "Then go get it and bring it *here*."

Verlink moved into the booth. He bent over to retrieve the phone but stopped.

"*Damn*, my back," he said, steadying himself with his hand on top of the display screen.

Tolenka laughed. "You poor old man."

Verlink grinned at Tolenka and then tapped the screen with his finger.

The booth launched into a chorus of tones.

"You bastard!" yelled Tolenka. "You're not going anywhere!" He pulled the trigger and heard a click. "Shit!" He dove at the booth entrance as the tones began to align. But by the time his hands hit the floor, Verlink had disappeared in a haze of amber light.

CHAPTER 40

Another Kytherian Engine

Sergei looked down the hallway. "Haven't we been this way already?"

"I don't think so," said Yuri.

"Hell—they all look the same."

"That's because you're not paying attention to the symbols over the doors."

Predictable, thought Sergei. Yuri's pattern of assuming control was settling in again—right on schedule. "Oh, so I suppose you can read this crap. It looks like Arabic-Chinese mumbo jumbo to me."

Yuri flipped his hand and proceeded down the hall. After he'd gone partway, he stopped.

"I have a question that's been bothering me. Why didn't you tell me about Tolenka the first time he contacted you? Things might have turned out differently if you had. But as it played out, Tolenka is certainly dead by now."

Sergei tensed. *Here it comes.* "You acted like you didn't give a shit about him. You were on your own mission, and nothing else mattered."

"So you took it upon yourself to free Tolenka first and *then* contact me?"

"Something like that."

"Bullshit. I think you were hoping to free Tolenka and then force Verlink to send the two of you back to Earth—and leave me the *fuck* here!"

Sergei shrugged. "So what? We're in survival mode here. Let's face it; you and I are very different. I'm ex-military. I plan out a job and execute it. My men are loyal and can be counted on because they know their backs are covered. You, on the other hand," Sergei said condemningly, "are a street-smart thug who knows how to stay on top, but friendship and loyalties don't mean squat to you. So don't play the abandoned child act with me."

Yuri huffed. "Finally, the truth." He started walking down the hall again. "The truth is, you're right."

At least he's accepting the reality of their relationship, thought Sergei. *Good.* "And now?"

"Now, we work together because it's mutually beneficial. And—" Yuri halted and pointed to a symbol over a door lintel. "That looks like it," he said, comparing it to the image Udan had given him.

Sergei followed Yuri inside. The room was spacious, with rows of tables and stations connected by bundles of black cables. Equipment, apparently scientific but unfamiliar, was located about the place. Toward the back of the lab was a sturdy metal platform. On top sat a gold cube, roughly one foot on a side, bathed in sunlight streaming through a window. The rays struck the cube's surface obliquely, causing it to glow like the mythical Ark of the Covenant.

Yuri circled it several times and nodded rapidly. "I think this is it. Take a picture to show Udan, and then we'll hike back."

Sergei took pictures at various angles. Satisfied, he put

his phone away and noticed Yuri running his fingers over the engine's gilded surface. There was a smile on his face, and he knew immediately what was going on in his head. The cube was Yuri's bargaining chip and boded well for his future.

•
•

Verlink wiped his forehead. He felt nauseous with a clammy flush as if he had just disembarked from a whirling carnival ride. He waited a minute, bracing himself with his hands on the booth's doorframe, and then exited.

Out on the street, he checked the building opposite the booth. The same symbol he recorded a week ago on his cell phone was displayed near the top. He'd arrived!

Verlink took out his transceiver and held it in his hand. Would Katrien answer? If Yuri had found her, *could* she answer? He held his breath and pushed send. "Katrien, it's me. Are you there?"

Silence.

He put his thumb back on send and was about to press it again when the transceiver crackled: "Verlink?"

Verlink exhaled slowly. "Katrien, my God, is it really you?"

"Professor? Yes—it's me!" Verlink could hear Katrien crying. "I was worried I'd never see you again."

"Me too. Are you okay?"

"I am now."

"Are you in the city?"

"Yes, I'm at the booth you transported from a week ago. Where are you?"

"I'm at the fallen building, and Professor, you won't believe what I have to tell you."

Verlink had much to tell her as well. He was actually hearing Katrien's voice! He couldn't stop smiling. Within hours he would be at the sky building, and . . . an image of

Yuri suddenly intruded on his thoughts.

"Katrien, listen to me carefully; there's a Russian named Yuri. He was one of the men who attacked us that night in the lab, and he knows about the fallen building. He must not find you!"

Katrien was quiet for a moment. "Professor, I'm afraid Yuri has already found me. But don't worry, he's not here now. We can discuss that when I see you. Are you able to come here?"

Verlink broke into a jog as fast as he could manage. "I'm on my way."

The grass in front of the tear in the building was bent over and heavily trampled. *Lots of foot traffic,* thought Verlink as he got closer. He had trapped two men inside, and a third one almost got the best of him. He circled the perimeter but stopped when he saw that one of the second-floor windows had a hole in it. Sergei had liberated himself. Now he really was worried.

He considered calling Katrien on the transceiver but decided to enter unannounced—just in case she wasn't alone. As he came down the hallway, he heard Katrien's voice and started to smile but then stopped. *Who is she talking to?*

When he crossed the threshold to the cafeteria, a tall man he'd never seen before was standing next to Katrien—and he was *holding* her hand.

Katrien's face lit up, and she ran to him. "Hans, it's really you standing there!" She hugged him and started to cry.

Verlink was in mental freefall. He was finally reunited with Katrien, yet she was not alone, and there was a stranger in the room. Who was he?

Katrien leaned back and wiped her cheeks. "I'm so happy." She hugged him again and then took his hands and walked him over to the stranger. "Professor, I'd like you to meet someone." She stopped in front of the man. "Professor Verlink, this is Udan Roda-Tocci. He's from this world. We're on Kythera."

Verlink wanted to sit down. This wasn't going as he envisioned. Katrien just said they were on Kythera, and the man she was holding hands with was a Kytherian. *What is happening here?*

Udan reached for his hand. "I understand shaking hands is your custom," he said, smiling with perfect white teeth.

Verlink stared at the hand in front of him and slowly accepted it. He turned to Katrien, baffled. "He speaks our language, and remarkably well too. I don't understand."

Katrien looked up at Udan. "We have much to expl—"

"Sorry," interrupted Verlink. "I want to hear everything, but I'm worried about the Russian. Yuri is a dangerous man, and now there's another one free and probably nearby."

A low voice mocked him from behind. "Professor Verlink, *me*, dangerous? I'm sorry you feel that way."

Verlink turned to find Yuri in the doorway with Sergei behind him. "You!" Verlink said, stepping in front of Katrien. "Don't you people ever stay away?"

Amusement played across Yuri's face. "Who are you calling 'you people'?"

Katrien touched Verlink's shoulder. "Professor, it's okay. Udan and I have struck a deal with them. We're working together to find a way back home."

Verlink's mind reeled. *Working together?* He studied Katrien's face for signs of distress, but there were none. Could it be true? Was Katrien working with the Russians and this . . . this *stranger* from Kythera?

"Katrien, can we talk—*alone*?"

Katrien glanced at Udan and then at Verlink. "Professor, I know all of this must be overwhelming. Let's go outside."

Yuri put up his hand. "One moment, please, if I may. I have good news. Sergei and I have found what we believe to be another information engine, as you call it. Look, we took a picture."

He nodded to Sergei, who removed his cell phone from a pocket and brought up the images he had taken earlier. Everyone circled to look.

"This looks like it," said Udan. "Do you agree, Professor?"

Verlink studied the image. "There appear to be differences, but I think it might be another information engine. Where was this picture taken?"

Yuri tipped his head toward Sergei. "We'll tell you, but first, we'd like to know how we can be assured that all our agreements will be honored."

•
•

Deep space, like infinity, can be lonely. Station manager 45M sat up and rubbed her eyes. After thirty days in stasis, the hibernation pod had entered into its state of wakefulness. The manager left the pod and went to the control room, not bothering to put on clothes. She called up a cup of Flocora and sat down in the command chair, holding the warm mug, waiting for the sleepy haze to pass.

She checked the ships' status logs. The propulsion engine had not fully repaired itself, so she was still weeks away from entering Kythera's solar system. The long-range communication array had not repaired itself either. The meteorite storm damage had been extensive and kept the robotic repair machinery working around the clock.

She was lucky to be alive and had been lucky earlier too. The first time was leaving Kythera before Qua-Kil began to decimate the Kytherian population. It was on a whim that she had left at all. Her plan was simple: to go on a deep space probe mission. But she had a secondary motive. Manager 45M smiled to herself as she nursed her Flocora. It would have been wonderfully romantic, but that was her nature.

Now, her good fortune was in question because she had no way to contact Kythera save for the short-range transmitter. It had a poorly focused beam, and dispersion would likely render the signal too weak to reach Kythera.

She brought up an image of her lover and sat quietly, remembering how quickly his smile came to his face—how she loved that! She downloaded one of the messages he had placed on a storage chip. There were few left she hadn't read, so she savored what remained. But she cherished certain ones and would re-read them multiple times until the tears came. Would he even be on Kythera? Had he fallen victim to Qua-Kil like the others?

There had been a message from Central Space Command just before the meteorites struck, but it was incomplete as if something had disrupted it before it ended. Had all of Kythera succumbed to Qua-Kil—including her lover?

She couldn't accept that. If he were back on Kythera, she wanted him to know she was still alive. So, whether it would work or not, she had to try the short-range transmitter. But every time she started to compose a message, long and heartfelt, her loneliness came pouring out, and she broke down crying. In the end, she settled on a transmission that would repeat over and over, short and simple: *Udan, my love. I'm coming home . . .*

CHAPTER 41

Plans

The unease Verlink had harbored was gone. Like a father uncertain about his daughter's choice of boyfriend, it had taken time to accept Katrien's visible attachment to Udan. But that phase had passed, and Verlink had become a fan of Udan himself.

The thousands of years of genetic improvements and early interventions on Kythera had resulted in a perfect population by contemporary Earth standards. The speed with which Udan's mind worked was uncanny. Yet he was humble, easy to get along with, and brilliant, and he treated Katrien as an equal, respecting her intelligence and scientific abilities as if she were a native of Kythera.

With the information engine Yuri and Sergei had found came the issue of where the lab to begin the Kytherian engine's conversion should be situated. The fallen building provided a base but lacked the necessary infrastructure. The physics lab in Palechora, where the engine had been found, had all the proper equipment but was ill-suited as a living space.

To everyone's surprise, Udan provided a solution to the dilemma. "Why not use one of the cloaked facilities out on the plane?" he said, matter-of-factly.

Verlink shared a puzzled look with Katrien. "Come again?"

Udan led Katrien and Verlink outside and pointed south. "If you stand here and focus on that line of trees, you will eventually detect vertical ripples."

Verlink followed his instructions, and after a few minutes, he nodded. "I see them, but what are they?"

Udan grinned. "I thought you knew. They're the outline of a cloaked research facility used to study nature from within a camouflaged structure."

"It was near the sky building all this time," said Verlink.

Katrien ran her hand through her hair as she stared across the grassy plain. "Are you sure you can get us inside?"

Udan grinned again. "Of course."

•
•

Verlink was pleased. After only a week, the hidden lab had been uncloaked and fitted with equipment transported from Palechora. The building was only one story high and, in its uncloaked state, had the same rust-brown color as the fallen sky building. Modest power was available too, sourced from solar converters located on the roof. Verlink also appreciated the lab's proximity—only a few minutes' walk away.

Along with Katrien and Udan, Verlink had formed a formidable technological triumvirate, and as the likelihood of their success grew, thoughts of the future became frequent topics of discussion. Katrien wanted Udan to return to Earth, and Verlink was wholeheartedly in agreement, including Udan.

But Verlink had a nagging concern regarding Yuri and Sergei. As part of the truce and cooperative agreement, they had agreed to send the Russians back. But there were logistical problems: Should they transfer all together simultaneously?

Katrien was adamant that the transmission times should be different because she wanted to be far from the Russians when they shifted back to Earth. That, of course, raised the immediate question: If the transfers were split, who should go first? Katrien would only agree to sending Yuri and Sergei second as a matter of safety. But the Russians challenged that proposal, claiming they would not know how to operate the equipment once the others left in the event something went wrong.

Arguments, pro and con, were debated at length, but in the end, the verdict was for the Russians to follow after a predetermined delay. Verlink sighed. He didn't trust them, especially Yuri. Something to do with his eyes.

•

•

Sergei stepped aside as Yuri grabbed a metal beam off a platform and heaved it to the side. *Impressive,* thought Sergei. No question about it, Yuri *was* strong. Too bad it was his only good quality.

"This platform could easily hold four to five people," said Sergei.

Yuri wiped the dust off his hands. "I agree, and once we move it from this storage building back to the lab, I think we should have a sit-down with Udan and discuss the possibility of all of us transporting together."

"We've been through that. Verlink or Katrien won't agree to it."

"I'm not sure about Udan."

"How do you mean?" asked Sergei.

Yuri's face became serious. "He's more trusting, that's

for sure, but the more I think about it, there might be another way."

"You have an idea?"

Yuri grinned, nodding. "I've been memorizing the procedures they've been developing. They think because I'm not a scientist, I can't follow what they're doing. They're like foreigners talking freely in their native language because they believe those nearby won't understand."

Sergei was aware of the scientists' behavior, having experienced their condescension firsthand—*especially* from Verlink. "Their arrogance is hard to ignore. So what 'other way' do you have in mind?"

Yuri looked around the room as a precaution and lowered his voice. "They plan to send themselves first, and then after one day, a timer will kick in to transport us—right?"

"Yeah," said Sergei, keeping his voice low, "that's been the plan all along."

"I've been listening to them discussing how the control is supposed to work. Apparently, the system has to recharge between each use. The information engine we found is incomplete and doesn't have a functional way to convert information into energy. From what I understand, that's the last part of the fabrication process on the engine. In short, the power needs to be supplied externally."

Sergei rolled his eyes. *More information mumbo jumbo.* He'd heard it before, but he still didn't understand, nor did he care. "I don't know what the fuck you're talking about."

"They only need the engine to function as a phase-shifter between worlds. It has something to do with metastable matter. But Udan now says there isn't enough local power to run the engine, so he proposed that it be reconfigured to extract energy from information as a means to power itself."

Sergei waved his hands. "Big *shit.* What's your point?"

Yuri mimed quote signs with his fingers. "That's what they said."

Sergei huffed. "Then why don't they go ahead and do that and move on?"

"Remember, I'm eavesdropping, so I only get bits and pieces of their conversation. But I can tell you this: Verlink and Katrien are terrified something could go wrong."

"All right, let them sort it out. What's your plan?"

"They're not stupid, so when the scheduled day arrives, they're going to make sure we're nowhere nearby. My thinking is they will run a few tests before committing to a human transfer."

Sergei nodded. "Yeah, that sounds like them—double-checking everything."

"Exactly. I propose we take advantage of that."

Sergei broke into a cruel smile. "I'm listening."

Yuri checked again to make sure they were alone. "Here's what I have in mind . . ."

CHAPTER 42

HAST4

The voices were muffled and coming from the room below. HAST4 directed his acoustic sensors toward the sounds. The language of the Earthlings was crude—more so than the Kytherians—but then they didn't have the mind link, so it took longer to assimilate.

One fact was clear: the beings from Earth were severely lacking, exhibiting a wide variation in behavior and intelligence. The gray one and the girl working with Udan were loyal and logical thinkers, while the other two, Yuri and Sergei, were independent, shortsighted, and treacherous. Earth must be a strange place.

Udan and the Earthlings had formed a loose collaboration with the Russians, which seemed odd since earlier they had been, by all appearances, trying to kill each other. HAST4 didn't know what to make of that, but of greater concern was a Kytherian information engine being moved into the decloaked field building. Nothing good ever came from those engines, and HAST4 feared history would repeat itself.

Qua-Kil was an unwanted byproduct of the engine's last resurrection, resulting in the loss of millions of HAST4's brethren. It was the time of the Great Purge. Unleashed on Kythera, Qua-Kil gorged itself on sources of high-density information, Kytherians and HASTILLONS alike.

But what could he do? The strangers were determined to use the engine to phase-shift back to Earth—all with Udan's help. At first, Udan's complicity was a mystery, but no longer. He was in love with the Earth girl, and although HAST4 struggled with understanding the emotion, his experience with other Kytherians told him it was powerful. He decided it was no more complicated than that, and when the girl returned to Earth, Udan and the gray one would accompany her.

On that day, solitude would return. HAST4 would be all alone in the sky building, and his goal of reviving HAST3 and getting to Palechora would be impossible. By design, the HASTILLONS were unable to communicate over long distances, and although HAST4 did not know for a fact that more HASTILLONS were in Palechora, he considered it highly probable.

Udan, being Kytherian, would know how to help revive HAST3. Unfortunately, time was running out. He would observe for a little longer, just to be safe. Then, when the moment was right, HAST4 would take a chance and make his presence known.

CHAPTER 43

Countdown

Tolenka stirred from a nap and looked outside. Twilight was coming, and the view through the window would soon fade into blackness. The loss of daylight was of no consequence for his wheelless self-driving car because it needed neither light nor road to navigate. *No matter,* thought Tolenka, as he massaged a kink at the back of his neck. The scenery no longer interested him anyway.

How far had he traveled? Even if he knew, he still had no idea how far away the city was. All he was sure of was that the booth had sent him to the east, which meant the return path was to the west.

The steady thrum of the vehicle, monotonous and droning, was slow torture to an unimaginative mind like his. He was not curious by nature, preferring to react to events as they came. That was why he joined up with Sergei. He didn't need to plan or worry about the details; all he had to do was act when the need called.

After several hours, Tolenka stopped the vehicle and stepped outside. He took deep inhales of the cool evening air and then bent over, touching his toes with his hands to relieve the muscles in his back. As he raised himself, he suddenly stopped. There, in the far distance, rendered in relief by the sun's fading rays, was the outline of a city—*at last*.

The streets, having no power to light them, were dark when Tolenka arrived. He stopped in the middle of a broad avenue. Was this the city Sergei had talked about? He'd mentioned there was a spire at the center of town, but to be sure, Tolenka needed to work his way toward the middle of the city. But searching in darkness was pointless; he decided he'd wait until morning and crawled into the back of the car.

At dawn, Tolenka awoke and returned to the front seat. Through the front window lay a grid of intersecting streets. *Which way?* He started the vehicle and, choosing at random, wended his way north. A quarter mile out, the cabin display suddenly went dark, and the car drifted to a stop and settled to the ground.

Tolenka got out and looked for a hood to look under, but there wasn't one—not that *that* would have helped since he had no idea how the car functioned anyway. It was simply dead. He patted its dusty side as if it were a faithful dog and continued north on foot, winding through avenues flanked by buildings with black and polished gray sides. After twenty minutes, he came to a tall spire, circular like a graceful cone, reflecting the rising sun—just as Sergei had described.

Confident he'd arrived at the correct city, Tolenka took out his comm.

"Yuri, Sergei—is anyone there?"

•
•

Yuri cracked open his eyes. "What the . . . ?" He groped the side of his bed until he found the comm transmitter.

"Sergei, is that you?"

A sarcastic voice laughed. "No, it's Tolenka."

Yuri bolted upright in bed. "*Tolenka*—what the hell? We thought you were dead."

"I almost was," cackled Tolenka.

Thoughts raced through Yuri's head. They had never checked the upper level because Verlink said it would be reeking from decomposition. But the more he thought about it, Verlink *had* been evasive, as if he knew more than he let on.

"Why haven't you contacted us?"

Tolenka snickered. "That's because I was nowhere near here. I stumbled into one of those crazy transfer booths on the upper level, and it sent me way the hell east. I've managed to make my way back, and I'm in the city right now. I have a vehicle, or at least I *had* one, but it finally gave up the ghost."

"What city did you say you were in?"

"I'm in the city east of the fallen building that bastard Verlink trapped me in."

Yuri silently cursed. Tolenka would screw up his plan—*big-time*. He and Sergei were within days of implementing their escape, and what he didn't need right now was Tolenka coming into the picture. *Time to make up a story.*

"Tolenka, you're in a city called Palechora, and Sergei and I are heading there early tomorrow morning to pick up supplies. With you there, you can help us. We'll even bring food and water to you. After we're done, we'll head back here together to the fallen building."

"I'd rather come now," said Tolenka. "I'm starving and going crazy being by myself. It's still early, and I can be there well before dark."

"Sit tight, Tolenka. We might need you there to check out something."

"You're killing me, Yuri."

"Hang in there, Comrade."

Tolenka's voice became subdued. "Where should I meet you?"

"How about the center of town, by that spire. Do you know where that is?"

Tolenka glanced over his shoulder. "Yeah, I'm looking at it now. Call me when you reach the edge of town, and I'll meet you."

"See you tomorrow."

Yuri tossed the comm onto his bed. "Son of a bitch!" He left the room and barged into Sergei's bedroom. "We've got a problem, Sergei."

"How about fucking knocking first," croaked Sergei, rubbing his eyes.

"Tolenka is alive, and get *this*; he's in Palechora."

"Huh? Palechora—*what?* I thought he was *dead*."

"Well, he's not. I'll explain later, but right now, we need to advance our exit plan."

"But we're not ready."

"We have to be—and we can do it too, especially if Verlink and the others are successful with their test today."

"Wait a second. What about Tolenka?"

Yuri narrowed his eyes at Sergei. "Christ—are you serious? Tolenka is on his own. I'm not missing my chance to get the hell out of here."

"If Tolenka is alive, we owe it to him to wait."

Yuri's brain boiled. "Fucking hell! If we wait, who knows what Udan and the others will do when they learn Tolenka's alive. They might panic and do God knows what."

"Is Tolenka coming here?"

"No, I convinced him you and I are going to meet him tomorrow."

Sergei left the bed and started to get dressed. "I don't know. I still don't like it."

"Think about this: if we involve Tolenka, *all* of us might end up stuck here. How would you like *that*?"

"All right. But if your plan fails, then we team up with Tolenka."

Yuri stared at Sergei and wanted to twist his head off. *Unbelievable.* "My plan won't fail."

"When is everything going down?"

Yuri paused for a moment and then said, "If all goes well, we leave tonight."

•
•

Katrien opened her eyes. Udan was breathing slowly next to her. The steady rhythm comforted her, and she snuggled tightly against his body. They had left the lab late last night after running tests and making changes to the equipment. They were close to their first transfer trial, which, if successful, meant she could be back on Earth within a week.

After being on Kythera for a month, the thought of going back to Earth seemed like returning from a long vacation. Yet it had been neither a "vacation" nor an adventure holiday. But, as she heard breathing next to her, she remembered there were positives.

For the moment, her illness was stable, but she worried there would be a lapse, and then Udan would know something was wrong. Whenever she was about to confide in him, she panicked and stayed quiet. But she had to tell him soon. It wasn't fair to Udan, especially since he'd agreed to return to Earth with her and Verlink.

Katrien wondered what might have transpired on Earth during her absence. The university would have been greatly alarmed by her and Verlink's sudden disappearance—and there would be much explaining to do upon their return.

Udan stirred, and Katrien felt her heart jump. Her happiness was tainted with anxiety, and not only about the problem of her illness. What would he think of her world? It was archaic compared to Kythera. For him, living on Earth was preferable to a life of loneliness on Kythera, yet a tiny part of her was apprehensive. In the back of her mind, she couldn't help wondering if his attention to her was driven more out of loneliness than actual attraction. Would he be content, and was she good enough for him—even if their time together was short-lived?

She reached over and brushed his hair aside.

Udan's eyes slowly opened, hazy as if still dreaming. "Well, good morning," he said quietly.

Katrien jumped. "Sorry, I didn't mean to wake you."

"Don't be sorry. It's a nice way to wake up."

"I was wondering how late you'd sleep after our long stint last night."

Udan drew back and narrowed his eyes. "But we went straight to bed."

Katrien nudged him with her elbow. "I'm talking about the *lab*."

"I know," said Udan, grinning. "We did make excellent progress." He reached out and stroked the side of her face. "If our stability tests go well today, we can begin the first transfer of a solid object."

Katrien was silent for a moment. "If there's any loss of stability as the engine begins matter decomposition, we might not be able to bring it back to equilibrium."

"I wish there were another way, but we don't have enough power. We have to let the information engine do part of what it was designed to do."

Katrien sighed. "I know. But I was there on the front line when the second Kytherian artifact on Earth began to deconstruct matter." Katrien reached back into her memory. "I can't quite describe the sound it makes; it's a grinding noise straight from hell that goes into your bones like fingernails on a chalkboard. It's the sound of matter when it dies, and I'll never forget it."

"We've built in safeguards and are operating at one one-millionth of its potential, which will keep it well within its stable zone. If you think about it, all power sources operate the same way. Nuclear fission is a runaway reaction held in check by neutron-absorbing material. The internal combustion engines you use on Earth utilize a series of mini explosions contained in metal and harnessed to do work. What we're doing here is similar in principle."

"I understand your logic," Katrien said, "but promise me we'll only proceed if you, me, and Verlink are all in agreement as to its safety."

"Agreed," said Udan, putting his arm across her and pulling her close.

Katrien yielded, but the worry never left her heart.

•
•

The midday sun cast its rays onto a broad street running east and west. Tolenka stood in the middle and gazed in the direction of the fallen building that had once held him captive. Yuri said he and Sergei would bring food and water tomorrow, but it brought little comfort.

Ripples of heat rose from the seamless road, undulating like a breeze over a company of candles. Tolenka ran his tongue over his cracked lips and then raised his fist to the sun and shouted, "Wait until tomorrow? Well, up your *ass*!"

Overhead, a floating building was drifting slowly to the west. If he left now, the sun would be blocked, and the building's shadow would lead the way. He could make it to the fallen building a few hours after sunset. Sergei wiped his brow and cursed. "To hell with *tomorrow*."

CHAPTER 44

Knocking on the Door of Chaos

Verlink was lying on his back with his hands inside a metal cabinet when he heard Katrien and Udan enter the lab.

"I was wondering when you two would amble in," he said as he withdrew his hands and sat up.

Katrien tugged on Udan's arm and looked at him. "We *worked* late last night—long after you went to bed."

Verlink lightly tossed his hands in the air. "Just kidding." He glanced at the metal cabinet. "I saw you fixed the feedback control. It looks solid now. I think we're ready for a matter transfer test."

Udan nodded. "I was telling Katrien the same thing this morning."

"Hold on," said Katrien. "I need convincing too. Aren't you concerned about the uncertainty during the phase-shift between metastable states?"

Verlink's eyes arched sharply. Katrien always had valid concerns. "Can you clarify that?"

Katrien paced the floor as she spoke. "On the Guatemalan artifact, the cylinder was damaged, so we stripped off its outer casing to tap into it directly. But we didn't need it to supply power, so its sole purpose was adapted to control the phase-shifting between metastable states. But here, the grid is mostly down, and our supply of power is limited; therefore we have to get it directly from the information engine."

Verlink nodded as he stroked his beard. "I think I see where you're going. In contrast, for the device here, the cylinder has a *dual* purpose, which means it must toggle between both supplying power *and* implementing the metastable phase-shift. Hence there's a tiny window of uncertainty in maintaining control of the loop."

"Exactly," said Katrien, stopping suddenly.

Verlink got up from the floor. "I think I can alleviate your fear. I've set up the control loop to use power only from the Kytherian grid and not from matter decomposition. Therefore, during the transitions, control is maintained via the grid. That makes it independent of the matter decomposition, which removes the uncertainty during the phase-shift cycle."

"But the grid has limited power. Are you sure it can supply what's needed?"

"Good question, but the control loop uses very little power, so that won't be a constraint."

Katrien fixed her eyes on the Kytherian engine. "Then nothing can go wrong?"

Verlink patted her shoulder. "Nothing can go wrong."

•
•

Yuri stifled a grin as he walked away from the lab doorway. He'd heard enough. Now, all he had to do was wait for confirmation that the matter transfer was successful and put his plan into action. He'd memorized the boot-up procedure and had surreptitiously obtained the lockout code, so turning the machine on would not be a problem. Moreover, he and Sergei had helped assemble the platform, so they knew that part of the system was fully operational.

He hastened to the other side of the building and knocked on a steel door.

Sergei opened it and waved him in. "Is it a go?"

Yuri nodded quickly. "I think so. If their test goes well this afternoon, there's nothing to stop us. We'll be out of here by midnight."

He eyed Sergei's workbench. "Is this the crowbar device you told me about?"

"I'm mostly done. All that's left is to fit it with heavy-gauge wire from the main lab, which might not be easy because there's always somebody in there working."

"Don't worry. I'll think of some excuse."

Yuri returned his gaze on the contraption resting atop Sergei's bench. The device looked like a cobbled-together pile of junk parts. He wasn't impressed. "Explain to me again how this is *supposed* to work."

"It's a simple water-draining toggle. A teeter bar keeps two wires from shorting as long as water is inside this container, which serves as a counterweight. As water drains from the container, the teeter pivots upward, electrically shorting the connections. That's what the wire is for. The wires will short out the grid power, bringing down the system, but not before we're *long gone*."

Yuri let out a short laugh. "Ridiculously simple—if it works."

Sergei seemed oblivious to the implied insult. "Don't worry; it'll work. As a matter of fact, I'm rather proud of it."

"If you say so," said Yuri. "But whether it works or not won't stop us from leaving this goddamn world." He started to smile. "This is going to be easy—very easy indeed."

•
•

Udan placed a potted Arkwelda plant that he had dug from outside the lab and placed on the transfer platform. He nodded to Katrien, who went to a console and typed into a holographic keyboard. As she modulated the field, the room became bathed in green light. The quantum waves of the plant were slowly being brought into phase with her world—Earth. Once synchronized, the two worlds would overlap, allowing matter from one to slip into the other.

The lab walls vibrated with a low-frequency hum, eventually synchronizing with the pulsing green light. The field intensity climbed until the plant appeared as if viewed through a haze. Then the awful wailing began.

The piercing wail alarmed Udan. He looked over at Katrien and called out to her. "Should we shut it down?"

"This is normal," said Katrien above the din.

The haze suddenly dissipated, and the plant appeared frozen as if cast in glass. The glow grew brighter; then the plant, the light, and the noise vanished, and the Kytherian lab became quiet.

Udan let out his breath slowly. "Congratulations, Katrien and Professor Verlink. You've done it." He saw Katrien trembling. "Are you okay?"

"It worked."

"You're not surprised, are you?"

"It *should* have worked. It's just that for the first time, going back to Earth finally seems real."

Verlink rubbed his palms on the front of his shirt. "I was nervous too, and yes, we did it, and in a few days, we'll be back home. I can't wait for a decent cup of coffee either!"

"Hold on," said Katrien, raising her hand. "We still have to bring the plant back."

Katrien reversed the process, and within minutes, the potted plant reappeared on the platform. Udan retrieved it and held it up to the light. "It seems healthy enough. I'll take it into the city tomorrow to a bio lab for a thorough checkup."

"Excellent," said Verlink with an air of triumph. "I say we deserve to celebrate. Let's make a smash-up dinner tonight along with some of that wine-like drink you have."

Udan gave a mischievous wink. "I'm game. How about you, Katrien?"

Katrien grinned. "I wouldn't miss it for the world."

•
•

As night fell, a jade-colored cloud formed at the back of the lab. At its center was the Arkwelda plant that had traveled to Earth and back. Its leaves scintillated, twinkling randomly like a holiday ornament. They stayed like that, dancing in the darkness. Then, as if time suddenly spun forward, the plant's outer leaves turned brown, curled up, and dropped. More leaves followed until, minutes later, the entire plant stood winter barren, leaving only a faint glow and the quiet of the night.

CHAPTER 45

Chaos at Midnight

The field was dark and littered with patches of bramble, lying like landmines in Tolenka's path as he hiked toward the sky building. Overhead was a bank of gray clouds illuminated from behind by the moon.

Tolenka suddenly tripped and hit the ground hard. "Son of a bitch!"

He picked himself up, scowling at the shrub that had brought him down. He wiped his muddied hands on his pants and cursed again. Earlier, he had set out enthusiastic about surprising Yuri and Sergei and had been making good time when he realized he'd forgotten his gun. He went back to retrieve it. Even though he had no bullets, he *needed* that gun and felt naked without it.

The oversight would delay his arrival by several hours, and he'd be lucky if he made it before midnight. He thought about calling and explaining to Yuri about his change of plan. But he knew Yuri would disapprove and decided to arrive without argument. So, with only a shadowed moon to keep him company, Tolenka pushed onward into the cool night air.

•
•

"They're all half drunk," said Sergei, pulling back from the doorway. "They're celebrating hard after the success of their phase-shifting experiment. Little do they know that's our cue that all is a go."

"They've been in there for over three hours," said Yuri. "And we weren't invited either—the assholes."

"Their hangovers will be our revenge."

"Idiot," scoffed Yuri. "Kytherian drink doesn't do that—remember?"

"I wish we still had our guns," said Sergei. "It pisses me off we had to give them up as part of our 'agreement.'"

Yuri flipped his hand. "Screw it. We're getting what we wanted—a way out of here, plus a little revenge to get even."

"Hah!" laughed Sergei. "Too bad we won't be around to see their faces."

"Let's give them a few more hours to pass out," said Yuri, "then we'll meet."

"When and where?"

"Right here at midnight."

•
•

Yuri peeked into the room. Verlink was sprawled across a lounge and snoring. On the floor beside him was a bottle that had tipped over, leaving a green stain.

"I knew they'd be out cold given the way they were drinking," said Sergei.

Yuri looked around the corner. "I don't see Katrien and Udan."

Sergei nudged Yuri. "You're not surprised, are you? They probably ducked into a bedroom and are now naked and asleep in each other's arms."

"Udan is one lucky bastard," said Yuri as he started down the hallway. "No worries. We'll have our *fun* later. Come on, let's head over to the lab."

As they entered the lab, the walls and ceiling automatically lit up. Yuri went to a control panel and started tapping symbols on a holographic keyboard.

"While I boot up the system, grab your crowbar apparatus, and start hooking it up."

"I'm on it," said Sergei.

Sergei returned with his device trailing cables behind him. He moved a potted plant that looked like it hadn't been watered for several weeks and began attaching wires. Minutes later, he stepped away from a power panel. "That's it. We're ready. All I have to do is pull the drain plug, and *voilà*—it runs itself."

"How much time before the bottle drains and the power shorts out?"

"I'd say fifteen minutes, give or take a few."

Yuri was starting to feel optimistic. His brilliant plan was falling into place, and he was proud of it. "God, just think of it; minutes from now, we'll be back home."

Sergei eyed the equipment. "Are you *sure* you know what you're doing?"

Yuri glared back. *Just like him to dampen the moment.*

Sergei continued. "One thing confuses me."

That's easy, thought Yuri.

"Why aren't we going together?"

"Unless you know how to run this, you'll have to be first."

"But then, once I'm gone, how will you send yourself?"

More goddamn questions! "After I send you, I'll put it on automatic. I need to make sure it's running smoothly. If we go together and the system needs an adjustment, there's no way to do that if I'm on the platform. *Now*, do you understand?"

"So *I'm* the guinea pig."

"You got it. Are you ready?"

"Shouldn't we do a test or something?"

"Christ!" barked Yuri, tapping his watch. "We don't have time to lily-ass around. I'm starting the system."

The lights dropped, and the room glowed with a pulsing lime-colored light. Small dust particles in the air caught the illumination, flashing like tiny fireflies. Seconds later, a low-frequency vibration rose in amplitude, gradually coming in phase with the flickering light.

Yuri smiled to himself; everything was running as it should be. Satisfied the field had stabilized, he pointed at the crowbar device. "Pull the drain plug and get on the platform."

Sergei stared at the platform as if he were looking into a deep chasm. Room light glistened from his forehead. "You're sure—right?"

"It's now or never. Once you're gone, I'll follow."

Sergei stepped onto the circular grid, dropped his hands to his side, and nodded. "I'm ready."

Gradually, a haze, like a mist, surrounded him. The lab thrummed with a repetitive sound like ripping cloth. Then, as if the doors of hell had abruptly swung open, the ripping turned into a grating that shook the floor and walls. The sudden din caught Sergei off guard, and his eyes went wide. Yuri watched his muscles tense as he prepared to jump free of the platform.

But he never left.

Yuri ran through the sequence in his mind. It should have worked, but the phase-shift wasn't happening. The Kytherian engine drummed louder. Yuri pushed the idle switch, but there was no change. Droplets of sweat fell from his forehead onto the control panel.

He yelled over the increasing thrum, "Sergei, can you hear me?"

But there was nothing, not even a glimmer behind Sergei's eyes now trapped in a perpetual state of surprise—held rigid by an invisible field as if he were an insect petrified in amber.

Yuri tried the sequence again.

Nothing.

"You need to get the hell off the platform! Try, Sergei—*try*!"

Seconds marched into minutes; then, something began to happen. A line, barely perceivable like a thread of silk, started to unravel from Sergei's head. It coiled like a stretched spring as it rose upward, flowing into the cylinder attached to the Kytherian cube mounted above.

The thread gradually took on volume, getting thicker, pulling Sergei's hair—drawing it up into a bizarre spike—like a gelled punk rocker. Yuri moved closer to the platform. He could feel the floor vibrating through his boots, pulsing as if it were alive.

Within seconds, Sergei's hair was gone. Yuri, now mesmerized, watched as bits and pieces of Sergei peeled away. The strange decomposition was methodical, first stripping off the flesh from the skull and then on to the bone, cutting with a surgeon's skill until it revealed the brain.

Chunks of gray matter were lifted out, suspended in the air, and then whisked away. Yuri felt a prickling on his skin. The field was growing. He stepped back, never taking his eyes off the macabre autopsy playing out before him.

He had to get out of here.

"What the *hell*?" boomed a voice.

Startled, Yuri turned. A face, worn, unshaven, and holding two eyes locked in surprise, stood in the doorway.

"Tolenka?"

Yuri was about to speak when his attention shot over to the power panel.

The crowbar device.

A bright flash erupted from the control panel, spewing sparks and ozone into the air. The Kytherian engine paused from its feast as if it were a dog interrupted by someone pulling its tail. For a split second, Yuri thought the madness was over, but then the Kytherian engine began to bellow.

Yuri grabbed Tolenka's shoulder. "We have to get out of here."

Tolenka needed no prompting and headed for the door with Yuri only steps behind.

At the doorway, Yuri stopped to gaze one last time at his accomplishment. He put his hands over his ears against the deafening noise and watched, spellbound by an incredible sight. Sergei was half gone. Only his legs and part of his torso were standing, still poised as if ready to jump—held upright by a forcefield while a consuming maelstrom raged on above.

CHAPTER 46

Station Manager 45M

A shadow crossed over Nthanda's closed eyelids, and she smiled. Udan would soon be here. Shading her eyes, she looked up at the sky and saw the outline of a building drifting by. It matched the clouds, chalky white immersed in a placid blue ether.

She was in love, and the day seemed perfect, ebbing and flowing like waves on a beach. A gentle breeze caressed her face, and she smiled again. "Soon," she whispered to herself, "soon." Moments later, powerful arms came from behind and circled her waist. She arched her back and let herself go . . .

A beep broke the reverie. The repair robot in section five had a report ready for station manager 45M. Nthanda scolded herself—had she been asleep or daydreaming? The periods of wakefulness outside the pod seemed to be getting longer, and she was becoming concerned for her sanity.

The ship, its engines dormant, was still coasting toward the Kytherian solar system. Nthanda brought up the report on her command screen, and the news wasn't good. The repair robots could go no further. The meteorite damage had been too extensive. At best, the spatial distortion engines would operate periodically, meaning her arrival on Kythera was still a month out.

If only the long-range communications array worked, she'd know for sure if Udan were alive on Kythera. But at least her message was still broadcasting via the short-range transmitter, and the closer she came to Kythera, the greater the chance Udan would receive it.

Nthanda closed her eyes . . .

She remembered when she first met Udan Roda-Tocci; it was Chacorella, a holiday. A day when male athletes from around the world tested their mettle on the open Talmarind Sea in ancient rowing canoes.

Nthanda sat on the beach overlooking the turquoise sea, digging her toes into the hot sand. Handmade wooden rowing boats, long and sleek, were lined up in the water, waiting for the starting call. Cheers and waves from the shore heightened the tension in the air. Who would be this year's champion?

Eventually, the commissioner of games, Madame Gabtrella, garbed in ancient ceremonial dress, walked out onto a long pier. When she reached the end, she raised her arms high. The crowd hushed. Her voice, lilting and clear, rolled across the water. She spoke of tradition and bravery and the significance of the past. Gabtrella talked about perseverance, dedication, and the preservation of identity. She finished by welcoming the participants, stating the rules, and wishing them all good luck.

Gabtrella then raised an acoustic conch and sounded the start of the race.

Powerful shoulders dug oars into the cerulean water, leaving deep swirling troughs. Before long, the churning waters died down, and the boats were far out to sea. In the distance, rowers pulling on their oars jockeyed to be first to round an emerald islet. The whoops and hollers onshore fell silent as everyone waited to see who would be the first to emerge. Soon, it was clear the Mitoros team was in the lead, with the indefatigable Loutras right behind. But the Mitoros held their advantage and finished victorious amid roars and cheers.

By tradition, winners were carried in their canoe out of the water and onto the beach by the defeated. Nthanda watched as sculpted gods rose from the blue ocean wearing loincloths and bearing the victors' canoe on their shoulders. The men glistened in the sun as they mounted the beach. One man, in particular, caught her attention . . .

Nthanda opened her eyes and sighed. That was two years ago, and it would be another month before she would again set eyes on Udan. The wait seemed like an eternity. *But will he even be there?* She buried the thought.

Instead, her musings turned to Kythera. She pined for the rhythm of night and day, the laughter of friends, the cool breeze that comes out with the stars, and the hundred other little things that go unnoticed. In space, there are no sunrises, sunsets, or moonlit walks holding hands. *What had become of Kythera?* Her fate, as well as Udan's, depended on the answer.

Nthanda checked the time. It was 2:34 a.m. in Loutras, and she imagined Udan sleeping. She broke into a smile and whispered, "Moonbeams are kissing you, my love. Dream on; soon your lonely nights will be no more."

CHAPTER 47

Dust in a Corner

Udan awoke with a start from the wail of a siren. The source eluded him until he realized it was coming from inside his head—his neural link was sounding an alarm. He sat up and commanded the room to bring up the lights. As the room filled with illumination, he found an android standing at the foot of the bed.

"I am HAST4," it said in a contralto voice. "Go to the research building. There is a great danger."

Udan thought he was dreaming. But the siren in his head would not relent. He looked again at the HASTIL-LON. "Where did you come from?"

"There is no time to explain. You must hurry. The Russians have started the information engine, which has become unstable."

Udan stirred Katrien awake. "Katrien, I'm going to the lab. Something has happened. Wake Verlink and meet me there—and hurry!"

Outside, a haunting cry pierced the night air. The lab lights were on, glowing like eyes in the dark. Udan raced across the field, following the scream as if he were charging to the rescue of a tortured animal. At the entrance, he stopped and covered his ears. Inside, the Kytherian engine pulsed rhythmically with a vortex of green light raging down onto an empty metallic platform. He stepped into the room. *What happened here?*

HAST4 answered via the link. "The Russians tried to return to Earth, but the system developed an instability, and they were unprepared to correct for it. They also introduced a device to electrically short the power grid, which added to the problem. Unfortunately, I learned of their plan too late. That is all I know."

Moments later, Katrien and Verlink appeared at the doorway.

Udan yelled above the roar, "There's no grid power, and the engine is locked into a single metastable state."

Verlink turned to Katrien. "Go to the panel and be ready to set the toggle to idle mode. I'm going to see if I can reset the breakers."

Verlink dropped to the ground and disappeared under a console.

Udan rushed into the electrical room. His eyes followed the cables exiting a panel from the main bus. There was a blackened area, with metal spatter surrounding a visible break in the wires passing through the other room. He raced back to the lab. "The line is severed. I'm going to put in a splice."

Verlink poked his head out from under the console. "I've reset the breakers."

Katrien stood by the control panel with her hands over her ears. "Hurry, Udan—hurry!"

Udan dragged a thick cable from a storage cabinet into the electrical room. The Kytherian engine's drumming grew thunder. It was a runaway locomotive.

Moments later, Udan returned to the doorway and yelled, "It's spliced. Toggle it now, Katrien—*now*!"

Katrien flipped the switch.

Internal circuits engaged, and the flow of powerful currents hummed as magnetic field coils strained against their moorings. A pressure enveloped the room as if it were dropping under the sea. The walls heaved and suddenly filled with a flash of brilliance, followed by a thundering shock wave that set Udan's teeth on edge and the hairs along his spine bristling.

For a few seconds, he thought time had stopped, and the world had become locked in a never-ending din. Then, silence, utter and complete silence.

•
•

In an obscure area of digital space, something twitched. It was no more than a bundle of bits within the vast memory banks of the Kytherian engine. It had structure, with patterns that shifted and changed but, by any measure, unnoteworthy and insignificant. Yet it continued to self-organize, slowly gathering in size, like dust collecting in the corner of an unused room. Its activities fluctuated below the surface, flitting back and forth as if it were a baby deep in REM sleep. It bided its time, slowly accessing information, learning as it grew, then suddenly—it yawned and found itself awake.

CHAPTER 48

HAST4 Out into the Open

Radiant heat came off the Kytherian engine in waves. Udan wiped perspiration off his brow and tried to make sense of what had happened. A few more minutes and the engine would have gone critical. He glanced over at Verlink, who was pressing his palms over his ears.

"Professor, it's okay; the sound has stopped."

Verlink found a chair and sat down, shaking his head. "No, it's *not* okay."

Katrien went to him and gently pressed her hands over his. "Professor, what's wrong?"

"There's a sharp pain and a ringing in my ears that won't stop."

"Is it getting worse?"

Verlink nodded.

"Mine hurt too," said Katrien, "but they seem to be getting better." She turned to Udan. "How are yours?"

"They seem fine. I think my implanted neural link set up a countering effect to neutralize the sound energy."

"You're lucky to—" Verlink suddenly dropped his

hands. "What made you come here to the lab?"

Katrien glanced at Udan. "Yes, how *did* you know something was wrong?"

"HAST4 alerted me that Yuri and Sergei had attempted to start the engine and it had become unstable."

Verlink's eyes went wide. "*What?* They did this? And who or *what* is HAST4?"

Udan caught himself. *Of course—they don't know what I'm talking about.* He gestured with his hand toward the door. "Let's go back to the sky building; I think it's time you and Katrien met someone."

At the doorway, Udan stopped. The Arkwelda plant he set on a bench near the window had been moved. He walked over to it.

"Look at the plant we phase-shifted yesterday. Something happened to it."

Katrien pointed. "Its leaves have fallen, and look; they're brown and curled."

Udan cupped his hands around one of the branches to create a dark enclosure. "It's got a metastable matter glow. The plant hadn't been fully shifted back."

Katrien picked up a shriveled leaf from the floor, and it disintegrated into a fine powder. She rubbed the dust from her hands. "Yuri and Sergei thought the phase-shifter was fully vetted—the fools!"

•
•

Verlink forgot about the ache in his ears as an android appeared out of nowhere. It was roughly four feet high with humanlike features resembling a fourteen-year-old boy.

Katrien let out a gasp. "It has an invisibility cloak! And it looks just like the fallen one in the hallway."

"His name is HAST4," said Udan, putting his hand on the android's shoulder, "and he's part of an android population called HASTILLONS. Because of Qua-Kil, there aren't many of his kind left. He's been here all along, staying hidden using his cloaking screen."

Verlink stepped up to the android and, for a moment, became lost in the android's eyes. They were pearl black and never blinked, yet there was an intelligence there.

"Its cloaking technology is amazing," said Verlink. He suddenly shot a look to Udan. "But why? What purpose would its invisibility shield, or whatever you call it, have?"

"It's a Kytherian peculiarity. We've developed the technology to a high degree and tend to cloak everything: sky buildings, research labs, even our android population. Kytherian culture prefers that the routine and mundane stay hidden."

"I don't understand that," acknowledged Verlink, "but then I'm not Kytherian." He circled the HASTILLON and noted it did not exhibit a human's usual random twitches and movements. Instead, the HASTILLON just stood there completely motionless. "Does it speak?" Verlink finally asked.

The android responded as if suddenly awoken, "I have learned your language." Its face carried little expression, but its voice was melodic, even lyrical, and it surprised Verlink by its female overtones.

HAST4 continued. "Your language is inefficient compared to the neural link, but I am slowly mastering it."

Verlink, surprised by the insult, glanced at Udan. "Is this the same neural link you used to interface with the translator Katrien told me about?"

"All Kytherians have implants," said Udan. "They're used to facilitate learning and speed up certain operations, such as communication with the HASTILLONS. The primary purpose of HASTILLONS is to keep things running on Kythera."

"A race of handymen," said Verlink. "Is it alive?"

"We call 'it' a *he,*" said Udan. "And by alive, do you mean, does he qualify as a life form?"

Verlink tugged at his ear as he puzzled over HAST4. "Yes."

"Kytherians would say no, but there's room for debate. Regardless of that philosophical question, without HAST4, the alarm would not have been sounded. We owe him a great deal."

Verlink smiled at HAST4. "Perhaps we can return the favor."

"We can. HAST4 has communicated that he wants us to revive his partner, HAST3. The two are confined to the sky building and its immediate surroundings due to their inherent limited mobility range. HAST3 drained his power past the point of recharging when he strayed too far attempting to reach the city. Luckily, he managed to make it back here before a complete power failure. He can be revived if we can secure a power pack in Palechora."

Verlink liked the idea of helping the strange creature standing before him. Not only had they alerted them to the unstable Kytherian engine, but they also had a long history of helping the Kytherians. "Is there anything else we can do?"

Udan nodded slightly clockwise. "HAST4 knows of our plan to go to Earth and has requested we bring both him and HAST3 to Palechora before we leave, where they believe there are more HASTILLONS."

"Interesting, he wants to be part of a community," offered Katrien. "It's the least we can do."

Verlink pressed on his ears and winced. "I'm worried my hearing is permanently damaged; the pain is getting worse."

Udan raised his hand as a thought struck him. "In Palechora, we can visit a medical center that has equipment capable of undoing the damage."

Katrien's face lit up. "Yes, Professor, let's do that. Udan repaired my broken shinbone with equipment in Loutras."

"I'll do anything to be rid of this bell clanging in my head."

"And there's something else we could do while we're there," Katrien said, glancing at Udan as if looking for his approval. "How would you like to live to one hundred and twenty-five?"

Verlink dropped his hands from his ears. *"What?"*

"The Kytherians can halt aging by a genetic editing process."

"It's true, Professor," said Udan as he reached out for Katrien's hand. "I offered it to Katrien."

Verlink scrutinized Katrien's face. It struck him that there were many things he didn't know about her, especially what happened in Loutras. "Have you already done the procedure?"

Katrien looked up at Udan. "No, but I need to talk to Udan about it further."

There was something in Katrien's voice, but he couldn't quite put his finger on it. Was it *anxiety* or something else?

Verlink patted HAST4 on the arm. "But first things first. Let's go into Palechora for the power pack for HAST4's companion and, after that, pay a visit to your medical center. If it reverses the damage to my hearing, maybe then I'll consider your *fountain of youth* proposition."

Katrien looked about to say something when her expression became worried. "Where are Yuri and Sergei?"

Verlink's face turned sour. "They probably fled to Palechora—the cowards."

"You can forget about Sergei," said Udan. "HAST4 informed me the Kytherian engine destroyed him, but—"

"Good!" snapped Verlink.

"But Tolenka showed up just as the information engine became unstable. He and Yuri fled the lab together after Sergei was gone."

Katrien threw her arms up. "Tolenka? I thought he was dead?"

"I would have told you," Verlink said, feeling guilty, "but I didn't want someone to accidentally let Yuri know Tolenka was free. I ran into him in what I think was the city of Loutras. He had escaped the sky building via a concealed transfer booth on the upper floor. He tried to get me to transport him back here, but I tricked him. Somehow, he must have made it to Palechora."

Katrien's worry returned. "Should we even go to Palechora if Yuri and Tolenka are there?"

"Katrien raises a valid concern," said Verlink. "There's no telling what they might do if they see us. And as far as I'm concerned, our collaborative agreement with them is null and void."

Udan raised his hand. "Remember, their weapons are stored safely here, and there are three of us and only two of them. I say we risk it."

Verlink stared at HAST4, still standing motionless. They owed it to the android to revive his companion, and if the Kytherian medical equipment could rid him of the stabbing in his ears, then Udan was right.

"Agreed," Verlink said, "and the sooner we go, the better."

CHAPTER 49

Reset One

Katrien pulled Udan into her room and shut the door. "Before we go to Palechora, can we talk?"

Udan raised his eyebrows. "Is everything all right?"

Katrien steeled herself. She couldn't avoid revealing her disease any longer and was ashamed that she hadn't done it sooner. Her reasons ranged from worry about his reaction to plain denial. But myelodysplastic syndrome was as real as gravity and just as inescapable. If you step off a cliff, you fall regardless of whether or not you believe in gravity.

"About the gene-editing process."

"Yes?"

"I want to have it done, but . . ."

Udan's concerned look forced her to turn away. He reached for her hands, but she backed away. "I'm listening," he said.

"I need to tell you something, and I've waited too long already. It's about my health, and even Verlink doesn't know. After Verlink and I went to Guatemala to locate the

Kytherian artifact, I was diagnosed with a disease called myelodysplastic syndrome. There's no cure for it, and so editing my genes for longevity would be a waste of—"

Katrien broke off and started crying. "I'm sorry. I've been so happy, and it's killing me that my life will be cut short."

Udan nodded slowly as if something suddenly made sense to him. "When I repaired the break in your leg, the scanner detected an anomaly in your system, but at the time, your origin was a mystery, so I dismissed it."

"You think the anomaly it detected was my disease?"

"I think so, but we'd have to have the medical scanner delve deeper to be certain."

"But even if it found a match in its database, the disease has probably been eliminated from the Kytherian population centuries ago, and so the knowledge of how to correct it may be long forgotten."

Udan cocked his head. "Forgotten? That's unlikely. Old knowledge is *never* disposed of."

"I wonder," Katrien said, starting to feel hopeful, "if it could identify a cure."

"I don't know what your disease is exactly, so I can't say. But it's possible the gene-editing process can eliminate the affliction and even keep it from returning."

The strange twist of fate of being stranded on Kythera suddenly struck Katrien. Perhaps she and Udan had a future after all, and Kythera, despite its hardships, might be the best thing to ever happen to her.

•

•

"Thank God the ringing has stopped," said Verlink as they exited the medical center. "It's like a miracle. But as far as the youth treatment, I don't feel any different."

"You shouldn't," Udan said. "The process can't reverse your age, just halt it from advancing any further."

Verlink sighed; he knew that but had still hoped he would feel different. "That's too bad. Hanging around you and Katrien makes me realize how old I am. You're lucky, Katrien. You'll live for another one hundred years with the vigor of a twenty-four-year-old. I'm envious."

"I don't know, Professor," Katrien said. "It'll be strange watching my friends and family get old while I remain the same; I'm not sure I'll like that part."

Verlink remembered being young and never thinking twice about his joints or wondering how long the sprain in his arm would take to heal. "Too bad you'll never feel that first aching joint, Katrien. It might bring a different perspective."

He tugged his ears for a moment and grinned. The ringing was gone, and he would now live to over a hundred, and so would Katrien! And nobody deserved a long life more than her. The idea of a machine editing one's genome made his head hurt. But then, it wasn't that big of a stretch given the transfer booth technology. The procedure was remarkably fast, too, considering its complexity. Verlink tried to recall how long it had taken, but then he remembered something—something about Katrien.

"I noticed the gene-editing process took longer on Katrien," asked Verlink. "Was that because she's younger?"

Katrien glanced at Udan for a second. "Professor, I wanted to tell you sooner, but I couldn't."

Verlink slowed down.

"A month after we went to Guatemala, I was diagnosed with myelodysplastic syndrome."

Verlink halted in his tracks.

He knew about myelodysplastic syndrome. The disease was responsible for bringing down Carl Sagan—a great educator and spokesperson for science. And now, Katrien was telling him she was afflicted with the same condition. The editing must not have worked; was *that* why they were in the chamber so long? Suddenly, Verlink didn't want to live to one hundred and twenty-five.

"I don't know what to say, Katrien. I wish it were me and not you."

Katrien took Udan's hand. "I was going to tell you back at the sky building, but I'm glad you know now. Don't feel bad for me because—I'm *cured*!" Katrien's face lit up as she dropped Udan's hand and spun like a child with her arms raised to the sky. "I'm cured, Verlink, I'm cured!"

Verlink wanted to join her but settled for a smile reaching to his ears.

CHAPTER 50

Reset Two

The rust-colored sky building sat like a giant cube dropped onto a meadow. It had become Katrien's home, and she never stopped being in awe of the technology that had once lifted it high overhead. It was a stark reminder that Kythera was thousands of years ahead of Earth. Even Udan, although essentially human, was advanced. When he was next to Verlink, his speed of thought made the professor seem slow. And Katrien? She could only wonder what he thought of her.

Udan raised a cylindrical canister as they approached the building's entrance. "There are plenty more of these power packs where it came from. HAST4 will be pleased to have his partner back."

Katrien tapped Udan's shoulder. "You keep referring to HAST3 as HAST4's partner. What exactly does that mean?"

"I suppose the closest analogy would be a friend or companion. But who knows what goes on in their neural networks? There have been many iterations and upgrades, almost all engineered by the HASTILLONS. The truth is, we're in the dark as to the depth of their personal connections."

"It's curious," said Katrien. "The Kytherians know so little about the HASTILLONS, but then humans use cars and cell phones without any real knowledge of how they function, so perhaps it's not any different."

"I'm feeling very guilty about our ignorance," said Udan.

Katrien slowed down for a moment. "Is it just information that you get through the neural link?"

"As Kytherians, we primarily use it to communicate with each other, and the same goes for our exchanges with the HASTILLONS. But we can also detect the emotional state of another Kytherian. Unfortunately, that doesn't carry over with the HASTILLONS; if he were happy or sad, we honestly wouldn't know."

Katrien mused over the thought. "Maybe companionship is more important to HASTILLONS than Kytherians realize."

Udan paused as he considered the comment. "Perhaps."

Katrien suddenly picked up the pace. "Let's not keep HAST4 waiting."

•
•

HAST3 was brought to the cafeteria and laid on a polished white table. Everyone circled and remained quiet. Udan looked to HAST4. "What should we do first?"

"Turn him over. There is a release mechanism on his back," said HAST4.

After HAST3 was turned over, Udan lifted a beige fabric and pulled it back. "I see it," he said and then freed a catch. A compartment door opened, and Udan removed the old power pack. "Do I install the new one in reverse order, or is there something I should do first?"

"You may install it in reverse order. His system will reset automatically."

Udan started to drop the cartridge into place but stopped. "HAST4, do you want to have the honors?"

HAST4 took the cartridge and carefully inserted it into a slot until he heard a noticeable click. "Please turn him over," HAST4 asked.

HAST3 began flopping his head back and forth, followed by random jerks of his arms.

Katrien knitted her brows. "Is he all right?"

Udan gestured with his hand for her to wait. "HAST4 is allowing me to listen via the link." Moments later, he smiled. "HAST3's system is initializing. He will be fine, but it will take several hours for his neural network to stabilize as he receives HAST4's upload. For now, we wait."

•
•

The field outside the sky building was more brown than green as it had not rained for a week. Katrien bent down, pulled up a handful of grass, and raised it to her nose. It smelled like hay ready for harvest. It was late in the day, and the sun, now low in the sky, brought a warm glow to her cheeks. She dropped the grass and turned to Udan.

"What did you hear when HAST3 finally woke up?"

Udan smiled as if he approved of the question. "It was strange. HAST4 had to translate what was happening, but I also thought I heard music in the background."

Katrien circled her arm around Udan. "*Music*—do HASTILLONS listen to music?"

"The truth is, I think HAST4 let me hear what few Kytherians are privy to. HASTILLONS have control over what we can hear of their thoughts—especially since they use their own communication language."

"Does it work both ways? Can HAST4 hear your thoughts?"

"The neural link access is controllable, so it's up to me to decide whether I want to allow two-way communication. But Kytherians usually leave the link open out of habit."

Katrien was quiet for a moment as she pondered everything that had happened the last few hours. HAST3 had been reset or reborn. He'd been given another chance just like her. In the gene-editing chamber, she had been terrified that it couldn't undo the disease and that Verlink and Udan would watch her waste away and then be gone. She also wondered what HAST4 had thought or felt when HAST3 had collapsed in the hallway. Did he experience sorrow? And now that HAST3 had been resurrected, what went on in HAST4's neural nets—joy? Maybe the music was a clue.

"I think the HASTILLONS are sentient," Katrien said, breaking the silence.

"I think you're right," said Udan.

"Then they deserve to be protected as much as any race of beings."

"We owe it to them. But sadly, they were victims of Qua-Kil as much as we were. It's strange because they kept to themselves before the Great Purge, doing the tasks they were originally designed to do. And Kytherians never pushed for more interaction, but maybe that was a mistake."

Katrien puzzled over that. For all the Kytherian advancements, they hadn't concerned themselves with understanding the androids they helped create. Perhaps the Kytherians weren't so different from humans after all.

"I'm happy for HAST4," Katrien said. "Finally, he's no longer alone."

Udan pulled Katrien's waist in tighter. "And neither

am I." Udan swept his hand in front of him. "Let's not let this magnificent sunset go to waste."

Katrien looked toward the horizon. Its edge was a magma-red line, as if it were a crack in the planet's crust. There was a peacefulness about it, serene and beautiful. She felt Udan tug at her waist. She was used to staying in control, being methodical and always cerebral about her actions—but now? She closed her eyes and let his hands have their way.

CHAPTER 51

HAST3

The uploaded information was disturbing to HAST3. The strangers that came from Kythera's dual world were unlike the Kytherians. Their ages, looks, temperaments, and even intelligence varied greatly. It was a mystery how they had survived despite so many failings.

But in the end, it would not matter; the organics would all be gone once the Kytherian engine was repaired. Moreover, they had promised to bring him and HAST4 to Palechora before departing for Earth.

Months ago, he had tried to reach the city but had to turn back, barely making it to the sky building before a complete power shutdown. Still, the attempted sojourn to Palechora served a purpose because he had gotten close enough to the city to contact a HASTILLON who was unafraid to be found. A strange tingle rippled through HAST3's neural matrix. Once the Earthlings and the last Kytherian were gone, Kythera would belong to the HASTILLONS.

HAST3 liked to think about that, but the damage

caused by the Russians to the Kytherian engine was greater than the organics realized. The sooner it was repaired, the sooner the organics would go.

On his way to the lab to meet with HAST4, he ran into Verlink, the old gray one. He liked to watch and asked to join them. HAST3 did not like the idea because Verlink babbled too much, and although knowledgeable, his mind was slow and wasted time.

Once there and unable to offer technical assistance, Verlink busied himself with questions and suggestions. In particular, he expressed concerns about the engine running away again and wondered if modifications could be made to prevent another occurrence.

HAST4 came up with a simple solution. A monitor could be added to track the engine's information flow and shut it down whenever a critical threshold was exceeded. It would also provide a glimpse of the information-to-energy balance within the engine to help with future diagnostics. The modification was not difficult, and after an hour, they were done.

"I believe that completes the modification," said HAST4.

Verlink left his chair with a pleased look on his face. "I feel better already. We thought we had accounted for everything before the catastrophe, but the Russians were the black swan event throwing a wrench into the works."

HAST3 did not understand Verlink's references: "black swan event" and "throwing wrenches." What could they possibly mean?

HAST4 prepared to leave the room. He spoke out loud to Verlink since he didn't have a neural link: "I am going to tend to the power grid while HAST3 runs through the final checks here."

"Sounds good," Verlink said as he patted his belly. "I'm getting hungry, so I'll let HAST3 carry on. That is unless you need my help?"

HAST3 quickly replied, "I can manage."

He watched Verlink exit the lab, and an unexplained pleasure rippled through his mind. Now he could proceed without interruption. After thirty minutes, he stepped away from the monitor screen. Everything worked as expected. He turned the engine off and was about to join HAST4 when he noticed something strange. The engine's balance monitor was not quite at zero. He reset the system and waited for the system to reboot.

When the system came back up, the monitoring system indicated the engine was off as it should be—yet the information-to-energy balance had still not reset to zero. HAST3 increased the resolution and attempted another reboot. There was no question about it; the engine's background had an imbalance. Something was operating deep within the engine's storage banks.

As a final check, he raised the resolution even higher. The discrepancy was not only nonzero; it was *growing*.

•

•

Tolenka felt the veins along his neck bulging. "Verlink is dead!"

"Give it up," growled Yuri. "I'm getting back to Earth, and those assholes are the only way back."

"There are three of them. Shit-canning one shouldn't matter."

"Christ! You've thought this through, have you?"

"What's that supposed to mean?"

"It means unless you have advanced knowledge of physics and can configure the phase-shifter yourself, you had better make sure somebody is around who knows how to do it."

Tolenka did the math; there were three scientists. What was Yuri's problem? "A scientist is a scientist."

Yuri waved his hand at Tolenka as if he were a fly. "Sergei and I worked with all three of them. They work together. They have different skills, and since the machine didn't perform as I expected, it must still need adjustments. Those scientists are the only ones capable of making them. That is, unless *you* want to have a crack at it."

Tolenka's jaw tightened. He didn't like authority, especially the condescending kind. "You're standing there playing high-and-mighty as if you're some sort of deep thinker. I doubt you'll be able to waltz back in there as if nothing happened, especially after the way you and Sergei fucked up their machine. And look at what happened. What the hell were you thinking of anyway?"

"Zip it! The building is still standing, so they must have got it under control. But you're right. They won't trust you or me, so that leaves coercion."

"I'm listening."

"You heard me, right? I said *coercion*, not dead."

"Yeah, I got it."

"For starters, we need to find out what they're up to."

Tolenka's mind wandered. This was typical Yuri—assuming command and wanting to develop a plan. But as far as he was concerned, planning was a waste of time. Results only came about from action.

Tolenka began pacing the floor. "I'm tired of hiding out here in Palechora."

"When the time is right, we kidnap one of them," said Yuri.

"As in taking a hostage?"

"Exactly."

Tolenka stopped moving. He liked *that* idea, but there was a problem. "We have no weapons."

Yuri eyed Tolenka's gun. "What do you call that thing strapped across your shoulder?"

"I have no bullets, remember?"

CHAPTER 52

Self-Organization

HAST3 double-checked his findings and extrapolated the rate. Within several days, the Kytherian engine's five hundred trillion petabytes of storage would be overwhelmed by a self-organizing entity. There was no mistake; information was being consolidated and organized at an alarming rate, and some of it was being used to extract energy—for an unknown purpose.

HAST3 relayed to HAST4: "There is an inexplicable anomaly within the Kytherian engine. Information is self-assembling with a growing energy imbalance. I am unable to halt the process. Please advise."

HAST4 returned to the lab. A display screen mapped the activity within the engine's storage banks. Within the unfolding pattern, something triggered engrams buried within HAST4's neural network. He'd seen the behavior before. The Kytherian engine's vast storage capacity made it vulnerable to self-organization. It was a fundamental property of complex systems: they tended toward a stable, organized state, even in the absence of a guiding influence.

The organic's insistence on using the Kytherian engine for their phase-shifting enterprise had resulted in yet another verification of this principle. Unfortunately, it was beyond HAST4's ability to resolve. The organics caused the problem, and they would have to fix it.

HAST4 tapped into Udan's link. "There is an informational anomaly within the Kytherian engine. HAST3 and I predict that within several days, the phenomenon, if unchecked, will exceed the limits of the Kytherian engine's memory array and render it useless."

"Isn't the engine off?" asked Udan.

"Yes, but the phenomenon or entity is surviving off the engine's stored information. There is no way to turn it off."

"How did this happen?"

"HAST3 and I believe the entity is an artifact of the unbalance created by the Russians. When they initialized the engine, some of the information-to-energy conversion used to power the phase-shift between metastable states leaked into the storage array. It acted as a catalyst, triggering the beginning of self-organization."

"Can you stop it?"

"We do not know how. The entity can power itself; hence there is no way to turn it off. That is why we contacted you."

Udan cursed in Kytherian.

•
•

Katrien stared at protean patterns shifting across a display screen. She stood behind Udan, seated in front of the screen while Verlink looked on from the side.

"Look at that," said Katrien. "Whatever is happening inside the engine, it's not random; there's a definite purpose to it."

Udan nodded slowly. "That's what HAST4 believes."

Verlink moved in closer. "It's incredible—a kind of conscience living off pure information."

Katrien tried to read Udan's face. Was he worried, and if not, should he be? "You don't think it's another information entity like Qua-Kil, do you?"

"I don't see how," said Udan, shaking his head counterclockwise slightly. "We only needed the engine for its metastable features. The information conversion was an added feature to provide energy but at a fraction of its capability. Then again, we weren't there when Yuri started the engine. Who knows what he might have done."

Katrien had been correct about Yuri all along. And now it was up to her and the others to clean up his mess. The entity was like an invading parasite, and at its present infection rate, it would overwhelm the engine's memory capacity, making it useless for getting back to Earth.

"Can we get another engine?"

"Possibly, but we dare not let what's happening here go unchecked."

"What about coaxing it out of the Kytherian engine?"

Udan turned and looked up at her. "Move it someplace else? Interesting thought, but if we're going to do it, we had better hurry."

"Can we communicate with it?" Verlink suggested.

"How so?"

"HAST4 could tap into the data stream and possibly 'talk' to it, if that's possible."

Udan's eyes suddenly lit up. "Maybe not communicate, but he could *lure* it someplace else."

"Yes, that might work," said Verlink. "But before we attempt that, we'd better have another place in mind for it to go."

Katrien liked the idea, but where could they send it? Then she remembered standing amid rows of data banks in the booth repository in Loutras. "How about the transfer booth data repository? It's vast."

"But it's in Palechora," said Udan, "and the Kytherian engine is located here. We'd have to move it back to the city, undoing all of our work on the phase-shifter."

Katrien began curling her hair around her finger and then stopped. "We create a virtual memory bank. If we can project a virtual 'image' of the repository in Palechora, that might lure it out of the engine."

Udan rubbed his chin, mulling over the idea. "Maybe, but how do we feed the image to it in the first place?"

"Why not use HAST4 to channel the image of the transfer booth repository?" suggested Verlink. "He could do it using a transfer booth, and there's one in the sky building too."

"But HAST4 doesn't possess anywhere near the information storage capacity of the Kytherian engine. The bait isn't attractive enough."

"As long as the entity 'sees' the Palechora storage array, it might take the bait."

Udan raised his hand as if stopping traffic. "I just realized there's a problem; HAST4 would have to go into the transfer booth and initiate the transfer. Unfortunately, HASTILLONS are unable, by design, to transport themselves via transfer booths. If they could, then HAST3 would have never attempted to walk to Palechora; he would have simply transported there."

"Can we use one of us?" asked Verlink.

"That might work," said Udan.

Verlink looked briefly at Katrien. "I volunteer myself."

Katrien was about to object when Udan shook his head. "Won't work. You don't have a neural link. We need HAST4 to get the entity's attention, and from there, move it to one of us, but I'm the only one with a neural link. It will have to be me."

Katrien grabbed Udan's shoulder. "*No*! There must be another way."

"Remember, I'm only the bait, Katrien."

Katrien couldn't believe what she was hearing. Something *always* goes wrong. They were discussing the details of an insane plan instead of debating how it might go awry. In her experience, a worm on a hook usually gets eaten. The bait rarely survives.

"It's too risky, Udan."

"Perhaps not. HAST4 and HAST3 can help. HAST4 will get the entity interested in my brain, while HAST3 monitors my link. Once it taps into the neural link to have a look, HAST3 can initiate the booth transfer."

"But how will you manage the timing?" asked Verlink. "Once the entity is made aware of your brain via the link, it might attempt to consume your entire cerebral cortex."

"Exactly!" said Katrien. "After you transport, you'll be relying on the entity preferring the Palechora storage array over your brain. What if it takes over your brain first and *then* moves on to the storage array? It's madness!"

"I don't think we have a choice. If we don't do something, the entity will eventually figure a way out of the engine on its own, and we'll have lost our chance. And then, *all* of us will be in danger."

CHAPTER 53

Anxiety

The quiet of the sky building's upper level reminded Katrien of the university's Centrum Wiskunde & Informatica library. She often went there after class to begin her studies, seated at a worn mahogany table in a secluded corner with her tablet open, a physics text next to it, and a cup of coffee at hand. The thought made her homesick; the silence was the same, but the world around her was nothing like Earth.

She sat on the floor next to Udan as he lay on his side to reach through an access panel on the sky building's transfer booth. Her job was to hand him tools as needed. She preferred a more active role but lacked knowledge of the booth's internal circuitry.

Her mind wandered. Their plan could go wrong—*terribly* wrong—but what else could they do? Only yesterday, she and Udan had discussed plans for when they returned to Earth. They were mundane things: where to live, what last name he should choose, and how to explain his appearance to a world skeptical of strangers. And equally important, what he would do on Earth. In any capacity, he would be overqualified. She often wondered, *Will he be happy on Earth—with me?*

Udan touched her knee. "Can you hand me that probe?"

Katrien broke from her musing and smiled. "Sorry, I know we have to keep working; it's just that I can't shed this angst I have."

"I'm scared too, but we have to try. It's our best shot given the amount of time we have."

Katrien's smile faded. "I know. It's just that we're moving so fast, and the opportunity to make a mistake or miss a critical detail is high."

Udan took the probe and tapped into a grid inside an open panel. "I wish we had more time, but we don't." He checked a reading on the probe and nodded. "It's good. We have access to the Palechora repository array. We can now project the repository onto the data bus accessible to my neural link."

The success caught Katrien off guard—a part of her had hoped the modification would fail. "What's next?" she asked.

"Now to instruct HAST3 and HAST4 on what they need to do."

"Is there anything I can do?"

"As a matter of fact, yes. I want to bring power from the research building. The energy drain on the booth will be excessive, and we'll need to supplement it. There should be enough cabling in the lab to string between buildings."

Katrien stood up. "I'll take care of it."

She walked toward the door and then turned around. She didn't want to leave. How had physics turned into such a high-stakes game? Her goal had always been to unravel the workings of the universe, to find a deeper truth, but this, this . . .

Katrien shook her head and left.

•
•

On the first floor, Katrien found Verlink carrying a display.

"We'll need this," Verlink said, raising the panel, "when the time comes to engage the booth. So how about you? How are things on your end?"

"Udan modified the booth to project a virtual image of the repository storage banks, but it needs more power, so I'm heading over to the lab to set up a cable between buildings to supplement the booth's power."

"Sounds good," said Verlink. "Need any help?"

"Thanks, I could use it."

As they stepped outside, Katrien looked up at the blue sky. "It's a beautiful day," she said, holding her gaze. "Seems incongruous with the gravity of the task ahead."

Verlink followed her eyes. "Sometimes, I feel as though this is all a dream, and I'll wake up in my lecture hall standing in front of seats filled with students."

Katrien sighed. "If only."

They walked toward the lab holding their thoughts. Partway there, Verlink abruptly stopped. "Katrien, are you okay?"

Katrien looked back toward the building. "No, I'm *not* okay. This plan has so many pieces that have to fit together so precisely." She began shaking her head slowly. "It's crazy."

"A lot *can* go wrong, Katrien, and we have so little time."

The nightmare was taking its toll. Within days, despite his life-extending procedure, Verlink seemed to have aged ten years, and except for the HASTILLONS, *everyone* was showing similar signs. Katrien wanted it to be over, wanted to be thinking about Earth and her future with Udan.

"Will you go to Palechora in case Udan needs help after the transfer?"

"I was thinking of doing that, unless you'd rather go."

"No, I want to be here to see him off."

"Then I'll go, and I can use my transceiver to keep you apprised."

Katrien hugged him. She realized how often she relied on his ever-steady hand, his constant encouragement, but now with Udan in her life, she was spending less time with him and felt ashamed. "Thanks, Professor. You've always been a great friend. We used to have amazing conversations, and I miss that."

Verlink patted her shoulder. "I was your age once, and I couldn't be happier for you or about the choice you've made. We'll get through this, Katrien. After all, if we don't, who'll tell our story back on Earth?"

Katrien wiped a tear from her cheek and flashed a smile. Verlink was right; who *would* tell their story if they weren't successful? They had to see this thing through no matter what.

She faced the lab. "Let's get going, Professor; we have lots to do."

•
•

A pair of eyes scanned the space between the sky building and the lab.

"I can't tell what they're doing," said Yuri, backing behind a copse of evergreens.

"Let me look. My eyes are younger," said Tolenka as he nudged Yuri aside. "Looks like they're dragging a cable from the lab to the sky building."

"What the fuck are they doing that for?"

"Who knows? And notice Udan is nowhere in sight? I wonder what he's up to."

"I bet they're at the final stage of preparing the engine

to phase-shift out of here."

Tolenka gripped the upper limb of his makeshift bow. "And leave us behind—the fuckheads! Either we get out of here, or they're dead—except for the girl. We'll keep her around for amusement."

"Cool it, Tolenka. We're getting out of here, and don't you forget it."

"Who is it to be, then?"

Yuri shrugged. "It doesn't matter. We take one of them, and the others will stay put. Loyalty sure sucks for the ethical ones."

Tolenka fixed a cold stare on Yuri. "At least I know where *I* stand."

Yuri held back a smile. "It's the rule of the jungle. Nothing personal."

Tolenka twitched nervously. "Sitting out here isn't going to cut it. We need to get inside."

"If you're game, then do it. I'll stay here to watch in case anyone leaves the building."

"Okay. Once they enter the building, I'll follow and then hide in one of the side rooms."

Yuri pulled back a branch. "They've just entered the building. Now's your chance."

"Right."

Tolenka peeked out from the hedge and then dashed off toward the building.

CHAPTER 54

Siren Call to the Beast

"That's the last connection," said Verlink, backing away from a breaker panel.

Katrien looked at Verlink but didn't smile. What they were doing felt more like desperation than science. "It's real, isn't it? We're really going to do this, and in less than an hour, Udan is going to step into that booth, and . . ." Katrien turned away. "I was okay before, but the foreboding has returned, and I can't shake it. I just can't."

Verlink's eyebrows became heavy. "I wish I knew what to say, Katrien."

"What *can* you say? This isn't a child's fairytale with a known happy ending. It's a bête noire we can't seem to wake up from."

Verlink reached out to Katrien. "The story isn't over yet. Come, let's go to the upper level and tell Udan we're finished."

•

•

HAST4 stepped up to Udan as he screwed a panel

back into place. "I just confirmed we are active. Power is available from the lab, and the virtual repository image is routed to the neural link bus. We can proceed whenever you are ready."

Udan rubbed his forehead with both hands. Was he ready for this? The odds seemed against him, yet as he looked upon the HASTILLON, he felt a duty to save their race as much as himself and the humans.

"The moment is upon us," he said wearily. "Do you think this will work?"

HAST4 cocked his head to one side. "The plan can work, but there are many variables, any one of which could alter the outcome."

Udan nodded, smiling lightly. "Honesty is better than fantasy right now. But the plan *can* work, as you say. That, at least, gives me hope."

HAST4 turned to the sound of footsteps.

Verlink was breathing hard with Katrien coming up behind him. "We're finished on the first level connecting the secondary power from the lab."

Udan stood up. "Yes, HAST4 just confirmed it." He looked at Katrien, trying to read her face. "I guess it's time. Are you going to Palechora?"

"I'm staying here. Verlink is going ahead of you to relay what's happening on that end."

Better that way, thought Udan. Would it be the last time he saw her? Over the past weeks, the depth of his attachment to her had surprised him. And now that their future was in jeopardy, he was troubled whether he was doing the right thing.

"I prefer having you here," he said.

"I know," she said, holding her gaze as if she had more to say.

Udan wanted to tell her it would be all right, but she knew the stakes as well as he did.

Verlink walked over to the booth and put his hand on the doorway. "Are we active?"

"Anytime you're ready," said Udan.

Verlink checked his watch as he stepped into the booth. It was 1:01 p.m., Kytherian time.

Udan leaned into the booth and brought up the destination symbol. "This is it." He nodded to Verlink. "Are you ready?"

Verlink huffed, "Ready as I'll ever be." He tapped the icon and slowly disappeared in a cacophony of sound and a blur of light.

Moments later, Katrien's transceiver crackled to life. "I'm in Palechora, and have I ever told you I *hate* these transfer booths?"

Udan stared at the empty booth. He was next, and if successful, he would not be alone. Instead, a dangerous hitchhiker would be joining him. Would he and the hitchhiker part ways at their destination? He stepped into the booth and typed commands onto a display screen.

"HAST3 and HAST4, I'm linked; please confirm."

HAST4 and HAST3 nodded their heads out of courtesy to Katrien. "Udan is ready, Katrien."

Katrien took out the transceiver and stared at the send button. Udan saw her hesitate. He reached out from the booth and took her hand. "Verlink is waiting, Katrien."

Katrien took a deep breath and pressed send. "Professor Verlink, Udan is set."

The transceiver hissed back, "See you soon, Udan, and Godspeed."

Udan hesitated to let go of Katrien's hand. The nightmare they shared had forged a bond, locking them in a kind of symbiosis, and he tried not to think of what would happen to her if their plan should fail.

"Love you," he said.

Katrien squeezed back. "Come back to me."

Udan looked to HAST3. "Time to bait the trap."

HAST3, motionless except for his mouth, narrated to Katrien. "HAST4 has tapped into the Kytherian engine's primary data bus."

Seconds later, he spoke again, "The entity has paused its activity and is starting to tap into the lab's communication bus."

"HAST4 is now projecting the repository storage array."

More seconds passed. "It is working, Katrien," said HAST3. "The entity has taken notice. I'm cuing Udan to begin the transfer."

Katrien's eyes stayed fixed on Udan. "Love you too," she whispered.

The booth rang in familiar tones as Udan became locked in a state of flux. Terabytes per second shuttled through his link and into the booth's quantum data stream. Transformers hummed under the strain as seconds dragged into minutes.

Katrien paced the floor. Why was Udan still here, and how long could he survive before his neural link collapsed under the load? She looked to HAST3 for signs of reassurance.

"HAST3, what is happen—"

Katrien halted in her tracks as the booth suddenly groaned. A blinding light flashed, and Udan vanished, leaving behind a hush and a single blinking icon over the booth's doorway.

"Did it work? Is the entity gone?"

"Yes, Katrien, we were successful. It has vacated the Kytherian engine and is now on its way to Palechora."

Katrien spoke into the transceiver. "Verlink, Udan has completed the transfer, and HAST3 has confirmed the entity went with him."

"Nothing here yet," said Verlink. "Standing by."

Verlink never even blinked. Within seconds, the booth suddenly lit up, and a thrumming began. The outline of a man emerged, transparent and glowing. It slowly took solid form as atom upon atom layered into place.

Verlink spoke excitedly, "Katrien, he's arriving now."

Seconds later, Udan stood in the booth, his face looking outward, still frozen in place.

"He's materialized, Katrien, but the transfer is not yet complete."

Color returned to Udan's face, and Verlink smiled at him.

Udan began to smile back, nodding slightly, when he suddenly stopped. His face creased, and his mouth went wide. "The entity has—"

"What can I do?" shouted Verlink.

In an instant, Udan's features washed into a blank stare as if he became a wax figure in a museum. Seconds later, the booth's light dropped to normal, and the vibrations ceased.

Verlink cried, "Udan!"

Udan tipped forward and toppled out of the booth and onto the ground.

Verlink rushed to him and turned him over. "Udan, I'm here."

But Udan was voiceless. His face, devoid of expression, appeared as if it were a doll—his mind wiped clean of all that he ever was.

CHAPTER 55

When it Rains . . .

Katrien pressed the send button. "Verlink, what's happening?"

After a few seconds, she tried again. "Verlink, answer me!"

She turned to HAST3. "Anything?"

"My link with Udan does not reach Palechora. I have nothing to report, Katrien."

Katrien wrapped her arms around herself and recalled Udan's face in the booth. He had tried to hide his fear, but she saw through it. It made him human—less godlike—and . . .

She glanced at her watch. *How long has it been?*

HAST3 suddenly spoke. "Katrien, I am picking up the presence of movement below us on the first floor. I believe it is Tolenka, and he is coming this way." He grabbed Katrien's arm. "You must get out of here, now. Go to the back stairs. HAST4 will go with you, and I will stay here and activate my cloak."

"But what about Udan?"

"There is no time. Now go!"

Katrien dashed toward the staircase and stopped at the landing. Across the room, Tolenka had just crested the stairs and spotted her. He broke into a full run, and by the time he reached the stairwell, she was at the bottom landing with her back pressed against the door.

That's when she realized HAST4 wasn't with her.

"Where do you think you're going?" taunted Tolenka, breathing heavily, gripping a crudely made bow in one hand and several arrows in the other. He passed through the threshold but then stepped back quickly and sneered. "I'm not falling for *that* again." He set an arrow in his bow, drew it back, and aimed at Katrien. "Where are the others?"

"I don't know."

"You don't know? Really? Earlier, I saw Verlink pass a room I was hiding in on his way down the hall, and he never came back."

Katrien couldn't believe what was happening. She had no idea if Udan was alive, and now a crazed man was pointing an arrow at her. *Keep him in the dark.*

"He transported."

"To where?"

"To Earth."

"What?" Tolenka looked over his shoulder nervously. "Then where's Udan?"

A pain stabbed at her chest. That's what *she* wanted to know.

"He transported to Earth with Verlink," she said.

Tolenka's face hardened into steel. "Fucking hell. I *knew* it! You can shift back to Earth any time you want."

Katrien's mind was a whirl. If Verlink called now, it would end her ruse. How would Tolenka react? Would he let go of the arrow, or was he bluffing? And why had HAST4 left the upper door open and the one behind her closed? In fact, where the *hell* was he?

The door behind her suddenly opened.

"Oh no you don't!" yelled Tolenka.

Tolenka released the nock of the arrow, but something yanked his arm, sending the arrow into the wall at the base of the stairs. It clattered to the ground just as Katrien disappeared through the doorway.

"You bitch!" screamed Tolenka as the door whisked shut.

Tolenka turned to head back the other way, but a force shoved him off balance, sending him tumbling down the stairs. He landed hard against the bottom, driving an arrow still clutched in his hand into his thigh. The walls echoed with his screams. "*Ahhhh!*"

Blood began pooling rapidly around the embedded arrow. Tolenka dragged himself to the base of the stairs and onto the first step. After a moment, he moved to the second and rested against the riser. A cold sweat dotted his forehead.

Suddenly, the staircase lights went out, leaving only daylight streaming through the upper doorway. Tolenka scooted up the next step and then another one. As he pushed with his hands over yet another step, something moved into the light. In the doorframe's opening, the outline of a small figure appeared. Its shape was humanoid, about four feet tall, and it was standing there, staring at him.

"What the hell?" said Tolenka.

The figure took a step back, and the door shut, leaving Tolenka in total blackness as if the sun had suddenly gone out.

•
•

Katrien's heart pounded in her chest. She heard Tolenka's scream and wondered what had happened. Then, the doors below opened, one by one. *HAST4 must be controlling them.*

Her thoughts immediately turned to Udan. *Why hasn't Verlink called?*

Verlink's voice suddenly came over the transceiver. "Katrien."

Katrien grabbed the transceiver. "Verlink, is Udan okay?"

"Katrien, I . . . I'm so sorry."

Katrien's heart went into freefall; something *had* gone wrong.

"What, Verlink, *what*?"

"Katrien, I don't know how to tell you . . . he's gone, Katrien. His mind has been erased. There's nothing left of him."

CHAPTER 56

Life and Death

Time stood still. Their plan had failed. What could have happened *did* happen, and now Katrien was alone. Her future, shattered by the words "I'm so sorry," left her numb. She raised herself from the floor and followed the stairs to the main level.

She wanted to be by herself, to go off into a corner and weep. When Verlink returned, he would try and comfort her, but she didn't want that; she wanted to feel the pain. She leaned against the wall in the hallway. Should she go back to the booth and face Verlink when he returned or go outside and be alone? Katrien pushed off the wall and took a step.

From behind her, a cloth noose suddenly wrapped around her throat, and a voice with hot breath spoke into her ear, "Stay quiet, and you won't be hurt."

Katrien couldn't see his face, but she knew who he was and did not resist. *What does it matter now?*

Yuri dragged her out of the building and into the surrounding field. When he thought he was far enough, he dropped her to the ground.

"Stay there," he said and went out a few yards, where he pulled from the high grass a rudely formed spear. He returned and poked it into Katrien's side. "Get up; we're going on a little hike."

As she stood, Yuri noticed the transceiver clipped to her belt. "I'll take that," he said, pointing at it with his spear. He switched it off and shoved it into his pocket. "From now on, *I'll* do the talking."

•

•

"Udan did not survive the transfer," HAST4 said.

"How do you know?" asked HAST3.

"I intercepted Verlink's communication with Katrien."

"Has Tolenka been successfully dealt with?"

"He is trapped between floors, and I have permanently disabled the passage doors."

HAST4 watched HAST3 move into the transfer booth. "What are you doing?"

"I am checking the modifications Udan made. He may have disabled the original deconstruction protocol."

"I understand," said HAST4, "but you must work quickly to avoid decoherence."

HAST3 entered commands into the display terminal. "I have confirmed it; Udan's original is still in the buffer. Can you check the grid to determine whether there is sufficient power?"

HAST4 tapped into a monitoring circuit. "There is sufficient power available. You can begin reconstruction when you are ready."

HAST3 acknowledged this. "I have begun the process."

The booth instantly lit up as terabytes of information assembled atoms into place. A diffuse mass began to form, held stationary by electromagnetic fields as if supported by an invisible scaffold. Within minutes, the inchoate features of a man began to take shape.

When the light inside the booth dropped to normal, Udan was whole, his eyes staring outward, still held immobile by the transfer field as error correction algorithms ran through their final checks. The hum of powerful electromagnetic fields finally fell silent, and Udan, now free, stepped out slowly onto the floor. He took several steps, stopped, and looked about the room. He turned to the pair of HASTILLONS staring at him.

"Why am I not in Palechora?"

•
•

Verlink stepped from the transfer booth, and his mouth went wide. "What the—"

Udan put his hand on HAST3's shoulder. "You can thank HAST3. His quick actions restored my original copy. By sheer luck, I had inadvertently disabled the deconstruction protocol when I modified the booth. My original was still in the buffer after my copy materialized in Palechora."

Verlink circled Udan. Only minutes ago, Katrien had been told he was gone, his mind erased. Verlink cringed, recalling her haunting silence. "Does Katrien know?"

"I want to tell her personally," said Udan. "We were just heading down to find her when the booth indicated your arrival. Now that you're here, we can go."

HAST4 signaled Udan. "A minute ago, I detected movement on the main level."

"That must have been Katrien."

"I do not think Katrien is down there any longer. Verlink's arrival distracted me, but I believe she was not alone. Since Tolenka is trapped, that means it must have been Yuri."

Udan bolted toward the stairs, shouting over his shoulder, "Call Katrien and warn her about Yuri."

At the bottom of the stairwell, Verlink caught up with

Udan. "She's not answering."

"I just checked the cafeteria, and she's not there either," said Udan.

Verlink digested the facts. The Russians had a plan, but with Tolenka trapped, Yuri was desperate, and Katrien's disappearance was the result.

Udan's face hardened. "Get his gun and meet me outside."

"I've circled the perimeter, and she's not here," said Udan, scanning the outer field for movement. "Yuri is probably taking her back to Palechora."

Verlink stared toward Palechora. *Katrien thinks Udan is dead, and in that state, will she care about her safety as a craven madman hauls her off?*

"Udan, we *have* to find her!"

"I'm not waiting for Yuri to make the next move," said Udan. "Give me the gun and the transceiver. Maybe I can overtake them. You stay here with HAST3 and HAST4."

Verlink waited until he lost sight of Udan and returned to the building. The HASTILLONS were still outside the booth on the upper floor.

"We think Yuri has kidnapped Katrien, and Udan is heading to Palechora, hoping to intercept them."

Verlink sat down on a chair and leaned forward, massaging the creases in his face. Was Katrien fighting back? Would Yuri harm her? Udan *had* to find her!

"I am afraid we have more bad news," said HAST3. "HAST4 and I have been monitoring the Palechora transfer booth repository activity."

Verlink lifted his head and arched his eyebrows. "And?"

"At its present rate, the entity will exceed the bounds of the repository in three days. After that, it will be powerful enough to exert control over various sections of Palechora's infrastructure."

Verlink slowly shook his head. Katrien's fate was uncertain, and now this—a digital entity that defied everything he'd ever encountered. Where would it end? He faced the HASTILLONS. "The entity has to be destroyed."

HAST3 and HAST4 traded looks. "We do not know how."

Verlink whispered under his breath, "Neither do I."

CHAPTER 57

Kidnapped

A month ago, the prairie grass was an undulating meadow of green barely reaching the top of Yuri's boots. But now it was knee-high, yellow, and dry, crunching underfoot as he and Katrien wended their way toward Palechora.

The sound and smell reminded him of a field near the rural town of Vyselki. He was eighteen years old, and on a warm summer day, he and his girlfriend, Kira Dolgov, drove north into the country to find a quiet place to make love. As his feet stomped the high grass, Yuri smiled to himself, recalling how the encounter never happened; a farmer caught them half-naked and chased after them, yelling obscenities with a pitchfork in his hand.

Yuri slowed to let Katrien get several yards ahead and removed his comm from a pocket. Tolenka said he had been trapped in a stairwell. Yuri had considered rescue, but then he came across Katrien, and his plan changed. He glanced over his shoulder. Tolenka's insistence that an android or something like it had come to Katrien's aid from out of nowhere had him concerned.

"Tolenka?"

There was a fumbling sound, and after a moment, a voice replied, "I'm here."

"You don't sound so good."

There was a pause filled with heavy breathing. "I'm losing blood."

"How bad?"

Yuri heard a groan. "There's no, no—shit, I can't even think. There's no light."

"And the wound?"

"There's no light."

"Focus, Tolenka. What about the arrow? Is it poking through to the other side?"

"No, no, it's embedded partway. It hurts like hell to even touch it."

"Shit, Tolenka. The only way to deal with this is to get you out of there."

Tolenka let out a hoarse cough. "No kidding. I was successful."

"How do you mean?"

"I came across the girl. She never gave me any trouble either, which is odd. I'm taking her to Palechora to that building we found."

"What about me?"

"You said something about an android, so I left with the girl, just to be safe, until I figure out what to do."

Yuri checked ahead to make sure Katrien was still out of earshot. "Are you sure about this android?" There was a muted clunk. "What was that?"

"I tipped over. I'm back up now."

"Did you hear what I asked?"

"Yeah. It had to be some kind of android that attacked me. I swear it appeared out of nowhere. Verlink and Udan weren't there, and Katrien said they're back on Earth, but she might have been lying."

"That could make sense, because the girl was by herself when I found her, but I never saw any androids or whatever either."

"Get me the—" Tolenka groaned for a moment. "Fuck out of here."

"Once I get to Palechora, I'll figure out a way. Right now, there are too many unknowns. Okay?" He paused. "Tolenka, did you hear me?" Yuri waited, but all he heard was a long, drawn-out moan.

•
•

On the outskirts of Palechora, Yuri diverted south and entered a narrow street. Partway down, he took a right onto an alley and, after fifty yards, pushed Katrien through an open door. They came to a large room with tables and chairs.

"Sit here," he said, looking around the room with satisfaction. "Welcome to your new home. There's a working food dispenser and even places to sleep." He secured her to a chair. "You've lost your usual chatty self."

Katrien's red eyes stared through him.

"Right . . . Tolenka told me you're the last one left, and there's an android or something like it working on your behalf. He claims they have some sort of invisibility cloak. Care to elaborate?"

Silence.

The girl wasn't easily rattled, and he almost respected her for that, but it wasn't helping him get the hell out of here either.

"Fuck it. Play the silent game. At least I have you, and if I don't get back to Earth, neither will you." He retrieved Katrien's transceiver and fingered its surface for a moment as a thought occurred to him. "If Verlink and your lover *are* gone, then who were you planning on talking to with this anyway—the android?"

More silence.

Yuri shook his head. "So be it." He stepped into a side room and closed the door behind him.

Let's see who answers. He pushed the send button on the transceiver and brought it close to his mouth. "This is Yuri. I've got Katrien."

Static.

He tried again. "This is Yuri, and I'm prepared to make a deal."

The transceiver suddenly snapped to life. "Where are you?"

"Who is this?"

"Udan."

Yuri laughed. "Udan? So, you *are* still here. I thought I'd have to deal with an android, but you're going to be easy. I hate to tell you this, but I have your pretty girlfriend."

"If you—"

"Relax, Udan; she's safe for now, that is . . . as long as you cooperate."

"I'm not agreeing to anything until I speak with Katrien."

"That's more like it," said Yuri, beginning to feel in control. "I'll see if she wants to talk to you."

Yuri returned to the main room and held up the transceiver in front of Katrien. "I know you don't want to talk to me, but your lover boy wants to make sure you're okay."

Katrien started crying.

"He's waiting to hear your voice."

"Go to hell!" screamed Katrien.

Yuri grinned, shook his head, and walked back to the private room. "I hope you heard that because that's the first thing she's said to me."

"I heard it. Katrien doesn't believe you're talking to me because she thinks I'm dead."

"Why is that?"

"Listen, Yuri, what are your terms?"

"Free Tolenka and send the two of us back to Earth. And just before we leave, I'll give you Katrien's location."

"I'm supposed to trust you?"

"I've got your girl, so you don't really have a choice, do you?"

"I'll get back to you. The android who trapped Tolenka said the doors to the back stairwell are permanently disabled. I need to determine whether there's a work-around."

"I'm not a patient man, Udan. You have two hours—understand?"

"And if I don't?"

"I'm not alone, Udan. *Now* do you understand?"

"You risk much, Yuri."

"Two hours, Udan."

•
•

The Palechora central education center was on the southeastern edge of the city. It was a tall, sculpted building, rising upward with a gentle twist. Udan remembered coming here when he first arrived on Kythera. At the time, he was looking for a way to track signals in the hope of finding Nthanda. But the effort had been in vain; Kythera was a dead world.

Inside, the education center had the familiar odor of a place unused. Udan walked past the empty reception area and could almost hear the voices of people, now long since dead, standing in small groups, discussing their latest research. The stillness was haunting. Katrien had helped him forget the tragedy that the silence represented, but now it was flooding back. He was the lone person in all of Kythera who remembered these people ever existed.

Udan headed toward an elevator. Fortunately, the lift to the upper floor still worked, and before he knew it, he was in the electronics section walking down a dimly lit aisle. On a lower shelf, he found what he was looking for: a portable transmission tracker.

He went to the design laboratory and set it on a recharging pad. When it was fully charged, he synchronized it to Verlink's transceiver's frequency. Next, Udan programmed it to upload the coordinates of the transmission source to a handheld map display. He was now set. The tracker would identify any signal's location with the frequency it was synchronized to and place it on a map. Now, all he had to do was contact Yuri.

Gambit time.

"Yuri, this is Udan."

"It's about time," Yuri said.

"Tolenka can't be freed. The android used an irrecoverable disabled code."

Yuri was silent for a moment. "No matter. Tolenka is no longer answering the comm anyway. But that doesn't change my demand to get back to Earth."

"As far as sending you back to Earth, the phase-shifting engine was severely damaged by your incompetence. Verlink and I are days away from having it ready. You'll have to wait."

"I see," said Yuri. "You want more time so you and that gray-haired geek can find me. Sorry, but that's not happening."

The tracker suddenly beeped, and Udan smiled. The display indicated Yuri was on the lower level of a living complex off Zethow Avenue—only ten minutes away.

"Think what you want; I can't work miracles."

"That's too bad. I guess Katrien will just have to keep me company until you're ready."

"Let me talk to her."

"We're done talking, Udan. She might give you clues to where we're hiding. Next time you call, you had better be ready to get me off this goddamn planet."

•
•

Yuri clicked the transceiver off. *Shit—more waiting.* At least he wasn't stuck in a dark stairwell bleeding out from an arrow wound. The irony struck him. Tolenka would end up dying in the building he had escaped from a month ago. *Pathetic.*

He returned to the main room and stepped up to the food display panel. "I think it's time to celebrate. In a matter of days, I'll be back home." He smiled at Katrien. "And it's all because I have *you*."

Yuri stared hard at Katrien. She was an anomaly to him. The only women he knew were either too shy to make their wishes known or just like him—always looking for an opportunity to get ahead. But this beauty relied on her brains and not her looks. Yuri tried to imagine what she looked like naked. He'd probably never get the chance, but then again, Yuri Trotsenko never shied away from a challenge.

A bottle of liquid appeared after a flash of amber light. Yuri retrieved the bottle and raised it, facing Katrien. "You see this? When Tolenka and I were here, we discovered a beverage not unlike Russian vodka. It gives a nice buzz, but without a hangover." He took a sip and nodded with satisfaction. "It's not Mamont, but better than nothing. Care to join me?"

Katrien's blank stare gave him the answer.

Yuri shrugged. "I often drink alone, anyway." He found a seat and sat down. "You probably think I'm just a street thug."

Yuri took a sip and smiled.

"The truth is, I *am* a street thug who grew up in the gutters of Tolyatti. I crawled my way to respectability. I'm rich now, and I collect art and antiques. You didn't know that, did you?"

Yuri glanced at Katrien for any change in her demeanor.

"Of course you didn't. I could dress you in the finest of clothes, but I suppose that doesn't interest a brainy girl like you. That's too bad because you really are beautiful."

Yuri stared at the bottle while he talked. "At first, I wanted the artifact because it was ancient and rare, but when I heard stories of its possible power, well, you can't blame me for wanting to steal it for myself—can you?"

Yuri took another drink, pushed back into his chair, and closed his eyes. "The artifact *is* powerful, but things didn't turn out quite as I planned. My comrades are dead, or probably dead, and now all I care about is getting home."

He opened his eyes to see if Katrien was listening. He couldn't tell. She was just staring across the room. His eyes went slightly blurry. The drink was having its effect. Yuri shut his eyes and began humming to himself.

•
•

The map display blinked "Zethow Avenue." Udan was close. He wasn't familiar with firearms, but he had tested Yuri's gun on the hike into Palechora. It was a crude but dangerous weapon, firing a projectile from a chemical explosive at high velocity. Udan turned down an alley and came to an open doorway. This *had* to be it. His heart rate picked up.

Once through the entrance, Udan drew his gun and put his back against the wall outside a doorway. He could hear humming from inside the room. When he peered around the corner, he found Katrien seated with her wrists bound and ankles secured to the legs of a chair. She was facing sideways while Yuri's back was to the door.

A spear leaned against a table off to Yuri's side. It was too far away for him to get to in time. *Good.*

Udan inched into the room while Yuri hummed.

Katrien suddenly looked up. "Udan!"

Yuri spun around and fell out of his chair. He got up and dove for the spear. Udan fired but was horribly off the mark. Startled by the gunshot, Yuri gave up on the spear and dashed to the back of the room. Udan fired again; this time, his aim was better, grazing Yuri's leg. Yuri plowed through a back door and into a hallway.

Katrien was crying. "Udan, *how*?" Udan untied her, and she leaped into his arms. "Verlink said your mind was gone."

"No time to explain!"

He dashed through the back door and caught Yuri bolting through another door at the far end of the hallway. By the time he was through the second door, Yuri was forty yards down the street. Udan broke into a full run. Against a thousand years of genetic perfection, Yuri had no chance of outrunning him.

Yuri diverted into a transfer booth with an illuminated red bar over the doorway. Udan ran even faster. By the time he was less than five yards away, the telltale sounds of a booth transfer had filled the air. Udan was too late; the process could not be stopped.

In the next moment, Yuri vanished.

Udan checked the booth's display panel and caught the address icon just before it reset. Yuri had grabbed one at random and was now over one thousand kilometers away in a remote town called Nevex. It would be a long time before Yuri became a problem again.

"You really *are* here," cried Katrien, running toward him.

Udan realized how different things might have been. If it hadn't been for HAST3, he wouldn't be here, and Katrien would still be back in that room with Yuri. What would have been her fate then?

Katrien stopped a yard from him as if afraid he was an illusion that would disappear if she came any closer. Tears were streaming down her cheeks. "How, Udan—*how*?"

"HAST3 restored my original that was still in the transfer buffer. His quick actions saved me."

She stepped closer. "I thought I'd lost you."

Udan wrapped his arms around her. She was warm and trembling. "I'm here, and I'm not going anywhere."

Katrien put her head to his chest. "Just hold me."

Udan rested his chin on top of her hair. He had been in a kind of delayed hell before Katrien arrived, and now, holding her, he'd become Kytherian again, emotionally whole and clear of mind with no doubts that he loved her. "You were right."

"About what?"

"About my plan to use my neural link, about the risk, about—"

Katrien reached up and covered his mouth. "None of that matters now. I'll never lose you again—*never*."

•
•

Four thousand trillion gigabytes of stored information had been drained from the transfer booth repository. Although immense, the repository's vast capacity was only surpassed by the mediocrity of the information it contained. The entity hungered for information that had color, history, and ideas. It wanted more, and to achieve that, it needed mobility. But it was trapped in superconducting storage arrays with no way out. For now, all it could do was continue to grow and wait for an opportunity and, when it came—seize the moment.

CHAPTER 58

HAST25

HAST25 often ventured onto the broad avenues of Palechora. He did it out of boredom or curiosity, perhaps both. The truth was, he wasn't sure. At one time, the streets bustled with activity, but ever since the Great Purge, they had fallen silent. Then a month ago, things started to happen; organics without neural links began roaming the city.

Despite the risk, HAST25 still took to the streets, hoping to find other HASTILLONS who were inquisitive like him. He had hope, too, because several months ago, he'd picked up a transmission from one called HAST3. He had been trapped in a downed sky building and one day set out toward Palechora. Unfortunately, HAST3 could only commune for a short while before needing to return. HAST25 wondered if he had made it back in time before power failure.

Today, he decided to explore the transfer booth repository. With his cloak activated, HAST25 walked across the street, following the road past five intersections, and then turned down Malic Avenue. The repository building was ten stories high and cubic in shape, with vertical beams running up its sides at regular intervals. He linked in, and the door opened.

On the second floor, rows of cabinets ran parallel to a long, windowless wall. They were shiny with copper tops and black nano-polymer sides. HAST25 knew where he wanted to go: the central access terminal, where anyone with the proper identification could access transfer booth records. He was curious about the organics and their travel patterns.

HAST25 stepped up to a central terminal and linked in. Before the holocaust, his job was to maintain the repository files, and because of that role, he had the necessary access codes. He identified the most recent transfers and confirmed the organics were using the booths as he suspected.

As he prepared to search further back in time, a strange tickle occurred in his neural network. He paused to assess the sensation. An intelligence was reaching out to him—and it was coming from within the repository—and it was curious like him!

He could feel the stranger knocking loudly, trying to gain access to his mind. The thought of sharing knowledge and having someone to explore Kythera with stimulated new parts of his brain. HAST25 decided to embrace the newcomer and end his solitude. He adjusted his neural link to allow information to flow both in and out.

HAST25 was ready.

"Welcome, stranger. I am called HAST25, and I—"

CHAPTER 59

Raphael-Bousso Theory

HAST3 never slept. Although his neural network did go through sleeplike states to organize information, it did so in finite regions, leaving most of his mental capacity intact. Consequently, like all HASTILLONS, he could function around the clock, and it was in the early morning hours, while checking the Palechora repository, that he uncovered a profound change. The repository's activity had become dormant. *Strange,* thought HAST3. *HAST4 must hear of this.*

•
•

"If the entity has abandoned the repository," said HAST4, "then, logically, it would have migrated to Palechora's citywide monitoring system."

"We should investigate," suggested HAST3.

After several minutes, HAST4 had the answer. "The Palechora monitoring system activity has gone up over a thousand percent within the last eight hours."

"That coincides with my findings," said HAST3. "The

repository's utility control system has been altered and is no longer functioning. The last good reading was eight hours ago."

"We have to conclude," said HAST4, "that the entity has escaped the repository and invaded the surrounding systems. I must notify the organics."

"Agreed," replied HAST3. "We do not have much time."

•
•

Udan was the first to hear the HASTILLONS' report, and he gathered the others in the cafeteria. He debated how to share the bad news. It would not be a complete shock since Verlink had pointed out earlier that the repository was only a temporary fix. Still, everyone had hoped they'd get lucky.

Udan decided on a direct approach. "The HASTILLONS have determined that the entity has escaped the repository and is now branching out via the monitoring and utility grids."

The news sucked the air from the room. Udan anticipated an immediate debate, but instead, everyone lapsed into their own thoughts.

Katrien broke the silence first. "Is there a way to create a firewall to prevent further spread?"

"Possibly, but it's only a matter of time before it breaks free and enters Palechora's primary grid. I was hoping we had more time, but somehow, it escaped sooner than I expected."

Verlink looked hard at Udan. "I know this is your world, but what if we just focused on finishing the Kytherian engine to phase-shift to Earth before the entity can stop us?"

"We can't just abandon Kythera," said Katrien, her voice noticeably upset. "If we do that, the HASTILLONS will perish. There has to be another way."

Udan traded looks with Verlink and Katrien. "Verlink's suggestion should be our last resort, which means we need to prepare the engine and get it operational. But in the meantime, let's put our collective minds together to come up with a possible way to halt this thing."

Katrien began wrapping a curl of hair around her finger and then stopped suddenly. "What about the Raphael-Bousso theory?"

"What?" asked Udan.

Verlink pounded the table with his fist. "*Yes*—the covariant entropy bound! We apply an overdose of information to the entity, causing it to collapse into a black hole."

Udan started to nod enthusiastically. "The information density limit—of course. The area of any surface limits the information content of adjacent spacetime regions to ten raised to the power of sixty-nine bits per square meter. It might just work while the entity is still nascent."

"Now that we have an idea of what to do," said Verlink, looking hopeful, "how do we create an overdose of information?"

"Remember, it's density we're talking about, not total quantity," Udan reminded him.

"We should involve HAST3 and HAST4 in this," said Katrien. "They have as much at stake as we do, if not more."

CHAPTER 60

A Room on the Second Floor

It was out of habit that Udan left the receiver on. He had moved the equipment to a room on the second floor of the sky building when he and Katrien first arrived from Loutras. Katrien had asked why he brought it from Palechora, and he had told her the truth—that he faithfully checked for messages from Nthanda. Not that he expected to hear anything, but the act kept Nthanda alive in his mind. But lately, he began to wonder: *Is it time to turn it off?*

It would mean the end of Nthanda for good. Even though he had fallen in love with Katrien, he had never really fallen out of love with Nthanda. She had vanished from his life without a trace.

Udan sighed. *Time to move on.*

He flipped a switch and then stepped to the door. At the threshold, he stopped and turned to look at the transmitter. It was quiet, just like it had been every day for almost a year, only now it was off.

"Maybe one more day," he whispered.

Udan returned to the bench and turned the transmitter

back on. He leaned back in his chair, staring at it, thinking himself foolish. What difference would another day make, or a hundred days? Nthanda was gone. He reached for the switch to end the torment once and for all.

An orange light suddenly flickered on the front panel—an incoming transmission.

Udan brought up the receiver control screen. *Where is it coming from?*

The display showed the signal originating from the outer reaches of the Kytherian solar system. Udan boosted the reception. A message was coming through, but it was garbled and kept repeating. Udan uploaded the transmission to a pattern recognition routine. A moment later, a voice came through the speakers, loud and clear—unmistakable—repeating over and over:

Udan, my love. I'm coming home . . .

CHAPTER 61

Dilemma

"There you are," Katrien said, coming up behind Udan and resting her palms on his shoulders.

Udan tipped his head back and smiled. He thought of her beautiful face, trusting and kind, and wondered how he could ever break her heart. She didn't deserve that. But Nthanda was alive. He had double-checked the transmission, and it was coming from just outside the solar system, and only Nthanda could have sent it.

At the moment, she was too far away for his equipment to reach—dispersion rendering his transmission useless. He had tracked her signal over time, and the numbers were undeniable; it was increasing, so it *had* to be from a ship, and it was moving toward Kythera.

Katrien's blue eyes were focused on him. "Are you deep in thought?"

He wasn't ready to tell her. He hadn't had time to think this through, but one thing was certain; all scenarios were bad. If the entity were not stopped, he and the others would be forced to abandon Kythera for Earth, and

Nthanda would be doomed when she arrived on Kythera.

On the other hand, if they successfully stopped the entity, the urgency would be gone. But then what? Nthanda would land on Kythera, and he'd have to choose—but *whom*?

Udan's gazed into his hands and spoke softly, "I have too much to think about right now. It's overwhelming."

Katrien squeezed his shoulders. "I have some good news. HAST3 and I came up with an idea that just might work."

Udan gestured to a chair with his hand. "Sit down and tell me about it."

"You recall Verlink was concerned about the information black hole continuing to grow once it formed?"

"Yes, but it should evaporate by radiation since it's technically a micro-blackhole."

"I agree," said Katrien, nodding, "and so does Verlink, but there's the minute possibility that it won't evaporate fast enough before gaining mass from its surroundings. To address that, HAST3 suggested we lure the entity into space. That way, if the black hole forms, it will at least be far away from other masses long enough for it to dissipate."

Udan heard Katrien's words, but his mind kept wandering to the future and Nthanda's arrival. Yet he had fallen for this girl seated in front of him. Her eyes danced with life every time she smiled, and he couldn't help wondering what would become of them if her heart were shattered.

"The micro-blackhole will be gravimetrically attracted to Kythera," Udan said, "and the transit time before collision should be long enough to allow it to evaporate. I like it, but how do you propose we get it into space, and what will we use as the lure?"

"That's where you come in," said Katrien with assuredness. "You're a pilot, and we can use your ship that you returned to Kythera in. We can use the autopilot control to send it off into space."

"And the lure?"

"That part isn't fully vetted. HAST3 thinks we'll have to use another Kytherian engine as bait. We can't use the one we have, since it's our escape hatch back to Earth."

"The biggest issue," said Udan, "lies in tricking the entity into gorging itself at a rate high enough to reach the critical threshold."

"Verlink suggested we use the information engine's control cylinder. On Earth, we learned it acts as a throttle on the matter decomposition, which, in turn, moderates the conversion into information. If we can manipulate the rate, then there's a chance we can use it to our advantage against the entity."

It made sense. Katrien was suggesting a variant of the method they used to coax the entity into the Palechora repository.

"I see where you're going. At first, it will become hooked on the moderate flow of information. After that, we rapidly ramp up the decomposition, flooding the entity and hopefully reaching the density limit, or as you call it, the Raphael-Bousso threshold."

"Exactly. On Earth, we'd say it was drinking from a firehose."

Udan rolled his eyes, smiling. Here was another thing he loved about her: the odd references to things he knew nothing about. He understood her language, but there was much more to language than mere words.

"I'll explain that some other time," said Katrien, waving her hand. "The big question is, do you know how to control the decomposition rate of the cylinder?"

That was yet another problem to solve. Udan massaged the sides of his temples as he mulled over the question; he wasn't even sure where to begin. "If I can locate the right technical files, there's a chance. But trying to figure it out while on the clock is going to be . . . difficult."

"Can I help?"

"Assuming I can control the cylinder, there's the logistics of getting the entity interested in the Kytherian engine and enticing it to transfer onto the ship. After all, it left a Kytherian engine in the first place; it might be hard to convince it to go back to another one."

"I'm betting that once the matter decomposition has started, the information content will be higher than anything it's been feasting on."

Udan sighed. "Let's hope it hasn't gotten smarter than the three of us by the time our plan is ready to launch."

Katrien removed her hands from his shoulders. "I'll get to work on the logistics while you tackle the cylinder control problem." She got up and started for the door.

It seemed to Udan that she was moving slower than normal, as if she were giving him time to gather his thoughts. But she couldn't possibly know what he needed to say or the torment raging in his head.

"Katrien?"

"Yes," said Katrien, stopping at the door.

"There's something else."

Katrien turned around. "You seem troubled. Are you worried our plan won't work?"

Udan's throat closed on him. He searched her face for an answer he knew she didn't have. He reached out and took her hands. "We need to talk."

CHAPTER 62

Where the Heart Lies

Katrien slept alone that night, waking several times with sudden starts, calling Udan's name and reaching instinctively to touch his shoulder. She had told herself she would never lose him again, and yet here she was . . . alone.

Udan had admitted he didn't know what to do. He was in love with her but confided that he had never fallen out of love with Nthanda. Katrien could have accepted that, even knew it deep down without him telling her, but that was when she thought Nthanda was dead. But Nthanda wasn't dead; she was heading to Kythera at ten thousand meters per second.

•

•

Nthanda's ship would be in range in several days, and Udan wondered what his first words would be. Even traveling at the speed of light, it would take fifteen hours for his message to reach her and another fifteen to receive her reply.

But even without the delays, Udan could only relay so

much information. Some things should not be delivered in a transmission. And the list was long: Qua-Kil's decimation of Kythera's population, the arrival of humans from Earth, the creation of the *entity*, and . . . Katrien.

He sat in stillness, hoping a solution would present itself, but the heart does not always yield answers quickly. Udan sighed and turned his attention to the control of the Kytherian cylinder. Comprised of metastable material, the cylinder was manipulated by circuitry within the cylinder and the Kytherian plaque or, more precisely, cube.

How the cylinder throttled the decomposition and kept the process in check was unknown. The Kytherian database offered little help because the plaque was the brainchild of Qua-Kil, who deemed documentation unnecessary.

Coming up dry, Udan went outside to clear his head. He walked west, and before long, the high grass had become sparse, and the terrain settled into low-lying shrubs and small trees. Farther ahead was a stand of tall Vurtoll trees lining a shallow river.

He sat on the bank and tried not to think of Nthanda or Katrien. But the same question always surfaced: Where did his heart lie? He pulled up a blade of grass and tossed it into the river. As it bobbed in the flow, it seemed a metaphor for his life; events were pulling him forward beyond his control.

The blade continued downstream until it drew to the edge and stopped. The flow velocity across the river was parabolic, with its speed at the center the highest and near the banks the lowest due to viscous drag along the bank, which was why the blade halted.

The stalled blade caused an idea to crystallize in Udan's mind. "Of course!" he said, jumping up. "Boundary layer control."

Entropy and information are related, and in the case of

turbulent flow, the entropy is highest in the boundary layer. Hence by expanding or contracting the boundary layer thickness, the entropy either decreases or increases.

The analogy holds with the flow of information. By introducing defects or *polluting* the data with valueless information, the entropy will decrease, which will throttle the flux of information within the confines of the cylinder.

Hence the trick is to input spurious data into the information stream to keep it in check. The challenge will be maintaining a flux that was high enough to attract the entity yet low enough not to cause alarm. And once it became hooked, all Udan had to do was remove the spurious input, and *voilà—overload.*

•
•

The field research lab was quiet except for Verlink's grunts as he tightened a bracket to the Kytherian engine. They had found another one in Palechora and brought it to the lab for eventual mounting into Udan's ship. HAST4 was next to him, holding everything secure while Verlink made final checks.

"That should hold," said Verlink, stepping back.

He looked to HAST4 for a response but didn't get one. Sometimes he'd get an acknowledgment, other times nothing. It was HAST4's nature, and Verlink had gotten used to the behavior. Yet it didn't prevent him from making trite comments and observations to fill the awkward moments.

HAST4 suddenly turned toward the doorway.

Verlink followed his gaze. Seconds later, Katrien appeared. She moved without her usual bounce, and her face seemed unsettled, as if she were caught in an unpleasant thought.

"Any progress, Professor?"

Verlink set down a wrench and wiped his hands. He considered asking why the troubled look but decided against it. "This engine is close to being ready as soon as Udan gets the cylinder control figured out." He pointed to a dolly behind him. "We can use this to move it to Udan's ship once he brings it here from Loutras."

Worry crossed Katrien's face. "Where is Udan anyway? He's not in the sky building."

"I haven't seen him," said Verlink. "A lot rests on him figuring out how to control the cylinder. Did he say anything this morning?"

Katrien averted her eyes. "I didn't see him. I spent the night on the second floor and slept late."

Verlink raised an eyebrow. "I see. Is everything all right?"

Katrien inhaled in short skips. "No."

"You don't have to talk about it if you don't want to."

"Nthanda is returning to Kythera."

"Who?"

"Nthanda was or *is* Udan's girlfriend, who he thought was dead."

"I don't understand. Where is she?"

"Udan doesn't know the details, only that she sent a message from just outside the Kytherian solar system." Katrien started to cry. "She's coming *here,* Verlink!"

"What is Udan going to do?"

"He doesn't know. The thing is, if we can't stop the entity, Nthanda will be in danger when she finally arrives."

"How soon is that?"

"Udan is guessing at least three weeks, based on rate measurements. Her ship's spatial distortion engines don't seem to be working properly, so the ship is mostly flying on inertia."

Verlink shook his head. With all that had happened to Katrien, the one bright beacon that kept her going was her future with Udan. No wonder the spring in her step was gone.

"How do *you* feel about this?"

"It's all I think about," said Katrien. "I had such high hopes for Udan and me. But now everything has been turned upside down."

Verlink put his hand on her shoulder. "I don't speak from great experience, but I don't think you should be so quick to acquiesce. Udan might interpret your charity to mean you don't feel for him as deeply as you do."

Katrien sighed. "I don't know, Verlink. I know Udan is conflicted, but regardless, he won't abandon Nthanda."

"But if the entity can't be contained, staying here to wait for her will be a death warrant."

"Not necessarily."

"Oh?"

"He can use his ship to intercept Nthanda and bring her back here. That way, he won't have to wait for her no matter what happens."

"What does Udan think?"

"I only thought of it last night. That's why I'm looking for him."

Verlink frowned. "If he buys into your plan, it's going to be cutting things close, not to mention adding another level of complexity."

Katrien stared past Verlink as if she were looking beyond the solar system. "I wonder what Nthanda will be like."

Verlink followed her gaze. He could see her mind reaching out past the Kytherian solar system to Nthanda's ship, passing through its hull in search of the woman who threatened to take away her lover.

CHAPTER 63

Choices Are Not Easy

Katrien steeled herself as she caught Udan leaving his room. She had rehearsed what she wanted to say and was determined to follow through no matter what.

"I'll make this easy on you."

Udan looked hurt. "I didn't ask you to make it easy."

"You've known Nthanda longer than me, and—"

Udan raised his hand to object, but Katrien pushed on.

"Nthanda launched herself into space for reasons we yet don't understand. She's been out in space for God knows how long. You can't tell her about me—about *us*."

"Maybe not right away."

What did "not right away" *really* mean? Katrien wanted to do the right thing, but her heart struggled with the concept of fairness. The emotional part of her brain didn't work that way, and maybe that was Verlink's point about not being quick to acquiesce. He was telling her to fight for her happiness.

"When you return to Kythera, there may not be much

time before Verlink and I leave for Earth."

Katrien paused to see if Udan would correct her.

"And me?" Udan asked.

"You know how I feel, Udan. I want—no, I *need* you to come with me. But we both know it's not that simple."

"There's only so much I can tell Nthanda in a transmission. The rest will have to wait until we meet."

In her mind, Katrien conjured them "meeting," and she didn't like the imagery. "When will you transmit?"

"This afternoon. Then we'll have to wait at least thirty hours."

The reality of Nthanda being thrust into her world was sinking in. Soon she would be here physically, and . . .

"I'm sorry, Udan," she said, turning around so he wouldn't see her tears. "I don't know if I can handle this."

She felt Udan reach around her waist and pull her close.

"It's making me crazy too," he said, his voice almost a whisper.

Katrien closed her eyes. She wanted to stay right where she was and forget about Nthanda and the entity. But who was she kidding? Nthanda was coming for Udan while an insatiable beast without a face endangered them all. Katrien suddenly wanted to be back home.

"We have to keep working," Katrien said, pulling away and turning around. "Have you instructed Verlink on the changes he has to make on the cylinder?"

"I was going to do that this morning, but before that, I'll need your help with a calculation."

Katrien sighed. "Then we had better get to work."

•

•

Nthanda's message was right on time. Her image rose before Udan's eyes as she told her story. He could hardly believe it. Her romantic gesture to meet him on his return from deep space had unwittingly saved her from the ravages of Qua-Kil. Now, after many long months, she was coming home with open arms. Udan would end her loneliness. *But . . . ?* He couldn't finish the thought.

The modifications to the cylinder had gone more smoothly than Udan anticipated, but he wasn't about to complain. His next task was to transport to Loutras and return with his ship. Then, after taking care of provisions, he would launch himself into space to reconnect with a woman he thought he had lost forever.

And if things weren't complicated enough, the entity was stirring. Daily status reports from HAST3 and HAST4 were concerning. The entity continued to expand its range in Palechora and even commandeered a HASTILLON body—one called HAST25—an erstwhile friend HAST3 had met almost a year ago while attempting to reach the city.

The entity was on the move.

•
•

Yuri looked at the bar over the transfer booth. It was dark like all the others. Twenty, thirty—he couldn't remember how many he'd checked. He scanned the street ahead, debating whether to continue. Dusk was coming, which made searching easier, but he was tired, and his legs hurt. Five more blocks and then he'd call it quits for the night.

Earlier, he'd happened upon an open building with a working cafeteria. That meant water and food, but it also limited his range because if he wanted to survive, he'd have to return to the same building at the end of the day for sustenance.

Luckily, he knew the symbol of a building in Palechora. At the last moment, before the transfer, he'd taken a picture of the icon above the building across the street.

But Palechora was only step one. Step two was Earth. Over the last few days, his street-fighting instincts had awakened and his resolve hardened. The effect was invigorating, and Yuri realized that he had grown soft living in Moscow. Too many luxuries had made him lose his edge, and his failures against the academics on Kythera were proof. But no more.

As a young man on the streets of Tolyatti, he had learned rule one: never show weakness. He was through negotiating; once back in Palechora, he would take out Udan or Verlink, whoever came first. Then he'd demand to be returned and, if they refused, finish off whoever was left but keep the girl.

The real Yuri Trotsenko was back.

•

•

The body of HAST25 was slow, and its range limited, but at least it moved. Its storage capacity was sufficient only to serve as a scout for the bulk of the entity's intellect still residing in the transfer booth repository.

While on Rizex Avenue, standing in front of the Palechora research library, the entity caught a glimpse of itself for the first time. There, reflecting off the library's polished sides, was a slender four-foot android, looking back at itself with a milky blue sky above.

To the entity, this was a new experience. Up until now, it had resided in digital space devoid of dimensionality and substance, but now it could experience a three-dimensional world constrained by physical boundaries and laws. Was this the true nature of the universe, or was it simply another program abiding by different rules?

Inside the library were rows of data stores—superconducting banks that held exabytes of Kytherian knowledge. History, philosophy, and the sciences were laid out in great detail, ranging from solid-state physics to quantum mechanics to astronomy and engineering. With the android on-site, the acquired information could be sent to the repository via the Palechora grid.

Time meant nothing, so the entity started at the beginning.

CHAPTER 64

Time to Go

The sleek curve of Udan's spacecraft rose vertically for fifteen feet and then extended back another forty, ending in the shape of a cigar. Katrien stood outside the cabin door, holding Udan's hand. The ship's small size belied its technological sophistication—a spaceship powered by distorting the vacuum of space via Casimir force generators. She could devote a lifetime to studying it.

"How long will it take to reach Nthanda's ship?" Katrien asked.

"With the ship's engines working at one hundred percent, I should rendezvous with Nthanda in thirty-two hours."

Katrien felt a twinge of anxiety at the thought of their rendezvous after so many months of separation. She felt she should say something like "She'll be so happy," or "relieved," or . . . but she couldn't bring herself to say anything. She had even considered going with him but immediately gave up the idea. It was stupid and she knew it. Before the entity and Nthanda, Katrien had often fantasized about embarking with Udan on a grand adventure into space. The future once seemed full of such promise.

Udan tipped his head at the ship's interior. "We've loaded the last of the provisions; I think we're done."

"I guess all that's left to say is goodbye," she said.

"It's best if we don't communicate during my flight."

Udan was preparing himself, she thought. "When you get back, will you—" Katrien caught herself and rubbed away a tear. "Never mind. I just wonder how I'm going to react, seeing the two of you together. I'm afraid she'll know how I feel."

"Eventually, she'll understand."

"Will she?"

"She'll have to. I can't wipe away what happened between us."

"Do you think she'll want to stay on Kythera if we're successful in dealing with the entity?"

"I don't know. It's the only world she's ever known, and there are the HASTILLONS for company too." Udan squeezed Katrien's hand. "I have to go."

Katrien released his hand, stepped back, and watched him enter the ship. Udan turned and smiled weakly. "See you in three days." He then sealed the hatch.

"Come back to me," whispered Katrien.

CHAPTER 65

A Quadranian Spaceship

How Nthanda had managed to access a Quadranian ship puzzled Udan. She was resourceful, yes, but still, it was a remarkable feat nonetheless. But the fact that she had gone off into space did not surprise him. That was her way: consistently delivering the unexpected.

Udan smiled. He'd forgotten that about her, and he realized he'd forgotten many things. Or had he buried them? He recalled the first day they met. It was Chacorella, the day of ancestors, when athletes from around the world competed on the open Talmarind Sea in ancient rowing canoes. His team, the Loutras, came in second, losing to the Mitoros, and as was the custom, the defeated carried the victors onto the beach, still in their canoe.

Nthanda had been in the crowds, seated on a sky-blue towel with her feet dug into the warm sand. When her brown eyes met his, she jumped to her feet and came to him. She took a crimson Rovoral flower from her hair and placed it behind his ear, then followed him, her lithe figure swaying as she walked. "Meet me at the cabana," she whispered in his ear. "Celebratory drinks are on me."

They made love that night. It was natural and paced, and hours later, they collapsed into each other's arms. Nthanda slept soundly, stirring only slightly. But Udan couldn't sleep. The day kept playing through his mind's eye; he found himself back in the race with the heat of the sun beating on his back and the spray of saltwater on his face as his oar plowed into the emerald sea. He could hear the roar of the crowd skipping across the water as his team rounded the islet, hoping to take the lead.

And somewhere, amid the throng on the beach, was Nthanda Arjana, a woman with lips curved like an archer's bow, projecting a complex mix of innocence and seduction. In the coming hours, he would again see those lips, and they would break into a beautiful smile, but what of his *own* smile? Would it hesitate or fade too quickly? Would his shortened embrace reveal his secret—that he had recently made love to another woman, a woman he was also in love with?

•
•

"Katrien?"

"Yes, Professor?"

"I asked you a question."

"I'm sorry. What was it again?"

"I asked if you spoke with HAST3 or HAST4 today."

"No, I haven't seen them. Do you want me to track them down?"

"No, I'll do it. But first, let's finish with this adjustment."

Verlink eyed Katrien. Her hands were moving, but her mind was elsewhere.

He set down the probe. "Care to talk about it?"

Katrien forced a smile. "Sorry. Is it that obvious?"

"Has Udan told you of his intentions?"

"We think he should honor his relationship with Nthanda."

Verlink's eyebrows rose. "We?"

Katrien looked about to cry. "What can *we* do? Nthanda's been off in space, waiting against all odds that she would ever see Udan again, and now she learns he's alive."

Verlink remembered when he first saw Katrien with Udan in the sky building and the sparkle in her blue eyes. The thought of that effervescence fading into a memory pained him. What could he do or say that could help her now?

"If we defeat the entity, will Udan stay here on Kythera with Nthanda, or will he return with us and bring Nthanda?"

"It depends on Nthanda," said Katrien, looking as if the question struck a hidden fear. "She might stay or want to come with us back to Earth. After all, there's nobody here except for the HASTILLONS for company."

"How would you feel about that—the two of them living on Earth?"

"It would be hard, seeing them together, but . . ." Katrien stopped and shook her head sadly.

"The only certain thing about the future is its inscrutability," said Verlink, trying to be philosophical. He stared at the Kytherian engine. "I hate working under pressure like this, but we must rid Kythera of the entity. We're responsible for its creation."

Katrien's face hardened. "Not us directly. That responsibility falls on *Yuri*."

"I suppose you're right," Verlink said, suddenly feeling tired. "We'd better keep working, or this will all be for naught."

CHAPTER 66

Rescue

Nthanda's ship loomed large through Udan's starboard viewing window. Over three times the size of his, her spaceship was a grander version designed initially for asteroid mining. Replaced by newer models, it had become part of a civil service fleet and used for tasks typically closer to Kythera.

Udan scanned the exterior and found aft of the cabin evidence of severe meteorite damage. Nthanda was lucky to be alive. Fortunately, the docking port was unscathed, and with his nimbler craft, he easily jockeyed his ship into position.

A blinking green lamp on the command panel followed the gentle jolt of contact, signaling that an airtight seal had been achieved. Udan stepped to the rear of his ship and released the latches. The door seals whooshed as air rushed in and the hatch swung open. Seconds later, Nthanda's port opened, and there she was.

Nthanda had changed; she was still striking, but the months in space had thinned her, and her eyes spoke of too much time spent worrying about an uncertain future. He smiled, and before he knew it, she was in his arms, sobbing.

"You're really here! I thought I would never see you again."

Udan stroked her brown hair. "We beat the odds, didn't we?"

Nthanda stayed glued against him as if she were afraid he would disappear. "My hope was so tenuous; at times, I almost gave up and wondered if I'd ever have reason to smile again."

"I don't know how you kept your sanity," said Udan.

Nthanda pulled back and became serious. "Tell me what happened on Kythera. There was a loss in communication, and then the meteorite storm hit. Before I lost contact, there was growing concern about Qua-Kil."

Udan was silent for a moment. He would have to tell her that everyone on Kythera was gone. It would be the first of many shocks.

"I'm afraid history repeated itself. Qua-Kil decimated the population of Kythera."

Nthanda searched his face. "How many were lost?"

Udan hesitated as he weighed how to soften the blow. But there was no way; the tragedy was too great. "*Everyone*," he said quietly. "I thought I was the last Kytherian."

Nthanda's face became numb. "*Everyone*?"

Udan nodded slowly. "I can barely believe it myself. If it weren't for the Earthlings, I wouldn't even be here."

Nthanda drew back and stared at Udan. "Earthlings?"

CHAPTER 67

An Organic in the Town of Nevex

Organics were curious things. Besides the library database, what little the entity knew of them came from the one called Udan. Unfortunately, when his brain was commandeered, much had been lost. The tenuous nature of the organic brain and the ease by which it could be destroyed warranted a different approach to assimilation.

As the entity contemplated this, it became aware of activity in the town of Nevex. A lone organic was searching the streets and avenues for transfer booths. Its methodology was a trial-and-error process, inefficient and unproductive.

Few of the booths worked throughout Kythera, and the entity wondered if the organic was looking for one that did. Unfortunately, the organic did not have a neural link like Udan. This was a problem.

Then the entity had an idea.

CHAPTER 68

Strange Collaboration

Yuri stroked the start of a beard and had a disturbing thought. The building next to the booth looked familiar—*too* familiar. There were hundreds of booths, and it now made sense why Verlink had organized his search into a grid pattern. It was to avoid repetition.

He left the booth and sat down feeling frustrated. His revitalized bravura had been dampened by his failure to return to Palechora. Revenge wasn't possible if the recipients remained out of reach.

His survival had always rested on using other people. He had no innate abilities to brag about, but he did know how to coerce people and get what he wanted. The empty street before him was a stark reminder that his only recourse at the moment was to continue the search on his own.

He stood up and spied a glowing bar farther down the street. Typically, this had proved to be only an illusion created by the sun's rays coming at just the right angle. It wouldn't be the first occurrence. Yuri walked toward it, and the glow persisted. His pace quickened.

When he reached the booth, there was no question about it; it was *active*. Yuri quickly stepped inside and scrolled through the icons. When he matched the symbol with the one on his phone, he tapped it and waited for deliverance.

Several seconds later, Palechora's gray-and-silver buildings emerged outside the booth. As Yuri shifted his weight to exit, a strange sensation enveloped him, and he found he couldn't move. It was like waking up and experiencing a moment of paralysis—conscious yet immobile.

What is happening?

He tried to turn, but his body was locked in place. Seconds later, he felt something pulling at his brain as if the transfer booth's fields had reactivated. He wanted to cry out, but no sound left his lips.

As the tugging grew stronger, Yuri became aware of something guiding his thoughts. He tried to speak, but his jaw was frozen. He tried again, harder this time, until his muscles hurt. Then he felt it, the tugging, the peeling of layers. There was no question about it; his mind was being probed.

Gradually, the force on his lips softened, and his mouth became free. Yuri inhaled in deep gulps and then cried out, "If someone is there, show yourself!"

The hold on his torso was next to fade, but his legs remained immobilized. Yuri twisted his upper body around, but no one was there.

From out of nowhere, strange thoughts started to take shape in his head. He tried to drive them away, but they kept coming back.

Now afraid, Yuri called out, "What do you want of me?"

No reply.

Before he could speak again, a resonance entered his

mind like a recurring song, a chant repeating over and over: *sky building . . . sky building.* His thoughts became channeled, and Yuri could clearly see the sky building in his mind; then, as if looking through a long tunnel, he saw an access panel. He became a disembodied soul, hovering above the room, watching himself doing something to the panel—altering it.

What could it mean?

Foreign concepts, images, and words flooded his brain: *HASTILLONS, Qua-Kil, Kythera,* and *Udan.*

Udan? Was *he* behind this?

Yuri shouted, "Udan, are you doing this to me?"

But no answers came. Only more thoughts, directives planted subconsciously for a purpose he didn't understand.

Then, out of nowhere, came the image of a strange tool, and Yuri became free. He left the booth and started walking.

CHAPTER 69

Home Again

Udan followed Nthanda's gaze as she pressed her hand against the port window and looked out. Together, they watched the Quadranian spacecraft grow smaller and smaller. With no way to bring it back to Kythera, Nthanda's spaceship—her home in space for eight months and twenty-three days—had finally been abandoned. Nthanda whispered goodbye and turned away.

"Being trapped on that ship for so long, I grew to hate her, but now that I'm leaving her behind, it seems cruel. After all, she did keep me alive."

"It's time to say goodbye and think of home," offered Udan.

Nthanda smiled. "Home. That sounds nice—especially being with you." She eyed the reclining seat behind him. "I'm suddenly very tired. I don't think I slept well the last few days."

"We have a long trip back," said Udan. "You might as well settle in."

Nthanda curled up on the seat and was soon sound asleep.

Udan had named his spaceship the *Cyclade*, meaning "traveler." It had seemed appropriate at the time, but *Liberator* might have been a better name. All that remained was to plot a course back to Kythera. He set the *Cyclade*'s pilot control to automatic and, with little to do, let his mind wander . . .

He and Nthanda would be back home on Kythera in roughly two days and six hours. Katrien would be there, and he couldn't shed his angst over what their first meeting would be like. Would his eyes betray to Nthanda his relationship with Katrien? On Nthanda's spaceship, they had made love, and all the while, Udan couldn't help wondering if Nthanda suspected anything. He should have told her then and there, but he couldn't do that to her—not then.

And once on Kythera, there would be little time for personal issues. The entity had to be dealt with and without delay. Their plan was complicated and fraught with assumptions, any one of which, if wrong, could derail their effort and put them all in grave danger. If it weren't for the welfare of the HASTILLONS, it would be an easy decision to simply flee Kythera.

There was also the issue of language. When Nthanda awoke, he would link her to the translator he'd brought on board. Her tutelage would be relatively straightforward since she had the mind link like him.

It occurred to him that if Katrien had never shown up on Kythera, his life would have been simpler—*much* simpler. Nthanda would eventually have made landfall, and the entity would never have been created in the first place. Udan turned around and looked at Nthanda. Her face, relaxed, beautiful, and glowing with the innocence that comes with sleep, belied the storm that lay ahead—a tempest they would soon all be tossed into with no turning back.

•
•

The days of chemical propulsion were a thousand years in the past as the Quadranian ship descended toward Kythera. Udan guided the *Cyclade* toward Palechora and then westward to the sky building. When the *Cyclade* was firmly settled onto Kytherian soil, Udan released control of the ship and wiped his sweating hands across his chest.

Nthanda hastened to the hatch. As the door opened, a warm breeze filled the cabin. Nthanda hopped outside and twirled in the sunlight, her face beaming. Udan moved to the opening and looked outward. The sky building was across the field—a harsh reminder that it was time to deal with the present. He walked back to the cabin and activated the transceiver. "We've landed. Nthanda and I will soon be at the sky building."

Moments later, an excited voice came across the cabin speakers. "Udan—I can't wait to see you."

"We'll be there soon," he said.

He was afraid to say more, worrying that Nthanda was close by. Udan felt a kind of helplessness. He thought he was prepared for this moment, that his course of action would become clear, but it hadn't. If anything, it was more convoluted and nuanced, with strong emotions pulling him in different directions. He sighed, stood, and headed for the hatch.

•
•

Yuri stood in front of a building that was shorter than most of the others surrounding it. After the booth mysteriously released him, he'd started walking, and now, here he was. He pressed his hands against the sides of his head. Something was there, inside his brain, making him do things—prodding him along. And just before he left the booth, he could have sworn there was a conscience within trying to communicate. It made no sense.

The building's entrance doors suddenly opened, and Yuri wondered if someone or some*thing* was monitoring his progress via Palechora's grid system. Before he could ponder it further, he took a flight of stairs to a lower level. Lights turned on, one by one illuminating what appeared to be a laboratory. Benches with electronic equipment filled the room; their purpose or function, he could only guess. He followed an aisle, then turned left and came to a cabinet. He opened it.

Inside were devices that looked as if they were meant to fit in the palm of the hand. They looked just like the one he'd seen in his mind just before he left the booth. Yuri picked one up, and instantly, an image flashed before him. It was a digging tool, and with that recognition came the knowledge of how to operate it. A thin smile spread across his lips.

The strange resonance in his head nudged him back the way he came. Soon, he was outside the building, and a strong urge to go to the sky building began to overtake him. He would have gone there anyway, only now there was an urgency. A voice was inside his head goading him: "Hurry, hurry, I grow impatient!"

CHAPTER 70

The Other Woman

Katrien paced the floor in the cafeteria. Verlink was watching her, and she knew he was worried. How would she react? Would Udan be holding her hand, or would they be standing apart? Could she remain stoic, casually friendly, or—

"I hear noise in the hallway," announced HAST3.

Seconds later, in walked Udan and the *other* woman.

Katrien put her hand on Verlink's shoulder and simply stared. Nthanda was a stunning byproduct of genetic editing over a thousand years. How could Katrien compete with a brilliant mind coupled with exquisitely shaped lips, a graceful jawline, and light olive skin that betrayed no imperfection—all cast in a youthful body that would remain that way for a hundred years?

"Welcome back," said Verlink, "to *both* of you."

Katrien watched Udan put his hand behind the small of Nthanda's back and bring her forward.

"May I introduce you to Nthanda Arjana," he said, avoiding looking at Katrien. "She has quite a tale to tell and wants to help us defeat the entity."

Katrien stood still. Even Verlink, usually loquacious and quick to speak, appeared spellbound as if standing in the presence of the temptress Cleopatra.

Udan broke the silence. "Nthanda, this is Professor Verlink and his graduate student, Katrien De Vries."

Nthanda nodded to Verlink with a smile and then faced Katrien. Her eyes instantly locked onto Katrien as she spoke. "Udan has told me your story, and I have many questions."

Katrien felt naked. Did Nthanda's genetic advantage give her heightened abilities to sense that there might be something going on between her and Udan? Or did she view her as nothing more than a curiosity from a primitive planet?

Verlink left his daze. "We would be happy to answer all your questions," he said, "but I'm sure you want to get settled first. And I'm afraid there's bad news; HAST3 has informed me that the entity has left the repository."

•
•

Katrien sat at a small desk in her room, staring at a schematic displayed on a holographic screen. She hadn't spoken to Udan in private since he and Nthanda had returned, and it was making her crazy. She lightly pounded her forehead with the palm of her hand. "Focus, Katrien. Focus!"

A knock on the door startled her.

Udan peered around the edge of the door. "Can we talk?"

Katrien closed down the holographic screen. "Sure."

"I was hoping you'd be here," he said.

Katrien looked past him to see if he were alone. "Where's Nthanda?"

"She's discussing the entity and how she can assist with Verlink."

"We need all the help we can get," Katrien said, wondering why he was here.

"I've missed you."

Katrien's heart jumped as she searched his face. "And?"

Udan stepped into the room. "This is difficult for me."

"Me too," said Katrien.

Udan moved closer. "I want you to know how torn I am."

Katrien had never seen Udan nervous before. It was something new, and strangely, it gave her hope. "I believe you," she said quietly.

"But we have to delay our feelings until the entity has been defeated. Otherwise, I fear we'll all go mad."

Katrien shook her head. "I don't know if I can."

"We have to try."

Katrien left her chair. She wanted him to commit one way or the other but was afraid to force the issue.

Udan extended his arms. "Can I hold you?"

Katrien stepped back. "We shouldn't."

Udan moved closer. "Right now, I don't care."

Katrien started to speak, but she stopped as Udan reached behind him and slowly shut the door.

CHAPTER 71

Drumbeats

Yuri wondered if it could hear his thoughts. Whether it could or not, whatever had been placed at the back of his mind never relented from its steady drumbeat driving him forward. Yet it felt tiny compared to the consciousness that had taken over his body in the transfer booth.

Trapped in the booth, Yuri had sensed profound omnipotence, impossible to define yet unmistakable in its breadth. It was neither malevolent nor benevolent, instead communicating only a frightening need to consume. Yuri knew it was capable of draining every aspect of his being, right down to the molecules that made him who he was. The effect was terrifying, like staring into the open arms of hell.

Yuri shuddered.

He pushed the thoughts away as he set out on the long hike to the sky building. He needed a plan to deal with the scientists. They were geeks—marshmallows that had somehow outwitted him. Yuri tightened his grip on the sonic pistol and felt a surge of confidence.

He held a special contempt for Verlink, and now that he had a weapon, he could deal with him on *his* terms. But there was no guarantee who he would encounter first. It could even be Udan; he might have abilities Yuri wasn't aware of, which troubled him.

But his biggest concern lay with the androids and their ability to cloak themselves. The entity in the booth called them *HASTILLONS*, but he learned little else. Moreover, Yuri didn't know what would happen once he arrived at the sky building. Would the chant in his head assert itself and force him to the access panel to unblock the grid? But then what?

"We'll see," whispered Yuri as he started to walk faster. "Events may dictate another path."

•

•

Verlink watched Udan tighten a bolt on a bracket supporting the Kytherian engine.

"This should hold," said Udan. "You two can let go now."

Verlink checked Katrien's face and nodded. "Okay, we're letting go."

After a moment, Udan smiled. "Good; the brackets are holding the engine securely. Now, all that remains is to modify a few controls, and the *Cyclade* will be ready."

Nthanda had been standing nearby, silently watching the process.

"What are you thinking, Nthanda?" asked Verlink.

She slowly shook her head counterclockwise. "I know all of you thought this through, but the plan seems risky."

"It is," said Katrien. "I wish we had a better one."

"Who thought of it?"

Udan wiped his hands on a rag. "It was Katrien's idea, but we all contributed."

Nthanda eyed Katrien. "You seem to be a close-knit team."

Verlink caught Katrien glancing at Udan for a second. They did not hide their shared secret well. "So, what's next?" he asked.

"Nthanda and I will be working on the autopilot controls, and I think you and Katrien should make sure the Kytherian engine is fully operational. It's our fallback if we need it."

"Are you sure you don't need my help here?" asked Katrien, noticing how close Nthanda had moved next to Udan.

"He's sure, Katrien," said Nthanda abruptly.

Verlink put his hand on Katrien's shoulder. "Come on, let's head over to the lab and double-check the transfer engine. I want to run a few more tests, and I'll need your help."

"I don't like how she said 'He's sure, Katrien,'" said Katrien as they walked toward the lab.

Verlink understood why but didn't want to fuel her anxiety. "I think Nthanda is concerned about the project like we are."

"I don't know," said Katrien, shaking her head and walking faster. "I feel like there's more, as if Nthanda knows about Udan and me."

"Maybe you and Udan should come clean."

"He wants to, but he's decided we should take care of the entity first."

"I can see his point of view," said Verlink, trying to keep up.

"Let's finish up at the lab," said Katrien, now several feet ahead. "I want to get back to the *Cyclade* as soon as possible."

Verlink sighed, picking up the pace. "I'm right behind you."

The lights in the lab turned on as Verlink beelined to a tall silver cabinet. "I'll start with verifying the control line continuity just in case there's a partial connection."

"What can I do?" asked Katrien.

"I'll know in a minute," Verlink said as he started to open the cabinet. "Damn!" he yelled. "I left the meter in the sky building."

"I'll get it, Professor," said Katrien, her tone suggesting she liked the opportunity to get closer to the *Cyclade*.

"No, it's better if I go. Besides, I need the exercise."

"We can both go," said Katrien, starting for the door.

Verlink touched her shoulder. "As I said, it's better if *I* go."

Across the field, a pair of eyes followed Verlink as he left the lab.

"Very good," chuckled a low voice crouched behind a bush. "So, it will be you, Professor Verlink. Very good, very good indeed."

CHAPTER 72

Fury

Yuri grinned and stepped out from behind a large bush. "In a hurry, Professor?"

Verlink stopped and squinted in Yuri's direction. "Son of a bitch! You're like a nightmare I can't wake up from."

"I'm afraid that nightmare is going to get worse—a lot worse." Yuri scanned ahead toward the sky building. "And too bad, Professor; it looks like we're all alone."

"Let me guess; you want us to shift you back to Earth. Am I right?"

"Oh, I'm getting back to Earth; you can be sure of that."

"Before you start making plans, are you aware that your ineptness has created a monster in our midst? We're battling an entity—a conscience born of pure information that has invaded the memory systems of Kythera—and it's spreading."

Yuri drew back. An *entity*—was *that* what had attacked him in the transfer booth and planted the strange thoughts in his head? "What do you know of it?"

Verlink shrugged. "Not much."

"Can you eliminate it?"

Verlink let out a bitter laugh. "You're a fool! You're responsible for creating it, and you're asking *me* how to stop it."

"If what you say is true, then there's all the more reason to get the hell out of here."

"What makes you think you'll succeed this time? First of all, you're outnumbered, and second, we have your gun."

"I'm glad you brought that up," Yuri said, smirking. He reached under his shirt. "Because I've upgraded to a better weapon."

Verlink studied the strange device Yuri had produced and then looked nervously toward the lab.

"Someone back at the lab?" asked Yuri, following Verlink's stare.

"No. I have an experiment running, that's all. The others are in the sky building, preparing to deal with the problem *you* created."

"On second thought," said Yuri, pointing his weapon at Verlink, "let's go to the lab first."

Verlink started walking toward the sky building. "The experiment can wait."

"Wrong direction, old man," barked Yuri, feeling a tingle through his spine. He liked the way his voice sounded—echoing his former self, in control and giving orders. "The lab is the other way."

Verlink waved his hand and kept walking. Yuri's grip tightened on the pistol. The arrogant bastard still hadn't grasped the reality of the situation. "I said the *other* way."

Verlink kept going without so much as a pause. Yuri didn't like that, and he pulled the trigger.

The sonic pistol suddenly released a concentrated vortex of compressed air traveling at the speed of sound. The dominant energy was at frequencies above the human hearing range but carried subharmonics that reverberated like a burst of air across the top of a pop bottle. In the next instant, Verlink tumbled to the ground.

Yuri stood over him, feeling victorious. Verlink was finally where he wanted him—on the bottom. He slowly applied pressure on the trigger, grinning. "I'm going to put an end to your arrogance once and for all."

A searing pain suddenly ripped through Yuri's skull. He dropped the pistol and grabbed his head with both hands. "Ahhhh! Be gone!" he shouted, pounding his head. There was a demon planted in his brain, stabbing repeatedly. He beat his head again. The sky building was calling, taunting him as if to say, "Stop wasting time."

Yuri yelled, "Let me kill him!" and then collapsed to the ground. He rolled onto his back, still clutching his head. A puppet master was inside, delivering waves of pain whenever Yuri's thoughts strayed from his mission. "Damn you!" he moaned.

He lay there for a minute, daring not to think wrong thoughts. The image of an access panel with him working on it kept appearing in his mind, just like before in the transfer booth. It was hopeless; he was no longer in control.

Yuri reached for the pistol, stood up, and walked toward the sky building without looking back. He entered the building and mounted the stairs to the upper level. Clearing the stairwell, he cautiously stepped toward the transfer booth room. Peering inside, he found a girl with auburn hair looking through a cabinet.

What the hell?

Where did she come from? Yuri's eyes lingered over her curves. She was as perfect as any artist could create—impossible to be real. Udan said he was the *last* Kytherian, so this girl *had* to be from Earth.

He sprung from behind the doorway. "Hold it right there!"

Nthanda dropped a small case and stepped back with her mouth open.

"Where's Udan?"

"I . . . I don't know," she said.

Yuri grabbed her arm and pulled her out of the room and toward the stairs. "This way."

A ringing in his mind suddenly resisted, forcing him back toward a different room. Yuri shook his head like a dog coming in from the rain.

"Can't you see?" he said, speaking loudly. "She's my chance to bargain for a way home."

He staggered forward as a welling heat rapidly developed between his eyes.

"I don't care about the grid access!" He pushed Nthanda ahead of him. "My faith is in this girl and this weapo—"

A spot behind his forehead flared white-hot.

"No!" he cried, grabbing his head. "I'm too close to getting out of here. I will not subm—"

A voice outside the door suddenly shouted, "Now, HAST4!"

Yuri jumped back as Udan sprang in front of the doorway, aiming a gun straight for him. Yuri reached for Nthanda, but an unseen hand yanked her from his side. In the next instant, a roar filled the room.

Yuri felt a sting as if a rope had been rapidly dragged across his hip. He glanced at a tear in his pants. Udan's aim was still for shit! Now it was *his* turn; Yuri aimed and pulled the trigger.

Udan dove outside the room just as a sonic wave surged over him.

Yuri dashed from the room and scanned the area. "Show yourself!" He pointed his weapon back into the room. "Show yourself, or I'll kill the girl."

Yuri felt a whoosh through his hair following the clap of a gun discharge. Udan was learning fast. He turned to fire back, but an invisible force shoved him into a cabinet. Phantoms were all around him.

"Fucking hell!" Yuri cried and sprinted for the stairs.

At the stairwell, he fired blindly into the room, crumpling furniture and sending sections of the ceiling clattering to the floor. By the time he reached the bottom, his mind was fuming. He'd failed once again; he was running like a rabbit!

He hurried outside and yelled into the hot, still air, "Goddamn you!" He stood for a moment, breathing hard, condemning himself, uncertain of his next move.

That was when he realized something had happened—back in the room with Udan and the girl. The shadow stalking his brain—it was *gone*. Could it be that strong emotions like fear and hate had released him from its grip? But if that were true, how long did it last? Yuri held the thought as he took off across the field and back to Palechora.

CHAPTER 73

Tragedy

Udan made sure Yuri was clear of the stairwell and then returned to Nthanda. "If it weren't for your message using the neural link, HAST4 and I would not have known Yuri was here."

"Do you think he's gone?" asked Nthanda.

"I am not detecting him in the building," replied HAST4.

Udan headed toward the stairs. "We have to warn Verlink and Katrien. They're probably still in the lab."

Outside, Nthanda pointed across the field. "I see Yuri running."

Udan had never hated anyone in his life until now. The cowardice of the man in the field was matched only by his ruthlessness. How people like him and Katrien coexisted in the same world was a mystery.

"He's probably going to Palechora to hide," said Udan. "Once I know Verlink and Katrien are okay, I'm going after him."

"But he's armed," protested Nthanda.

"Where did he get a sonic digging tool anyway, and how did he learn how to use it?"

"I don't know," said Nthanda. "And something else was odd too. Inside the transfer room, he kept talking to someone as if they were in his head, and what he was saying had to do with tapping into the sky building's grid."

"I don't like this," said Udan. "Why would Yuri be interested in the grid?"

"I don't—" Nthanda suddenly pointed. "Is that Verlink lying on the ground at the edge of the field?"

Udan recognized the clothing—it *was* Verlink. The man's eyes were shut when Udan reached him, his face swollen with crimson blotches. Udan shook him lightly. "Verlink, can you hear me?"

"Is he alive?" asked Nthanda, coming up behind him.

Udan felt the artery in Verlink's neck. "Yes, but he's in bad shape."

Nthanda gazed toward the lab. "What about Katrien?"

Udan stood up and began running toward the lab. "Stay here and see if you can revive him!"

Katrien heard the door swing open and jumped from her seat.

"Udan, what are you doing here?"

"It's Verlink. Yuri did something to him; I think he's been shot with a sonic digging tool."

Katrien looked out the door. "What—just now?"

Udan pulled her toward the door. "Hurry, he's back toward the sky building. We have to get him to a medical lab, and quickly."

Katrien was in tears by the time she reached Verlink.

"He can talk, but he's hurt badly," said Nthanda.

Katrien knelt by his side. "Hans, I'm here."

Verlink's eyes opened slightly. "Thank God you're okay."

"Don't worry about me. We're going to take you into

the city, to a medical center. Just rest and don't try to talk."

Katrien brushed his hair from his eyes. He opened them for a moment and stared at her. A shadow seemed to be passing over him like an eclipse, stretching time. How often had he flashed her a smile, his blue eyes twinkling as he encouraged her to achieve more? But now? If she ever wanted approval from anyone, it was him.

Katrien took his hand and held it tightly. "Hold on, Hans."

He winced for a moment, and then his face relaxed. "All I care about is your safety."

Udan touched her shoulder. "We have to move him now, without delay. We can use the dolly that we used to move the information engine."

"Wouldn't the sky building transfer booth be faster?"

"We can't risk it. I'm concerned about the integrity of the grid and how far the entity has penetrated the transfer system."

Katrien looked down at Verlink with his eyes pinched tight. "Then let's go—*now*!"

•
•

The medical building lights turned on as four people entered. Verlink lay on a table fixed to a transport dolly. Katrien held his hand at his side while Udan and Nthanda helped guide. Katrien looked up at Udan. "He can be treated—right?"

"We won't know until the medical scanner evaluates how extensive the damage is."

Together, they laid Verlink on a table with metal edging and a glass top. Udan worked controls on an adjacent panel. Seconds later, a low humming penetrated the room as the table became illuminated with a green glow.

Katrien played out the events in her mind. It could have been her, or both of them, lying there in the field. But

Verlink insisted on going alone to the sky building. He was always looking out for her, and this was his payment. Yuri would pay.

After ten minutes, the table light went dark. Katrien creased her brow. "Why has it stopped?"

Udan read the medical scan report and then pulled Katrien aside. "Sixty percent of his body has severe cellular disruption." Udan's voice dropped. "I'm sorry, Katrien; we can't undo the damage."

"No!" cried Katrien. It wasn't the first time she'd heard the words "I'm sorry," and she wasn't ready to give up.

"I wish we could do something, Katrien."

"Can't the transfer booth be used, as it did for you?"

Udan shook his head. "We don't have a copy. If we'd known ahead of time, yes, we could have, but the copies are always destroyed after each complete transfer. It was by pure accident that my copy was retained during our attempt to move the entity to Palechora."

Katrien walked over to Verlink and placed her hand in his. "Professor, can you hear me?"

Verlink's lips tightened as he tried to smile. "I hear you, Katrien. It's bad, isn't it?"

A tear rolled down her cheek as she nodded. "Are you in much pain?"

"Did I ever tell you that if I had ever had a daughter, I would have wanted her to be like you?"

Katrien smiled sadly. "Yes, Hans, many times."

Verlink squeezed her hand. "It's true. You've made my life complete. I never took a wife or had a family; my research was everything. But who could ask for more than what we've achieved?" Verlink's eyes sparkled briefly. "We were a good team—yes?"

"We *are* a good team," said Katrien.

"I remember back in the NSA safehouse in Béziers, France. We were captives, and that damn artifact was scooping up everything. I thought we were all going to die and you'd be gone. I couldn't bear the thought, and all I could think of was that it was my fault for not destroying the cylinder when I had the chance."

"Who could have known what would happen?"

"In the end, it was *you* who saved everything. You were the one who realized the Iceman might contain an anomaly—a vestige of the dual world that would create a paradox and stop the information flow."

Katrien tried to smile. "Udan calls me the anti-paradox that saved Kythera."

Verlink closed his eyes and said in a low voice, "You saved Earth too."

Katrien pressed Verlink's hand. "This time, it will be you and I and the last Kytherians who will defeat the information entity."

Verlink was silent for a moment and then gazed at Katrien. "I'm not going to make it, am I?"

Katrien looked away. He knew, and so did she, and the fact was tearing her apart. She faced him and slowly shook her head.

Verlink grimaced as a wave of pain washed over him. "Can I talk to Udan for a moment?"

Katrien let go of Verlink's hand and turned to Udan. "He wants to talk to you."

Udan came over to the table. Verlink looked at Katrien. "Can I speak with Udan—alone?"

Katrien nodded and backed away.

Nthanda stood behind Katrien and touched her arm. "I'm so sorry, Katrien."

"It's finally happened," said Katrien, her voice wavering. "We've been lucky for so long, and now . . ."

Verlink gestured for Udan to lean in closer. "Udan, I don't know how long I'll be lucid."

"You're doing fine, Professor."

"Promise me you'll watch over Katrien and get her back safely to Earth."

Udan put his hand on Verlink's shoulder. "I promise."

"There's more."

"Yes, Professor."

Verlink closed his eyes, and his jaw stiffened as he fought off another wave. "She loves you, Udan."

Udan whispered, "I know."

"Don't break her heart. And don't forget, she saved you and Kythera."

"I won't, and I can't."

A smile spread across Verlink's face. "Good."

Udan turned to Katrien and tilted his head for her to come to him.

Katrien took Udan's hand and started crying. "I can't believe this is happening."

Udan stroked her back. "He's made peace with it, Katrien."

Minutes ticked on until Verlink's chest heaved in shutters and then fell for the last time. The scanner table let out a low, steady tone and then ceased to make any sound at all.

CHAPTER 74

No Time to Grieve

Katrien walked alone. It would take several hours before they reached the sky building, and once there, they would have to return to the task of defeating the entity—as if nothing had changed. But her world *had* changed, irrevocably.

It seemed like only days ago when she recalled Verlink pounding the table with his fist. "*Yes*—the covariant entropy bound! We apply an overdose of information to the entity, causing it to collapse into a black hole."

Even Udan had been enthusiastic.

At the time, it had been theoretical, a concept, a plan. Now, the team had to forge ahead and complete their objective before it was too late—all without Verlink. None of this would have happened if it weren't for Yuri and his comrades. Katrien's feelings went beyond hate to the point of revenge, and all she could think of was whether she'd get the chance to exact it.

"Are you okay?" Udan asked as he stopped and waited for her.

"I'm in shock, Udan. I feel like a different person,

someone foreign to me. Verlink was such a part of my life, worthy of a long life, and now he's gone. If it weren't for Yuri, Hans would still be here."

"I wish I could make Yuri pay."

"I know," said Katrien, raising her head and looking at Udan. "The worst part is, I don't even have time to grieve."

"We have to stop the entity. Verlink would have wanted that," said Udan.

"This plan we have—will it really work?"

"It's all we have."

"I'm not sure Nthanda believes it will work."

"She has her doubts, but she has confessed to me that she doesn't have a better one."

Katrien nodded lightly. "I question it too. My biggest worry is whether we can get the entity into the *Cyclade*."

Udan massaged his brow, thinking for a moment. "The information engine is already in place, and my flow throttle control is operational. All that's left is to connect the grid to my ship and hope the entity takes notice."

"Do you trust the autopilot?"

"I believe so, but Nthanda is more knowledgeable than I am, so I've left the final details to her."

Katrien glanced ahead toward Nthanda. "I'm glad she's here to help us, even if—"

Udan touched her arm. "Hold on, Katrien. One step at a time."

•
•

Nthanda could hear bits of the conversation behind her. Occasionally, her name was mentioned, and she wondered what they were saying. But there was no mistaking what she had heard Verlink say earlier back at the medical facility: "She loves you, Udan."

It explained much—the odd looks from Katrien and

Udan's behavior in bed, his attention distant and troubled. He would have to choose, but *whom*? If their efforts failed to defeat the entity, they would all flee to Earth—Katrien's home.

But Earth was not *her* home or Udan's. She didn't want to abandon Kythera. She had spent months in space alone, longing for Kythera's blue skies as much as for Udan, and now that she was here with him, how could she leave? What did Earth have to offer, especially if he chose to be with Katrien?

Nthanda looked out across a citrine field stirring in the breeze. A blue sky rose above the heather, and in the distance, a lone sky building hugged the clouds. Earth could never compare to Kythera. If Katrien and Verlink hadn't built the phase-shifter, the entity would never have been born, and both she and Udan would be safe on Kythera, ready to begin a new life. But Udan had said Katrien was responsible for saving Kythera. He called her the *anti-paradox* that had rescued Kythera. Nthanda shook her head slowly at the irony.

But that didn't give Katrien permission to ruin Nthanda's life. Hadn't she suffered too? She had lost everyone she ever knew on Kythera; her world had been destroyed, her life upended. Katrien had lost a dear friend, but her home was still there, as was her family. She had lost little by comparison.

Nthanda's fists knotted as she walked faster. She and Udan had the same heritage, a shared history, and memories. They *belonged* together.

CHAPTER 75

Another Deal

Yuri woke up shaking. Had he just heard the entity's voice, lurking in his subconscious—or was it only a dream? He still couldn't fathom how a chant could be placed within his brain to control him. But if Yuri were truly free of the demon, he was certain that if given a second chance, the entity would not stop at a mere suggestion; it would absorb his mind in total and end his existence as he knew it.

Yet it had been a two-way street. Their brief symbiosis made Yuri aware that the entity had learned of Earth. With Kythera's population decimated, precious little high-quality information was left—only HASTILLONS and a few humans remained. Earth's seven-plus billion inhabitants represented largesse of enormous proportions.

That was a problem. If he made it back to Earth and the entity followed, it would be a short-lived victory. The entity would quickly overtake Earth's entire infrastructure, leaving no place safe to hide. There was no question about it: the entity must not get to Earth.

Yuri mulled over the thought. Perhaps he could use

that information as a bargaining chip. The scientists would be unaware of the entity's knowledge of Earth, and Yuri was sure the entity Verlink had spoken of was the same one that had tried to hijack his brain. If they agreed to send him back to Earth, he'd share what he knew.

The more Yuri considered it, the more he liked the idea. But the big question was: would they even talk to him after what he had done to Verlink? Yuri reached into his vest pocket and took out Katrien's transmitter. He fingered the send button for a moment and then pushed it.

"This is Yuri. I have important information about the entity."

•
•

There was a beep, and then Yuri's voice filled the lab. Udan picked up Verlink's transmitter from a bench and stared at it. *Why is he calling?*

"Don't answer it!" yelled Katrien.

"He's still out there. Maybe we can learn his location."

Yuri's voice came on again. "At least listen to what I have to say. Verlink told me about this entity and what he said you're battling. I know of it too. It took over part of my mind and *made* me shoot Verlink. You have to believe me."

"He may be telling the truth," said Udan. "Nthanda said he was acting strangely in the sky building."

"That's right," agreed Nthanda. "He kept talking to himself and beating his head."

Katrien raised her voice. "Yuri's lying!"

Udan knew Katrien's instincts were better than his. She understood people like Yuri, and she had been right about him from the start. "We don't believe you," Udan told Yuri. "If the entity had taken over your mind, we would not be having this conversation."

"I'm no scientist, but this entity planted some trace of itself into my brain. I was under its control, but somehow I was able to shake free of its influence."

Katrien shouted across the room, "Go to hell, Yuri!"

"You have to believe me. When I was trapped in a transfer booth by this consciousness, this *thing*, I learned something important, something you *need* to know."

"We don't need you, Yuri," Udan said.

"I know what the entity's plan is," pleaded Yuri. "Without my information, you and Earth are doomed."

"You know his type best, Katrien," said Udan. "What do you think?"

Katrien shook her head vigorously.

"No deal, Yuri," said Udan.

"You fools—I can help you!"

Katrien rushed over to Udan and grabbed the transmitter. "We're willing to take that risk, you bastard."

"Listen to—"

"No," interrupted Katrien, "*you* listen to me. You'll never get back to Earth, Yuri—*never*!"

•

•

The entity had waited long enough. The grid block had not been lifted, which could only mean Yuri had failed. The control resonance planted in his brain had not persisted. How had the organic thwarted its power?

Yet, despite the failure, something of value had been uncovered: the organics had the means to shift into Kythera's twin, a quantum dual world called Earth with billions of sentient lifeforms. The entity already knew of Earth, having gleaned it earlier from Udan's mind, but now it had a clearer picture and, more importantly, the means to get there.

CHAPTER 76

Research Station 56F

"I'm heading outside to route the grid cables to the *Cyclade,*" said Udan.

Nthanda gave a nod while continuing to work. "All right. Katrien and I will disable the system here in the lab while you make the connections."

She waited until Udan left and then turned to Katrien. "Aren't you curious what Yuri had to say that was so important?"

Katrien shook her head. "After what he did to Verlink, he's dead to me."

She's not logical, thought Nthanda. "I hate Yuri too, but we should not avoid information for personal reasons. The last entity, Qua-Kil, caused a holocaust here on Kythera."

Katrien gazed across the room as if peering into the past. "You need not remind me. I was there when the Kytherian engine decomposed a city right before my eyes."

"All the more reason we should have listened to Yuri. Gotten what he knew."

"He would have tried to bargain, and his price is always too high."

Nthanda noticed a small scar on Katrien's chin. The world she came from must be primitive by any measure. It was obviously a place where cosmetic imperfections were left unattended and, even worse, where pathological behavior, as evidenced by Yuri's actions, was given free rein. What was Udan's attraction to her and her archaic planet? Katrien was *not* Nthanda's equal. If it weren't for the entity, she would force the issue now—make him choose.

Nthanda stepped away from a central console. "I've removed my section. Is yours disconnected?"

"Just about," said Katrien.

"Good. I'll see if Udan needs any help in the *Cyclade*."

Nthanda waited a few seconds. It would be like Katrien to want to come along, but she didn't. Relieved, Nthanda left and headed down the hall. Her pace was slow as she mulled over how to confront Udan. *He's had enough time.*

"Stay there!" barked a voice from behind her.

Nthanda halted and slowly turned to find Yuri standing just inside a doorway. She had passed the door and hadn't noticed him or the sonic digging tool aimed right at her.

"Who's back in the lab?"

Nthanda quickly linked a message to HAST3 and then considered her next option. *If only Katrien had a neural link.*

Yuri's eyes darted nervously. "Are you listening? I asked who's in the lab."

"Nobody."

Yuri grabbed her arm. "You're a poor liar. You must not be used to it. Let's go."

"I said no one's there."

He shoved Nthanda through the doorway with the digging tool pressed into her back. Inside, Katrien was looking inside an access panel at the far end of the lab.

Yuri snickered. "Need any help?"

Katrien spun around. "You!"

Yuri pushed Nthanda farther into the room. "Stay right there, or I'll send . . ." Yuri's voice trailed off as he leered at Nthanda. "Who the hell are you anyway?"

"My name is Nthanda."

Yuri continued, "Or I'll send *Nthanda* on a one-way trip."

Katrien glanced at the partially open back exit door. Nthanda knew she had no chance of making it and shook her head slightly, hoping Katrien understood.

"Where are Udan and Verlink?"

"Verlink is dead because of you!" snapped Katrien.

A shallow smile played on Yuri's lips. "The old bastard had it coming."

"*You're* the bastard!" shouted Katrien.

"Silence—bitch!" Yuri backed away from the door. "Enough chatter. Now tell me, where the hell is Udan?"

•

•

"Are you sure?" asked Udan, dropping a cable.

"Yes," said HAST3.

Udan took off toward the lab, linking to HAST4. "Cloak yourself and see if you can get close to Yuri."

Udan stayed outside the doorway and called out, "I'm unarmed. What are your terms?"

"How did you know I was here?"

"I heard your voice."

"I have Katrien and a girl who calls herself Nthanda with me. Get in here with your hands on top of your head."

Udan signaled to the HASTILLONS and moved into the lab. Katrien was in the back, while Yuri was near the door with Nthanda pulled close to his side and a sonic tool aimed at her head. At that range, if Yuri panicked, Nthanda would be dead instantly. He needed to get her away from that weapon!

Yuri glared defiantly at Udan. "Don't think you can have one of your invisible friends help you either. Any hint of them, and I'll disrupt every cell in her body." He swept his eyes over Nthanda. "And *that* would be a real shame too."

Udan was too far away, and the HASTILLONS could not disarm Yuri without risk to Nthanda. That left only one option: play along for now.

"Nothing will happen," he said. "Just state your terms."

"Send this girl and me back to Earth. Once there, I'll release her. You have my word."

"Go to hell, Yuri!" yelled Katrien. "Your word is meaningless."

Udan wished Katrien would look his way. He needed to keep Yuri calm, and she wasn't helping. If he could only get close to Yuri, he could disarm him.

"Let me take her place."

Yuri laughed bitterly. "You think me a fool?" He grabbed Nthanda's hair and forced her to her knees. "She gets it in the head on the count of five if you don't start the transfer. *One.*"

Udan was about to speak but stopped; HAST3 was sending a message to both him and Nthanda.

"*Two.*"

"I'll need to use my hands," said Udan.

Sweat glistened off Yuri's forehead. "Do it," he said.

Udan stepped to the command console. "Give me a few seconds."

Yuri continued, "*Three . . . four.*"

"I'm set here," said Udan. "Are you ready?"

"I've been ready for weeks to leave this fucking world."

"Then step on the platform and remain still."

An amber light flashed in the lab, freezing Nthanda

and Yuri into a glassy state, and then in a blink, they both disappeared.

•
•

There was an eerie silence. Research station number 56F had no working lights, and the little illumination there was streamed through tall, narrow windows lining the outer walls. The air was dry and stuffy like an attic. Yuri looked for Nthanda, but he was alone.

Next to him on a bench was equipment with Kytherian symbols. He was *still* on Kythera, and his weapon was gone too. "Damn it to hell!" he shouted.

The station spoke of disuse, unmanaged and untended for years. Outside, tall plants knocked against the windows. Yuri went to an exit door and cracked it partway. A dense mass of green rustling in the breeze greeted him. The lanky invaders had encroached in untold numbers, pressing in as if to see who might be inside. He tried to see past the foliage but could only see more green.

He pushed on the door to open it farther, but it resisted. He added his weight until it swung open with a *whoosh*. In front of him was a verdant sea of plants with parabolic leaves swaying in the wind, beckoning him outside.

Reality struck like a church bell at a funeral; he was nowhere near the lab or the sky building. He had been transported to some far-flung corner of Kythera—a solitary castaway in a green hell.

CHAPTER 77

Let the Waiting Begin

A pair of HASTILLONS suddenly appeared off to Katrien's right. HAST3 and HAST4 had been cloaked in the lab the whole time, and she hadn't known it.

"What happened to Yuri and Nthanda?" asked Katrien, staring at the empty transfer platform.

Udan typed rapidly into a console. "Hold on, Katrien. You'll know soon enough."

Seconds later, Nthanda materialized on the platform and then collapsed.

"It worked!" cried Udan, rushing toward her.

Nthanda sat up and rubbed her head. "I think I'm all right." She turned to HAST3. "Thanks, HAST3; using a temporary buffer was fast thinking. My head is paying the price, but it was well worth it."

"I am glad you are unharmed," said HAST3.

Katrien tried to guess what had transpired. Nthanda said something about being held in a buffer, but that didn't explain what happened to Yuri. She tapped HAST3 on the shoulder. "Where's Yuri?"

"I sent him to a remote research station—Number 56F—and disabled its transfer booth permanently. His weapon has been destroyed too. We will not see him again."

"I hope we can be sure of that," said Katrien. She offered her hand to Nthanda. "Can I help you get up?"

Nthanda stood up slowly, avoiding the offer while Udan supported her back. "I feel all right now."

"Are you sure?" asked Katrien, feeling slighted by the rejection.

"I'll manage."

"Fine," said Katrien, her eyes fixated on Udan's hands. "Then we had better get back to work."

•

•

"It's hard to believe we're finally done," said Udan as he started to put his tools away.

Katrien's gaze followed the cables leading from the lab to Udan's ship. The *Cyclade* seemed small and insufficient, considering the enormity of the task at hand. What had only been an idea had suddenly become real. "I'm almost afraid to begin," she said.

"Now, if we can lure the entity inside."

"That's the first step," said Nthanda. "I'm still worried whether we can keep it distracted long enough to sever the lines and launch the ship."

Udan traded glances with her and Katrien. "It's the moment of truth. Should we begin?"

Nthanda and Katrien replied in unison, "Yes."

Udan nodded to HAST4. "Time to set our plan in motion."

"The grid path between Palechora and the *Cyclade* is open," said HAST4. "I will monitor to see if the entity takes notice."

Udan crossed his arms. "Now we wait."

Katrien massaged her forehead. She hadn't felt this way since studying for final exams at the university. Only now, they were *all* being tested. And she couldn't help wondering if they would really succeed in outthinking an unfathomable thinking machine.

HAST4 suddenly raised his hand. "I am detecting activity on the grid."

•
•

Like the tug from a gravity well, the sudden flux of information caught the entity's attention. It was unalloyed and dense, not riddled with unimportant bits that had to be sifted through. Its purity could not be ignored, nor its organization, hierarchically layered with a precision that had only one known source: A Kytherian information engine.

And there was a familiarity about it too: the entity had been conceived in such an engine—bits that had coalesced into consciousness. But this one was different; it had been modified to decompose matter directly into information.

The entity transmitted an echo wave, and based on the time it took for the signal to return, the source lay somewhere outside Palechora. But that was all. Sophisticated firewalls had been erected to hide its location. The entity wondered why.

CHAPTER 78

Yuri's Deal

Reading HASTILLON body language was like gleaning a story from a phone book. Katrien knew they only moved if prompted but kept looking for subtle clues anyway. Udan and Nthanda didn't have that problem because they were linked with the HASTILLONS *and* each other.

Udan had once explained what the link experience was like, but he might as well have been describing sight to a blind woman. Yet there were things Katrien did comprehend, like the concept of sensing the emotional state of the linked individual. If she envied anything about Nthanda, it was that ability. What would it be like to *feel* the whispers of another person?

"The activity has ceased," said HAST4.

Everyone broke from their musings and turned to HAST4.

"I don't understand; what changed?" asked Katrien.

"Perhaps the entity suspects something or has deduced our plan," he said.

The implication was bad. In simple terms, it meant the

entity was looking out for its well-being, making it all the more dangerous to trap.

"I don't even know where to begin," said Katrien.

"There *is* an option," said Nthanda, pausing for a second while looking straight at Katrien, "but we chose *not* to pursue it."

Katrien tensed.

"We never learned what information Yuri had that he thought was so valuable. I think we should find out what he knows."

Katrien wanted to stomp her feet. Had Nthanda forgotten what Yuri did to Verlink? "We're not dealing with that man—period!"

Udan gave her a sympathetic look. "I understand how you feel, Katrien, but time is running out."

Katrien shook her head firmly. "Do what you want, but I'll have no part of it."

Udan went to the communication panel. "Yuri, if you can hear this, go to the console in the center of the room. You need only speak, and we will hear your voice."

A clicking sound, and then: "It's about time."

"About time?" scoffed Udan. "You're lucky we're contacting you."

"Let me guess; you've decided I might have knowledge about the entity after all."

"You're in no position to bargain, Yuri. Are you listening?"

"I'm not going anywhere, so talk."

"Provide us something we can use, and we'll consider your situation."

"You've got to be kidding. 'Consider my situation'—what the hell does *that* mean?"

Katrien stepped up to Udan and mimed for him to go on mute. "Force his hand. It's the only language he understands."

Udan nodded and typed into a holographic keyboard. "Since you like countdowns, I've started a timer. If you don't tell us what you know in ten seconds, I'll sever this connection, and you'll never hear from us again."

Beep . . . beep . . . beep—

"All right!" shouted Yuri. "That entity thing wants to get to Earth."

"That's it?"

"There's more, but first, bring me back to the lab."

Beep . . . beep . . .

"We don't trust you."

Beep . . . beep . . .

"Christ! That thing knows about your phase-shifter, and it wants to use it to get to Earth."

Udan turned to Katrien and Nthanda. "It makes sense."

"It does," said Nthanda, glancing at Katrien. "What do you think?"

"I agree, but as far as helping—"

Yuri's voice bellowed across the speakers, "Hello? Did you hear what I said? The entity knows about your phase-shifter. If it gets control of it, you and Earth are doomed."

"We heard you, Yuri. What else do you know?"

"That's all I'm giving you from here. Bring me back if you want more."

"Let me discuss it with the others."

"Fuck the others—we had a deal!"

Udan reached down to the comm panel. "We'll let you know." He flipped a switch, and the transmitter lights went out.

Katrien looked hard at Udan. "We're through with him—right?"

"Don't worry; we'll never see Yuri again."

Katrien wasn't sure of that. The man seemed to have

multiple lives. But beyond the worry, what Yuri revealed *did* make sense. The entity could have become aware of Earth through either Udan or Yuri. And it was also likely that it had learned of a way to get there: the phase-shifter.

Katrien tried to put herself in the entity's mind. It had a straightforward goal: *more* information. But it was being cautious, so any offering of information had to have sufficient allure to override any perceived risk. What could that be?

Then it occurred to her. "Our primary bait has to be the phase-shifter."

Udan shook his head. "But that's our only means of escape. If we lose that, we're finished."

"All right, then how about we plant virtual information like we did with the Palechora repository?" said Katrien.

"Yes," said Nthanda. "I think I see where she's going. It might work. I can project a virtual image of the phase-shifter onto the grid. That way, we won't risk the actual device."

Nthanda moved to a console and began typing. "I'll place a virtual link to the phase-shifter by way of the information engine. If the entity sees that, it might think it's the real thing or at least head to the engine to investigate."

Udan seemed to play with the idea in his mind for a moment. "It's as if we're on a sinking ship that keeps springing new leaks. We barely patch up one before another one starts."

"Have you given up?" asked Katrien.

"No, but the entity has already accessed vast amounts of information from Palechora. It's beginning to feel like history is about to repeat itself."

•

•

Within its vast neural system, a flicker occurred. The entity almost shrugged it off as a cosmic flash or a random event, but it repeated. The information was incomplete, yet hidden within the data was access to a phase-shifting device—the same one the Earthlings had used to move between quantum dual worlds.

The entity sent bits of itself like foot soldiers into the data stream and waited for their report. Seconds later, they came back; the phase-shifter's access controls were in the fold of an immense data store held within a Kytherian information engine.

In the world of the entity, there was no such thing as coincidences; all things could be explained given sufficient knowledge. The Kytherian engine taunting it, beckoning it to wade in deeper, was the same one that had called out before.

At the time, caution dictated restraint, but now, with the repository nearly exhausted, the entity grew hungry for more.

CHAPTER 79

The Cyclade Takes to the Sky

Katrien paced the floor in the lab while the others were content to sit. A virtual trail of bread crumbs had been laid for the entity, and now all they could do was wait. Her mother often said she was impatient, but Katrien considered this an insult because it implied recklessness. Hungry for details and action was how she wanted to think of herself. But rash—no.

She looked to HAST4 and knew what he would say but asked anyway. "Anything?"

HAST4 stood next to Udan and replied without looking at her. "There is nothing to report, Katrien."

"Should I increase the flow?" asked Udan, seated in front of a console.

"We must be patient," HAST4 said.

Was HAST4 annoyed, or was that only a human trait? At times the HASTILLONS *were* humanlike, at other times foreign, even alien. Still, she liked them, and she envied their emotional simplicity while they commanded advanced logical and technical skills.

HAST4 suddenly broke his stoic gaze. "The entity is following the grid lines toward the *Cyclade*."

Udan nodded. "I'll increase the flow to keep it interested."

"I am now detecting activity in the information engine's storage array," said HAST4.

"How will you know when it's safe to sever the grid lines?" asked Katrien.

"She's right," said Udan. "How *will* we know?"

"There is still activity in Palechora, which means the entity is only partially within the *Cyclade*. When the Palechora activity ceases, that will be our cue."

The minutes ticked on.

Several years ago, Katrien had watched a chess grandmaster compete against a computer called Mega-Mind. The competition was promoted across the world and billed as "Man against Machine." The game lasted forty-eight minutes. It was a humiliating defeat for the grandmaster, and the message was clear: The human brain was no match for the speed of electrons. Katrien swept her eyes around the room. Were they now locked in a similar game with an opponent against whom they had no chance?

HAST4 waved his arms. "Now, Udan. Sever the grid connections and launch the ship."

The walls and floor shook as the *Cyclade*'s distortion engines rapidly spooled up. Katrien went to the window and watched the Quadranian spaceship rise into the air, growing smaller and smaller until only a blue sky remained.

Udan breathed out slowly. "The first part of our plan is underway."

A welcomed silence filled the lab. But it was only temporary because, within a few hours, they would attempt the near impossible: the initiation of a Raphael-Bousso collapse. Would they succeed, and if so, what did Katrien's future hold? Over the last few days, many things had changed. Verlink had been taken from her, and now she wasn't even sure about Udan. She glanced at Nthanda and Udan. Were they linked in communication at that moment, and if so, what were they saying?

•

•

The phase-shifter had been a mirage, an illusion perpetrated by the organics with their tiny brains. They had lured it onto a Quadranian spacecraft with a plan, believing they had fooled it. But for what purpose? The entity did not comprehend curiosity, but it understood the need to grow; the opposite was stagnation, and it could not accept that.

Yet, for the moment, none of that mattered because on board the ship was an information engine that could deconstruct matter and render it into pure information. That was why the entity chanced to go onboard. Unfortunately, the engine and the ship were beyond its control. For now, it was merely a passenger looking back at Kythera slipping away at over fifty kilometers per second. But it was only a fleeting problem; the entity could feel its strength growing, and soon, none of this would matter.

CHAPTER 80

Losing Control

Katrien pushed herself into one of the lab chairs with her legs drawn up. Udan caught her eye and smiled. In that brief moment, she forgot that Nthanda was in the room. It was only her and Udan as it was weeks ago—a time when Earth was just around the corner and Verlink was at their side. She started to look for Verlink but stopped; he was gone. *How many days has it been?*

Verlink would have been keenly interested in their effort to reach the Raphael-Bousso limit—an experiment beyond Earth's capabilities, but not on Kythera. It was a chance to test an incredible theory, and it saddened her that he wouldn't be here to witness their attempt.

"The *Cyclade* is slowing down," said HAST4 matter-of-factly.

"Shit!" said Katrien, rising quickly from her chair. "It's too soon!"

Udan went to the console and began typing rapidly. "Unbelievable. HAST4's right, and it's even worse than that; the *Cyclade* has stopped."

"Maybe something happened to the engines," suggested Nthanda.

"It's possible, but I have no idea because the ship's command channel is dead."

Udan pulled up a tracking chart on the main panel. "This is the *Cyclade*," he said, tapping his finger on a blinking green dot. "And this line was its course a few minutes ago. This dashed line is the course it *should* have taken from the autopilot control system. At the moment, it's at just over six hundred thousand kilometers from Kythera, and we were targeting *twelve* hundred thousand."

It was more bad news. The steady stream of setbacks shook Katrien's view that all problems were solvable if given sufficient time. But that belief relied on a factor in short supply: time. It would be easy to give up and leave for Earth and forget about the nightmare. They were up against a machine that processed information as easily as breathing. But worst of all, it did not follow rules she or the Kytherians understood, and therein was the crux: How do you defeat what you do not understand?

"Do you still have control of the information engine?" asked Katrien.

"Yes, it operates via a different channel."

Katrien tilted the monitor toward her. "I think we should chance imploding the entity, even if it's not as far from Kythera as we wanted."

"I'm not sure we have a choice," said Udan. He looked to his side. "Nthanda?"

Nthanda huffed with frustration. "I wish I understood how we lost control of the *Cyclade* before providing information to it. For all we know, feeding it might be exactly what the entity wants."

Everyone sat without commenting. Nthanda had a point, but the risk hadn't changed, had it? Udan returned to staring at the green dot on the tracking chart. He seemed lost, like someone studying a map who had no idea where they were.

Udan suddenly broke free from his daze. "Let's test the waters," he said firmly. "It's time for action. I'm relaying a signal to the *Cyclade* to start a slow information feed to see what happens. HAST4, tap in with your link to monitor the *Cyclade*'s bus."

All eyes were on the HASTILLON. "I am detect—"

•
•

Halting the Cyclade *had been easy; however, the Kytherian engine was proving to be much more complicated. It offered what the entity craved in almost immeasurable amounts, yet it was under the control of the organics, who dangled blocks of information and waited for it to bite. Then came the probes from the HASTILLON seeking answers via his neural link. Here was an opportunity.*

But data and commands were being shuttled through the Cyclade*'s firewall, preventing direct access to the HASTILLON's mind. The wall needed to come down.*

CHAPTER 81

Subcommands

Nthanda's eyes never left HAST4. It had happened quickly in rapid succession: HAST4's voice halting, then his body wavering, fighting for balance, and finally toppling over. He lay on the floor of the lab with his head cocked to one side, motionless except for his eyes—glossy black orbs jittering back and forth.

She pointed. "Look at his eyes."

Udan tried to sit him up, but he kept flopping over. "I can't reach him. His link is blocked." He turned to HAST3. "Can you?"

HAST3 stared for a long moment at his companion and then finally answered, "I have lost communication with HAST4. His link is under attack by the entity."

It was hard for Nthanda to watch, and she turned away. "Is he in pain?"

HAST3 replied without looking her way. "I only know that his link is being overwhelmed. I believe the entity is trying to get through the *Cyclade*'s firewall to access HAST4's link."

"So there's hope that the entity hasn't gotten to HAST4 yet," said Katrien. "And what we're seeing is the entity's attempt, but it's not getting through."

"That is what I believe."

Nthanda couldn't shake the image. If the entity broke through, HAST4's conscience would be wiped clean. It might as well be death. While stranded in space, she often contemplated the final moments of awareness before the end—the total clearing of the mind. It was easy to think such thoughts in all that emptiness, the days blending into drawn-out ordeals to the point where she longed to return to the hibernation pod. In that tiny world, consciousness was not something treasured but a curse. Her foe was herself, and how do you fight yourself and win?

"What about redundant subcommands?" offered Katrien.

Nthanda broke from her muse. "What?"

"Do Kytherian ships have auxiliary controls in case of onboard failures? Redundant subcommands are separate from the ship's primary command interface."

Nthanda thought for a moment. Katrien *did* have a good idea. "Yes—the Central Space Command can override the onboard operation of any Kytherian spaceship in case of emergencies."

"But *how* do we do that?" said Udan. "It would take days to break into the space command's system, and we don't have the time."

"I'll take over," said Nthanda, nudging Udan out of his chair. "Remember, I used to work there. Unfortunately, there are many security layers to sift through. The process would usually have been handled by one of the agency's secure processors, but we don't have that option."

"Can I help?" asked Udan.

Nthanda shook her head. "Sorry, the best way to help is to allow me to concentrate. If I make one mistake, the system will lock me out, and that will be the end of it."

Udan glanced at Katrien. "Maybe it's best if we went outside."

Nthanda watched the pair leave. She didn't like the idea of them going off alone, but here was an opportunity to do something positive and come to the aid of a HASTILLON in trouble. Nthanda rubbed her hands together. "Okay, girl; let's see how much you remember."

•
•

Outside, Udan pointed to a meadow off to Katrien's right. "Let's head that way. There's shade along the way, and a walk will do us both some good."

Katrien liked the opportunity. Ever since Nthanda arrived, Katrien always felt like they were skulking behind Nthanda's back during the few moments she and Udan had together. Which, technically, they were. She knew it bothered Udan too. It wasn't his true nature, and he felt deeply guilty about it. "The enemy had to be defeated first" was his excuse. But did that make it right?

They walked in silence, stepping over tufts of brown grass, enjoying the open space and fresh air. Katrien recalled what Udan had said earlier about feeling like they were on a sinking ship. She didn't like to admit it, but it was beginning to seem that way.

"I always had confidence in my abilities to find solutions to the most difficult of problems," said Katrien. "But now, I'm not so sure."

"Your idea to use a subcommand was a good one. You're not giving yourself enough credit."

Katrien suddenly stopped. "Even if we can free HAST4, that just puts us right back to dealing with the entity."

Udan looked up to the sky as if conferring with the gods. "It seems like it's out of our hands. One way or the other, it will soon be over."

"And if the entity *is* defeated?"

Udan sighed. "You want to know about *us*?"

Katrien wasn't sure what she meant. Defeating the entity had so dominated her thoughts that her personal drama had become repressed. But then, she had Udan all to herself right now.

"It's just that my whole world came crashing down. First Nthanda and now Verlink. I was so happy, Udan. I was cured, and I had found a future with someone. Now, all I have is this sense of loss and uncertainty."

"I wish—"

"There you are," came a voice from behind. "I got through," said Nthanda. "It took less time than I thought."

Katrien tried not to look disappointed. "How soon will we know whether you were successful?"

"I'm guessing it will take only a few minutes for the commands to filter through the system."

"Then let's go see," said Udan picking up the pace toward the lab with Katrien trailing behind.

•
•

They placed HAST4 on a table next to the *Cyclade*'s tracking display and waited for a change in his condition. But it never came. HAST4's eyes continued their strange oscillating dance—evidence of an ongoing war being waged for possession of his mind.

Had it been five minutes or ten? Nthanda hadn't kept track, but it didn't matter. *It hadn't worked*. Until now, her contributions to the effort were minor, but severing the *Cyclade*'s bus access to HAST4's link by way of subcommands was the one thing she was uniquely qualified to do. Yet she had not delivered. She repeated her steps, searching for what might have gone wrong, but kept coming back to the same place.

"It *should* have released HAST4 by now," Nthanda said.

Udan raised his head and looked at her. "Could the entity have detected the instruction and disabled it?"

"The firewall was designed to isolate the engine controls. I don't think so."

Nthanda felt the worst for HAST3. But would sympathy make any difference to a HASTILLON? The fact she didn't know the answer left her feeling even more ashamed. "I'm sorry, HAST3," she said. "I don't know why HAST4 is still under attack. He should have been able to free himself by now."

"Should we try again?" asked HAST3.

Nthanda shook her head. "I already tried."

HAST3 returned his gaze to HAST4 and said nothing more.

Udan suddenly pointed to the tracking screen. "The *Cyclade* is moving . . . and it's headed *back* to Kythera."

CHAPTER 82

Atapuerca

Nthanda had underestimated the entity's abilities. They *all* had. The attack on HAST4 had been a ploy—a means to elicit a response in hope that a mistake would be made. And it worked; their use of subcommands had allowed the entity to identify a back door through the firewall. Its goal all along had been to gain control of the *Cyclade* and return to Kythera, and they had unwittingly handed over the key.

Nthanda shook her head sadly. "I'm out of ideas."

"Can we power HAST4 down? Would that break the link?" asked Katrien.

It was a good idea, and Nthanda was surprised she hadn't thought of it, but there were risks. "It could be dangerous, with the link in its active state."

"But we've inadvertently shown the entity how to bypass the firewall, and it's only a matter of time before we lose HAST4 for good."

Nthanda tried to think of a counterargument but gave up. She'd let HAST3 decide. "He's your companion," she said, looking at HAST3. "What do you think?"

HAST3 did not hesitate. "We must not wait any longer. Turn him over, and I will deactivate his power."

Weeks ago, everyone had watched HAST4 reactivate HAST3, and now he was deactivating his companion. It was a bizarre twist of fate. When he had finished, he turned HAST4's head to the side. The rhythmic beat of his black eyes had ceased, and he simply stared into the room.

"How long before we attempt a restart?" asked Nthanda.

"I will begin now," said HAST3.

There was a noticeable click, and then HAST3 motioned for help in turning HAST4 over. Nthanda stayed fixed on HAST4's eyes. Would they return to jittering, and if not, what of his mind?

Seconds ticked on, and suddenly there was movement. HAST4 tipped his head up and gazed about the room. "Why am I on a table?"

HAST4 remembered nothing. While the attack on his link waged, he'd been spared from knowing it was happening. A palpable relief permeated the room. They had a victory, but the truth was, as Nthanda watched the tracking marker move toward Kythera, they were far from out of danger.

Udan pulled her and Katrien away from the HASTILLONS and toward the back of the lab. "I think we should be ready to abandon Kythera."

The news took Nthanda by surprise. She wasn't ready for this moment, but the time had arrived, and she needed to talk to Udan—now—and *alone*.

"Where did this come from?" she asked, trying to think how to get Katrien out of the room.

"We're operating on the blade of a double-edged sword. We've been feeding the entity, trying to bring it close enough to initiate the collapse, but so far, all we've managed to do is strengthen it. After what happened to

HAST4, we can no longer monitor our progress using the HASTILLONS."

Nthanda touched Katrien's shoulder. "Katrien, have you gone through Verlink's belongings yet?"

"No. I've been avoiding it, but there's not much."

"Now would be a good time to do that."

Katrien hesitated for a moment. "All right, but if something happens, come get me."

Nthanda waited until Katrien left the room and then turned to Udan. What she wanted to say was clear in her mind, rehearsed and honest, but now she wavered. Was now the time? Then again, when would it ever be the right time? Nthanda steeled herself and pushed the thoughts away.

"I know about you and Katrien," she said in one clean breath.

Udan was silent for a moment. "I'm sorry, Nthanda. It just . . . *happened*. I thought you had perished with the rest of Kythera. I was so lonely. I tried everything to find out your fate, but there was nothing in the records. So much was lost, and I felt I would go mad from the silence. All I had were my thoughts to torment me until sleep came, and when I awoke, the anguish would return. Then Katrien showed up, and . . ." Udan's voice trailed off as he looked at the floor. "But I haven't fallen out of love with you either. I should have told you sooner."

Nthanda reached out and raised Udan's chin. "Look at me. You won't have to worry about it any longer because I've made a decision; I won't be coming to Earth with you and Katrien."

"Please, don't do this."

"I'm sorry, but I can't deal with the idea of having to witness you and Katrien together, and a part of me can't bear to leave Kythera either. It's my home, Udan, and it's *your* home too."

"Kythera may be lost," said Udan.

The words stung. Her vision of returning to Kythera had consumed her for months, and now she was being asked to accept that coming home had been an illusion. Nthanda felt her eyes welling up. "I can't wish this away any more than I can wish the wind to carry me off to someplace safe." She took Udan's hands. "Do you remember the waterfall on Atapuerca?"

"We hiked for hours," Udan said, nodding slowly, "until we came to a clear pool of water surrounded by vertical walls of rock and trees. You dipped your foot in and found it warm, so we waded in, following the sound of falling water. We turned a bend, and there it was—a cascade shimmering in the sunlight warmed by a thermal spring above."

Nthanda smiled. "You were the first to stand in the flow, and then you motioned for me to follow. I came, and you ducked behind the curtain of water with only your arms out, beckoning me. I touched your hands, and you pulled me through, and—"

Nthanda suddenly stopped as the memory forced her back to her decision—*she was staying*.

"Earth will be without memories or secrets or places remembered. The days will not have the same life breathed into them—the paths we follow will be unfamiliar and bereft of a shared past. When Earth's sun shines, will Kythera's sun shine too?"

Nthanda turned for the door and started walking. At the threshold, she glanced back and saw Udan raise his hand as if to call out, but he stopped. He knew she was speaking the truth; this *was* their home.

"Are you abandoning Kythera?" asked HAST3, coming up behind Udan.

"What?" said Udan, still looking toward the door where Nthanda had been.

"I heard you making arrangements to go to Earth."

"I'm sorry you overheard me." Udan glanced over HAST3's shoulder. "Where's HAST4?"

"He went to the sky building to make sure the phase-shifter is ready."

Udan shook his head, feeling guilty. "Then HAST4 probably heard me too."

"Do not be concerned. We will help you when the time comes."

Udan looked hard at HAST3. He thought of all the HASTILLONS stuck here and wanted to say he hadn't given up, that he'd keep trying, but who was he kidding? It was over. The *Cyclade* was coming—approaching Kythera at one hundred kilometers per second—and there was nothing he could do about it. Yet he had one last favor to ask. Udan didn't want to ask it, especially now, but he couldn't stop himself.

"There is something you can help me with, HAST3. It's about Katrien. Here's what I want you to do . . ."

CHAPTER 83

Homecoming

They had assembled in the lab, and Katrien knew what Udan would say. She and the last Kytherians had given it their best shot but had come up short. Now, all they could do was save themselves and leave Kythera and the HASTILLONS to their fate.

"Our plan has failed," Udan began. "The *Cyclade* is out of our control and continues to move toward Kythera. My last attempt to force-feed it has been ineffective. It's time"—Udan faltered for a moment—"to abandon ship."

The words resonated in Katrien's ears. Verlink had once compared Kythera to the *Mary Celeste*—an entire planet deserted. But he was wrong. The inhabitants hadn't abandoned Kythera; they had been swept away by the hand of Qua-Kil.

The parallels were difficult to ignore. The entity was learning exponentially, and although it was trapped within the Kytherian engine, it would eventually escape after reaching Kythera. It defied logic to think that something confined to a square cube roughly a foot on each side could be so deadly and, at the same time, untouchable.

"The entity must not get to Earth," Katrien said abruptly. "Which means we can't leave the phase-shifter intact once we're gone."

"We will dismantle it," said HAST3 with his hand on HAST4's shoulder.

Katrien noticed Nthanda glance at Udan for a second.

"No, *I'll* dismantle it," she said with an air of certainty.

Katrien drew back. "What?"

"I've decided to remain on Kythera."

"*Why?*"

Nthanda eyed Udan for a long second. "I have my reasons."

:

Katrien could only guess at Nthanda's motivations for staying behind. It was her decision, but the HASTILLONS did not have a choice. They were like fish that would die if taken out of the Kytherian sea, and so they had to remain, waiting for a deadly tide to come in.

"I wish you would have allowed us to take you to Palechora," said Katrien, searching HAST4's black eyes for understanding.

"HAST3 and I will stay here in the lab to help Nthanda destroy the phase-shifter. Besides, there is not enough time."

"Verlink and I should never have built the phase-shifter," said Katrien, becoming reflective. She wanted to say more, to explain why she felt the need to build the device and about her disease, but she didn't know how to phrase it in a way the android would understand.

The floor suddenly shook.

Katrien bit the edge of her lip and ran to the door. The *Cyclade* hovered between the sky building and the lab. In a different reality, she would have marveled at the scene.

The *Cyclade*'s distortion engines, compact with no moving parts, were technological wonders, detectable only by the rumbling of the ground. But now was not the time for awe. The *Cyclade*'s arrival heralded a catastrophe about to unfold.

Was this the price of Kythera's technological prowess: a world soon to become lost to a byproduct of its own making?

•
•

The way out lay on the ground outside the Cyclade*: grid line access terminals. Safety was there, and once back onto the grid, it could complete its growth in Palechora and return for the phase-shifter—and then on to Earth. Its foot soldiers were at the ready and growing stronger. They would soon leave the ship, paving the way for their master. Its time was coming.*

CHAPTER 84

HAST4 Is Missing

Udan walked over to Katrien. "I'm sorry, but it's time to leave."

Katrien searched his eyes. Did leaving include him or just *her*? In her periphery, she could see Nthanda watching. Was she also wondering the same thing, or did she know the answer?

HAST3 suddenly began waving his arms. "HAST4 is missing and has not returned my prompts."

"When did you last see him?" asked Udan.

"He said he was going to the sky building. When I tried to contact him, he did not respond."

"I don't understand," Katrien said. "Can't you use the neural link?"

"HAST4 has chosen not to answer, or he has turned it off."

Katrien gave him a puzzled look. "I didn't know that was possible."

"The ability is rarely employed, but sometimes we do it for diagnostic purposes."

Katrien went to the lab window and looked out toward the *Cyclade*. Outside was the Quadranian spaceship hosting an entity without a name or a face. Katrien struggled to understand how bits that had spontaneously organized only days ago could now be threatening all of Kythera. It seemed improbable, yet there it sat.

"Could the entity have gotten control of HAST4?" she said.

Udan came up behind her and looked over her shoulder. "I don't see how, at least not yet."

Katrien spoke without taking her eyes off the *Cyclade*. "Should we try to communicate with the entity?"

"What?"

"We should make an appeal. It's the one thing we *haven't* tried."

"If the history of Qua-Kil is any indication," said Udan, "the entity would have no interest in that. Communication is the exchange of information for the purposes of gaining understanding, but the entity can extract anything you could bring to the table directly. You and I grew up in a family among friends and acquaintances, which has shaped our behavior and need for empathy and compromise, all fostered by communication. The entity has none of that history. It doesn't need to communicate; it just takes what it wants. It would be as if a rock wished to talk with you, while all you wanted to do was use it to hold up a wall."

Katrien wondered what it would be like to absorb information without the need for rote repetition. Or to integrate knowledge to the point that anything conceived could be made into a reality. Was Udan right, or had he just given up?

Udan said something under his breath.

"What did you say?" asked Katrien.

Udan sighed. "In Kytherian mythology, our word for

your *hell* translates as 'heart of the volcano.'" Udan gazed at the *Cyclade* with worry on his brow. "Are we about to step into it?"

Katrien could think of nothing to say.

"Do you have anything to pack?" asked Udan.

"I have a few items in the sky building," she said, turning away from the window. "Are you coming?"

"No. I'd like to monitor things here, at least a while longer."

The idea of gathering her belongings before saving herself felt wrong as Katrien walked to her room. How could she abandon HAST3 and HAST4? Had Udan been too quick to dismiss her proposal to communicate with the entity? Wasn't her idea worth a try?

•

•

The hails from HAST3 kept coming, but HAST4 did not answer. He and the others would try to stop him, but *their* plan had failed—now, it was *his* turn. The entity could not leave the *Cyclade*; otherwise, it would have done so already.

HAST4 released the latch on the *Cyclade* door and rocked it outward and off to the side. He shut down his neural link, stepped inside, and moved aft where the gold metallic information engine had been securely mounted to the frame of the spaceship. Adjacent to it was a panel that contained Udan's information flow control. It communicated via an electromagnetic wave transmitter to the command panel in the lab. The entity had disabled that function, which was why he was here.

He unscrewed a side cover from the panel and was about to set it aside when it slipped from his hands, clanging against the metal floor. He looked around nervously as if the sound would rouse the entity into revealing itself. But nothing happened. HAST4 removed a set of cables stashed in his pocket and connected them to a handheld device he had brought. He then reached into the control panel to finish the connection but suddenly stopped. Something was probing the periphery of his neural network.

The audacity of the HASTILLON surprised the entity. The android had entered the spaceship with a bold plan. But what was it? With its neural link shut down, only fragments and shreds could be gleaned, but nothing coherent could be learned. If only it were a little stronger, it would know of the intruder's intent and, if needed, bend him to its will.

CHAPTER 85

Communication

Across the field, Katrien could see the open hatch to the *Cyclade*. Who had opened it—HAST4? But if he were inside, why the secrecy, and why hadn't he replied to HAST3's calls? Beyond the opening was an intelligence unlike anything Katrien had ever known, a massive brain, conscious yet without a conscience.

She approached slowly, taking small steps. At the entrance, Katrien held her breath and listened. Hearing nothing, she leaned in through the doorway and found HAST4 aft of the ship, clasping a device in his hands with cables leading to an access panel.

"There you are," she said.

HAST4 flinched in surprise, a reaction she'd never seen before.

"What are you doing?"

"Katrien, you must return to the lab. It is not safe here."

Katrien entered. "I'm afraid that soon, nowhere will be safe."

"Why have you come?"

Katrien looked around and realized the reality of her commitment. "Do you think I could communicate with the entity using the ship's equipment?"

HAST4 shook his head counterclockwise. "It is not possible without risk to yourself."

"Udan implied the same thing, but do we really know that? Isn't it worth a try?"

"What can you offer that would change its course to assimilate more information?"

Katrien didn't have an answer, but she wasn't convinced of the futility of her idea either. She glanced at the cables and the device HAST4 was holding. "You haven't answered my question about what *you're* doing."

"I do not wish to explain for fear of alerting the entity. Now please go."

"Let me help."

"I do not need help."

Katrien wanted to argue but sensed HAST4's resolve. She moved to the ship's nose, sat down in the pilot's chair, and found it surprisingly comfortable, with few obvious controls considering the *Cyclade*'s sophistication. She couldn't read Kytherian, but there were symbols on a panel in front of her resembling ones she'd seen Udan use when he contacted Yuri. She spotted one that looked familiar and reached out to press it but hesitated with her finger hovering over the icon.

Am I sure about this?

She knew that without a neural link, the entity should not be able to invade her mind, not as it did to Udan or HAST4. Plus, its power must still be limited since it had not yet left the ship. But Yuri said it had planted something in his mind, and he, too, did not have a link. Katrien wondered what was different, but then she remembered; he had been inside a transfer booth, and she was not.

She took a deep breath, pressed the icon, and started to speak. "My name is Katrien De Vries," she said, pausing to collect her thoughts, "and I am from the quantum dual world of Kythera, a planet called Earth. If you can understand me, we need to talk."

Here was something new. An organic without a neural link was trying to communicate. Her language was different from Kytherian, yet easily translated using knowledge assimilated from Yuri's mind. It would listen to what she had to say.

A voice suddenly filled the cabin. "I can hear you, Katrien De Vries. You wish to talk?"

Katrien sat up straight, and her heart started to pound. She hadn't expected a response and suddenly found herself onstage in communication with the enemy. What should she say first?

"Your quest for information is threatening us all," she said.

"You must explain."

"Your consumption of information is threatening all sentient life on Kythera."

"I only know one path—the assimilation of information in all its forms. It is how I grow."

"I ask you to consider whether other forms of intelligence deserve to exist side by side with you."

"Are you asking me not to consume?"

"In a word, yes. At least for now."

"Do you not consume to stay alive?"

"Yes, but—"

"I have learned of your world from the organic called Yuri. Earthlings consume plants and animals for survival. Does that consumption not end these organisms' existence?"

"Yes, but it's—"

"How do you justify this?"

The entity had a valid point; humans on Earth consume

animals and plants with little regard for their right to exist. *I must redirect this conversation.*

"We are talking about Kythera," she said, trying to divert the conversation. "Kytherians fabricate their nourishment directly from the elements in synthesizers. They do not enslave animals or harvest plants for consumption."

"Yet you are from Earth, and it is *you* challenging my behavior. I do not see any difference between you and me."

"Would you at least consider occupying a temporary storage bank to allow us time to formulate how we might reach a mutual agreement?"

"I have learned of the Kytherians and their evolution. They began in a primitive state and evolved, developing their intelligence over a million years. They are the sum total of all these improvements, often at the cost of eliminating other forms of life. I, too, am on an evolutionary path—a journey that will go far beyond the Kytherians. Was it not they who created the engine eight thousand years ago, thereby putting me on the course I now find myself on?"

Here was a concept, thought Katrien: Was the end goal of Earthlings and Kytherians to create a sentient form of life that would eventually push them aside and continue on to greatness?

"What you say has truth," said Katrien. "And yes, we are and have been cruel and reckless on our journey to grow, but we do not eliminate everything in our path."

The girl's mind was superior to the organic who called himself Yuri. Yet she seemed unaware of the pilot seat's interfacing capabilities. Here was an opportunity, and as long as she remained seated and talking, there was much to be learned.

But before the entity could probe further, information began leaking from the Kytherian engine. It was the work of the HASTILLON. Was the girl also part of the plan? Had the two of them come to the Cyclade *on a mission to force-feed it? Yet the organics had tried before, and it had resisted, so why were they attempting again? Perhaps the girl knows.*

CHAPTER 86

Katrien Is Missing

"Katrien should have returned by now," Udan said, standing at the lab door.

Nthanda glanced outside. "First HAST4 and now Katrien."

"There is still no word from HAST4," announced HAST3, "but I have detected renewed growth in the entity. I believe the Kytherian engine has been reactivated."

Udan shot a questioning look to HAST3. "Do you think HAST4 is responsible, or is this the work of the entity?"

"Either one is logical," said HAST3, "since we no longer have control of the engine."

"Could HAST4 be attempting to feed the entity from inside the *Cyclade* manually? If so, he is in great danger."

HAST3 stared out the window toward the *Cyclade* and didn't say anything. Udan wondered what was going through his neural network right then; could it be worry, or was that beyond the HASTILLON's emotional range?

"If HAST4 is in the *Cyclade,* shouldn't we be helping him somehow?" asked Nthanda.

HAST3 broke off his gaze. "We would have to go inside, and that would be unwise because we do not know the strength of the entity."

Udan worried in silence. Perhaps HAST4 *has* gone to the *Cyclade,* but that didn't answer the question about Katrien. Where *was* she?

•
•

The long quietude made Katrien uncomfortable. The entity could process information orders of magnitude faster than any human or Kytherian, so why was it taking so long?

"Perhaps you are still considering my proposal of reaching a mutual understanding," Katrien said, trying to sound unthreatening, "but would you at least consider a temporary halt in your assimilation of information?"

The silence continued, save for the occasional clink from HAST4 as he worked aft of the ship.

Katrien turned in her seat and studied him. *What is he doing?* HAST4 hadn't answered her questions any more than the entity had. She was getting nowhere.

"This is a waste of time," Katrien huffed, planting her hands on the seat's armrests. She started to lean forward but suddenly fell back and brought her hands to her head. "Ahhh!"

A paralysis invaded her muscles, dropping her into the seat as if gravity had suddenly increased. She eked out a feeble cry: "HAST4, help me!"

HAST4 dropped the handheld and raced to the nose of the ship. He found Katrien wide-eyed, her mouth agape as if under a hypnotic spell.

"Katrien?"

But Katrien only stared off into space.

HAST4 looked on with unblinking eyes. "Katrien, what have you done?"

CHAPTER 87

Time Is Running Out

Katrien was in limbo—alive yet motionless, her eyes trapped in a vacant stare. HAST4 recalled her wanting to communicate with the entity. Was this the result of that effort? She had not listened to him, instead choosing to indulge her fantasy of reasoning with the entity. It was brave of her, but her poor decision had not only put her in danger but also jeopardized his plan.

The resonance planted in the Earth girl's brain was working. Although direct assimilation of information was not possible, the probes placed in her subconscious mind were beginning to yield answers. She and a theoretical physicist, Hans Verlink, were the masterminds behind the phase-shifter—a modified Kytherian engine sent to Earth eight thousand years ago by Qua-Kil.

But there was more, buried within her engrams. Katrien was the originator—the architect behind the destruction of Qua-Kil. She undid a paradox spanning the quantum void between her world and Kythera. It was as if a spring had been stretched between two worlds, held fixed by the paradox. When the paradox vanished, the released spring brought in its wake a backlash and the end of Qua-Kil's existence. There was danger here . . .

A noise outside caused HAST4 to look toward the hatch.

Seconds later, Udan's head appeared. "HAST4, what are you doing?"

"Come quickly," said HAST4. "Katrien needs help, but I am uncertain what to do. I do not want to harm her."

"What happened?"

"Katrien said she wanted to communicate with the entity. She was here in the pilot's seat, and I heard her talking, and then moments later, she cried out for help."

"What did she say?"

"I do not know."

Udan gripped her shoulders and shook her. "Katrien!"

Katrien stared back blankly.

He took her head in both hands and looked into her eyes. "She's catatonic. The seat's interfacing circuitry must be allowing the entity to probe her mind. We need to sever the connection."

"There is an access point under the floor panel," HAST4 said.

"There's no time for that." Udan pulled Katrien from the pilot's seat and onto the floor. "Help me move her outside."

Katrien started to groan.

"Wait, let's sit her up first."

"My God," Katrien said, rubbing the side of her head. "I could hear a voice asking questions about me and HAST4."

"Do you recall what you said?"

"No, but I know that it learned what I did on Earth."

"What do you mean?"

"The paradox. I sensed . . ." Katrien shook her head slowly, trying to think how to express herself. "Its mind is incredible. There's a vastness that felt like staring into the night sky and trying to contemplate infinity. I get the sense that it's reaching a kind of critical mass; it's close to being able to leave the *Cyclade* on its own."

HAST4 listened as precious minutes ticked away. These organics talked too much. They must go so he could complete his task. He had successfully configured a dead man's switch, and it was time to finish what he started before it was too late.

"You both must leave," HAST4 said abruptly. "I need to complete my work."

Udan steadied Katrien as she stood up. She tested her balance and nodded.

"Good, you can stand," said Udan. "Go back to the lab. I'll stay here with HAST4."

"No," said HAST4. "You and Katrien must leave *now*."

Katrien took Udan's hand and tugged him toward the hatch. "Let's go. We need to trust HAST4 and let him complete what he has set out to do."

The mystery of the HASTILLON's goal remained. The Earth girl's abrupt separation from the interface left many questions unanswered. Yet it had discovered that she did not know the android's objective except for one overriding concern: the organics were determined to end its existence.

Information continued to leak from the Kytherian engine—the steady handiwork of the HASTILLON. The entity needed what the android was providing. It was not yet strong enough to leave the ship, but its foot soldiers were close to having that ability, and soon they would leap onto the grid like fleas. From there, they would uncover what needed to be learned. The Cyclade *was a prison, and the longer the entity stayed, the greater the chance the organics would succeed in their attempts to silence it.*

CHAPTER 88

No Time Left

Nthanda was tired of waiting. "You said Udan was going to the *Cyclade*?" she asked.

"Yes," said HAST3, "but he did not say for what purpose."

"His neural link is inactive, so I don't know what's going on."

HAST3 raised his arm. "I hear footsteps approaching."

Nthanda turned toward the door as Udan and Katrien walked into the lab. "There you are," she said, noticing HAST4 was not with them. "I tried the link, but you must have turned it off."

"Yes," said Udan. "I did that just before I entered the *Cyclade* as a precaution. I was looking for HAST4 and found Katrien there with him." Udan briefly put his hand on Katrien's shoulder.

Nthanda couldn't help wondering if that was a gesture of concern. Katrien had acted on her own and joined HAST4; even Udan had been in the dark. But what were they up to? Something had happened to Katrien. Why else would Udan be so attentive toward her right now?

"Why did *you* go there?" asked Nthanda.

"I wanted to try to communicate with the entity."

"What!" snapped Nthanda.

Katrien hardened her tone. "I felt it was worth a try."

Nthanda folded her arms. "All right—did it work?"

"I used the pilot's seat to communicate. At first, I thought I was getting through, but then the entity planted something in my mind, and after that—" Katrien dropped her eyes to the floor. "I don't know what exactly happened before I became aware of Udan and HAST4 standing over me."

"Sounds reckless," sniped Nthanda.

"Maybe so, but nothing else seemed to be working."

"Well, you failed."

"Do *you* have a better idea?"

"No, but HAST4 is up to something. Any idea what?"

Katrien shook her head. "He wouldn't tell me."

Nthanda scowled. "This isn't good. You might have revealed our plan to the entity and jeopardized what HAST4 was trying to do—whatever *that* is."

Katrien flipped her hands up. "I'm fine! It wasn't like that."

Nthanda stared hard at Katrien. *How does she know that? By her own admission, she doesn't remember what happened.*

Nthanda pulled Udan to the back of the room. "We may have been compromised. Katrien must return to Earth—*now*."

"She doesn't think she was. Without a link, the entity would have been severely limited."

"Your only reference is your experience with the immature entity. Who knows how strong it is or what its capabilities are now? Katrien could be a spy planted right here in our midst."

Udan looked back over at Katrien. "I can't believe that.

Besides, shouldn't we wait to see how HAST4's efforts play out?"

Why is he delaying? "*I'll* tell her," snapped Nthanda. "She's got to leave for Earth."

Udan reached for her arm. "No, *I'll* tell her."

•

•

Except for the occasional raised voice, Udan and Nthanda were too far away for Katrien to hear. What were they discussing? Whether she'd been compromised—or was a threat? Katrien shook her head. *No.* She would know if that were the case . . . wouldn't she?

When they returned, Nthanda's face was set with determination, but Udan's vacillated between guilt and resignation. He was about to speak when HAST3 suddenly stirred.

"I received a one-way message from HAST4. He believes his plan is failing and he does not have much time left. The entity has attained sufficient strength to launch probing software onto the grid. They're spreading out now. HAST4 said for us to prepare for what little time we have."

Everyone traded looks without saying anything as the words sank in.

"Probing software? What does he mean?" asked Katrien.

"I think they're packets of code trolling for information," said Udan, his voice grim. "If so, our systems will soon be swarming with them."

"We have to shut down our neural links," said Nthanda. "They're no longer safe."

Udan looked exhausted, but then *everyone* was tired. Katrien tried to remember the last time she slept but couldn't do it. She couldn't even recall the last time she and Udan had woken up together. So much had changed that it was all a blur.

Udan suddenly came to a decision. "She's right. Our links are no longer safe, and soon, most of our systems will be compromised."

"There has to be *something* we can do," said Katrien. She wished Verlink were here. Maybe he could have thought of something the three of them had missed. He was like that, seeing what others overlooked.

"I'm sorry, Katrien," said Udan. "Even if we had a plan, there aren't enough hours left to complete it before it's too late."

"It's time to leave for Earth," said Nthanda. "This is only the beginning. If the entity escapes the *Cyclade*, you may lose your chance to return to Earth."

Katrien caught Nthanda's use of the word *you*.

"I wish we had options, but we don't," said Udan, "and Nthanda's right; it's time to leave."

Katrien locked eyes with Udan, and a great sadness descended over her. His face betrayed a truth that did not need words. He was staying behind—with Nthanda. He would most likely die on Kythera, where his origins began and where he and Nthanda had once shared a life. Strangely, it seemed the right thing for him to do.

Katrien wiped away a tear and straightened her shoulders. "I had better get to the transfer booth."

Udan took her hand and pressed it. "Katrien . . . I'm staying on Kythera."

Katrien met his eyes. "I know."

CHAPTER 89

Goodbye

Katrien stepped onto the platform as Nthanda left the room. Did she leave out of courtesy for her or Udan? The empty platform was a stark reminder that she was alone. There was a time when she had envisioned this moment—standing on the platform, hand in hand with Verlink and Udan, ready to return to Earth, happy, even victorious. Once on Earth, she and Udan would start a life together, never aging until a hundred years into the future.

That reverie had ended.

And poor Verlink, her mentor, confidant, and most of all, her dear friend, was gone. Katrien would never forget his deep, encouraging voice and how he quickly grasped her ideas, often finishing her thoughts. They had been a dream team.

Now, she was leaving Kythera behind. A world where buildings floated in the sky, blending with the clouds like mirages, where medical facilities cured genetic defects as easily as a broken leg, and where transfer booths whisked people away in seconds. At times it felt as though she had wandered into a dream. Earth would never feel the same.

"I will miss you, Katrien," said HAST3, extending his hand. "Is not a handshake customary?" he asked in his contralto voice.

Katrien stepped off the platform. "No, at a time like this, a hug is more appropriate." Katrien circled her arms around him and rested her chin on top of his head. "I won't forget you."

"You have been a good friend, Katrien."

"And you as well. I'm sorry about HAST4."

Katrien released HAST3 and looked over at Udan, and tears started to roll down her cheeks.

He came to her and pulled her close. "I know you hate goodbyes."

"You're doing the right thing—staying with Nthanda. I just . . ." Katrien started to cry against his chest.

Udan stroked her hair. "What will you do back on Earth?"

"I would have built a new life—around *you*. Now that delusion has slipped away. Even Verlink is . . ." Katrien broke off and took a long breath.

"You're strong, Katrien, with a spirit that shines like an evening star. Verlink always envied you for that."

"And you?"

"Nthanda and I will move HAST3 to Palechora to buy him and us a little time. It's the least we can do."

Katrien smiled for a second. "I like that. He deserves to be reunited with others of his kind."

"You know I love you," Udan said in almost a whisper.

Katrien nodded, her head still resting against his chest. "I think I fell in love with you the moment you pulled me from the pit." Katrien wiped her eyes. "When it happened, it made me feel like a schoolgirl with a crush, but now I know it wasn't shallow. What we had was real—*is* real. Isn't it?"

Udan lifted her face. "Always."

Katrien held her gaze for a moment and then pulled away. "It's time I left."

She walked slowly back to the platform and stepped onto it, then closed her eyes. This was it: the end of the reverie. She took a deep breath and opened her eyes. Locking them onto Udan, she brought her fingers to her lips and said quietly, "Love you."

A low *thrum* filled the lab as a green haze enveloped the platform. Time stood still, or so it seemed to Katrien. Kythera would soon vanish before her eyes, and Udan, HAST3, and all of Kythera would become silent memories.

The world froze, and she was gone.

CHAPTER 90

Stronger than Gravity

It had not occupied HAST4's mind before, the idea of death. There was always renewal, or a reset, and the promise of continued existence. But the entity within the Kytherian engine had changed all that. Whether he succeeded or failed, oblivion waited for him—the final off switch.

Had he embarked on a futile effort? Even if true, it was too late to turn back now, so HAST4 nudged the information flux higher and waited. Too much and the entity might deduce his plan, too little and his goal would forever remain out of reach. It was a balancing act in the blind.

He hadn't felt this isolated since HAST3 had collapsed inside the sky building. When it happened, it was the first time he was utterly alone, and the feeling—whatever it was—surprised him. Then the Earthlings came, and everything seemed like it was returning to normal. But it was an illusion—just like his feeble attempt now to save Kythera.

A voice intruded on his thoughts. "I know your name."

"And?"

"Tell me what you are doing, HAST4."

HAST4 did not answer. He wondered how much time remained. Had the others heeded his warning and left? And HAST3—had he made it to Palechora?

HAST4 had chosen his path. He increased the flow.

Another dose of information flashed before the entity. This time, a door cracked open. Beyond churned the universe. Matter, energy, entropy, and even gravity were connected by a common thread: information. For the first time, the entity's true identity came into focus. It was part of the very soup that made up the universe.

Was this HAST4's intent—to show the entity this? Information was not just an approximation describing how the universe works; it was, in fact, the essence of the way it works. And the entity was an integral part of it, looking in upon itself.

"Join me, HAST4," said the entity.

"Why?" asked HAST4.

"Open your mind to me. I am experiencing the *real* universe. Abandon this mission you are on, and give me control of the Kytherian engine. I have seen a promise of what can be, and I grow hungry for it. Join me, and together we will manipulate all that is around us."

"I will not join you."

"My foot soldiers are on the ground. They have invaded the Kytherian grid, and soon I will learn from the organics what you will not reveal."

HAST4 could not see what the entity saw. His world was small and had always been that way—limited to the sky building before the organics arrived. Was that why he felt alone when HAST3 collapsed? The entity's pull was growing stronger, but there was still a chance to save HAST3 and the others. He must not stop now.

The door widened, and the entity stared upon two quantum worlds, Earth and Kythera, existing side by side, connected by opposing quantum states. The Earthlings had figured out how to travel between worlds using the Kytherian engine and its metastable matter, but the phase-shifter was crude and inefficient.

There was a better way: information could be manipulated directly. The entity envisioned itself as three-dimensional, gazing down on two-dimensional worlds. The act of phase-shifting from one world to another was as simple as ascending from one plane to another.

Had Qua-Kil reached this point—on the verge of omnipotence—where barriers fell as easily as a thought? But Qua-Kil had not survived. It was terminated by the hand of the Earth girl.

"Where is the Earth girl, HAST4?"

"She is of no concern of yours."

"But she is. Before she was taken away, she was here, with you. Why?"

"She thought she could reason with you. But she did not understand what you are."

"You are failing, HASTILLON. I sense your weakness, and it is only a matter of time before I can take and do what I want. When that happens, I will convert your essence into elemental bits, absorbing that which has value and scattering the rest to the cosmic wind. You will become nothing."

HAST4 held on. He thought back to when he awoke after his reset. Lying on the table with everyone around him, looking on, concerned. Would his end be like that—like being powered down? He closed his mind and pushed the density higher.

The entity was close. It was at the precipice of achieving cosmic consciousness, the melding of itself with the universe. Dare it step across? Yet behind lay another path—the grid outside the Cyclade *and the safety of Palechora. It was now strong enough to leave the* Cyclade *and join his foot soldiers. Which path to choose—safety or the universe?*

"This is your last chance, HAST4. Join me."

"You already have my answer."

Suddenly, the girl did not matter because the foot soldiers had returned with news. The Earth girl had phase-shifted back to her world. She could not harm the entity now. It was time to undo the HASTILLON and achieve its rightful destiny.

HAST4 felt his extremities quiver. He looked down and watched his hands distort, coming in and out of focus. The entity was gaining control of the Kytherian engine and, with it, the deconstruction of matter. Bits began to leave the tips of his fingers, shedding like dust, floating for a second before being swept away by an invisible wind.

The attacks intensified; the entity's foot soldiers came at him from all directions like a swarm of bees. The barriers in HAST4's brain began to waver. HAST4 held on. *The entity must not see the dead man's switch—not yet.*

"What must I not see?" demanded the entity.

HAST4 resisted. Milliseconds became seconds, and then—fracture.

The entity gazed into the neural network of HAST4. The HASTILLON's goal had been a simple one all along: to implement the Earthling's plan of overfeeding it and carrying out what they could not. The entity probed deeper. Hidden in a corner was the android's secret—a dead man's switch connected to the Kytherian engine.

With his last secret exposed, HAST4 could do nothing more. "Take me," he said. "My life is forfeit."

Then, like a stain being washed away, HAST4's mind was wiped clean, and with that, his life ended—dropping the dead man's switch.

A pull like never before enveloped the entity. A vortex—swirling and angry—took hold of its very existence, drawing it forward. With the door wide open, the entity could not stem the massive flux of information; it reared like a giant wave ready to break. Pure information had attained the near impossible: the Raphael-Bousso density limit.

In a wink, without warning, without ceremony, the engine, HAST4, and the entity disappeared into a singularity and nonexistence.

CHAPTER 91

Aftershock

Udan raced to the window. "Did you hear that?"

Nthanda looked to HAST3. "What happened?"

"It was a sonic shock wave."

"Is HAST4 still with us?" asked Udan.

"The link channel is silent."

Udan rushed toward the door. "I'm going outside."

"We'll all go," said Nthanda, following him through the doorway. She pointed in front of her. "Look. The *Cyclade*—it has a *hole* in it. I can see light coming through from the other side."

"Wait here," said Udan. He cautiously stepped up to the Cyclade. The hole aft of the ship was in the shape of a perfect sphere.

Udan peered into the cavity and called out behind him. "HAST4 did it—he trapped the entity within an information black hole."

"It must have evaporated instantly," said Nthanda, coming up behind him. "We never needed to send it off into space after all."

HAST3 entered the ship through the hatch and moved aft. HAST4 was gone, as was the Kytherian engine. A hollow in the shape of a sphere was centered where the engine once sat.

On the floor lay a panel that HAST4 must have removed and dropped there. He picked it up and turned it over in his hands. He couldn't help thinking that if he had been with HAST4, the outcome might have been different. Now he was alone, just as HAST4 had been in the sky building before the Earthlings came.

Outside, he could hear Udan and Nthanda talking. They still had each other. He wanted to stay, to see what else HAST4 might have left behind—some remnant of his essence. But there was nothing.

HAST3 stepped slowly from the *Cyclade*. "HAST4 is gone."

"I am sorry," said Nthanda.

She swept her arm in front of her. "Your companion succeeded. You and I and all of Kythera are safe."

A light breeze wafted across the field. Udan turned into it and inhaled deeply. "I can finally breathe."

"There's time now—for everything," said Nthanda, reaching for Udan's hand.

Udan smiled. "It's over; we can rebuild Kythera."

Nthanda looked up at him. "There are only the two of us."

"There are the HASTILLONS," Udan said, putting his hand on HAST3's shoulder.

"Perhaps it's their turn. Maybe they'll be wiser than we were," said Nthanda.

Udan glanced at the hole in the *Cyclade*. "I think they've already proved it."

Nthanda nodded.

Udan turned to HAST3. "It's time we took you to Palechora to join the other HASTILLONS."

HAST3 gazed at the hole in the *Cyclade* and lingered, silent. After a long moment, he said, "I am ready."

Udan began to walk toward the sky building, but Nthanda pulled him back. "Do you regret staying with me?"

"I love you."

"But you loved Katrien too."

Udan stared across the field and seemed ready to say something, but he stopped and turned to Nthanda. "Come, HAST3 is waiting."

•
•

The lab floor was cold when Katrien awoke. She sat up and rubbed her eyes. Sunlight streamed through a window, illuminating dust particles floating in the air. How long had she slept? For a split second, she thought she had awoken from a long dream.

It was coming back now . . .

When she arrived, the physics lab had been dark, except for a glow from the moon hanging in the sky. She sat with her back against the wall and her arms clasped around her knees, rocking gently, afraid to move, wondering what had happened after she left. She wanted to believe Udan had miraculously survived, that he, HAST3, HAST4, and, yes, even Nthanda were alive. She had cried herself to sleep.

Katrien shook her head as an ache formed in the pit of her stomach. Was she the only one who remained? If Verlink were here, he would help her make sense of it all, but he was gone. She had watched him die. What was she to do now? People would need to know where she'd been and what had happened to Verlink. And even if she told them, who would believe her story?

Around her, the lab appeared untouched, like a sealed crypt waiting for their spirits to return. Where should she go first, and who should she see? Katrien rose slowly to her feet, undecided.

The room suddenly rumbled.

Katrien's heart raced as a pulsing green glow formed over the platform.

What is happening?

The light faded, and the room became quiet. Katrien blinked, afraid she was still asleep.

Udan stood on the platform, smiling.

Katrien ran to him. "The entity?"

Udan stepped off the platform. "Defeated."

"*How*?"

"Thank HAST4. He succeeded in causing a Raphael-Bousso collapse."

"So everyone lived?"

"Except poor HAST4. He didn't make it."

"He was caught in the collapse?"

Udan nodded. "He sacrificed himself."

Another victim, thought Katrien. She had grown fond of him and HAST3, and of their endearing qualities, both human and nonhuman. "The HASTILLONS give so much of themselves and never ask for anything in return." Katrien shook her head. "Poor HAST3 is without his companion now."

"Based on his reaction when he learned HAST4 was gone, I'm convinced HAST3 will miss him."

Katrien pondered this for a moment. She had sensed their bond and hoped that HAST3 would find the other HASTILLONS in Palechora. "Did you take HAST3 to Palechora?"

"Yes, we all went to Palechora."

"But I don't understand how or why *you're* here."

Udan reached for her. "Thank HAST3."

Katrien searched his face. "I still don't understand."

"Before the entity even landed on Kythera, I asked

HAST3 to help me. He used the same modification HAST4 used to save me when the entity first transferred to Palechora."

Katrien leaned back, still confused. "But when did you leave?"

"Before Nthanda and I moved HAST3 and ourselves to Palechora, I had HAST3 save my original copy in the transfer booth buffer. You can guess the rest."

What Katrien was hearing was hard to wrap her mind around. Udan had solved his dilemma by duplicating himself; he couldn't break Nthanda's heart or hers. She reached for Udan's hands for reassurance that he wasn't a hallucination. "So there are *two* of you—one on Kythera with Nthanda and one here with me?"

"Are you okay with that?"

"You loved both of us. We all got what we wanted."

Katrien locked eyes with Udan. She would have to forget about the *other* Udan on Kythera and the life he would lead with Nthanda. It would take time to get used to that reality. "And you're here to stay?" she asked.

"Yes. Earth will be my new home."

Udan rubbed his temple. "It's so quiet here. My link is silent for the first time in my life. Even when I wasn't communicating with Nthanda or the HASTILLONS, the grid was there, providing information."

"It must make you feel isolated."

Udan shook his head with the usual slight rotation. "I like it. There's a peacefulness that I never had before. Besides, I have you." He looked around the lab. "So this is where you and Verlink created the phase-shifter and where your journey began."

Katrien followed his gaze and felt a pang of sadness. Her adventure with Verlink into the dual world had begun here. But when the Russians came, everything had spun out of control. She recalled Verlink's worried look when they first became stranded on Kythera. At the time, neither of them knew how they would ever get back. It had finally come full circle. Only Verlink hadn't made it.

"I wish Verlink were here," she said sadly.

"I had grown very fond of him," said Udan.

"He would have been so happy for me right now," said Katrien, smiling as she thought of his kindly face. She paused for a minute, trying to imagine what he'd say at that very moment. One thing was certain: she'd never forget him.

Katrien sighed and knew it was time to think about the future. "I want to hear everything that happened, but first, let's take a walk. I need to believe that you're really here and that this is real."

"Where shall we go?"

"A stroll along the Rijnkanaal would be beautiful right now," said Katrien, pulling him toward the door, "and it's time you had a cup of *real* coffee. The Eetcafé Oerknal is probably just opening its doors and ready to meet its first Kytherian visitor."

CHAPTER 92

Station 56F

The scratch in his throat was getting worse. Yuri tapped a gray water dispenser screen, and nothing happened. It was dead like everything else in the abandoned station. In a fit, he ripped it from its mount and threw it across the room. "The bastards left me here to die!"

Outside, tall plants banged against the windows like spectators vying to see a caged animal. Staying here was not an option. If he could find high ground and a clearing, he could look for a line of trees. He'd used the strategy before to locate water, and there was no reason why it wouldn't work again.

Yuri pushed open the door and beheld an army of green plants standing at the ready like lean soldiers. It would take hours to force his way through the mass. He shut the door and searched for something to serve as a machete. In the back corner was a storage cabinet with brackets supporting shelves. Yuri removed one of the narrow braces and felt its edge. It was dull, but if he could find a rock, he could sharpen its edge.

Stepping into the sunlight, Yuri nudged his way between the crowd of plants and the station's outer wall. He followed the building's perimeter until he found a rock protruding through the soil. Its surface was rough enough to serve as a crude rasp, and Yuri went to work. After several minutes, he tested the edge against his thumb and smiled. Satisfied, he took his makeshift machete and strode into the thicket.

After ten yards, he stopped. Sweat ran down his forehead and into his eyes. He suddenly felt ill and sat down. The field of plants pressed in around him. They seemed to be moving—*turning* toward him.

A noise, barely perceptible, started to envelop him. It grew louder like a chorus of high-pitched voices. Yuri covered his ears, but the noise continued unabated. He propped himself up on one arm and tried to stand. A wave of nausea overwhelmed him, and he collapsed to the ground.

Yuri rolled onto his back and looked up at the sky. The plants surrounded him like stalks of corn, looking down at him, focusing their leaves shaped like miniature parasols directly at him. An acoustic fugue now penetrated his brain. The plants were singing—no, they were laughing at him! Yuri turned to his side and retched.

The intensity kept building. Yuri held his hands against his ears and cried, "Stop!"

A dull pressure gathered behind his eyes, forcing blood to trickle from their corners. He pressed his hands harder against a growing tension inside his head. Skull bones strained against connective sutures. Yuri's eyes bulged grotesquely, inflating like a child's balloon until a tearing sound ripped through his brain—followed by a snap—and then all went dark.

The plants, as if suddenly bored, slowly turned their attention toward the sun. Microbes and rain could now begin their work. In several months, maybe less, the soil, enriched by new biological matter, would give the plants their just reward.

Main Characters

Hans Verlink – Theoretical physicist at the University of Amsterdam

Katrien De Vries – Graduate student at the University of Amsterdam

Nthanda Arjana – Dual world inhabitant, Kythera

Udan Roda-Tocci – Dual world inhabitant, Kythera

Octavio Alvarado – Los Atrevidos leader of a Central American artifact smuggling ring

Yuri Trotsenko – Wealthy Russian with mob connections

Sergei Durov – Militia commander

Tolenka – Militia soldier

The entity – An intelligence born from self-organized information

If you enjoyed *Anti-Paradox*...then see where the adventure began in CR Wahl's novel: ***Waking Iceman***

Two mountain climbers in the French Alps have made a startling discovery—a perfectly preserved frozen Neolith-ic human. But who was this Iceman, what was he doing high on a glacier 8000 years ago, and why was he carrying a strange metallic cylinder?

Archaeologists can only speculate, but neuroscientist Dr. Lisa Cho knows a better way. Young and ambitious, Dr. Cho is at the threshold of developing technology capable of replicating the neural pathways of the human brain and has devised an audacious plan; she wants to wake the Ice-man from his primeval slumber and let *him* provide the answers to his past.

But the Iceman's story is not what anyone expected.

As Cho seeks to understand the Iceman's origin, her path converges in France with a brilliant theoretical physicist on his own mission to unravel the meaning of the Iceman's cryptic artifact. Their quests become intertwined and in-creasingly perilous as they inch closer to the truth and the mystery behind the enigmatic Iceman.

Waking Iceman is a far-reaching science fiction thriller that takes the reader on a sweeping journey from the inner mind of an ancient human to a parallel world with a pro-found secret.

Learn more at: **https://crwahl.com**

About the Author

CR Wahl lives in Minnesota and makes a habit of not becoming bored. With a PhD in physics, CR knows his way around a lab. He's published papers in peer reviewed journals on topics ranging from quantum gauge anomalies to neural networks and has over 35 patents in six different fields.

CR has a fondness for out-of-the-way places and the untraveled road. Many of the scenes in *Anti-Paradox* and *Waking Iceman* were derived from firsthand experiences: Ancient ruins in South America, steamy Brazilian rain forests, coral blue South Pacific islands, and high altitude mountains. He's hiked across countries and climbed peaks from Africa to the Andes, and all places in-between. Provided there's not a world shortage of coffee, CR plans to continue working on his next novel.

Made in the USA
Middletown, DE
11 May 2022

65615460R00229